ID0364108

Enid Blyton's
BACK TO
ST CLARE'S

The Enid Blyton Newsletter

Would you like to receive The Enid Blyton Newsletter? It has lots of news about Enid Blyton books, videos, plays, etc. There are also puzzles and a page for your letters. It is published three times a year and is free for children who live in the United Kingdom and Ireland. If you would like to receive it for a year, please write to: The Enid Blyton Newsletter, PO Box 357, London WC2E 9HQ sending your name and address. (UK and Ireland only.)

THE ENID BLYTON TRUST
FOR CHILDREN

We hope you will enjoy this book. Please think for a moment about those children who are too ill to do the exciting things you and your friends do.

Help them by sending a donation, large or small, to THE ENID BLYTON TRUST FOR CHILDREN. The Trust will use all your gifts to help children who are sick or handicapped and need to be made happy and comfortable.

Please send your postal order or cheque to:
The Enid Blyton Trust for Children,
Bedford House,
3 Bedford Street,
London WC2E 9HD

Thank you very much for your help.

Enid Blyton's
BACK TO
ST CLARE'S

containing
The Second Form at St Clare's
Claudine at St Clare's
Fifth Formers of St Clare's

complete and unabridged

DEAN

The Second Form at St Clare's first published 1944
Claudine at St Clare's first published 1944
Fifth Formers of St Clare's first published 1945
This edition published 1993 by Dean
an imprint of Reed Consumer Books Limited
Michelin House, 81 Fulham Road London SW3 6RB
and Auckland, Melbourne, Singapore and Toronto
Reprinted 1995

Copyright © Darrell Waters Limited 1944, 1945

ISBN 0 603 55110 6

Enid Blyton is a registered trademark of Darrell Waters Limited

A CIP catalogue record for this title is available from the
British Library

All rights reserved. No part of this publication may be
reproduced, stored in a retrieval system, or transmitted in any
form or by any means, electronic, mechanical,
photocopying, recording or otherwise, without the
permission of the copyright holders

Printed in Great Britain by The Bath Press

THE SECOND FORM
AT ST CLARE'S

CONTENTS

1   OFF TO SCHOOL AGAIN

THE last week of the summer holidays flew by, and the twins, Pat and Isabel O'Sullivan, seemed to be in a rush of buying clothes, fitting them on, looking out lacrosse sticks, finding lacrosse boots, and hunting for all kinds of things that seemed to have completely disappeared.

'Where *is* my knitting-bag?' said Pat, turning a whole drawer-full of things upside down. 'I know I brought it home at the end of last term.'

'I can only find *one* of my lacrosse boots,' wailed Isabel. 'Mummy, have you seen the other?'

'Yes, it came back from the bootmaker's yesterday,' said Mrs. O'Sullivan. 'Where did you put it?'

'Packing to go to school is always much more muddling than packing to come back home,' said Pat. 'I say, Isabel—won't it be fun to be in the second form this term?'

'Who is your form-teacher there?' asked their mother, unpacking half Pat's things and packing them all over again.

'Miss Jenks,' said Pat. 'I'll be sorry to leave Miss Roberts and the first form, in some ways. We did have fun there.'

'I bet we'll have some fun in Miss Jenks's class too,' said Isabel. 'I don't think she's quite so strict as Miss Roberts.'

'Don't you believe it!' said Isabel, trying to cram a tin of toffees into a corner. 'She may not have Miss Roberts's sarcastic tongue—but she's all there! Don't you remember how she used to deal with Tessie when Tessie used to try on her pretend-sneezes ? '

'Yes—sent her to Matron for a large dose of awful medicine, supposed to stop a cold ! ' giggled Pat. ' All the same, I bet we'll get away with quite a lot of things in Miss Jenks's form.'

'I hope you mean to work,' said Mrs. O'Sullivan, putting in the top tray of Isabel's trunk. ' I was quite pleased with last term's report. Don't let me have a bad one as soon as you go up into another form, will you ? '

'We'll work all right, Mummy,' said Pat. ' I can tell you, the teachers at St. Clare's aren't easy-going where work is concerned. They keep our noses to the grind-stone ! Mam'zelle's the worst. She really seems to think we ought to learn to talk French better than we speak English ! '

' No wonder your French accent is so much improved, then,' said Mrs. O'Sullivan, with a laugh. ' Now Pat— let me see if I can possibly shut your trunk. You'd better sit on it whilst I try to shut the clasps.'

The trunk wouldn't shut. Mrs. O'Sullivan opened it again and looked inside. ' You can't take all those books,' she said, firmly.

' Mummy, I *must*,' said Pat. ' And I simply must take those games too—we love jigsaws in the winter term.'

' Well, Pat, all I can say is, you'd better take books, games, toffees, biscuits and knitting things, and leave behind your clothes,' said the twins' mother. ' Now—be sensible—take out three books and we can shut the trunk.'

Pat took out three books, and, when Mrs. O'Sullivan was not looking, put them hurriedly into Isabel's trunk. Her own trunk now shut down fairly easily, and was locked. Then Mrs. O'Sullivan went to Isabel's.

'This won't shut, either,' she said. 'Gracious, the things you girls take back with you to boarding-school nowadays! When *I* . . .'

'When *you* were a girl you only took a small case, and that held everything!' chanted the twins, who had heard these remarks before. 'Mummy, we'll *both* sit on Isabel's trunk, shall we?'

Mrs. O'Sullivan opened the trunk and firmly removed three books from the top layer. She looked at them in surprise. 'I seem to have seen these before!' she said. The twins giggled. They sat on the trunk and it shut with a groan.

'And now to pack your hand-bag with night-things in,' said Mrs. O'Sullivan, looking at the school-list to make sure nothing had been forgotten. 'That won't take long.'

Night-gowns, tooth-brushes, face-flannels and sponges went into small bags. Then the twins were ready. They were both dressed neatly in their school winter uniforms of grey, with blue blouses and scarlet ties. They put on grey coats and grey felt hats with the school ribbon round, and looked at each other.

'Two good little St. Clare girls,' said Pat, looking demure.

'Not so very good,' said her mother, with a smile. 'Now—there is the car at the door, ready to take us to the station. Have we really got everything? You must write and tell me if you want anything else.'

'Oh, we're sure to want lots of things!' said Pat. 'You're a darling, the way you send us things. It's fun to be going back to St. Clare's. I'm awfully glad you sent us there, Mummy.'

'And how you hated going at first!' said Mrs. O'Sullivan, remembering the fuss the twins had made, because they had wanted to go to another, much more expensive school.

' Yes—we made up our minds to be so awful that the school wouldn't keep us,' said Pat. 'And we *were* awful too—but we couldn't keep it up. St. Clare's was too much for us—we just *had* to be decent in the end ! '

' Do come on,' said Isabel. ' We shall miss the train ! I'm longing to meet all the girls in London, and see them again, aren't you, Pat ? I do like the journey down to St. Clare's.'

They were off at last. They had to travel to London, and go to the station where the St. Clare train started. The whole train was reserved for the St. Clare girls, for it was a big school.

There was a terrific noise on the platform, where scores of girls were waiting for the train. Their mothers were there to bid them good-bye, and teachers moved about, trying to collect the girls together. Porters shoved luggage into the van, and every one was excited.

' Bobby ! Oh, there's Bobby ! ' yelled Pat, as soon as they arrived on the crowded platform. ' And Janet too. Hie, Bobby, hie, Janet ! '

' Hallo, twins ! ' cried Bobby. Her merry eyes crinkled up as she smiled.

' It's good to see your turn-up nose again,' said Pat, slipping her arm through Bobby's. ' Hallo, Janet ! Got any more tricks from that brother of yours ? '

' Wait and see,' grinned Janet. A mistress came up at that moment and overheard the remarks.

' Ah—did I hear the word TRICKS, Janet ? ' she said. ' Well, just remember you're in *my* form this term, and there are really Terrible Punishments for tricks like yours ! '

' Yes, Miss Jenks,' grinned Janet. ' I'll remember. Are all the others here yet ? '

'All but Doris,' said Miss Jenks. 'Ah, there she is. Now we must get into the train. The guard is looking rather worried, I see.'

'Carlotta! Get into our carriage!' yelled Bobby, seeing the dark-eyed, dark-haired girl running down the platform. 'What sort of hols. did you have? Did you go back to the circus?'

Carlotta was a source of great attraction and admiration to the girls, for she had once been a circus-girl, and her understanding and handling of horses was marvellous. Now she had to settle down at St. Clare's, and learn many things she had never heard of. She had found her first term very difficult, but at the end of it she was firm friends with most of her form, and the mistresses were pleased with her. She ran up to the twins and Bobby, her vivid little face glowing with pleasure.

'Hallo!' she said. 'I'll get into your carriage. Oh, look—there's your cousin Alison. She looks rather miserable.'

'I *feel* miserable,' said Alison O'Sullivan, coming up, looking very woe-begone. 'I shall miss my friend Sadie dreadfully this term.'

Sadie had been an American girl with no ideas in her head at all beyond clothes and the cinema. She had had a very bad influence on Alison, but, as she was not coming back that term, it was to be hoped that the feather-headed Alison would pull herself together a little, and try to do better. She was a pretty little thing who easily burst into tears. Her cousins welcomed her warmly.

'Hallo, Alison! Don't fret about Sadie. You'll soon find other friends.'

They all got into the carriage. Doris arrived, panting. Hilary Wentworth, who had been head of the first form, flung herself down in a corner seat. She was very much

wondering if she would be head of the second form.   She
was a trustworthy and responsible girl who liked being
head.

' Hallo, everybody,' she said.   ' Nice to see you all
again.   Well, Carlotta—been riding in the Ring, I
suppose !   Lucky kid ! '

' You know I don't belong to a circus any more,' said
Carlotta.   ' I went to spend my holidays with my father
and my grandmother.   My father seems to like me quite
a lot—but my grandmother found a lot of fault with my
manners.   She says I must pay more attention to them
this term even than to my lessons !   You must all help
me ! '

' Oh no ! ' said Pat, with a laugh.   ' We don't want
you any different from what you are, my dear, hot-
tempered, entirely natural, perfectly honest little Carlotta !
We get more fun out of you than out of anyone.   We
don't want you changed one little bit !   Any more than
we want Bobby changed.   We shall expect some marvellous tricks from you this term, Bobby.'

' Right,' said Bobby.   ' But I tell you here and now,
I'm going to work too ! '

' Miss Jenks will see to that,' said Hilary.   ' Remember
we shall no longer be in the bottom form.   We've got to
work for exams. and pass them ! '

' We're off ! ' said Pat, leaning out of the window.
' Good-bye, Mummy !   We'll write on Sunday ! '

The train steamed slowly out of the station.   The girls
drew in their heads.   All the carriages were full of
chatterers, talking about the wonderful hols. they had
had, the places they had been to, and what sort of term
it would be.

' Any new girls ? ' said Isabel.   ' I haven't seen one.'

' I think there's only one,' said Bobby.   ' We saw a
miserable-looking creature standing a little way up the

platform—I don't know whether she'll be second form or first form. Not second, I hope—she looked such a misery!'

'Alison's doing her hair again already,' said Pat. 'Alison! Put your comb away. Girls, I think we'll have to make it a rule that Alison doesn't do her hair more than fifty times a day!'

Every one laughed. It was good to be back, good to be all together once more. The winter term was going to be fun!

2   IN THE SECOND FORM

IT was very strange at first to be in the second form, instead of the first. The twins felt very important, and looked down on the first-formers, feeling that they were very young and unimportant. But the third-formers also looked down on the second form, so things soon shook themselves out, and every one settled down.

'It's funny to go to the second form class-room instead of to Miss Roberts's room,' said Pat. ' I keep on going to the first form room, as I always used to do.'

'So do I,' said Janet. 'Miss Roberts is beginning to think we're doing it on purpose. We'd better be careful.'

' There's a whole lot of new girls in the first form, after all,' said Pat. ' Miss Roberts must have collected them altogether on the train. That's why we didn't see them. There's about twelve!'

'I shall never know all their names,' said Isabel. 'Anyway—they're only little kids—some of them not yet fourteen!'

'All the first-formers have been moved up,' said Bobby.
'Except young Pam—and she's only just fourteen. I
bet she'll be head of the first form!'

Pam Boardman had been new the term before, and was
a very hard-working child. As Bobby said, she was
made head of the first form, and was extremely proud of
the honour. She had many new girls under her, and was
eager to help them all.

Only two girls had been left down in the second form—
Elsie Fanshawe and Anna Johnson. The girls who had
just come up were sorry to see them there, for they were
not much liked. Elsie Fanshawe was spiteful, and Anna
Johnson was lazy.

'I suppose one of them will be head girl,' said Hilary,
with a grimace. 'Well—I don't fancy either of them,
do you, Bobby?'

'They both think themselves very superior to us,' said
Bobby. 'Just because they've been second-formers for
a year.'

'*I* should be ashamed,' said Carlotta. 'I would not
like to spend more than a year in any form. But Anna
is so lazy she will never get up into the third form, I'm
sure!'

'I believe Miss Jenks didn't send them up because she
hoped they'd buck up a bit if they were heads,' said Pat.
'I rather think she's going to make them joint head girls.
We shall have to look out if Elsie's head—she's really
catty.'

'We've got that Misery-girl in our form after all,' said
Bobby, looking at the new girl, who was standing mourn-
fully not far off, looking at nothing. 'She never says a
word, but looks as if she'll burst into tears at any moment!'

The Misery-girl, as the others called her, was named
Gladys Hillman. The girls tried to make her talk and
Bobbie did her best to make her laugh, but Gladys took

no notice of any one. She walked by herself, seemed to
dream all the time, and hardly spoke a word.

'Better leave her alone,' said Hilary. 'Perhaps she's
homesick.'

Not many of the St. Clare girls felt home-sick when
they returned to school, because it was all so jolly and
friendly, and there was so much to do that there seemed
no time to miss home and parents. The beginning of
term was always fun—new books given out, new girls to
size up, new desks to sit in, and sometimes new forms to
go to.

'There's a new mistress,' said Bobby, in excitement.
'She's to take Elocution and Drama! Look—there she
is—isn't she dark?'

Miss Quentin certainly was dark, and extremely good
looking. She had black piercing eyes, and a beautiful
voice. Alison thought she was wonderful.

'You *would*!' said Bobby. 'You'll be doing your
hair like Miss Quentin next, swept over your brow and
round your ears. There'll always be some one for you to
copy, my dear Alison! Do you remember last term how
you copied everything your dear friend Sadie did?'

Alison flushed. She was always being teased and she
never seemed to get used to it. She turned away with a
toss of her pretty head. The others laughed at her.
There was nothing bad in Alison—but on the other hand
there was nothing very good either. She was, as Pat so
often said, 'just a pretty little feather-head!'

The second form soon settled down with Miss Jenks.
At first it seemed strange to them not to have Miss
Roberts teaching them for most of the morning. They
missed her dry remarks and crisp words of praise. Miss
Jenks was not so shrewd as Miss Roberts, nor was she so
cool when angry. She could not bear the slightest hint
of rudeness, and she had no sympathy at all for 'frills

and fancies' as she put it.   No girl dared to fuss her hair
out too much, or to wear anything but a plain gold bar
for a brooch in Miss Jenks's class.

'Alison is in for a bad time!' grinned Bobby one
morning, when Alison had been sent to remove a bow
from her hair and a brooch from her collar.

'So is Carlotta!' said Pat.   'Miss Jenks doesn't like
frills and fancies—but she doesn't like untidiness either!
Just *look* at your hair, Carlotta.   It's wild enough in the
ordinary way—but it looks like a golliwog's hair at the
moment.'

'Does it really?' said Carlotta, who never cared in the
least what she looked like.   'Well, those sums we had
to do were so hard I just had to clutch my hair all the
time!'

'Old Mam'zelle's still the same,' said Isabel.   'Funny,
old, hot-tempered, flat-footed thing—but I like her all the
same.   She always gives us *some* excitement—and I bet
she will this term, too.   Do you remember how she and
Carlotta nearly came to blows last term?'

Yes—the summer term had been a very exciting one.
The girls looked at Mam'zelle and remembered all the
jokes they had played on her.   Dear old Mam'zelle, she
always fell for everything.   She was very terrifying when
she lost her temper, but she had a great sense of humour,
and when her short-sighted eyes twinkled behind their
glasses, the girls felt a real fondness for her.

'Ah,' said Mam'zelle, looking round the second form.
'Ah!   You are now the second form—very important,
very responsible, and very hard-working, *n'est ce pas?*
The first-formers, they are babies, they know nothing—
but as soon as you arrive in the second form, you are big
girls, you know a great deal.   Your French will be quite
per-r-r-rfect!   And Doris—ah, even Doris will be able
to roll her R's in the proper French way!'

Every one laughed. Poor Doris, always bottom at oral French, could never roll her R's. Doris grinned. She was a dunce, but nobody minded. She was a wonderful mimic and could keep the whole form in roars of laughter when she liked.

'R-r-r-r-r-r !' said Carlotta, unexpectedly. She sounded like an aeroplane taking off, and Mam'zelle frowned.

'You are now in the second form, Carlotta,' she said, coldly. 'We do not do those things here.'

'No, Mam'zelle,' said Carlotta, meekly. 'Of course not.'

'Tricks and jokes are not performed in any form higher than the first,' warned Mam'zelle. 'Whilst you are first-form babies, one does not expect much from you—but as soon as you leave the bottom form behind, it is different. We expect you to behave with dignity. One day the head-girl may be one of you here, and it is not too soon to prepare for such an honour.'

Winifred James, the much-admired head-girl, had left, and Belinda Towers, the sports captain, had taken her place. This was a very popular choice, for Belinda was well known by the whole school, and very much liked. As sports captain she knew practically all the girls, and this would be a great help to her as head-girl. She was not so gentle and quiet as Winifred, and many girls were afraid of her out-spokenness, but there was no doubt she would make an excellent head-girl.

Belinda visited every common room in turn and made the same short speech to the girls there.

'You all know I'm head-girl now—and I'm still sports-captain too. You can come to me if you're in a spot of trouble at any time and I'll help if I can. You'll all have to toe the mark where games are concerned, because I want to put St. Clare's right on the map this winter, with lacrosse. We must win every match we play !

We've got some fine players for a school team, but I want every form to supply players for the second and third match-teams too. So buck up, all of you, and practise hard.'

Alison groaned as Belinda went out of the second form common room. ' Why *do* we have to play games ? ' she said. ' They just make us hot and untidy and tired.'

' You forget they do other things as well,' said Janet. ' We have to learn to work together as a team—each one for his side, helping the others, not each one for himself. That sort of thing is especially good for *you*, my dear Alison—you'd sit in a corner and look at yourself in the mirror all day long if you could—and a fat lot of good that would do to you or anybody else.'

' Oh, be quiet,' said Alison. ' You're always getting at me ! '

It *was* fun to be back again, and to hear all the familiar school chatter, to groan over prep., to eat enormous teas, to talk about lacrosse, to laugh at somebody's joke, and to look forward to the class you liked the best—painting, maybe, or music, or elocution—or even maths !

There was a surprise for the second form at the end of the first week. Another new girl appeared ! She arrived at tea-time, with red eyes and a sulky mouth. She looked defiantly at every one as she took her place at the second form table.

' This is Mirabel Unwin,' said Miss Jenks. ' She has arrived rather late for beginning of term—but still, better late than never, Mirabel.'

' I didn't want to come at all,' said Mirabel, in a loud voice. ' They tried to make me come on the right day but I wouldn't. I only came now because my father promised I could leave at half-term if I'd come now. I suppose he thought once he got me here I'd stay. But I shan't.'

'That will do, Mirabel,' said Miss Jenks, soothingly.
'You are tired and over-wrought. Don't say any more.
You will soon settle down and be happy.'

'No, I shan't,' said the surprising Mirabel. 'I shan't
settle down and I shan't be happy. I shan't try at
anything, because what's the use if I'm leaving at half-
term?'

'Well, we'll see,' said Miss Jenks. 'Be sensible now
and eat some tea. You must be hungry.'

The girls stared at Mirabel. They were not used to
people who shouted their private affairs out in public.
They thought Mirabel was rather shocking—but rather
exciting too.

'I thought she was another Misery-girl at first, but I
believe she's just spoilt and peevish,' said Pat. 'I say—
the second form is going to be quite an exciting place this
term!'

3   TWO HEAD-GIRLS AND
TWO NEW GIRLS

MISS JENKS made both the old second-formers into
joint head-girls of the form. She and Miss Theobald,
the Head Mistress, had had a talk about them, and had
decided that perhaps it would be the making of them.

'Elsie is a spiteful type,' said Miss Jenks. 'She has
never been popular, though she would have liked to be
—so she gets back at the others by being spiteful and
saying nasty things. And Anna is bone-lazy—won't do a
thing if she can help it!'

'Well, a little responsibility may be good for them,'
said Miss Theobald, thoughtfully. 'It will give Elsie a

sense of importance, and bring out any good in her—
and Anna will have to bestir herself if she wants to keep
her position. Let them both try.'

'I don't know how they will work together,' said Miss
Jenks, doubtfully. 'They don't like each other very
much.'

'Let them try,' said Miss Theobald. 'Elsie is quick,
and she may stir Anna up a bit—and Anna is too lazy
to be spiteful, so perhaps she will be good for Elsie in
that way. But I too have my doubts!'

Elsie Fanshawe was delighted to be a joint head-girl—
though, of course, she would very much rather have been
the only one. Still, after being thoroughly disliked and
kept down by the whole of the second form, it was quite
a change to be top-dog!

'Now I can jolly well keep the others down and make
them look up to *me*,' thought Elsie, pleased. 'I can get
some of my own back. These silly little first-formers,
who have just come up, have got to learn to knuckle under
a bit. I can make Anna agree with all I do—lazy thing!
I'll have every single one of the rules kept, and I'll
make a few of my own, if I want to—and I'll report
any one who gets out of hand. It's worth-while not
going up into the third form, to be top of the second!'

The others guessed a little what Elsie was thinking.
Although they had not known the girl very well when
they were first-formers, they had heard the others talking
about her. They knew Elsie would try to 'get her own
back'.

'Just what a head-girl shouldn't do,' said Janet. 'She
should try and set some sort of example to the others,
or what's the use of being a leader? Look at old Hilary,
when she was head of the first form! She was a good
sport and joined in everything—but she always knew
where to draw the line without getting our backs up.'

'I can't bear Elsie,' said Carlotta. 'I would like to slap her hard.'

'Oh Carlotta! Have you still got that habit?' said Bobby, pretending to be shocked. 'Really, a second-former, too! What *would* Elsie say!'

Elsie overheard the last remark. 'What would I say to what?' she asked, coming up.

'Oh, nothing—Carlotta was simply saying she'd like to slap some one,' said Bobby, with a grin.

'Please understand, Carlotta, that you are in the second form now,' said Elsie, in a cold voice. 'We don't even *talk* of slapping people!'

'Yes, we do,' said Carlotta. 'Wouldn't you like to know whom I want to slap, dear Elsie?'

Elsie heard the danger-note in Carlotta's high voice, and put her nose in the air.

'I'm not interested in your slapping habits,' she said, and walked off.

'Shut up now, Carlotta,' said Bobby. 'Don't go and get all wild and Spanish again. You were bad enough with Prudence last term!'

'Well, thank goodness old Sour-Milk Prudence was expelled!' said Carlotta. 'I wouldn't have stayed if she had come back!'

It was the hour when all the second form were in their common room, playing, working or chattering. They loved being together like that. The wireless blared at one end of the room, and Doris and Bobby danced a ridiculous dance to the music. Gladys Hillman sat in a corner, looking as miserable as usual. Nobody could make anything of her. Isabel looked at her and felt sorry. She went over to her.

'Come and dance,' she said. Gladys shook her head.

'What's the matter?' asked Isabel. 'Are you home-sick? You'll soon get over it.'

'Don't bother me,' said Gladys. 'I don't bother you.'

'Yes, you do,' said Isabel. 'You bother me a lot.
I can't bear to see you sitting here all alone, looking so
miserable. Haven't you been to boarding-school before ? '

'No,' said Gladys. Her eyes filled with tears. Isabel
felt a little impatient with her. Hadn't she any courage
at all ?

'You don't seem to enjoy a single thing,' said Isabel.
'Don't you like any lesson specially—or games—or something ? '

'I like acting,' said Gladys, unexpectedly. 'And I
like lacrosse. That's all. But I don't like them here.
I don't like anything here.'

She wouldn't say any more, and Isabel gave her up.
She went across to Pat. 'Hopeless ! ' she said. 'Just a
mass of self-pity and tears ! She'll fade away and we'll
never notice she's gone if she doesn't buck up ! I'd
almost rather have that rude Mirabel than Gladys.'

Mirabel had been the source of much annoyance and
amusement to the second form. She was rude to the
point of being unbearable, and reminded every one every
day that she wasn't going to stay a day beyond half-
term.

'Don't tell me that any more,' begged Bobby. 'You
can't imagine how glad I am you're going at half-term.
It's the only bright spot I can see. But I warn you—
don't be too rude to Mam'zelle, or sparks will fly—and
don't get on the high horse too much with our dear
head-girl, Elsie Fanshawe, or you'll get the worst of it.
Elsie is pretty clever you know, and you're rather stupid.'

'No, I'm not ! ' flashed Mirabel, angrily. 'I only seem
stupid because I don't *want* to try—but you should hear
me play the piano and the violin ! *Then* you'd see ! '

'Why, you don't even *learn* music ! ' said Bobby.
'And I've never seen you open your mouth in the singing

class. We all came to the conclusion that you couldn't
sing a note.'

' That's all *you* know ! ' said Mirabel, rudely. ' Golly,
what a school this is ! I always knew boarding-school
would be awful—but it's worse than I expected. I hate
living with a lot of rude girls who think they're the cat's
whiskers just because they've been here a year or two ! '

' Oh, you make me tired,' said Bobby, and walked off.
' Really, what with you and the Misery-girl, and spiteful
old Elsie we're badly off this term ! '

Miss Jenks kept a very firm hand on Mirabel. ' You
may not intend to work,' she said, ' but you are not
going to stop the others from working ! You will do
one of three things, my dear Mirabel—you will stay in
the classroom and work—or you will stay in the classroom and do nothing at all, not even say a word—or
you will go and stand *out*side the classroom till the lesson
is finished ! '

At first Mirabel thought it was marvellous to defy Miss
Jenks and be sent outside. But she soon found it weari-
some to stand there so long, waiting for the others to
come out. Also, she was always a little afraid that the
Head Mistress, Miss Theobald, would come along. Loudly
as Mirabel declared that she cared for nobody, nobody
at all at silly St. Clare's, she *was* in awe of the quiet
Head Mistress.

' Did you tell Miss Theobald that you didn't mean to
stay here longer than half-term ? ' asked Pat. Every girl
had to go to see the Head Mistress when she arrived
on the first day.

' Of course I did ! ' said Mirabel, tossing her head.
' I told her *I* didn't care for anyone, not even the Head ! '

This was untrue. Mirabel had meant to say quite a
lot—but Miss Theobald had somehow said it first. She
had looked gravely at the red-eyed girl when she had

come in, and had told her to sit down. Mirabel opened
her mouth to speak, but Miss Theobald silenced her.

'I must finish this letter,' she said.   'Then we will talk.'

She kept Mirabel waiting for ten minutes. The girl
studied the Head's calm face, and felt a little awed. It
would be difficult to be rude to someone like this. The
longer she waited, the more difficult it would be to say
what she had meant to say.

Miss Theobald raised her head at last.   'Well, Mirabel,'
she said, 'I know you feel upset, angry and defiant.
Your father insisted you should come away to school
because you are spoilt and make his home unbearable.
You also domineer over your smaller brother and sister.
He chose St. Clare's because he thought we might be
able to do something for you.   No—don't interrupt me.
Believe me, I know all you want to say—but you don't
know what *I* have to say.'

There was a pause.   Even defiant Mirabel did not dare
to say a word.

'We have had many difficult girls here,' said Miss
Theobald.   'We rather pride ourselves on getting the
best out of them. You see, Mirabel, difficult children
often have fine things hidden in their characters—things
that perhaps more ordinary children don't possess . . .'

'What things?' asked Mirabel, interested in spite of
herself.

'Well—sometimes difficult children have a great talent
for something—a gift for art or drama, a talent for music
—or maybe they have some great quality—out-standing
courage, perhaps. Well, I don't know if this is the case
with you, or whether you are just a spoilt and unruly
girl—we shall see. All I want to say now is—give yourself a chance and let me see if there *is* anything worth-
while in you this half-term. If there is not, we don't
want you to stay. We shall be glad for you to go.'

This was so unexpected that Mirabel again had nothing to say. She had meant to say that nothing on earth would make her stay at St. Clare's beyond the half-term—but here was Miss Theobald saying that she didn't want to keep her longer than that—unless—unless she was worth-while! Worth-while!

'I don't care if I'm worth-while or not!' thought Mirabel to herself, indignantly. 'And how dare Daddy write and tell Miss Theobald those things about me? Why couldn't he keep our affairs to himself?'

Mirabel voiced this thought aloud. 'I think it was horrid of my father to tell you things about me,' she said, in a trembling voice.

'They were said in confidence to some one who under-stood," said Miss Theobald. 'Have you kept your own tongue quiet about *your* private affairs this afternoon, Mirabel? No—I rather think you gave yourself away to the whole school at tea-time when you arrived!'

Mirabel flushed. Yes—she had said far too much. She always did. She could not keep control over her tongue.

'You may go,' said Miss Theobald, picking up her pen again. 'And remember—it is not *St. Clare's* which is on trial—it is *you*! I hope I shall not say good-bye to you and rejoice to see the last of you at half-term. But—I shall not be surprised if I do!'

Mirabel went out of the room, her ears tingling, her face still red. She had been used to getting all her own way, to letting her rough tongue say what it pleased, and to ruling her parents and brother and sister as she pleased. When her father had at last declared in anger that she must go away, there had been a royal battle between them. The spoilt girl had imagined she could rule the roost at St. Clare's too. But she certainly could not rule Miss Theobald!

'Never mind—I'll lead everyone else a dance!' she thought. 'I'll show Daddy and the others that I mean what I say! I won't be sent away from home if I don't want to go.'

And so Mirabel set herself to be as annoying as possible, to spoil things for the others, and to try and domineer in the classroom, as she had always done at home. But she had not bargained for the treatment she got at last from an exasperated class.

4   MIRABEL IS A NUISANCE

THE second form did not so much mind when Mirabel was annoying in classes they disliked, such as the maths. class, which they found difficult that term—or even in Mam'zelle's class when she took irregular French verbs, hated by every girl. But they did dislike it when she spoilt, or tried to spoil, the English class, or the Art Class.

'It spoils our reading of *The Tempest*, when you make idiotic remarks, or flop about in your seat and make Miss Jenks keep on saying "Sit up!"' said Hilary, angrily. 'Either behave badly enough to get sent out of the room at once, idiot, or else keep quiet.'

'And if you dare to upset your paint-water all over somebody again, and make us lose ten minutes of the art class whilst we all get ticked off by Miss Walker I'll scrag you,' said Carlotta, all in one breath. 'We wouldn't mind so much if you did something really funny, like Bobby or Janet did last term—what you do *isn't* funny—just idiotic, spoiling things for the whole class.'

' I shall do what I like,' said Mirabel.

' You will not,' said Elsie, spitefully. ' I'm head-girl of this form—with Anna—and we say you are to behave yourself, or we'll know the reason why.'

' You do know the reason why,' said Mirabel, pertly.

' Any one would think you were six years old, the way you behave,' said Bobby, in disgust. ' Well—I warn you—you'll be sorry if you keep on like this. We're all getting tired of you.'

The explosion came during the Drama class. This was taken by the new teacher, Miss Quentin, and was really rather an exciting class. The girls were to write and act their own play. Dark-eyed Miss Quentin was full of good suggestions, and the play was almost written.

The new teacher was not much good at discipline. She relied on her good looks and rather charming manner, and on the interest of her lessons, to help her to discipline her classes. Alison adored her, and, as the girls had already foreseen, was copying her in everything, from her little tricks of speech, to the way she did her hair.

Most of the girls liked Miss Quentin, though they did not very much respect the way she coaxed them to behave when they became a little unruly. They really preferred the downright methods of Miss Roberts or Miss Jenks. Mirabel, of course, soon found that Miss Quentin was quite unable to keep her in order.

' Your turn now, Mirabel dear,' Miss Quentin would say, smiling brightly at her. Mirabel would pretend not to hear, and Miss Quentin would raise her voice slightly.

' Mirabel! Your turn now, dear! '

The class disliked Miss Quentin's ' dears ' and ' lambs ' and other names—except Alison. She loved them. They all looked at Mirabel impatiently. She was always losing time like this, when they wanted to get on.

Mirabel would pretend to come back to earth with a

start, fumble for the place, be gently helped by Miss
Quentin, and at last say something, usually incorrect.
When there was any acting to be done she came in at
the wrong moment, said the wrong lines, and altogether
behaved in a most annoying manner. Miss Quentin was
at a loss to know how to deal with her.

'Mirabel! I have never yet sent a girl out of my
class,' she would say, in such a sorrowful voice that it
quite wrung Alison's heart. 'Now come—pull yourself
together and try again.'

One morning Alison was waiting to act a part she
loved. She had rehearsed it over and over again to
herself, acting it, as she thought, to perfection. She was
longing for her turn to come, so that she might gloat
over the sugared words of praise she felt sure would
drop from Miss Quentin's lips.

There were ten more minutes to go—just about time
for Alison's turn to come. And then Mirabel chose to
be stupid again, saying her lines incorrectly, doing the
wrong things so that Miss Quentin had to make her speak
and act two or three times. The teacher, following her
usual rule of being patient and encouraging, wasted
nearly all the precious ten minutes on Mirabel.

Alison cast her eye on the clock, and bit her lip. All
her rehearsing would be wasted now. How she hated
that stupid Mirabel, holding up every class in order to
be annoying.

'Now Mirabel *dear*," said Miss Quentin, in her charming, patient voice, 'say it like this . . .'

It was too much for Alison. She stamped her
foot. 'Mirabel! Stop fooling! It's hateful the way
you take Miss Quentin in—and she's so patient too.
You've wasted half the time—and now I shan't have
my turn.'

'Poor little Alison!' said Mirabel, mockingly. 'She

so badly wanted to show off to her precious Miss Quentin, and hear her say " Well done, *darling* ! " '

There was a dead silence. Then Alison burst into a flood of tears, and Carlotta boxed Mirabel's ears very neatly and smartly. Miss Quentin stared in horror.

' Girls ! Girls ! What are you thinking of ? Carlotta ! You amaze me. I cannot have this behaviour, I really cannot. Carlotta, apologize at once to Mirabel.'

' Certainly not,' said Carlotta. ' I don't mean to be rude to *you*, Miss Quentin—but you must see for yourself that Mirabel deserved it. I knew no-one else but me would dare to do it—and it's been coming to Mirabel for quite a long time.'

The bell rang for the next class. Miss Quentin was most relieved. She had no idea how to tackle things of this sort. She gathered up her books quickly.

' There is no time to say any more, girls,' she said. ' I must go to my next class. Carlotta, I still insist that you put things right with Mirabel by apologizing.'

She went out of the room in a flurry. Carlotta grinned round at the others. ' Well ! ' she said, ' don't stand staring at me like that as if I'd done something awful. You know quite well you've all wanted to box Mirabel's ears yourselves. We're as tired of her as we can be. It's a pity half-term isn't here and we can see the back of her.'

' Carlotta, you shouldn't do things like that,' said Janet. ' Alison, for pity's sake, stop howling. Mirabel, you deserved it, and now perhaps you'll shut up and behave properly.'

Mirabel had gone rather white. She had not attempted to hit back at Carlotta. ' If you think that will stop me doing what I like to spoil things for anybody you're mistaken,' she said, at last, in a tight kind of voice. ' It'll make me worse.'

' I suppose it will,' said Hilary. ' Well—I'll give you a warning. If you don't stop being an idiot, *we* shall make things uncomfortable for *you*. I don't mean we shall box your ears. We shan't. But there are other ways.'

Mirabel said no more—but as she made no attempt that day or the following to behave sensibly, the girls made up their minds that they must carry out their threat.

They met in one of the music-rooms. Elsie Fanshawe was pleased. This excited her—it gladdened her spiteful nature, and added to her sense of importance, for, as she was one of the head-girls, she could direct every one in what they had to do.

' We've met together to decide how to get back at Mirabel,' she began.

Hilary interrupted her. ' Well—not exactly " get back ", Elsie,' she said. ' It's more to prevent her from going on disgracing herself and our class.'

' Call it what you like,' said Elsie, impatiently. ' Now —what I propose is this : we'll take her books from her desk and hide them. We'll make her an apple-pie bed each night. We'll stitch up the pockets and sleeves of her out-door coat. We'll put stones into her Wellingtons. We'll . . .'

' It all sounds rather spiteful,' said Hilary, doubtfully. ' Need we do quite so many things ? I know Mirabel is perfectly sickening and needs a good lesson—but don't let's make ourselves as bad as she is ! '

' Well—do as you like,' said Elsie, rather sneeringly. ' If you're too goody-goody to follow the lead of your head-girls, well, there will be plenty of us who'll do what I say.'

' I bet Anna didn't think of any of those things,' said Bobby, looking at the plump, placid Anna, sitting beside Elsie.

The meeting discussed the matter a little more, and

Carlotta boxed Mirabel's ears very smartly

then, at the sound of a school-bell, broke up. Only
Gladys had said nothing. She had sat, as usual, in a
kind of dream, paying hardly any attention to what was
said. The girls were becoming so used to the Misery-girl,
as they called her, that they really hardly noticed whether
she was there or not.

'Well,' said Hilary, as the girls ran off to change for
games, 'I suppose we must do something to teach Mirabel
that two can play at being annoying—but somehow a lot
of spitefulness seems to have got mixed up in it.'

'It's bound to, with Elsie Fanshawe to lead us!' said
Bobby. 'I wish she wasn't our head-girl. She's not
the right sort. As for Anna, she's no use at all—just a
lazy lump!'

'Mirabel's going to have a few shocks from now on,'
said Alison, who was more pleased than anyone to think
of the tricks that were to be played on Mirabel. 'I for
one will do everything with the greatest pleasure!'

'I hope your darling Miss Quentin will be pleased
with you!' said Bobby, with a grin, and scampered off
to the field before Alison could think of any reply.

5   MIRABEL AND THE MISERY-GIRL

IT was not pleasant to be thought a tiresome nuisance
by girls and teachers alike. Mirabel was getting tired of
her defiant pose. Nobody had ever thought it was funny,
as she had hoped. Nobody had ever laughed. They had
just got impatient. The girl began to feel sorry she had
ever started her irritating behaviour.

A great feeling of misery overtook her the evening of
the day she had been slapped by Carlotta. She felt that
no one liked her, and certainly no one loved her. Hadn't
her own father sent her away ? And her mother had agreed
to it ! How could she put up with that ? There was no
way to answer things like that except by being defiant.

Mirabel felt that she did not want to be with the others
that evening in the noisy common room. She stole away
by herself to one of the music-rooms. She had spoken
truly when she had told Bobby that she could play the
piano and the violin. She loved music, and was a really
good performer on the piano, and a beautiful player of
the violin. But because of her defiant obstinacy, she
had refused to learn either of the instruments at St.
Clare's, when he father had spoken to her about them.

'You can learn well there,' he had told her. 'There
are excellent teachers of bth.'

'What's the use !' Mirabel had flashed back at him.
'I'm only going to be there for half a term—and you
don't want to have to pay full fees for two lots of music
lessons, do you, as well as full fees for the ordinary
lessons ? '

'Very well. Have it your own way,' said her father.
So nothing had been said about learning music, and the
girl had missed her weekly lessons very much. Music
had always helped her strong, domineering nature—and
now, without it, she felt lost. She was depressed and
unhappy to-night—her mind longed for something to
fasten on, something to love. She thought of her violin
at home, and wished with all her heart that she had
brought it with her.

It was dark in the music-room. Mirabel did not turn
on the light, for she was afraid somebody passing might
see her, and she did not want any company just then.
She leaned her arms on a little table and thought.

Her hands touched something—a violin case. Something in the feel of it stirred her, and suddenly, with hands that trembled a little, she undid the strap and took out the violin inside. She put it lovingly under her chin, and groped for the bow.

And then the little dark music-room was full of music, as Mirabel played to herself. She played to comfort herself, to forget herself, and the notes filled the little room, and made it beautiful.

'That's better,' said Mirabel at last. 'That's much better! I didn't know how much I'd missed my music. I wonder whereabouts the piano is. I'll play that too. Why didn't I think of this before?'

She groped her way to the piano, and began to finger the notes gently in the darkness. She played from memory, and chose melodies that were sad and yearning, to match her own mood.

She thought she was alone, and she put her whole heart into her playing. Then suddenly she heard a sound in the room beside her, and she stopped at once, her heart thumping. She heard a stifled sob.

'Who's there?' said Mirabel, in a low voice. There was no answer. Someone began softly to grope her way to the door. Mirabel felt a stir of anger. Who was it spying on her? Who had come into the room like that? She jumped up and grabbed wildly at the some one near the door. She caught a blouse sleeve and held on.

'Who is it?' she said.

'Me—Gladys,' said a voice. 'I was in here alone—when you came in. I didn't know you were going to play. But you played such beautiful music I had to stay—and then it got sad, and I cried.'

'You're always crying,' said Mirabel, impatiently. 'What's the matter?'

'I shan't tell you,' said Gladys. 'You'll only tell the

others, and they'd laugh. They call me Misery-girl, I know. It's hateful. They'd be Misery-girls too if they were like me.'

'Like *you*—why, what's the matter with you?' asked Mirabel, her curiosity aroused. 'Look here—tell me. I shan't jeer at you or anything.'

'Well, don't turn on the light then,' said Gladys. 'You'll think I'm very feeble, so I'd rather tell you in the dark.'

'You *are* a queer fish,' said Mirabel. 'Come on— what's the matter?'

'It's my mother,' said Gladys. 'She's awfully ill—in hospital—and I don't know if she'll get better. I simply can't tell you how much I love her, and how much I miss her. I haven't a father, or brothers or sisters— only my mother. I've never been away from her even for a night till now. I know it sounds silly to you— you'll call me babyish and mother's girl—and so I am, I suppose. But you see, Mother and I haven't had any one but each other—and I'm so terribly, terribly home-sick, and want to be with Mother so much. . . .'

Gladys burst into sobs again, and cried so miserably that Mirabel forgot her own troubles for the moment and put her arm awkwardly round the girl. She saw how little courage Gladys had got—she saw how little she tried to face what had come to her—and she felt a little scornful. But no one could help feeling sorry for the miserable girl. Mirabel had no idea what to do for the best.

'Well,' she said, saying the first thing that came into her head, 'well, how would you like to be *me*! Sent away from home by your mother and father because they didn't want you, and said you upset your brother and sister and made every one unhappy! That's what *I've* got to put up with! I'm not so lucky as you, I think!'

Gladys raised her head, and for the first time forgot her unhappiness in her scorn of Mirabel.

'*You* unlucky ! Don't be silly—you don't know how lucky you are ! To have a father *and* a mother, a brother *and* a sister, all to love and to love you. And I only have my mother and even she is taken away from me ! Mirabel, you deserve to be sent away from home if you can't understand that families should love one another ! I can tell you, if I had all those people to love *I* wouldn't behave so badly to them that they'd send me away. You ought to be ashamed of yourself.'

Coming from the silent Gladys, this was most astonishing. Mirabel stared into the darkness, not knowing what to say. Gladys got up and went to the door.

'I'm sorry,' she said, in a muffled voice. 'You're unhappy—and I'm unhappy—and I should be sorry for you, and comfort you. But you made your own unhappiness—and I didn't make mine. That's the difference between us.'

The door banged and Mirabel was alone. She sat still in surprise. Who would have thought that Gladys could say all that ? Mirabel thought back to her own home. She saw the golden head of her little sister, the dark one of her brother, bent over home-work. She saw the gentle, patient face of her mother, who always gave in to every one. She remembered the good-humoured face of her father, changed to a sad and angry countenance because of her own continual insistence on her own way.

'It was Mother's fault for giving in to me,' she thought. 'And Harry and Joan should have stood up to me. But it's difficult for younger ones to stand up for themselves —and after all, I *am* difficult. I wish I was home now. I'm lonely here, and I've behaved like an idiot. I know Mother would always love me—and yet I've been beastly to her—and turned Daddy against me too. Harry and

Joan will be glad I've gone.   Nobody in the world wants
me or loves me.'

Self-pity brings tears more quickly to the eyes than
anything else.   Mirabel put her head on the table and
wept.   She forgot Gladys and her trouble.   She only felt
sorry for herself.   She dried her eyes after a while, and
sat up.

'I shall stop behaving badly,' she thought.   'I shall
leave at half-term and go back home and try to do
better.   I'm tired of being silly.   I'll turn over a new leaf
tomorrow, and perhaps the girls will feel more friendly.'

She got up and switched on the light.   Her watch
showed five minutes to nine—almost bed-time.   She sat
down at the piano and played to herself for a while, and
then, when the nine-o'clock bell sounded, made her way
upstairs to bed, full of good resolutions.   She began to
make pictures of how nice the girls would be to her
when they found she was turning over a new leaf.   Perhaps the twins would find she was somebody worth
knowing after all.

Poor Mirabel !   When she got into bed that night, she
found that she could only get her legs half-way down
it !   The girls had made a beautiful apple-pie bed, and,
not content with that, Elsie had put a spray of holly
across the bend of the sheet.   Mirabel gave a shout of
dismay as the holly pricked her toes.

' Oh !   Who's put this beastly thing into my bed ?
It's scratched my foot horribly ! '

Mirabel had never had an apple-pie bed made for her
before.   She could not imagine what had happened.   She
tried to force her legs down to the bottom of the bed,
but only succeeded in tearing the sheet.

The girls were in fits of laughter.   They soon saw that
Mirabel had not experienced an apple-pie bed before,
and had no idea that the top sheet had been tucked

under the bolster, and then folded in half, half-way down
the bed, and brought back to fold over the blanket.
Doris rolled on her bed in glee, and even placid Anna
squealed with joy.

' Golly ! You'll have to report that tear to Matron
in the morning,' said Elsie, when she heard the sheet
torn in half. ' You idiot ! You might have guessed that
would happen. You'll spend the next sewing-class mending a long rent.'

Mirabel threw the holly at Elsie. She had now discovered what had happened, and was angry and hurt.
She got into bed and drew the covers round her. The
others chuckled a little and then one by one fell asleep.

In the morning Mirabel awoke early. She lay and
thought over what she had decided the night before.
It wasn't going to be easy to make a complete change-
over, but she didn't see anything else to do. She simply
could NOT go on being idiotic. Once you were ashamed
of yourself, you had to stop. If you didn't, then you
really were an idiot.

So, full of good resolutions still, Mirabel went to her
classes. She would work well. She would give Mam'zelle
a great surprise. She would please Miss Jenks. She
would make up for her rudeness to Miss Quentin. She
would even be decent to that wild little Carlotta, and
forgive her for that box on the ears. The girls would
see she wasn't so bad as they thought she was, and
they would turn over a new leaf too, and be friendly to
her. Everything would be lovely again—and at the half-
term she would leave, and people would be sorry to see
her go !

It was with these pleasant thoughts that poor Mirabel
entered on a day of horrid shocks and unpleasant surprises !

ALISON and Elsie were the two who enjoyed punishing
Mirabel more than any of the others. Elsie because she
was naturally spiteful, and Alison because she had been
so annoyed at losing her turn in Miss Quentin's class.

'I'll sew up the sleeves of Mirabel's coat,' said Alison
to Elsie. 'I'll do them awfully tightly. She'll be
furious!'

'I'll take out some of her books and hide them,' said
Elsie. 'Anna, go and find Mirabel's Wellington boots and
put small pebbles inside—right in the toes.'

'Oh, can't some one else do that?' said Anna. 'I
shall have to go down to the games-room to get the boots.
Bobbie, you go.'

Elsie went to the classroom before morning school and
removed various books and exercise papers. There was
no one else in the room. The girl spitefully dropped ink
on to a maths. paper that Mirabel had done. 'This will
teach her to behave better!' said Elsie to herself.
'Now—where shall I put the books?'

She decided to put them at the back of the handwork
upboard, and cover them with the loose raffia there.
So into the cupboard went the books, and then Elsie,
having a few minutes to spare, looked round for something
else to do.

She saw the List of Classroom Duties hung up on the
wall and went to read them. It was Mirabel's turn that
week to keep the vases well-filled with water. Elsie
pursed up her lips spitefully.

'I'll empty out the water—and then, when the flowers
begin to droop, Miss Jenks will notice and Mirabel will

get ticked off for forgetting the water,' thought Elsie. So out of the window went the water from the four big vases. The flowers were hurriedly replaced just as the first bell went for lessons.

The second form trooped in to take their places. Alison went to hold the door for Miss Jenks. Mirabel took a look round at the girls, hoping to get a smile from some one. She was longing to say that she meant to turn over a new leaf. But nobody looked at her except Elsie, who nudged Anna and then turned away.

'She's coming!' hissed Alison. The class stopped lounging over their desks and talking. They stood up and waited in silence. Miss Jenks was very strict about politeness and good manners in her class.

'Good morning, girls,' said the mistress, putting her books on her desk. 'Sit, please. We will . . . good gracious, Alison, what is that you are wearing on your left wrist?'

'A bracelet,' said Alison, sulkily. The girls looked at it and giggled. It was very like one that Miss Quentin wore. Alison loved to wear anything that even remotely resembled her beloved Miss Quentin's belongings.

'Alison, I am getting tired of asking you to remove bows and brooches and bracelets and goodness knows what,' said Miss Jenks. 'What with putting up with Mirabel's stupidities, and your vanities, I'm going really grey!'

Miss Jenks had flaming red hair, with not a scrap of grey in it. The girls smiled, but were not certain enough of Miss Jenks's temper that day to laugh out loud.

'Bring me that bracelet, Alison,' said Miss Jenks, in a tired voice. 'You can have it back in a week's time providing that during that time I haven't had to remove any other frills and fancies from you.'

Alison sulkily gave up the bracelet. She knew it was

the rule that no jewellery should be worn with school
uniform, but the little feather-head was always trimming
herself up with something or other.

'And now please get out your maths. books and the
exercise you did for prep. and we will go on to the next
page of sums,' said Miss Jenks. 'It's much the same as
the one we did yesterday. Work them out, please, and
if there is any difficulty, let me know. Come up one by
one as I call you, with your maths. exercise paper, and I
will correct it at my desk with you.'

The class got busy. Desks were opened and books got
out. Pencils were taken from boxes. Exercise books
were opened, and there was a general air of getting down
to hard work.

Mirabel hunted all through her desk for her maths.
book. How curious! It didn't seem to be there.
'Have you borrowed my maths. book?' she asked Janet
in a whisper.

'No whispering,' said Miss Jenks, who had ears like a
lynx. 'What is it, Mirabel? One of your usual inter-
ruptions, I suppose.'

'No, Miss Jenks,' said Mirabel, meekly. 'I can't find
my maths. book, that's all.'

'Mirabel, you're always pretending you can't find this
and that,' said Miss Jenks. 'Get your book at once and
begin.'

'But, Miss Jenks, it really isn't here,' said Mirabel,
hunting frantically through her desk again. The girls
nudged one another and grinned. They all knew where
it was—at the back of the handwork cupboard. Mirabel
might look through her desk all day but she wouldn't
find her book.

'Share Janet's book, then,' said Miss Jenks, shortly,
only half-believing Mirabel. Mirabel heaved a sigh of
relief, and opened her arithmetic book to copy down the

sums from Janet's text-book. She put ready her maths. paper, which she had done in prep. the night before, to show to Miss Jenks. But as she turned it over the right way, she stared at it in horror. It was covered with ink-spots !

' Just as I've made up my mind to turn over a new leaf, all these things happen ! ' thought Mirabel in dismay. ' I can't imagine how I got that ink on my paper. Miss Jenks will never believe I didn't know it was there.'

Mirabel was right—Miss Jenks didn't believe it ! She looked in disgust at the untidy paper. She would not even correct it.

' Another of your nice little ways, I suppose,' she said. ' Do it again, please.'

' Miss Jenks, I really didn't make all those ink-spots,' said Mirabel. But she had given in too many badly-done papers before, on purpose, for Miss Jenks suddenly to believe her now.

' I don't want to discuss the matter,' said Miss Jenks. ' Do it all again, and let me have it this evening, without any mess on it at all.'

Mirabel went back to her desk. She caught Elsie's spiteful smile, but she did not guess yet that there was a campaign against her. She sat down, angry and puzzled.

The French class came next, and Mirabel discovered, to her dismay, that not only her French books, but also the French paper she had written out the day before as homework, had disappeared. She hunted through her desk again and again, and Mam'zelle grew sarcastic.

' Mirabel, is it possible for you to come out of your desk before the lesson is ended? Soon I shall forget what your face is like.'

' Mam'zelle, I'm sorry, but I can't seem to find the French paper I did yesterday,' said Mirabel, emerging from her desk flushed and worried.

If there was one thing that Mam'zelle could not stand, it was the non-appearance of any work she had set the class to do. She frowned, and her glasses slid down her big nose. The girls watched gleefully. The knew the signs of gathering wrath. Mam'zelle replaced her glasses on the bridge of her nose.

'Ah, Mirabel ! You cannot seem to find the work you did, you say ?   How many times have I heard that excuse since I have been here at St. Clare's ?   A thousand times, ten thousand times ! You have not done the work. Do not deny it, I know.   You are a tiresome girl—you have been tiresome ever since the first day you came. You will always be tiresome. You will give me that work before the end of the morning or you will not play lacrosse this afternoon.'

'But, Mam'zelle, I really *did* do it ! ' protested Mirabel, almost in tears.   ' I can't find my ordinary French books, either. They're gone.'

'Always this Mirabel holds up my class ! ' cried Mam'zelle, raising her hands to the ceiling and wagging them in a way that made Doris long to imitate her at once. ' She loses things—she looks for them—she makes excuses—I cannot bear this girl.'

'Nor can anybody,' said Alison, delighted at the success of the trick. Mirabel flashed an angry glance at her. She was beginning to wonder if the girls had had anything to do with the mysterious disappearance of her things.

'It's too bad all this happening now,' she thought. ' Mam'zelle might believe me.   I really am speaking the truth.'

But Mirabel had so often been silly and untruthful that she had only herself to blame now if no one believed her when she did actually tell the truth.   She tried once more with Mam'zelle.

'Please do believe me, Mam'zelle,' she begged. 'Elsie saw me doing the paper last night. Didn't you, Elsie?'

'Indeed I didn't,' said Elsie, maliciously.

'Ah, this untruthful Mirabel!' cried Mam'zelle. 'You will do me the paper once because you have not done it—and again you will do it for me because you have told an untruth.'

Mirabel saw her time at break going. She would have to do the two papers then. She looked round the class for sympathy. Usually, comforting glances were sent from one girl to another, when somebody got into trouble. But there were no comforting glances for Mirabel. Every one was glad that the Nuisance was in trouble.

Poor Mirabel! Her troubles were never-ending that morning. Miss Jenks noticed all the drooping flowers in the waterless vases, during the next lesson, and spoke sharply about it.

'Who is Room-Monitor this week?'

'I am,' said Mirabel.

'Well, look at the flowers,' said Miss Jenks. 'It doesn't seem as if they can have a drop of water in the vases, by the look of them.'

'Why, I filled them all up yesterday,' said Mirabel, indignantly. 'I did really.'

Miss Jenks went to the nearest vase and tipped it up. 'Not a drop of water,' she said. 'I suppose you will suggest next that somebody has emptied all the vases, Mirabel?'

It flashed across the girl's mind that some one might actually have done that, to pay her back for all the annoying things she had done. But it seemed such a mean trick—to make flowers die in order to get somebody into trouble! She flushed and said nothing.

'I suppose you thought I would let you miss part of the lesson whilst you filled up the flowers,' said Miss Jenks, in disgust. 'Hilary, have you finished answering the

questions on the blackboard ?   Good—then just go and
get some water for the vases, will you ? '

Mirabel spent the whole of break doing the French paper
twice over.   She guessed now, by the grins and nudges
among the girls, that most of her troubles were due to
them, and she was angry and hurt.   ' Just as I had made
up my mind to be decent ! ' she thought, as she wrote out
the French papers quickly.   ' It's beastly of every one.'

She was late for games because she could not put on
her coat in time to go to the field with the others.   Alison
had sewn up the sleeves well and truly—so tightly that
it was impossible to break the stitches.   Mirabel had to
go and hunt for a pair of scissors to cut the sewn-up
sleeves.   She was almost in tears.

And then, when she put on her Wellingtons to go across
the muddy field-path, she squealed in pain.   Nasty little
pebbles made her hobble along—and at last she had to stop,
take off the boots, and empty the pebbles into the hedge.

Miss Wilton, the sports mistress, had already started
the lacrosse game going.   ' You're late, Mirabel,' she
called.   ' Stand aside until half-time.   If you can't bother
to be in time, you can miss part of the game.'

It was cold standing and watching.   Mirabel felt
miserable.   Everybody and everything was against her.
What was the use of trying to be different ?

Miss Wilton took her to task at half-time.   ' Why were
you so late ?   You know the time perfectly well.   You
were almost fifteen minutes after the others ! '

She waited to hear Mirabel's excuse.   The other girls
listened.   They had not bargained for Miss Wilton
enquiring into the matter.   Alison felt uncomfortable.
She didn't want to get into trouble for sewing up Mirabel's
coat-sleeves.   She did not want another bad report.
Last term's had been very poor, and her father had had
a good many things to say that were not pleasant to hear.

Mirabel opened her mouth to pour out her woes—how her coat-sleeves had been sewn up—stones put into her Wellingtons—and goodness knows what else done to her ! Then she shut her mouth again. How often had she scolded her young brother and sister for telling tales of her when she had made things unpleasant for them ? She had always said that a tale-bearer was some one quite impossible.

'The girls deserve to have tales told about them,' thought Mirabel, 'but I shan't make myself into something I hate just to get back on them.'

So she said nothing at all.

'Well,' said Miss Wilton, impatiently, 'as you have no excuse, it seems, take off your coat and join in the second half of the game. But next time, if you are late, you will not play in the game at all—you can just go back to school and ask Miss Jenks to give you something to do.'

The game went on. One or two of the girls began to feel uncomfortable. It was decent of Mirabel not to give them away. You couldn't attack people if they behaved well. 'It's time we stopped going for Mirabel,' thought Hilary. 'I'll tell Elsie so tonight !'

7   A MEETING IN THE COMMON ROOM

ANOTHER meeting, this time called by Hilary, was held that night. It was held in the common room. Every one was there but Mirabel, who was doing her maths. paper all over again in the classroom.

'What's the meeting for?' asked Elsie, half-indignant that any one but herself should call a meeting.

'It's about Mirabel,' said Hilary. 'You know, she didn't split on us when she had the chance to—so I vote we stop playing tricks on her now. Anyway, we pretty well put her through it today!'

'We're certainly not going to stop,' said Elsie, at once. 'What, stop when she's only just begun to learn her lesson! She'll be as bad as ever if we don't go on showing her we can make things just as tiresome for her as she has made them for us!'

'No, we've done enough,' said Hilary. 'It makes me feel rather mean. I rather wish we hadn't done *quite* so many things—and anyway, I don't know who spilt ink over her maths. paper, and took the water out of the flowers. We didn't arrange that. Who did it?'

There was a silence. Elsie went red. She did not dare to say she had done anything more than had already been arranged—the others might think her spiteful, or mean.

'I believe it was Elsie!' said Carlotta, suddenly. 'Look how red she's gone!'

Every one looked. Elsie scowled. 'Of course I didn't do anything,' she said. 'I don't think we did nearly enough. I think a girl who openly says she's jolly well going to make herself too beastly to stay more than half a term ought to be well shown up!'

'Well, she *has* been shown up—by her own self!' said Janet. 'No one would have known anything about her or her private affairs if she hadn't gone round yelling them out! I think Hilary is right—we won't do anything more.'

'You talk as if Hilary is head-girl,' said Elsie, spitefully.

'Well—so she was in the first form,' said Bobby, losing her temper. 'And let me tell you she was a much better one than you, Elsie.'

'Don't forget that Anna is head-girl too,' said Pat. Anna smiled sleepily. Bobby turned on her at once.

'As if anyone can remember that Anna is head-girl, or anything! What's the good of a head-girl who is always too lazy to do a single thing? We've got two head-girls in this form—and one is spiteful and catty and over-bearing—and the other is fat and lazy!'

'Shut up, Bobby,' said Hilary, uncomfortably. 'It's no good losing your temper like that. Let's get back to the point—and that is, we're not going to persecute Mirabel any more. Let's give her a chance and see if today's lessons have taught her anything. She knows well enough we have all been working against her—and that must be a very horrid experience.'

'Hilary Wentworth—if you don't stop talking as if *you* were head of this form, you'll be sorry,' said Elsie, angered by Bobby's candid speech. 'Anna—for heaven's sake sit up and back me up.'

'But I don't think you're right,' said Anna, in her gentle voice. 'I don't want to persecute Mirabel, either. I don't feel spiteful towards her now.'

'You're too lazy to feel anything,' said Elsie, surprised and furious at Anna's unexpected refusal to back her up. 'You know perfectly well that as head-girls we must work together—and it's an unwritten rule that the form go by what we say.'

'Well, I can't work with you in this,' said Anna. 'I may be fat and lazy and all the other things you probably think about me, and don't say—but I am not catty. So *I* say, as head-girl of the form—we will NOT continue with our tricks against Mirabel.'

'Well!' said Pat, 'this is going to be difficult—two head-girls, each saying different! I suppose we'd better put it to the vote, which girl we follow. Now—hands up for Anna and doing what she says!'

Every single hand went up at once. Anna grinned
and for once sat up really straight. Elsie went white.

' Now—hands up those who wish to follow Elsie,' said
Pat. Not a single hand went up, of course. Elsie stood
up angrily.

' This is what comes of having to stay down with a lot
of half-baked first-formers ! ' she said, her voice trembling.
' Well—I'll tell you who emptied the water out of the
vases—and dropped ink on Mirabel's maths. paper—it was
your precious Anna ! If you want to follow a girl who
does things like that, and then is ashamed to own up to
them, well, you can ! '

She flung herself out of the room and slammed the
door loudly. Anna raised her well-marked eye-brows.

' Well, girls,' she said, in her rather drawling voice, ' I
assure you I am not guilty.'

Every one believed her. Anna might be lazy and not
bother herself or undertake any kind of responsibility—
but at least she was truthful and honest.

' I'm not going to count Elsie as head-girl any more,'
said Isabel. ' We'll have only Anna. Come on, Anna—
stir yourself, and settle things one way or another.'

' Poor Anna—she will have to open her eyes and wake
up at last,' said Carlotta's high voice, rather maliciously.
Anna stood up suddenly.

' Well—I'm just as tired of Elsie's spite and cattiness
as you are,' she said. ' So if you'll do with just me as
head-girl, I'll wake up a bit. It's not been easy trying
to work in with Elsie. I'm not going to give her away—
but I just can't bear some of the things she says and does.
Now—it's not enough just to stop persecuting Mirabel—
can't we do something positive—I mean, something to
put her right, instead of just stopping her being wrong?'

Every one gaped at Anna. This was the first time the
big, sleepy-eyed girl had ever made such a long speech.

or suggested anything of her own accord.   Hilary thought her suggestion was excellent.

'Yes—that's the way to do things really,' she agreed. 'It's not enough to stop things going wrong—you've got to set them going the other way—on the right road.   But I don't for the life of me see how.   Mirabel is terribly difficult.   I can't see that she's any good at anything at all.   There isn't anything to work on.'

'She's bad at lessons—no good at games—hopeless at art—poor at gym,' said Isabel.   'If there was *something* she was good at, we could make it our starting-point—you know, praise her up a bit, and give her some self-respect. That's what people need when things have gone wrong.'

Then the second form had a great surprise.   The Misery-girl spoke, in her rather timid little voice!

'Mirabel *is* good at something!   *Awfully* good!'

Every one stared at Gladys in double-amazement, astonished that she should have spoken at all, and amazed to hear what she said.   Gladys seemed to shrink under the gaze of so many pairs of eyes.   She wished she had not spoken—but she had been interested, in spite of herself, in the scene that had been going on—and she had suddenly felt that she would like to help stupid Mirabel. After all—she had put her arm round her the night before, and had been kind in her own awkward way.

'What do you mean?' said Anna.

'Well—she's frightfully good at music,' stammered Gladys, horrified now to think she had to speak to so many girls at once.

'How do you know?' asked Janet.   'She's never played any instrument here—and she doesn't even open her mouth in the singing-class.'

'I know because I've heard her,' said Gladys.   'She was in the music-room last night—you know, the one next to the boot-cupboard—and first she played a violin—oh, most beautifully—and then she played the piano. And it was all in the dark too.'

' In the *dark* ! ' said Carlotta, in surprise. ' Whatever were you two doing there in the dark ? How queer ! Do you usually go and sit in the music-rooms in the dark ? '

Gladys didn't know what to say. She couldn't confess that she often went to the lonely little music-rooms by herself when she felt extra homesick—the girls would laugh at her, and she couldn't bear that. She stared at Carlotta and said nothing.

' Well, can't you answer ? ' said Carlotta, impatiently. ' Do you often go and listen to Mirabel playing in the dark ? '

' No—of course not,' said Gladys. ' I—I just happened to be there—when Mirabel came in—and she didn't see me. So I heard her playing, you see.'

The girls looked at one another. So Gladys disappeared into the dark little music-rooms at night—all alone. What a queer girl she was ! They looked at her thin white little face, and two or three of them felt a pang of sympathy for the Misery-girl and her lonely thoughts, whatever they might be. Nobody laughed or teased her about being in the dark in the music-room. Even down-right Carlotta made no remark about it.

' You know,' said Janet, looking round at the little company of girls, ' Mirabel reminds me in some ways of the O'Sullivan twins ! '

' What do you mean ? ' said Pat, indignantly.

' Well—don't you remember how awfully difficult you were a year ago, when you first came to St. Clare's,' said Janet. ' You just made up your minds to be awkward, and you were ! You ought to understand Mirabel's point of view, and be able to tell us how to tackle her. What made you two change your ideas and want to stay here ? '

' Oh—as soon as we realized we were acting stupidly—

and you were friendly to us—we just sort of settled down and loved everything,' said Pat, trying to remember that first exciting term.

' Right,' said Anna, taking charge of the meeting again. ' That's just what *we*'ll do ! We think Mirabel was decent for not splitting on us today—so we'll be friendly towards her now instead of beastly—and perhaps if we get her to play to us, and praise her up a bit—she'll settle down too. What about it ? '

' Yes, Anna ! ' said every one, Gladys too. Hilary gazed in surprise at Anna. She would never have thought that sleepy Anna could have come to the fore like this— why, she really seemed to be taking a keen interest in everything ! And taking the lead too. Perhaps it would be a good thing that the class had broken away from Elsie's leadership. Anna seemed as if she was going to take the chance offered to her by the unexpected quarrel.

' Sh ! Here comes Mirabel ! ' said Pat, as the door opened. At once the girls began to chatter and gabble about anything that came into their heads. Mirabel looked at them suspiciously. She felt sure they had been discussing her ! Horrid things. Well—if they had been planning fresh tricks to play on her, she would go back to her old ways and upset every single class she could !

8   MIRABEL GIVES THE FORM A SURPRISE

THE twins talked together that night when they were in bed. Their beds were next to one another and they could whisper without any one else hearing what they said.

'We ought to have a few excitements now!' whispered Pat. 'I bet Elsie won't sit down under this! She'll find some way of getting back at Anna—and all of us as well!'

'I hope Mirabel will be sensible now,' said Isabel. 'She looked most suspiciously at all of us, I thought—and she hardly answered Janet at all when she spoke to her.'

'Well, I'm not surprised, really,' said Pat, with a yawn. 'After all—we did do an awful lot of things to her today. It was funny at first—but I didn't like it much afterwards—even though I must say I think Mirabel deserved a little rough-handling. I say—didn't you think it was funny, Gladys speaking up like that—and admitting she was in the music-room all alone? Funny kid, isn't she?'

'Pat, what Janet said was quite true,' said Isabel, speaking rather loudly.

'Sh! Don't speak so loud,' whispered Pat. 'What do you mean?'

'Well, you know—we did behave a little bit like Mirabel—and we did hate it when every one disliked us —it was a miserable feeling,' said Isabel. 'So let's make a bee-line for Mirabel tomorrow, and buck her up a bit. St. Clare's has done a lot for us—let's do a bit for Mirabel.'

'Pat! Isabel! If you don't stop talking at once, I'll report you to Miss Jenks tomorrow!' suddenly came Elsie's sharp voice through the darkness.

'You can't. You're not head-girl,' came Carlotta's cheeky voice, before the twins could answer.

'I'll report you too, for untidy drawers and cupboard,' said Elsie, furiously.

'Well—it will only be the fiftieth time, I should think,' said Carlotta, lazily. 'Go ahead, Miss Catty Elsie!'

There was a delighted squeal of laughter from the dormitory at this. Elsie sat up in bed, furious.

'Carlotta! If you dare to talk like a low-down circus girl to me . . .'' she began. But at that every one sat up in bed, indignant.

'Listen!' began Bobby, 'any one who calls Carlotta low-down deserves a spanking with a hair-brush! We're all proud of Carlotta—remember how she saved Sadie from being kidnapped last term! It's *you* who are low-down, Elsie! Now—just you remember what I said about that hair-brush!'

Elsie was furious. She began to tell Bobby exactly what she thought of her. She forgot to keep her voice low, and when Miss Jenks came along to see that all was quiet in the dormitory, she was amazed to hear a voice going on and on in the darkness—an angry voice, a spiteful voice!

She switched on the light and stood in silence by the door. Every girl was sitting up in bed. Elsie's voice died away in horror. She stared wide-eyed at Miss Jenks.

'Who was that talking just now?' enquired Miss Jenks, in her cool voice.

Nobody answered. Elsie simply could not bear to own up. She swallowed hard, hoping that Miss Jenks would deliver a general lecture and go. Miss Jenks didn't. She just stood and waited.

'Who is in charge of this dormitory?' she asked. 'Oh you, I suppose, Elsie—as you are one of the head-girls for this form. Well—as the culprit does not seem to have enough courage to own up, perhaps you, as head-girl, will see to it that the girl is punished by going to bed one hour earlier tomorrow. Will you?'

'Yes, Miss Jenks,' answered Elsie, in a very subdued tone. There was a smothered giggle from Carlotta's bed, hurriedly turned into a loud cough.

'You seem to have a cold, Carlotta,' said Miss Jenks, pretending to be quite concerned. 'Perhaps you had better go to Matron tomorrow morning and get a dose of medicine for it.'

'Oh, I shall be quite all right tomorrow morning, Miss Jenks, thank you,' Carlotta hurriedly assured her.

'Good night, girls,' said Miss Jenks, and switched off the light. As soon as her footsteps had died away, the girls began to giggle and whisper.

'Elsie! See you put yourself to bed an hour earlier tomorrow!' whispered Carlotta.

Elsie lay in bed, her cheeks burning. Why hadn't she owned up? Then she wouldn't have been so humiliated! She jolly well wouldn't go to bed early the next night, anyway. She shut her ears with her fingers, so as not to hear what the girls were whispering. She did not dare to tell them to stop—and as for threatening to report them—well, that would make them laugh all the more!

Every one felt scornful of Elsie—but they also thought the whole thing was funny. The girls were quite determined that Elsie *should* go to bed early the next night. They were not going to let her off the punishment she had meekly promised to give to wreak on the culprit!

The next day the twins gave Mirabel a cheerful grin at the breakfast-table. She smiled back, surprised and warmed. She had been expecting a few more tricks, and the unexpected smile surprised her very much.

After breakfast Pat and Isabel spoke to Mirabel. 'Did you hear about the row in our dormitory last night?' asked Pat.

'I knew there was something up,' said Mirabel. 'I heard the others talking about it. What was it?'

The twins told Mirabel about Elsie and Miss Jenks, and the girl smiled. 'Thanks for telling me,' she said,

'It was funny. I say—is the form going to do beastly
things to me today? You know, I'd just decided to
turn over a new leaf—when you did all those things.'

'Had you really decided to change?' said Pat, in
surprise. 'Well—don't worry—we're not going to get
back at you any more. But for goodness' sake do your
bit too. It's pretty sickening having class after class
upset, you know. You may feel in a temper about
your home-affairs—but that really isn't any reason for
venting your temper on the class!'

'No—I see that now,' said Mirabel. 'I'm an idiot—
always have been. Well—I bet you'll be glad to see the
back of me at half-term.'

'Wait and see,' said Isabel. 'I say—our form is giving
a concert next week, in aid of the Red Cross. Every
one is to do something. Could you play the violin for
us, do you think? And perhaps the piano too?'

'How do you know I play?' asked Mirabel, in surprise.
But at that moment Miss Jenks bustled the whole class
off for a nature-walk, and Mirabel found herself walking
with the timid Gladys, who, remembering the night in
the dark music-room, felt afraid to say a word. Mirabel
felt awkward too, so the two hardly exchanged a single
word.

The twins, when the chance came, hurriedly told the
rest of the form that they had asked Mirabel to play at
the concert planned for the following week. Every form
had been asked to get up something in aid of the Red
Cross, and this was to be the second form's contribution.

'Did she say she would?' asked Bobby.

'No—but we'll put her name down on the programme,'
said Pat. 'I bet she will! She was quite nice this
morning.'

Mirabel found her books back in her desk that day.
Anna had taken them from their hiding-place and put

them back. Elsie had scowled, but had said nothing. She didn't know whom she hated most—Anna—or that saucy Carlotta!

When the programme for the Red Cross concert was drawn up that evening, Isabel called across to Mirabel.

' Hie, Mirabel! I've put you down for a violin solo, and a piano solo. What will you play? Can you tell us the names of the pieces? '

' I haven't my violin here,' said Mirabel, hesitatingly.

' Pooh—you can easily send a telegram home for it,' said Pat. ' And Anna will lend you hers to practise on this week—won't you, Anna? '

' Of course,' said Anna. ' I'll go and get it now and you can see if you like the feel of it. It's a good one.'

Anna went to fetch her violin. She took it out of its case and put it into Mirabel's hands. As she had said, it was a good one. Mirabel drew the bow across it lovingly.

' Play something,' said Isabel. And then, as in the dark music-room, Mirabel played some of the melodies she loved. She forgot the girls in the common room, she forgot St. Clare's, she forgot herself. She was a real little musician, and she put all her heart into the music she loved.

The girls listened spell-bound. Two or three girls in the school played the violin very well—but Mirabel made it speak. The notes rang out pure and true, and Anna was amazed that her violin could produce such music.

When Mirabel stopped, every one clapped frantically. ' I say! You *are* marvellous! ' said Pat, her eyes shining. ' Golly—you'll make every one sit up at the concert next week, I can tell you. Now go and play something on the piano. Go on. You simply must! '

Mirabel looked round at the admiring audience, with flushed cheeks and bright eyes. Only Elsie Fanshawe did not applaud. She sat at a table, reading a book, taking no notice at all.

'Go on, Mirabel—play us something on the piano!' insisted Pat.

Mirabel went across to the old piano in the common room. It was there for the girls to strum on, if they wanted to. Usually dance music or popular songs were hammered out on it—but tonight something quite different was played!

Mirabel's long, sensitive fingers ran over the notes, and one of Chopin's nocturnes filled the quiet common room. Most of the girls loved good music, and they listened in delight. Gladys shut her eyes. Music always stirred her very much, though she learnt no instrument, and knew little about it.

The notes died away. The girls sat up, pleased. 'Look here—play that at the concert next week,' said Hilary. 'It's heavenly. I heard it on the wireless in the hols.—but you play it much better!'

'I don't,' said Mirabel, red with embarrassment and pleasure. 'All right—I'll play it. And if you really want me to play something on the violin too I'll send a telegram tomorrow asking for my own violin to be sent. Anna's *is* a lovely one—but I'm more at home with my own.'

'Good,' said Isabel. 'I say—aren't you a dark horse —never saying a word about your music—keeping it up your sleeve like that! You've got a real gift. I wish *I* had a gift. You're lucky!'

Mirabel went to help Isabel to draw up the programme. Her words echoed in her mind. 'You've got a real gift!' She remembered Miss Theobald's words too. 'Difficult children often have some hidden quality—some gift—something to make them worth-while!'

Nobody at home thought her worth-while—or surely

they wouldn't have sent her away! But she *was* worth-
while! See how the girls loved hearing her play. It
was a pity she hadn't accepted her father's offer to learn
music at St. Clare's. She had no other gift but music,
and she had refused to develop that, out of obstinacy.

'I bet you could pass any music exam. you went in
for,' said Isabel, handing Mirabel a few programmes to
print. 'Nobody in our form is specially good at music.
It's a pity you don't learn. You would be a credit to
us—you'd make some of the top-formers sit up, I bet!
And I guess you'd win the music-prize.'

'Well—I'll certainly send that telegram tomorrow,'
said Mirabel, printing the programmes neatly. She felt
happy for the first time that term. It was nice to be
working in friendliness with some one like Isabel. It
was lovely to be praised for something. Nobody thought
a great deal of her music at home, because none of them
were musical—except her brother—and dear me, how
she snubbed him! Mirabel felt annoyed with herself
when she remembered that. She ought to have encouraged him.

'I really must have been tiresome,' she thought.
'Well—going away from home does make you see things
clearly. When I go back at half-term I'll show them
I'm not as bad as they think!'

That night, at eight o'clock, all the second form winked
at one another. If Elsie was going to bed an hour earlier,
it was time she went. But she showed no sign. She
had come back from supper and had settled down to read
again, saying nothing to anybody.

'Bedtime for little girls!' said Carlotta. Elsie took
no notice.

'Naughty girls must go to bed early,' said Bobby,
loudly. Elsie did not move.

The girls looked at one another. It was quite clear

that Elsie was not going to get up and go. She had
not only been afraid to own up to Miss Jenks the night
before—but she was now going to evade the punishment !

To every one's surprise Anna spoke. 'Elsie !' she
said. 'You know perfectly well what you have to do.
Don't make us all ashamed of you.'

'You can't talk to *me* like that !' said Elsie, turning
over a page.

'I can,' said Anna, calmly. 'I am head-girl of the
form. I have the right to tell you what to do.'

'You haven't,' said Elsie, furiously. 'I'm head-girl
too.'

'You're not, you're not !' cried a dozen voices. 'We
only recognize Anna as head-girl now. We don't want
you !'

'Only Miss Jenks can decide a thing like that,' said
Elsie, looking round at the girls.

'Perhaps you are right,' said Anna, in her slow voice.
'Come with me and we will let Miss Jenks decide.'

Hilary looked at Anna in admiration. She knew that
this was the one thing that would defeat Elsie. On no
account would Elsie go to Miss Jenks at the moment !
It would be far too humiliating.

Elsie hesitated. The girls waited. They knew Elsie
would not consent to go with Anna. Anna stood up as
if she was going.

'I'm not going to Miss Jenks,' said Elsie, in a low
voice.

'I thought not,' said Anna, and sat down again.
'Well—either Miss Jenks decides this matter or the girls
do. I don't mind.'

'*We*'ll decide—we've already decided !' said Janet.
'Anna is our head-girl, and we don't want Elsie. And
that being so, Elsie—you'll just do as Anna says, and
go off to bed. It's your own silly fault.'

That was too much for Elsie. Her obstinacy rose up
and she pursed her thin lips. ' I'm not going,' she said.
' I'm not obeying Anna. She may be your head-girl—
but I won't admit she's mine ! '

' Right,' said Carlotta, cheerfully, getting up. ' Come
on, Bobby—Janet—twins. Get hold of Elsie, and we'll
bump her all the way upstairs to bed ! We can't have
her disobeying Miss Jenks's orders like this ! My word
—won't the third form stare when we go by with poor
Elsie ! '

' No—don't ! ' cried Elsie, in dismay, jumping to her
feet. She knew the wild little Carlotta would stop at
nothing. ' I'll go. I'll go. But I hate you all ! '

She burst into tears, and with loud sobs went to the
door. Carlotta sat down. When Elsie had gone, she
looked round.

' I didn't really mean us to bump her up the stairs
to bed,' she said, ' but I guessed she'd go of her own
accord if I suggested it.'

' She'll be awful tomorrow,' said Bobby. Anna shook
her big head.

' No,' she said. ' I know Elsie. She will begin to feel
a martyr, and terribly sorry for herself. She will try to
get our sympathy by being subdued and meek.'

' Yes—I think you're right,' said Janet. ' Well—the
best thing is not to take any notice of her at all. We
don't want to get spiteful—just let's leave her alone and
take no notice at all.'

' That's the best thing,' said Anna. She took up her
knitting again. ' Oh dear—being the only head-girl is
very wearing. There seem so many things to decide ! '

THE next morning Mirabel wanted to send her telegram.
Anna told her what to do.

'You'll have to go and get permission from Miss Theobald. Then you can slip down into the town with somebody after morning school,' she said. 'I'll go with you
if you like.'

Mirabel went to ask permission. She knocked at Miss
Theobald's door and was told to come in. The Head
Mistress looked up. She did not smile.

'What is it, Mirabel?' she asked.

'Please, Miss Theobald, may I send a telegram home?'
asked Mirabel.

Still Miss Theobald did not smile or unbend in any
way. She looked really stern. Mirabel began to feel
very uncomfortable.

'What is the telegram about?' she asked. 'You
know that you cannot leave before half-term. There is
no sense in upsetting your household with telegrams.'

'It's nothing to do with my leaving,' said Mirabel.
'It's—it's—well, Miss Theobald, I just want to ask my
mother if she'll send my violin, that's all.'

The head looked surprised. 'Your violin?' she said.
'Why? You don't learn music, do you?'

'No,' said Mirabel. 'I wish I did now. But I
wouldn't when Daddy gave me the chance. You see—
the second form are giving a concert for the Red Cross
next week—and I said I would play for them. I'd like
my own violin to play on. It's a beauty.'

Miss Theobald looked at Mirabel. 'So you *have* a gift,
Mirabel!' she said. 'You remember what I said to

you ? I wonder if there is anything worth-while in you after all ! '

Mirabel went red. She stood on first one foot and then on another. She felt certain that Miss Theobald had had bad reports of her from every mistress.

' I'm not sure that I shall let you ask for your violin,' said Miss Theobald at last. ' I hear that you misbehave at practically every class. You try to spoil everything, it seems. How do I know that you will behave at the concert ? '

' I will,' said Mirabel, earnestly. ' You won't believe me, perhaps—but I've turned over a new leaf now. I've got tired of being silly.'

' I see,' said Miss Theobald. ' You've stopped misbehaving just because you're tired of it—not because you're ashamed of it, or want to do better, or want us to think well of you. Only just because you're tired of it. You disgust me, Mirabel. Go, please. I'm disappointed in you. I had hoped that possibly you might turn over a new leaf for some better motive. I thought I saw some courage in you, some real intelligence that might help you to realize your foolishness and selfishness in behaving as you did. Now I see that you have none—you only stop because you yourself are tired of misbehaviour, and, possibly, are tired also of having the others unfriendly towards you. Please go.'

Mirabel was struck with horror at the cold, stern words. She had felt so pleased with herself to think she was turning over a new leaf. She *had* been ashamed of herself. She hadn't only got tired of being silly. She opened her mouth to defend herself, but the sight of Miss Theobald's stern face frightened her. She went out of the room without a word.

Miss Theobald sat and thought for a few minutes.

Then she rang her bell. 'Ask Miss Jenks to come to me for a few minutes,' she told the maid.

Miss Jenks soon appeared. 'Sit down for a moment,' said Miss Theobald. 'I want to talk to you about Mirabel Unwin. I have had continual bad reports from you about her. Is there any improvement at all?'

'Yes,' said Miss Jenks at once. 'She seems suddenly to be settling down. I don't quite know why. Has anything happened? I saw her just now, and she looked as if she had been crying.'

'Probably she had,' said Miss Theobald, and told Miss Jenks what had just passed between her and Mirabel.

'I should like to know if the girl has suddenly changed for the right reasons, or the wrong ones,' she said. 'Perhaps the head-girls could tell me. Send them, will you?'

'There seems to be some sort of upset between the two head-girls of my form,' said Miss Jenks. 'I don't think Elsie Fanshawe has gone down very well with the first-formers who came up into my form. But Anna seems unexpectedly to be showing some signs of responsibility and leadership. I'll go and send the two girls to you. Perhaps they can tell you more about Mirabel. Personally I think we might give her a chance now, and let her have her violin.'

She left the room and went to find Anna and Elsie. They were in the common room with the others. As the door opened and Miss Jenks appeared all the girls rose to their feet and stopped chattering. Janet turned off the wireless.

'Miss Theobald wants the two head-girls to go to her for a few minutes,' said Miss Jenks in her cool voice. 'Will you go at once, please?'

She left the room. There was a silence. Anna stood up to go. So did Elsie. But quick as thought Carlotta pulled her down again to her chair.

'You're not head-girl, Elsie. You know you're not.
We won't have you—and if we won't have you, then
Anna is the only head-girl. You are not going to Miss
Theobald!'

'Don't be an idiot!' snapped Elsie, scrambling up
again. 'You know I've got to go. I can't tell Miss
Theobald I'm no longer head-girl.'

'Well, Anna can,' said Hilary. 'It's unfortunate,
Elsie—but we all happen to think the same about this.
You were a bad head-girl—and we won't accept you.
You wouldn't let Miss Jenks decide it—you accepted *our*
decision—and you've got to abide by it. Anna must go
alone.'

'She's not to, she's not to,' said Elsie, half-crying.
'It's shameful. What will Miss Theobald think?'

'You should have thought of these things before,' said
Hilary. 'Anna, go. Say as little as you can about
Elsie, of course—but please let it be understood that you
are the only head-girl of the second form now.'

Anna went. Elsie saw that the whole of the second
form would stop her by force if she tried to follow. So
she lay back in her chair, looking as forlorn and miserable
as she could, letting the tears trickle down her cheeks.
She hoped that the girls would feel uncomfortable, and
very sorry. But nobody did. In fact, they took no
notice of her at all, and went on cheerfully chattering
among themselves. It was Saturday morning, and except
for an hour's lessons, they were free to do as they chose.

Mirabel was not there. She had had a shock, and it
had upset her very much. She did not want anyone to
see that she had been crying, so she had gone to the
cloakroom to bathe her eyes. She came out of the room
just as Anna passed it on her way to the Head. Anna
spoke to her.

'Hallo! Did you get permission from the Head to

send for your violin? I'll come down to the post-office with you if you like.'

'I didn't get permission,' said Mirabel, miserably. 'Anna, Miss Theobald was awful to me. She thinks I've only turned over a new leaf because I was tired of being an idiot. But I haven't. I'm awfully ashamed of myself now. It was dreadful having you all doing beastly things to me the very day I'd made up my mind to do better —and now even Miss Theobald is against me. What's the use of trying? It's just no good at all. I shan't play at the concert. I shan't do anything.'

Anna stared at Mirabel, surprised. 'Look here, I can't wait now,' she said. 'I've been sent for by the Head. But I'll have a talk with you afterwards, see? I'm awfully sorry, Mirabel. Really I am. Cheer up.'

She ran down the passage to Miss Theobald's drawing-room and knocked.

'Come in!' said the Head's pleasant voice. Anna entered, half-scared. Miss Theobald was kind and just —but her wisdom and dignity awed every girl, and it was quite an ordeal to go for any kind of interview.

'Good morning, Anna,' said Miss Theobald. 'Where is Elsie Fanshawe?'

'Elsie isn't head-girl now, Miss Theobald,' said Anna, feeling awkward. Miss Theobald looked most surprised.

'I hadn't heard this,' she said. 'Why isn't she?'

'We all decided that she wasn't quite fit to be at present,' said Anna, finding it difficult to explain without giving Elsie away too much.

'Miss Jenks knows nothing of this,' said the Head. 'Why didn't you ask her advice?'

'Elsie didn't want us to,' said Anna. 'She said she would rather accept our decision, without us taking matters any further. It's—it's rather difficult to explain, Miss Theobald, without telling tales.'

' Did Hilary Wentworth and the O'Sullivan twins agree to this ? ' asked the Head. She had great faith in the fairness and common sense of these three girls.

' Oh yes,' said Anna. ' I wouldn't have done it myself —I'm too lazy, I'm afraid. But once the girls wanted me to accept responsibility and carry on without Elsie, I had to take it.'

' Of course,' said Miss Theobald, sensing in Anna something better and stronger than she had known before in the lazy slow-moving girl. ' Well—I won't ask any more questions, Anna. I think probably the second form are right—all I hope is that some good will come out of this for Elsie. I can see an improvement in *you* already ! '

Anna blushed. Responsibility was a nuisance—but it did bring definite rewards, not the least of which was an added self-respect.

' Anna, I sent for you because I want to ask you about Mirabel Unwin,' said Miss Theobald. ' I always take the head-girls of any form into my confidence, as you know. Will you tell me what your opinion is of Mirabel—whether it is bad or good—anything that can help me in dealing with her. You know all the details as to why she was sent here because she has told the whole school ! '

Anna seldom wasted words. She said shortly what Miss Theobald wanted to know. ' Mirabel has been awfully tiresome, and the second form punished her for it. She's ashamed of herself now—and she wants to show us she's some good. Could you let her send for her violin ? '

' Very well,' said Miss Theobald, smiling at Anna's directness. ' I refused her permission a little while ago. Will you, as head-girl, tell her I have changed my mind, and she can go down and send off the telegram. Tell her too, that I shall like to hear her play at the second form concert.'

'Yes, Miss Theobald,' said Anna. 'Thank you.' The girl left the room, pleased. For the first time in her lazy life she felt that she had some importance. The Head had sent for her and actually listened to her. It was worth making an effort, if people like Miss Theobald appreciated it.

She went to look for Mirabel. She found her in the common room, reading rather soberly, her eyes still red.

'Mirabel! Come on down to the post-office and send that telegram,' said Anna. 'Miss Theobald says you may. And she says she will look forward to hearing you play at the concert next week.'

Mirabel looked up, astonished and delighted. This was a lovely surprise after having her hopes dashed and her good resolutions misunderstood. She stood up, glowing.

'Anna! It's because of you Miss Theobald said I could send the telegram. Thanks awfully. You're a brick.'

'It wasn't altogether me,' said Anna. 'Hurry up and get your coat on. We haven't much time.'

They hurried down to the post-office. The telegram was sent off—and caused much surprise in Mirabel's home!

'She wants her violin!' said her mother, in astonishment. 'Why, she must be settling down a bit. I *am* glad!'

So the violin was packed up, registered and sent off at once. It arrived on the Monday of the week following, and Mirabel unpacked it joyfully. Her own violin! Now she would be able to play beautifully. She would show the second form what real music was!

'And I'll astonish Miss Theobald a bit too,' thought Mirabel. 'She'll see I have a real gift—even if I haven't anything else! I'd like her to think I was worth-while —I really would.'

THE second form were very busy preparing for their concert. They were going to charge sixpence for the tickets, and all the first form, most of the third form, and even a few of the higher form girls had promised to come. All the mistresses had promised too. It was to be quite a big affair.

The girls were to manage everything themselves. They prepared the programmes and the tickets. Isabel drew a fine big poster and coloured it. She put it up in the big assembly room where every one could see it.

The concert was to be held in the gym, where there was a fine platform. The second form grew quite excited about it. Too excited for Mam'zelle's liking. She could not bear to feel that the class were thinking about something else in her lessons.

'Isabel! Pat! Did you not sleep last night, that you dream so this morning? What was the question I have just asked the class?'

The twins stared at Mam'zelle in alarm. Neither of them had heard the question. Carlotta whispered softly.

'She said, "Has anyone here seen my glasses?",' whispered Carlotta, grinning. This was quite untrue, as everyone knew! But the twins fell into the trap at once. They stared innocently at Mam'zelle, seeing her glasses perched as usual on her big nose.

'Well?' said Mam'zelle, sharply. 'What did I ask the class?'

'You asked if we had seen your glasses anywhere,' said Pat, 'but they are on your nose, Mam'zelle.'

There was a squeal of laughter from the class. Mam'zelle

banged on her desk angrily. '*Ah, que vous êtes abominable!*' she cried. '*Insupportable!*'

The twins glared at Carlotta, who was holding her sides. She shook her head at them, tears of laughter in her eyes. ' Wait till break, you wretch!' said Pat.

'*Taisez-vous!*' said Mam'zelle. 'Pat! Isabel! Of what were you thinking just now when I addressed the class? Be truthful!'

'Well, Mam'zelle—I was thinking of the concert our form is holding on Saturday,' said Pat. 'I'm sorry. My thoughts just wandered away.'

' So did mine,' said Isabel.

' If they wander away again I shall not come to the concert,' threatened Mam'zelle. There was a loud and universal groan.

' We shan't hold the concert unless you come!'

' You *must* come, Mam'zelle! You laugh louder than any one!'

' I will come if you write me a nice composition,' said Mam'zelle, suddenly beaming again. ' You shall write me a beautiful essay and tell me all that is to happen at this wonderful concert. With no mistakes at all. That will please me greatly. That shall be your prep. for tomorrow.'

The girls groaned again. French essays were awful to do—and this one would be difficult. Anyway, the idea had put Mam'zelle into a better temper, so that was something!

Two girls were doing nothing in the concert at all. Elsie had refused to do anything, and had announced her intention of not even coming. And nobody had asked the little Misery-girl to do anything. Every one felt certain that Gladys would not and could not do a thing. They thought it would be kinder to leave her out altogether.

Gladys was hurt because she was not asked, yet glad

Isabel painted a big poster for the concert

that she was not pressed to do anything. She shut more and more up into herself, only spoke when she was spoken to, and was so quiet in every lesson that the teachers hardly knew she was there. Only in Miss Quentin's class did she show any real animation. Not that Miss Quentin ever asked her to act a part, because, like everyone else, Miss Quentin always passed over Gladys, thinking that such a little mouse could never do anything !

But Gladys watched the others acting, and for once in a way forgot to brood over her troubles when she saw Bobby strutting across the room as a king or duke, and Carlotta playing the part of a jester.

Alison adored Miss Quentin's classes. She really did work hard in those—harder than she worked in any one else's. For one thing she was pretty and graceful, and parts such as princesses or fairies were given naturally to her, and for another thing, she lived for Miss Quentin's words of praise. She thought Miss Quentin was ' just wonderful ! '

The preparations for the concert went on well. Doris was to give some of her clever imitations. She meant to mimic Mam'zelle, who had all kinds of mannerisms which were a joy to the class. She meant to imitate Clara, the cook, a jolly, rough-and-ready person much liked by the girls. And she meant to dress up as Matron, and imitate her doling out advice and medicine to various girls.

' Doris, you really are a scream,' said Bobby, enjoying the girl's clever performance in rehearsal. ' You ought to be on the stage.'

' I'm going to be a doctor,' said Doris.

' Oh—well, you'll be a jolly good one because you'll make all your patients scream with laughter ! ' said Bobby.

Every one was doing something—either reciting, playing

the piano or violin, singing or dancing—every one, that is except Elsie and Gladys. Carlotta was going to give a display of acrobatics. She was marvellous at such circus tricks as turning cart-wheels, walking on her hands and so on.

'You and Doris, Carlotta, will be the hits of the evening,' said Pat. She and Isabel were going to give a dialogue, supposed to be funny, but they both felt it was not nearly so good as any one else's contribution. Bobby was to do conjuring tricks ! She was very good at these, and had a lot of idiotic patter that fell from her lips in a never-ending torrent.

'I bet Mirabel will be a hit too,' said Janet, after the girl had played her concert piece to them, during rehearsal. 'Good thing we found out she could play ! '

'By the way—how *did* you find out ? ' asked Mirabel, putting her violin into its case. 'I kept meaning to ask you. I didn't think anybody knew.'

'Yes—somebody did,' said Janet, looking round to see if Gladys was in the room ; but she was not. 'It was Gladys who told us.'

'*Gladys !* ' said Mirabel, suddenly remembering the night in the dark music-room. 'Yes—of course—she heard me that night.'

'She said you were in the dark,' said Pat. 'So that means she was too. Funny kid, isn't she, sitting about in dark rooms all by herself. She really is a little misery. I can't think what's the matter with her. She never tells anyone. If she did, we might help her a bit—get a smile out of her occasionally, or something.'

'Oh—she told me what's the matter,' said Mirabel, remembering everything Gladys had said.

'*Did* she ? ' said Bobby, in surprise. 'Well, what *is* the matter with her ? '

'It's her mother,' said Mirabel. 'She's in hospital—

awfully ill—perhaps she's going to die.   Gladys said she's
only got her mother—no father or brothers or sisters—
and they were sort of all-in-all to one another.   She'd
never been away from her mother even for a night till
she was sent here when her mother went to hospital.
She said she was awfully homesick, and missed her mother
terribly.   I suppose she thinks every day she may hear
bad news or something.'

The girls heard all this in silence.   They felt sorry and
uncomfortable.   The little Misery-girl really did have
something to worry about.   Everyone there but Carlotta
had mothers they loved—and fathers—and most of them
had brothers and sisters.   Even slow-minded Anna, who
had little imagination, knew for one short moment the
sort of heartache that Gladys carried with her day and
night.

' Why didn't you tell us this ? ' asked Bobby.

' I didn't remember it till now,' said Mirabel.

' Well, I think you should have told us at once,' said
Hilary.   ' We might have been decenter to Gladys.   She's
a poor little thing, without any courage or spunk—but
we haven't exactly made things any easier for her.   You
really are to blame for not having told us, Mirabel.'

Mirabel was really conscience-stricken.   She couldn't
think how she could have forgotten Gladys's troubles.
She had been so wrapped up in her own, and then, when
the girls had become friendly and helped her, she had
been so happy that she had not given a thought to the
little Misery-girl.   She stared unhappily at Hilary.

' I'm sorry,' she said.   ' I *should* have told you.   All
the same, I don't think Gladys would like it if she knew
that everyone knew about her troubles.   So don't tell
her you know.   Just be nicé to her and notice her a
bit.'

The second form received this advice in silence.

Mirabel sensed that they did not think very much of her for forgetting another person's troubles. She said no more, but went off to put her violin away.

'I wonder where Gladys is,' she thought. 'I've a good mind to hunt for her and ask her if she's heard any news of her mother lately. After all, it might help a bit if someone shares the news with her.'

Mirabel went to look for Gladys. She could not seem to find the girl anywhere. It was puzzling.

'Well, she simply *must* be somewhere!' said Mirabel to herself. 'I wonder if she's up in the boxrooms. I saw her coming down from there the other day and wondered whatever had taken her there.'

She went up the stairs to the top of the school. Trunks and bags were kept in the attics, but little else. There was a light showing under the door of one of the attics— and from the room came a voice.

It didn't sound like Gladys's voice. It was deep and strong. Mirabel listened in surprise. The voice was declaiming one of the speeches in *The Tempest*, which the second form were taking that term with Miss Jenks.

'That's not Gladys,' thought Mirabel. 'I wonder who it is. Ah—now there's a different voice. There must be two or three people there. But who can they be? Only the second form are doing *The Tempest* this term—and all but Gladys were at rehearsal this evening.'

A third voice spoke, gentle and feminine. Mirabel could bear it no longer. She really must see who the speakers were. They were declaiming Shakespeare's words beautifully.

She opened the door. The voice stopped at once. Mirabel stared into the room, expecting to see three or four people there, rehearsing the play. But there was only one person there—Gladys!

'Golly! It's only you!' said Mirabel, in astonishment.

' I thought there must be lots here.   I heard all kinds of different voices.   Was it *you* ? '

' Yes,' said Gladys.   ' Go away.   Can't I even do this in peace ? '

' What are you doing ? ' asked Mirabel, going into the room and shutting the door.   ' Do tell me.   It sounded fine.   Do you know it all by heart ? '

' Yes, I do,' said Gladys.   ' I love acting.   I always have.   But Miss Quentin never gives me a chance in the Drama class.   I could act the parts well.   I know I could. You see me act Bobby's part in that play we're doing with Miss Quentin ! '

And before Mirabel's astonished eyes, the girl began to act the part that had been given to Bobby.   But she acted it superbly.   She *was* the part !   The little Misery-girl faded, and another character came into the attic, someone with a resonant voice, a strong character, and a fierce face.   It was extraordinary.

Mirabel stood and gaped.   Her astonishment and admiration were so plain that Gladys was impelled to show her another part in the play—Carlotta's part.   Here again she was twice as good as the fiery Carlotta, and her voice, wild and strong, quite different from Gladys's usual meek, milk-and-water voice, rang through the attic.

' Gladys !   You're simply marvellous ! ' said Mirabel. ' You're to come and show the girls.   Come on.   Come on downstairs at once.   I never saw anything like it in my life   *You* to act like that !   Who would have thought it ?   You're such a mouse, and your voice is so quiet—and yet, when you act, you're Somebody, and you quite frighten me.   You simply *must* come down and show the girls what you can do.'

' No,' said Gladys, becoming herself again and looking nalf the size she had seemed two minutes before.

' Oh, Gladys,' said Mirabel, suddenly remembering why

she had been looking for the girl. ' Gladys—how's your mother ? I do hope you've got good news.'

' Thank you—it's just about the same,' said Gladys. ' Mother can't even write to me, she's so ill. If I could just get a letter from her, it would be something ! '

' Does she get *your* letters ? ' asked Mirabel.

' Of course,' said Gladys. ' I keep telling her how much I miss her, and how lonely and unhappy I am without her.'

' But, Gladys—how silly ! ' said Mirabel.

' What do you mean ? ' asked Gladys, half indignantly. ' Mother wants to know that.'

' I should have thought she would have been much gladder to think you were trying to settle down and be happy,' said Mirabel. ' It must make her very miserable indeed to feel you are so lonely and sad. I should think it would make her worse.'

' It won't,' said Gladys, her eyes filling with tears. ' If she thought I was happy here, and getting other interests, she would think I was forgetting her.'

' I do think you're silly, Gladys,' said Mirabel, wishing she was Hilary or Anna, so that she might know the best way of tackling some one like Gladys. ' Don't you want your mother to be proud of you ? She'll think you are an awful coward—no spunk at all—just giving in like this, and weeping and wailing.'

' Oh, you *are* hateful ! ' cried Gladys. ' As if my mother would ever think things like that of me, ever ! Go away. I won't come down with you. And don't you dare to tell any one what you saw me doing. It's my secret. You'd no right to come spying like that. Go away.'

Mirabel looked at Gladys's angry little face, and wondered what to do or say. She hadn't done any good, that was certain. ' I suppose I haven't got the character to help people properly, like Hilary or Anna,' thought Mirabel, going soberly downstairs. ' I've got a lot to learn.   When I go home at half-term next week, I'll really try and do better.'

She went down to the library to get a book.   But, as she hunted through the shelves, she kept thinking of Gladys.   She couldn't just do nothing.   If she, Mirabel, couldn't help Gladys, maybe somebody else could. Hilary could.   She was always so sensible.   So was Bobby—and the twins, too.   She would go and tell them what had happened, and leave it to them to do what they could.   Mirabel was beginning to have a very low opinion of herself and her powers.

She left the library and went to find Hilary.   She was lucky enough to see her in a music-room with Bobby, Janet and the twins, practising something for the concert. Good !   This was just the chance to tell them what had happened !

11   A DISAPPOINTMENT FOR THE SECOND FORM

'I SAY !' said Mirabel, opening the door. 'Can I interrupt a moment ? '

'I suppose so,' said Bobby. 'What's up ? '

'It's about Gladys,' said Mirabel, and she told them how she had found the girl acting all by herself in the box-room.   Then she went on to tell them what she had said to Gladys, and how she had failed to help her—only made her angry.

'Well,' said Hilary, listening intently. 'I think, Mirabel, you gave Gladys some very sound advice. Really I do.   Of course Gladys ought to stop moaning to her mother.   She must find a little pluck somewhere, or she'll go to pieces. You did right to say that it would help her mother if she knew Gladys was settling down, and trying to do well.'

' Oh—I'm glad you think that,' said Mirabel. ' I'm not so good as you are at knowing what to do for the best for people. By the way—Gladys said she didn't want· me to tell everybody.'

' Well, you haven't,' said Hilary. ' You've only told us five—and we understand perfectly. But, Mirabel, as it seems that Gladys has taken *you* into her confidence and nobody else, I think you'd better go on tackling the matter ! '

' Yes ! ' said all the others.

' Oh *no*,' said Mirabel, horrified. ' I came to ask *you* to help. I'm no good at this sort of thing.'

' Well, it's time you were,' said Hilary, firmly. ' Now come on, Mirabel—we all tried to help you when you needed it—you've got to do the same to Gladys. Be friends with her, and buck her up—and if you can persuade her to show us how she can act, we'll all listen and applaud —and she must be in the concert ! '

' She can't be. It's the day after tomorrow, and all the programmes are written out,' objected Isabel. ' We really can't write them all out again.'

' She wouldn't want to be in the concert, anyhow,' said Mirabel. ' All right, Hilary—I'll do what I can. But I really am very bad at this sort of thing.'

It was distasteful to Mirabel to mention the matter to Gladys again. She always felt awkward at anything involving tact or understanding in another's troubles. She would very much rather have left it to the others. Still, once she said she would do a thing, she did it.

Gladys was surprised, and not too pleased to find Mirabel always at her elbow the next day. ' Gladys, I didn't mean to make you angry,' Mirabel said, when they were alone for a few minutes. ' I'm clumsy in what I say. I know I am. But I really and truly am sympathetic. I don't expect I can help at all—but I'd like to.'

' Well,' said Gladys, looking at Mirabel's earnest face, ' I *was* angry yesterday. Nobody likes being told they're cowardly. But I thought it all over and in some ways I think you're right. I shouldn't keep writing to my mother and telling her how miserable and lonely I am. I know it would worry her—and that might keep her from getting well.'

' Yes, it might,' said Mirabel, pleased that what she had said had, after all, had some effect on Gladys. ' I say— look here—wouldn't she be *thrilled* if she knew you were in the concert—acting like that—being clapped by everybody ! I do wish you'd let the girls see you act.'

Gladys hesitated. She did know, quite certainly, that her mother would be pleased to hear of any success she made—but she was such a mouse, so afraid of everything— it would be a real ordeal to show off in front of the girls. And, of course, she couldn't possibly be in the concert ! She would be scared out of her life !

Mirabel saw her hesitate, and she went on pressing her. ' Gladys ! Come on—be a sport. Look—if you'll show what you can do, and get the girls to put you into the concert, *I'll* write to your mother myself and tell her how well you did. See ? Because I know you'll do well. And then think how pleased she'll be ! '

The thought of Mirabel actually writing to her mother for her touched Gladys more than anything else could have done. She stared at Mirabel's earnest face, and tried to blink back the tears that came far too easily.

' You are a good sort,' she said, rather chokily. ' You really are. I thought at first you were such a selfish, cold-hearted sort of girl—but you're not. Be friends with me, Mirabel. You haven't any friend here and neither have I. I'll do anything you ask me, if you'll be friends.'

'Well,' said Mirabel, remembering that it was the half-term the following week, 'I'm leaving soon, you know—at half-term. I never meant to stay longer than that. So it's not much use your being friends with me really—because I'll soon be gone.'

'Oh,' said Gladys, turning away. 'That's just my luck. People I like always go away.'

'Now don't start that sort of thing again,' said Mirabel, half-impatiently. 'All right. I'll be your friend till I go—but mind, you've got to be sensible and do what I say. And the first thing I say is—you've got to show the girls how you can act !'

It was quite pleasant to have some one taking such an interest in her ! Gladys felt warmed, and looked grate-fully at Mirabel. She was a weak, timid character—Mirabel was strong and decided, even though she was often wrong.

'Yes—I will show the girls if you want me to,' Gladys said.

'Well, after tea, in the common room this evening, you show them,' said Mirabel. 'I'll clap like anything at the end, so you needn't be afraid. Perhaps the girls will put you in the concert after all, when they see how good you are. Isabel said something about not being able to alter the programmes—but I'm sure it could be done. I could help.'

Mirabel felt rather proud of having got her own way with Gladys. She told Hilary and the others, and they looked forward with interest to seeing what Gladys could do that evening.

It certainly was a surprise to every one ! Gladys looked terribly nervous at first, and her voice shook. But in a minute or two, as she forgot herself, and threw

herself heart and soul into the part she was acting, it
seemed as if the little Misery-girl was no longer there—
but some one quite different, that nobody had seen before !

Gladys acted many parts from different Shakespeare
plays—Lady Macbeth—Miranda—Malvolio—Hamlet.
She knew them all by heart. Her mother had been very
fond of Shakespeare's works, and the two of them had
studied them together evening after evening. Gladys's
dead father had been a fine actor, and Gladys had inherited
the gift.

Gladys stopped at last, changing from Bottom the
Weaver to her own timid self. The girls roared with
delight at her, and clapped loudly.

'You monkey ! Fancy not telling us you could do all
that ! ' said Pat. ' You'll bring the house down at the
concert ! I say—we simply MUST put her in ! Can't
we possibly ? '

' Please, please don't,' begged Gladys in alarm. ' I
couldn't possibly do it in front of most of the school.
Well, I might, if I'd more time to rehearse with you.
But the concert's tomorrow. I should die if you made
me be in it ! Please don't ! '

' Well—if you feel so strongly about it, I suppose we'll
have to leave you out,' said Janet. ' Is there, by any
chance, anything else you've kept us in the dark about ?
Can you paint marvellous pictures—or work wonderful
sums in your head ? '

Gladys laughed—the first laugh since she had been at
St. Clare's. ' There's only one other thing I'm good at,'
she said. ' That's lacrosse.'

' Well, you don't seem to have shone there to any great
extent,' said Bobby, in surprise.

' I know. I didn't bother,' said Gladys. ' I just didn't
care whether I ran fast or not, or scored a goal, or anything. That's why Miss Wilton kept making me goal-

keeper, I expect. She thought I was only good for stopping goals, not for anything else. But I *can* play well, if I try. I was in the top team at my day school.'

'Good,' said Mirabel. 'We'll make you shoot dozens of goals and then you can write that to your mother, too.'

'Sorry about your mother, Gladys,' said Hilary. 'Tell us any news you get. We're all interested.'

Gladys went to bed really happy that night. She had a friend. She had been clapped and applauded. She had thrown off her reserve, and let the other girls speak to her of her mother. Things didn't seem so bad now. For the first time she fell asleep without lying and worrying.

In the middle of the night, five of the girls lay and tossed restlessly. Pat and Isabel, Doris, Bobby and Carlotta could not sleep. Their throats hurt them. They coughed and sneezed. It was most annoying—because the concert was to be the next evening !

'I shan't be able to speak a word,' thought Doris, as she tried to ease her throat. 'This really is bad luck. I can't possibly be in the concert. Blow ! I was so looking forward to it.'

In the morning all five went along to Matron, feeling very miserable and sorry for themselves. She took their temperatures.

'You've got the horrid cold that has been running round the school,' she said, briskly. 'You've all got temperatures except Carlotta—and it would take a lot to give *her* one ! But she can go to bed just the same. To the san, all of you.'

'But Matron—it's the concert tonight !' said Bobby, hoarsely. 'We can't possibly go to bed.'

'Put your coats on and your hats and scarves,' said Matron, taking no notice of Bobby at all. 'And go across to the san, immediately. You've all got the same feverish cold, that's plain—caught the chill watching lacrosse in that cold wind the other day, I suppose—so the germ found you easy prey. Bobby, are you deaf? Go and get your coat and hat at once and don't stand arguing.'

It never was any good trying to argue with Matron. She had dealt with girls for many, many years, and bed and warmth and the right medicine in her opinion cured most things very quickly. So, concert or no concert, the five girls were bundled into bed in the san, and there they lay, moaning about the concert and wondering what was going to happen.

It didn't take the rest of the form long to decide what was to happen.

'We can't *possibly* hold the concert without those five!' said Hilary.

'Doris was one of the stars,' said Janet.

'*And* Bobby,' said Hilary. 'And Carlotta too. It would be a very weak affair without those three. We'll have to postpone it. We'll have it next week.'

'We can't,' said Anna. 'The third form are having theirs.'

'Well, the week after then,' said Hilary. 'That will give the invalids time to get over their colds. I hope nobody else feels like sneezing or coughing! If they do, for goodness' sake go to the san, and get it over, so that we can have the concert all right in a fortnight's time!'

'Gladys can be in it this time!' said Kathleen. 'That makes another good performer.'

'Oh, good!' said Anna, looking at Gladys. 'That will be fine. You'll have loads of time to practise and rehearse now, Gladys.'

Gladys couldn't help feeling thrilled. She did love acting—and it would be fun to rehearse with the others. It hadn't been nice to be left out. Now she would be able to join in, and would be clapped just as the others were. There would be a lot to tell her mother when she wrote. She felt a wave of gratitude welling up for Mirabel. It was Mirabel who had made all this possible for her.

She went up to Mirabel and slipped her arm through hers. ' It's a pity about the others, isn't it ? ' she said. ' But they'll be better in a fortnight—and I *shall* like being in the concert now. I shall clap like anything when your turn comes, Mirabel. I think you'll be the best of us all.'

Mirabel did not smile. She looked rather cold and blank. Gladys wondered what the matter was.

' How many pieces are you going to play ? ' she asked. ' Do you want me to turn over the pages for you at the piano ? '

' I shan't *be* in the concert,' said Mirabel, in a funny, even voice. ' You know I'm going home at half-term— and by the time the concert comes, I'll be gone. I feel disappointed, of course—so don't keep on rubbing it in ! '

She took her arm from Gladys's and walked off. How sickening everything was !

12   GLADYS TACKLES MIRABEL

THE second form seemed to have dwindled considerably now that five of them were away. Hilary and Alison went down with the cold the next day, so there were many empty desks. The concert was put off for two weeks, and the second form girls felt very flat and gloomy.

Elsie was the only one who was at all pleased. She had consistently refused to take any interest at all in the concert, and she felt glad that this disappointment had come upon the others. As Anna had predicted, Elsie had adopted a martyr-like attitude, looking left-out and miserable all day long. But no one took the slightest notice of her.

The girl's pride was hurt. She had not liked to ask Anna what she had said to Miss Theobald on the day when both of them had been sent for. But it was clear to her now, that not only the girls no longer regarded her as one of their heads, but Miss Jenks also appeared to think that only Anna was head-girl. It was most exasperating. Elsie sometimes wished she was like Carlotta and could slap and box people's ears when she felt like it! She would box the ears of every one in the form!

The seven girls in the san had a bad time for the first day or two, and then, when their temperatures went down, they sat up and recovered their spirits. It was fun for so many to be together. They could play games and talk.

' It's half-term next week,' said Isabel. ' Our mother's coming over to take us out.'

' So's mine,' said Doris. ' Carlotta, is your father coming to take you out ? '

' Yes—and my grandmother too,' said Carlotta, gloomily. ' I get on with my father all right now—but I just seem to go all common and bad-mannered with my grandmother. I remember all my circus ways, and she just hates them. Oh dear—I meant to try and get terribly good-mannered this term, and not box any one's ears or lose my temper or anything.'

Mirabel is supposed to be going at half-term, isn't she ? ' said Bobby, suddenly. ' She won't be in the concert then—and she won't know if she's been chosen

to play in any of the lacrosse matches, either—and she'll
miss the birthday feast that Carlotta's going to give.'

' She's an idiot,' said Doris.   ' She can't think straight.
That's what's the matter with her.'

' She wouldn't be a bad sort if she made up her mind
to shake down and be sensible,' said Pat.   ' I quite like
her now.   And I must say she's good to that timid little
Gladys.   When Kathleen came in to see us yesterday,
she said that Mirabel really does look after her and walk
with her—and Gladys is like a little dog with her—trots
after her and does everything she's told.'

' Well, who would have thought that those two would
pair up ! ' said Isabel.   ' And there's another astonishing
thing too—who would have thought that lazy old Anna
would pull herself together as she has done ! '

By that week-end the seven invalids were very much
better.   They could not possibly have attended the
concert, if theirs had been postponed only a week, so it
was just as well that it had been put off for three weeks.
They would be well enough to go to the third form's
concert, which was on the Thursday before half-term.

Mirabel was looking very glum.   Half-term seemed to
be coming quickly.   The postponing of the concert had
been a bitter disappointment.   It was dull without half
the class at lessons.

The only bright spot was her new friendship with
Gladys.   The girl was showing unsuspected sides of her
character to Mirabel.   She could make excellent jokes,
and had a fine sense of humour.   She was fun to walk
with because she could keep up a merry chatter.   She
seemed to have quite thrown off her pre-occupation with
her own troubles.   She really was very fond of Mirabel,
and the girl, although embarrassed at any show of affection in the ordinary way, liked to feel Gladys slipping
her arm through hers.

'Mirabel! You won't really go home at half-term,
will you?' Gladys said that week-end. 'There are only
a few days more. It's lovely being friends with you.
Don't go, will you?'

'Of course I'm going,' said Mirabel, impatiently. 'I
told you I'd made up my mind to go at half-term, even
before I arrived here! And I'm not going back on that.
I never go back on what I've said.'

'No. I know you don't,' said Gladys, with a sigh.
'It's only people like me who change their minds and
alter what they meant to do. But I do wish you weren't
going, Mirabel.'

Gladys said the same thing to Hilary that day, when
she went to see her in the san. 'I do so wish Mirabel
wasn't going,' she said. 'I feel a different person since
she was nice to me, and all of you clapped me that time
I acted for you.'

'What's she got to go for?' said Hilary. 'She has
settled down all right. She's happy. She's one of us
now, and she enjoys life here. Whatever does she want
to go home at half-term for, now she's all right?'

'Well, you see,' said Gladys, earnestly, 'she can't go
back on what she said. She *said* she was going home at
half-term—she made up her mind about that—so she
she can't *possibly* change her mind, can she? She's such
a strong character, you see.'

'Well, it's strong characters who ought to be able to
change their minds at times,' said Hilary. '*I* call it
weak to stick to something when you know it's silly.
And it *is* silly for Mirabel to go back home now. We
want her for the concert. She knows that She's just
being weak, not strong!'

Gladys was astonished to hear this. It seemed to make
things quite different. Weak little Gladys had thought
that strong characters must be able to make right deci-

sions and carry them out—but now she saw that a strong character could do something wrong or stupid because it was too proud to unmake a decision! It was something quite new to her. She stared at Hilary.

'I wish you'd say that to Mirabel,' she said.

'Say it yourself,' said Hilary. 'You're her friend, aren't you? Well, *you* tell her!'

'She wouldn't listen to *me*,' said Gladys.

'What you mean is—you're afraid to tackle her!' said Hilary, with a laugh. 'Go on, Mouse—take the bull by the horns—and if you really do care for Mirabel and want her for your friend, don't be afraid of telling her what you think. Get a little spunk!'

Poor Gladys! Every one always seemed to be telling her to get a little 'spunk.' It was something she was sure she would never possess. She had been such a mother's girl that now it was difficult for her to stand on her own feet.

'All the same—it's no good having a friend unless you'll do something for them,' thought Gladys, trying to screw up her courage. 'I shall lose Mirabel if I don't tackle her—and if I lose her because she's angry with me for tackling her, well, I shan't be any worse off. So I'll do it.'

It wasn't easy. It never is easy for a timid person to tackle a strong one, especially if it is to point out that the strong one is wrong. Gladys went to Mirabel and slipped her arm through hers.

'Mirabel,' she said, 'I've been thinking over what you said about going home—and not changing your mind and all that—and I really do think you're wrong.'

'That's my own business,' said Mirabel, rather roughly.

'No, it isn't. It's mine too,' said Gladys, hoping her voice would not begin to tremble. 'You're my friend, and I don't want you to go.'

'I've told you I can't change my mind.   I never do,'
said Mirabel.   'Don't bother me.'

'If you were really as strong a character as you make
out, you *would* change your mind,' said Gladys, boldly.
'You know you could stay here happily now—but you're
too proud to own you've been silly—and you call it being
strong enough not to change your mind!'

'Gladys!   How *dare* you talk to me like this!' cried
Mirabel, astonished and angry.   'Anybody would think
you are Miss Theobald—picking me to pieces—telling me
I'm no good—not worth-while!'

'I'm not telling you that,' said Gladys, getting distressed.   'I'm only saying—don't let your pride stand
in the way of your happiness.   That's all.'

Mirabel wrenched her arm out of Gladys's and walked
off, red in the face.   How dare Gladys say things like
that to her?   She put on her hat and coat and went out
into the school grounds, fuming.

Gladys stared after her, miserable.   'I knew it wouldn't
be any good,' she thought.   'Of course Mirabel wouldn't
let me say things like that.   Now she won't even be
friends with me for the last two or three days before she
goes!'

Mirabel walked round the grounds, hot and angry.
But, as her anger died, her mind began to work more
calmly.   There was a great deal in what Gladys had said.
'Though how that timid little thing ever thought that
all out beats me!' said Mirabel to herself.   'There must
be more in her than I thought.   And the way she stood
up to me too!   She *has* come on.   She must like me a
lot to make up her mind to go for me like that, in order
to try and make me change my mind, so that she can
still have me for a friend.'

The wind cooled her hot cheeks.   She sat on the wall
and looked down over the valley.   It was very pleasant

*"How dare Gladys say anything like that to me," thought
Mirabel*

there. It would be marvellous in the summer. St. Clare's *was* fun—there was no doubt about that.

'Now, let's think things out calmly,' said Mirabel to herself. 'I was angry because my family sent me away because I didn't fit in at home—and I vowed to get back as soon as I could just to show them they couldn't send me away! Now I like being here—and I see that I *am* better away from home, and shall go back really thrilled to see every one. I dare say I'll learn lots of things here I ought to have learnt before—thinking of other people, not always having my own way and things like that. Well then—what is stopping me from staying here?'

She gazed down on the valley, and did not like to think out the answer. But she had to.

'All that is stopping me is, as Gladys pointed out, my pride. I'm too proud to tell Daddy that I'll stay. I was so angry at being sent away that I wanted to pay them out by coming back as soon as possible and being beastly. And I think I'm a strong character! Golly, all this makes me sound as hateful as catty Elsie!'

She stayed for a few minutes longer and then she sprang down from the wall. She went into the school building and took off her out-door things. She went straight to Miss Theobald's room and knocked at the door.

'Come in!' said Miss Theobald. She was talking to Miss Jenks and Mam'zelle. Mirabel was a little taken aback when she saw all three teachers there—but what she had come to say had to be said, no matter how many people were in the room.

'Miss Theobald,' she said, rather loudly. 'May I stay on, please, and not go home at the half-term? Would you let me? I like being here, and I'm sorry I was so silly at first.'

Miss Theobald looked at the girl, and smiled her nicest smile, warm and friendly.

'Yes—we shall be very glad to have you,' she said.
'Isn't that so, Miss Jenks—Mam'zelle?'

'It is,' said Miss Jenks and nodded kindly at Mirabel.

'Ha!' said Mam'zelle, '*c'est bien, ca!* I too am pleased.'

'I will telephone to your parents,' said Miss Theobald. 'I am glad, Mirabel, that you have something "worthwhile" in you—no, I don't mean your music! Something better than that. Well done!'

Praise like this was very sweet. Mirabel walked out of the room, warm and happy. She knew she had a great deal to learn—things would go wrong, and she would make mistakes—but nothing could take that moment from her.

She went to find Gladys. She found her curled up in a corner of the common room, looking rather small and woe-begone. She went over to her and gave her an unexpected hug.

'Well, old thing! I'm staying on! I've just been to tell Miss Theobald. And all because you ticked me off like that, and set me thinking!'

Half in tears Gladys returned the hug. It was marvellous. She, a weak person, had summoned up enough strength to tackle a strong one—and had actually got what she wanted. It was too good to be true.

'You'll be in the concert!' she said. 'And you'll come to Carlotta's feast. What fun we'll have! Oh Mirabel I'm so proud of you!'

'I'm rather proud of you too,' said Mirabel, awkwardly. 'You gave me a surprise, telling me home-truths like that. You're a good sort of friend to have.'

'What a lot I shall have to write and tell my mother!' said Gladys. 'And I say—won't every one be pleased you've changed your mind and are staying on!'

The girls *were* pleased. They had begun to like Mirabel

now, and they admired her for being able to alter her
mind and own that she had been wrong. Soon they
would forget Mirabel's extraordinary behaviour the first
few weeks of the term.

Only one girl was displeased. That was Elsie. Why
should such a fuss be made of that ridiculous Mirabel
who had behaved so badly, and who had been partly
the cause of Elsie's disgrace? Elsie brooded over this
and cast many spiteful glances at Mirabel, wondering
what she could do to pay her out for being popular,
when she, Elsie, was never taken any notice of at all!

But Mirabel was thick-skinned. She neither saw nor
felt Elsie's hostility, but looked forward happily to the
remainder of the term at St. Clare's.

13   HALF-TERM HOLIDAY

HALF-TERM came and went. It was a pleasant break
for every one. Most parents came to take out the girls
for some kind of treat, and those that lived near enough
went home for a day or two. Alison's parents were away
so she went out with the twins and their mother.

'Well, how are you all getting on this term?' asked
Mrs. O'Sullivan. 'Working hard, I hope?'

But nobody said anything about work. The twins
poured out their news about the concert, and about
lacrosse, and how Carlotta was going to have a feast on
her birthday. Alison talked of nothing but her beloved
Miss Quentin.

'She's awfully clever,' said Alison. 'It's lovely

learning Drama under her. She says I have the making
of a good little actress.'

' Oh do shut up talking about Miss Quentin,' groaned
Pat. 'Mummy, last term Alison was all over Sadie
Greene, that American girl—who, by the way, has never
even *written* to you, Alison! And this term it's Miss
Quentin! Isn't there any medicine or pill we can give
Alison to stop her raving about people? '

Alison had been very hurt that her ' best ' friend,
Sadie, had not taken the trouble to write to her at all.
She thought it was mean of Pat to remind her of it.

' Well, Miss Quentin wouldn't be like that,' she said.
' I've made her promise to write to me every week in the
holidays. She's loyal, I know. I think she's marvellous.'

' She's beautiful, she's wonderful, she's marvellous, she's
magnificent,' said Isabel, with a grin. ' But the thing
is—what does she think of *you*, Alison? Not much, I
bet! You're always going about thinking somebody is
wonderful—you never seem to imagine they might be
bored with you.'

The idea of her beloved Miss Quentin being bored with
her made Alison hot and angry. She glared at the twins.
Mrs. O'Sullivan saw the look.

' Now, now,' she said, ' don't let's waste our precious
time in quarrelling, please. I've no doubt Miss Quentin
is a very admirable person and I'm sure Alison works
hard in *her* class, at least, if she doesn't in anyone else's.'

Mirabel's father and mother came over to see her at
half-term, and took her out to lunch, a theatre, and tea
afterwards. Mirabel was intensely excited at the thought
of seeing them. She forgot all about the temper in which
she had been when she had parted from them. She
forgot the horrid things she had said, and the threats
she had made. She stood at the front door, eagerly
waiting for them.

When they arrived, they were startled by some one who hurled herself at them, flung her arms round them, and exclaimed in a choky voice, ' Mummy ! Daddy ! It's lovely to see you again ! '

Her mother and father looked at the excited girl, whose eyes shone with welcome. This was a different Mirabel altogether ! They hugged the girl, and looked with interest at the school. Neither of them had seen it. It had been a very sudden decision on Mirabel's father's part to send Mirabel away, and he had chosen a school recommended to him very highly by a friend. It had all been done in such a hurry that the parents had not had time to see the school itself.

' What a lovely place ! ' said Mrs. Unwin. ' Is there time to look round ? '

' Mummy, you simply *must* see everything,' cried Mirabel, and she dragged her parents all over the school, from top to bottom, even showing them the bathroom where she had her nightly bath. There was great pride in the girl's voice. Her parents exchanged happy glances with each other. It was quite plain to them that Mirabel was extremely proud of St. Clare's already, and felt it to be her own splendid school.

' Daddy, I'm so pleased you chose St. Clare's,' said Mirabel, when they came back to the front door at last. ' It's marvellous. It really is.' She looked at her parents and hesitated a little. She had something to say that was difficult. Mirabel hated saying she was sorry about anything.

' You know—I really am sorry I was so awful at home,' said the girl, rushing her words out. ' I can see you all better now, because I'm far away from you—and I think I was awful to every one.'

' We've forgotten it all,' said her father. ' We shall never remember it again. All that matters to us is that

you are happy—and will be happy when you come home
again. We felt so proud when Miss Theobald let us
know that you wanted to stay on. She said one or two
nice things about you.'

'Did she really?' asked Mirabel, pleased. 'I hated
her at first—she said some awful things to me—but now
I think she's fine. Oh Mummy—I do wish you'd brought
Joan and Harry with you! I did want to see them.'

'They wanted to see you too,' said her mother. 'But
it was too far to bring them. Now—what about
going? We shall never get any lunch if we don't
start soon.'

'Mummy—would you do something for me?' asked
Mirabel, suddenly. 'I've got a friend here—and her
mother's ill in hospital, so there's no one to take her
out for a half-term treat. Could she possibly come with
us, do you think?'

'Of course,' said Mrs. Unwin, surprised and pleased to
think that her difficult daughter had actually made a
friend. She wondered what the friend would be like.
She had never liked Mirabel's chosen friends before—
they had always been noisy, impolite and out-of-hand—
a little like Mirabel herself.

'I'll go and get her,' said Mirabel. She ran off to find
Gladys. She was getting ready for the school lunch,
feeling a little lonely, for nearly all the other girls had
left for the half-term holiday.

Mirabel rushed at her. 'Gladys! You're to come
with me! Go and ask Miss Jenks if you can come,
quickly! Mummy and Daddy say you can come.'

A shock of joy ran through Gladys. She felt nervous
of meeting Mirabel's parents—but to think that Mirabel
wanted her to come was marvellous. Her depression
fell away from her at once, and she stared in joy at her
friend. She had had few treats in her life, and it did

seem to her that going out to lunch and a theatre was too good to be true.

'Gladys, don't stand staring there!' cried Mirabel, impatiently. 'Hurry up. Go and find Miss Jenks. I'll get your out-door things.'

In three minutes Gladys was at the front door with Mirabel, red with shyness, hardly able to say a word. Mr. and Mrs. Unwin took a look at the nervous girl, and were astonished. So this was Mirabel's friend—well, what a change from the tiresome girls she had chosen before! They took a liking to Gladys immediately, and Mrs. Unwin smiled a motherly smile at her.

In some ways Mrs. Unwin resembled Gladys's own mother. Both were the gentle, kindly type, and Gladys warmed to Mrs. Unwin at once. In no time at all she was telling Mrs. Unwin all about her own mother, revelling in the understanding and kindness of Mirabel's mother.

'I say! I do think you've got a nice mother!' she whispered to Mirabel, when they went to wash their hands at the hotel, before lunch. 'Next to mine, she's the nicest I've ever met. And isn't your father jolly? I feel a bit afraid of him but I do like him. Aren't you lucky?'

Mirabel was pleased. She was seeing her mother and father with different eyes, now that she had been away from them for some weeks. It was pleasant to hear some one liking them so much. She squeezed her friend's arm.

'It's fun having you,' she said. 'I'm glad my people like you.'

A real surprise was in store for Gladys. When Mrs. Unwin asked her what hospital her mother was in, she heard Gladys's answer with astonishment.

'Why—that's quite near where my sister lives. I often go over to see my sister—and perhaps I could go to the hospital and find out how your mother is. I might even see her, if she is allowed visitors.'

Gladys stared at Mrs. Unwin, red with delight. It would bring her mother much closer somehow, if she knew some one was going to the very hospital where her mother was. And just suppose she was allowed to see her! Mrs. Unwin could write and tell her about it.

'Oh thank you,' said the girl. 'If you only could! It would be marvellous!'

The half-term went all too quickly. All the girls enjoyed it. It was a very pleasant break indeed, and they went back to school full of chatter about what they had done.

'Hallo!' said the twins, meeting Carlotta when they arrived back. 'How did *you* get on? Was your grand-mother very stand-offish?'

'No—she seemed quite pleased with me,' said Carlotta, grinning. 'I didn't walk on my hands or do anything she disapproves of—and I made my hair so tidy you wouldn't know me. I was most frightfully polite to her, and my father was awfully pleased with me. He gave me a pound note for my birthday!'

'Gracious!' said Pat. 'What luck!'

'And my grandmother told me I could order anything I liked for my birthday party, at the shop in the town,' said Carlotta, her eyes lighting up with delighted expec-tancy. 'I say—won't we order lots of things! She gave me some things out of her store cupboard too. I've got a big box in the cupboard in our dormitory. I don't know what's in it yet, but I bet my grandmother has given me plenty.'

'How gorgeous!' said the twins. 'You sound as if you've got enough to feed the whole school.'

'No—just our form,' said Carlotta. 'And I'm not sure yet if we'll have it properly, in the afternoon at tea-time—or whether we'll make it really exciting, and go in for a midnight feast again. I think we ought to have a midnight feast every term, you know! School doesn't seem really complete without that!'

It looked as if the latter half of the term was going to be exciting. There was the concert to look forward to that week—several lacrosse matches—and now Carlotta's feast! All the girls glowed. What fun they had!

Bobby had a secret, and so had Janet. They had gone out together with Bobby's parents, and with Janet's brother, whose half-term holiday was the same week-end. He was as much of a monkey as Janet, always up to tricks. He had given Janet and Bobby an old trick to play on Mam'zelle. It was a curious looking thing, consisting of a long stretch of narrow rubber tubing, with a little bladder on one end, and an indiarubber bulb on the other, which, when pressed, sent air down the tube into the little bladder, which at once expanded and became big.

'But what's it for?' asked the twins, in curiosity.

'You put the bladder under some one's plate at meal-time,' giggled Bobby, 'and run the tubing under the table-cloth. Then, when you press the bulb, the bladder fills and up tips the plate. Imagine Mam'zelle's astonishment when her plate starts dancing about! We shall all be in fits of laughter!'

This was really something to look forward to as well. Mam'zelle was a marvellous person to play tricks on. She was always taken in, and had caused more enjoyment than all the mistresses in the school put together.

'Oh Bobby! Let's do it soon,' begged Doris. 'Do let's. We haven't played any tricks this term, at all.'

'Well, after all, we *are* the second form,' said Janet, teasingly.

'Bobby will be playing tricks when she's head-girl!'

said Isabel. ' I'm surprised she has gone as far as half-term without thinking of any.'

' Oh, I've *thought* of plenty,' said Bobby. ' But Miss Jenks isn't an easy person to play about with. She doesn't keep her temper like Miss Roberts did. She flares up suddenly, and I don't particularly want to be sent to Miss Theobald now I'm in the second form. It may have escaped your notice that I'm working hard this term ! Don't forget I'm not Don't-Care Bobby as I was last term. I'm using my brains for other things besides tricks and jokes.'

' Let's have a rehearsal for the concert,' said Pat. ' We've only got a few days now. Bring your violin, Mirabel—and Gladys, make up your mind what you're going to act, out of all the hundreds of parts you seem able to play. Come on, everybody—let's enjoy ourselves !

14   A MARVELLOUS SHOW

THE days flew by, and the night of the concert came. Miss Jenks had to be lenient with the second form, because she could see that they really did mean their show to be a great success. Mam'zelle was the only teacher who would not make allowances, so the class groaned and worked for her as best they could.

' It is bad to have concerts in the middle of the term,' Mam'zelle grumbled to Miss Jenks. ' These girls, they think of anything but their work. Now, when I was a schoolgirl . . .'

' You worked all day, and you worked all night, you

had no games, you prepared no concerts. . . .' chanted Miss Jenks, with her wide smile. The teachers had heard a thousand times of Mam'zelle's hard-worked youth.

'There are other things as important as lessons,' said Miss Roberts. 'We are not out to cram facts and knowledge into the girls' heads all day long, but to help them to form strong and kindly characters too. This concert now, that you grumble at—it is making the second form work together in a wonderful way, it is bringing out all kinds of unexpected talent—look at Mirabel and Gladys, for instance—and it will help a great cause. It makes the girls resourceful and ingenious too—you should see the costume Doris has made for herself as Matron and as cook.'

Mam'zelle did not know that Doris was going to imitate her as well. The other mistresses guessed it and they were looking forward to it. They all liked Mam'zelle, and admired her sense of humour. She could take a joke against herself very well.

'The third form concert was quite good,' said Miss Lewis, the history teacher. 'But I think the second form will be more entertaining. The third form were rather high-brow, and didn't provide a single laugh for any one. I fancy we shall find plenty to laugh at this Saturday !'

The second form were getting very excited. Only Elsie was apart from all the thrills and enjoyment. The girl still obstinately refused to take part in anything, and would not even be prompter.

'But Elsie, every one will think it very funny that you are the only second-former out of things,' said Pat, impatiently. 'We keep on offering you things to do, and you keep turning them down. I think it's very decent of us to be so patient with you.'

'I'll take part on one condition,' said Elsie, sullenly.

'What ? ' asked Bobby, coming up.

'That you let me be head-girl again with Anna,' said

Elsie. ' You've punished me for weeks now, by taking away my authority as head-girl. Isn't it about time you let me have it back again ? '

' Well—we'll ask the rest of the form,' said Pat. So that night in the common room, before a rehearsal was held, Anna put the question to the meeting.

' Elsie says she will take part in the concert if we let her be joint head-girl again. What does every one think about it ? '

' Why should she bargain with us ? ' cried Carlotta. ' It is we who should bargain with her ! We should say " You can be head-girl again if you show that you are worthy of it ! " '

' Quite right,' called Doris.

' Look how she has behaved all these weeks,' said Janet. ' Has she tried to give us a better opinion of her ? Has she shown us she could be trusted to lead us again ? No —all she has done is to look spiteful, be catty when she has a chance, pose as a martyr and hope she'll get our sympathy. Well, she hasn't. We've just taken no notice at all, and she hasn't liked it.'

' I don't see why we should bother with her,' said Isabel. ' I really don't.'

' Will you show in the usual way whether you would like her again or not ? ' asked Anna. ' Hands up those who will give Elsie another chance as head-girl.'

Not a single hand went up. Anna grinned. ' Well,' she said, ' that's that. Elsie will have to put up with it. She hasn't come at all well out of this, I must say. I would have been willing to work with her again, if you'd said so—but I'm glad I haven't got to.'

Elsie was not there, and nobody bothered to fetch her to tell her what had happened. They began their rehearsal and were soon busy criticizing and applauding as one after another performed. Gladys was by now used to an audience and she acted as naturally as every one else. She and Doris were both natural actresses, though in a different way. Doris could imitate any one she had seen, but not act a part—and Gladys, quite unable to imitate any one around her, was excellent at interpreting any part in a play. The two admired each other and Gladys was fast making another friend.

'Well—I really think we've got everything all right now,' said Bobby at last. 'It *will* be fun! Doris, you'll bring the house down with your imitation of Mam'zelle. I only hope Mam'zelle won't mind. But I don't think she will.'

The door opened and Elsie came in. 'You held the rehearsal without me,' she said. 'What do you want me to do at the concert?'

'Well, Elsie—you said you would only be in it if we recognized you as head-girl again,' said Anna, rather awkwardly. 'We put the question to the second form, and I'm afraid they decided not to give you the chance. So we didn't think you'd want to help with the concert, in that case.'

'Couldn't you have told me you wouldn't have me as head-girl, and still let me be in the concert?' said Elsie.

The others stared at her. 'Don't be silly,' said Bobby, at last. 'That's not the point. The point is, you always refused, and then wanted to make a bargain with us—and we wouldn't make it. I suppose you're beginning to feel very awkward about being left out of the concert in front of the whole school, so you're climbing down a bit, and want to help even if we won't accept you as head-girl again. Well—help if you like—but don't expect us to fall on your neck and give you a warm welcome, because we shan't.'

This was a long speech and Elsie listened to it in growing anger. All that Bobby said was true. Elsie was now

beginning to feel horrified at being left out. Every one
in the school would notice it. They would whisper about
her. They would nudge one another as she passed.
Elsie couldn't bear it. But neither had she the strength
to over-rule her rage and accept Bobby's luke-warm offer
to let her help. She made a curious explosive noise of
rage and walked out of the room.

Doris immediately imitated the explosive noise, and the
whole form burst into laughter. Elsie heard the squeals,
and stopped. She felt inclined to go back and hit out
at every one. Then a wave of self pity overcame her
and she burst into tears.

The concert was an enormous success. Half the school
was there and all the mistresses. The curtain was drawn
at exactly eight o'clock, and everything went like clock-
work. The third form had been late in starting, and
there had been long intervals between the various turns,
which had bored the audience. But the second form were
most efficient.

Turn after turn was put on and loudly applauded.
Mirabel's playing was encored twice. The girl was so
thrilled at her success that she could hardly speak for joy.
Her piano-playing was really excellent, and as for her
violin solo, it amazed every one, even the four music-
teachers, who were by now used to gifted children
springing up in their classes at times.

Carlotta's acrobatics were hailed with delight by the
whole school. Every one knew that Carlotta had once
been a circus-girl, and they clapped till their hands
smarted when she did some of her graceful circus-tricks.
The first-formers gaped in admiration and secretly
determined to try out all the acrobatics themselves.

Gladys got an encore too. When the nervous, white-
faced girl stepped on to the stage, the audience waited,
rather critical, expecting to be bored. But before their

eyes the girl changed into the characters she acted, and
held the whole school spell-bound.   She was really gifted,
there was no doubt about it.

The most surprised person in the whole of the audience
was Miss Quentin.   She took the Drama class herself,
and prided herself on knowing the capacities of everyone
in the second form.   Privately she had thought that Doris
and Carlotta were the only ones worth teaching—and now
here was the quiet little mouse, Gladys, bringing down
the house with her polished and beautiful interpretations
of many of the most difficult parts in Shakespeare's plays !

Miss Theobald leaned across to Miss Quentin.   ' I must
congratulate you on one of your pupil's performances ! '
she said, in her quiet voice.   ' I can see that you must
have helped the child a great deal.   She could never have
done all this by herself.   It is amazing.'

Miss Quentin was not honest enough to say that she
was as astonished as Miss Theobald.   She loved praise
as much as Alison did, and she nodded her head, pretending that she had taught Gladys all that she knew.
Secretly she made up her mind to cultivate Gladys
Hillman and give her the most important part in the play
the second form were doing with her.   She knew Alison
had hoped for it—but she couldn't help that.   Gladys
must certainly have it.   Then Miss Quentin could take
all the credit to herself for the excellent performance she
was sure Gladys would give !

The concert went on.   The twins were applauded and
so was Janet.   The first-formers loved Bobby's conjuring
tricks, and her ceaseless, ridiculous patter, and gave her
an encore !   But it was Doris who was the real star of
the evening !

When she stepped on to the stage, dressed up as the
jolly, fat old cook, there was a roar of delighted laughter.
Doris pretended to make a pudding, keeping up a mono-

logue in the cook's Irish accent, bringing in all the phrases that the girls knew so well. They squealed with laughter.

Then she altered her cook's uniform deftly—and lo and behold, there was Matron ! Bobby ran on with some big bottles of medicine and a thermometer, and Doris proceeded to imitate Matron interviewing various girls sent to her for treatment or inspection.

Matron was in the audience, shaking with laughter. The girls roared with delight, missing many of Doris's jokes because they could not stop laughing. She was extremely clever and extremely funny.

' She should be on the stage,' said Matron, wiping her streaming eyes. ' Oh, am I really as funny as that ? It's time I retired if I'm such a joke. This girl will be the death of me ! Wait till she comes for medicine ! I'll get my own back then ! '

Doris went off the stage, grinning. The audience looked at the next item she was to do—another impersonation. Who ?

They knew as soon as she appeared again. She had made herself plump with padding. She had scraped back her hair into a bun, put on enormous flat-heeled shoes, secretly borrowed from Mam'zelle's room, and wore glasses crookedly on her nose.

' Mam'zelle ! ' shrieked the girls, in delight. ' Marvellous ! '

Doris approached the edge of the stage and addressed the girls in Mam'zelle's identical voice, taking off her English accent to perfection. The audience roared with laughter as Doris scolded them for misbehaviour.

'C'est abominable !' she finished. Then she turned away, re-arranged some things on a desk behind, and proceeded to take a lesson in the way that Mam'zelle took it, with hands wagging towards the ceiling, and her glasses slipping down over her nose.

Every one looked at Mam'zelle herself to see how she was taking it. Mam'zelle was lying back in her chair, helpless with laughter, tears pouring down her cheeks. The girls felt a warm wave of liking for her—how nice she was to laugh at some one taking off her little foibles and mannerisms! The girls had to laugh at Mam'zelle's squeals as much as at Doris's acting.

It was a marvellous show and a great success. Every one had loved it, and crowded round at the end to clap the performers on the back, and congratulate them. It was pleasant for both Mirabel and Gladys to feel these pats and hear the generous words of praise.

' Mother will hardly believe it all,' said Gladys to herself, her face shining with delight. ' I must tell her every single thing. And wasn't Mirabel's playing good? I clapped till my hands were sore.'

' We've made four pounds, three shillings and sixpence by selling tickets, programmes and getting in extra subscriptions,' announced Anna. ' Isn't that good? I bet no form will do as well as that.'

The second form enjoyed coffee and biscuits for a treat after the show, generously provided by Matron and Mam'zelle. ' Though why we should do this for a form whose chief success is putting up Mam'zelle and myself to be laughed at, I really don't know!' said Matron, beaming round. ' By the way—where's Elsie? She wasn't in the concert, and I don't see her now.'

The second form were so elated by their success that they wanted Elsie to join in the coffee and biscuits. But she was nowhere to be found.

She was in bed, alone—but not asleep; the only girl who had not shared in or applauded her form's success! Poor Elsie—her thoughts were very bitter that night, as she heard the echoes of laughter from the concert-room!

THE next big event was Carlotta's birthday. She was fifteen, and planned a really good feast. She had opened the box of goodies given to her by her grandmother, and it had proved to be even better than the second form had hoped.

'Sardines!' said Bobby, taking out three or four of the oblong tins. 'And what's this—an ENORMOUS tin of pine-apple chunks. It's ages since I've tasted pine-apple. And what a fine big tin!'

'Bars of chocolate-cream!' said Janet. 'Enough to feed the whole school, I should think!'

'Tins of prawns!' cried Hilary. 'I say—I do like prawns. Golly — prawns and pine-apple — what a heavenly mixture that would be!'

'Here's a ginger-bread cake,' said Alison. 'Isn't it big? Carlotta, I must say you own a first-class grandmother! Mine's good for a cake and a bottle of boiled sweets, but that's about all. Yours is Super!'

'Well, she's only just begun to be super,' said Carlotta, with a grin. 'When she didn't approve of me, she handed me out two shillings and a new hair-slide. See what happens when she *does* approve of me!'

'Let's teach Carlotta some really marvellous manners,' said Janet, 'so that she will make a wonderful impression on her grandmother in the Christmas hols. She'll come back with half a grocer's shop then, I should think!'

'Oh, I say—what's this?' said Bobby, pulling out what looked like a large medicine bottle full of a yellow liquid. She read the label on it, then laughed.

'Do listen. "One table-spoonful of this to be taken

"Sardines!" said Bobby, "and a huge tin of pineapple."

by each girl after the birthday feast!'' Oh Carlotta, your grandmother is a scream.'

'Did you say you could go down to the tuck-shop in the town and order anything else you liked for your birthday?' asked Hilary, looking at the fine selection of things spread out on the floor. 'I shouldn't think you want anything else, do you?'

'I'd like a good big birthday cake with fifteen candles on,' said Carlotta. 'I know candles are childish when you're fifteen, but I can't help it. I think a cake looks so pretty when they are all lighted. And, if we have the party at night, we can let the cake-candles light us!'

'Are we *really* going to have the feast at night?' asked Mirabel, thrilled. 'I've often read of midnight feasts in school-stories, but I didn't really think they happened.'

'Of course they happen!' said Bobby. 'You wait and see what we'll do.'

'I must order heaps and heaps of ginger-pop,' said Carlotta. 'I always feel I can drink a lot at night. And I'll get lemonade too. And buns we can butter and put jam on. I like those. It's a pity we can't cook kippers too. I do like kippers.'

Every one laughed. Carlotta loved kippers and pine-apple, two things she had had a good deal of in her circus days. She had often described to the girls how lovely frying kippers smelt, being cooked on a stove in the open-air, in the dark of the night after a show.

'No, Carlotta—we must draw the line at kippers,' said Anna. 'The smell would wake the whole school. You know how we smell kippers frying even when Cook has the kitchen and the scullery door shut.'

Elsie heard all the talk about Carlotta's birthday. She knew there was to be a feast or a party of some sort. She saw the amount of goodies taken out of Carlotta's box, and she wondered if she was going to be asked or not.

The others debated the point when Elsie was not in the room.

'Are we going to ask Catty Elsie, or not?' said Pat.

'Not,' said almost every one.

'Oh, yes, let's,' said easy-going Anna. 'She likes good things as much as any one.'

'I daresay—but we don't want her spiteful face glowering at us all the time,' said Isabel.

At this moment Elsie came to the door of the common room. She stood outside, listening. She was always wondering if the others were discussing her. This time they were!

'Well, as it's my birthday I can choose my own guests,' said Carlotta. 'It's for me to say whether I'll ask Catty Elsie or not.'

'Yes—all right—*you* say, Carlotta!' cried half a dozen voices at once.

'Well—I say this—I'll ask her, but at the same time I'll tell her she's got to drop this awful pose of being a miserable martyr and act sensibly,' said Carlotta. 'She goes about looking like a wet dish-cloth. I'm sure every one in the school must laugh at her. She's a disgrace to our form. Anyway, I'll ask her to the feast, and see if she's properly grateful, and will behave herself.'

'Yes, do that,' said Anna, who was as tired as any one else of seeing Elsie walking about looking as if she was going to weep at any moment. 'Maybe she learnt her lesson when she was left out of the concert. Perhaps she will jump at the chance of being friends again.'

'Poor Catty Elsie,' said Doris, and she began to imitate Elsie's rather high, silly voice, tearful and excited. Every one roared with laughter.

They had no idea at all that Elsie was outside the door, listening. They would have been very scornful of her if they had known that, for eaves-dropping was not looked on favourably by any member of the second form. They had very strict ideas of honour and liked to keep to them.

Elsie forgot that those who listen behind doors seldom hear any good of themselves. She stood there, trembling with anger and self-pity, hating all the girls who tossed her name about so scornfully, and laughed at her so unkindly.

A movement towards the door made her hurry away quickly. She turned a corner and went into a cloak-room, pretending to fetch a pair of shoes. The second-formers, pouring out of their common room to go to a Nature meeting, did not guess that she had overheard nearly all they had said.

There was no time then to ask Elsie to the party, for the girls were already late for the meeting. Elsie joined them, and sat sulkily silent whilst the second- and third-formers decided various matters concerning the Nature-Club. She didn't hear a word that was said. She remembered instead what she had just overheard, and looked with rage at Carlotta and the others. How she wished she could punish them in some way !

That night Carlotta went up to where Elsie was sewing in the common room. ' Elsie ! I expect you know I'm having a birthday soon, don't you ? '

' I should think the whole school knows,' said Elsie, spitefully.

' Well—I'm having a party or a feast of some kind,' said Carlotta. ' And every one is coming. The thing is— I'd like you to come too—but only if you'll pull yourself together and act sensibly. We're all tired of the way you're behaving. Come on, Elsie, now—can't you have a bit of common sense and be one of us ? We don't like you a bit as you are now, but we are quite willing to change our ideas of you, if you'll be sensible.'

' Very kind of you, *very* kind of you indeed,' said Elsie,

in a trembling, sarcastic voice. 'The great Carlotta is *most* bountiful and condescending ! And I know I should be very grateful and bow before her, thanking her for her great kindness ! '

' Don't be an idiot,' said Carlotta, uncomfortably.

' I'm not,' said Elsie, changing her tone of voice and almost snarling at the surprised Carlotta. ' I'm just saying—" No, thanks ! *I'm* not coming to your beastly feast." Ho—be a good little girl and you can come to the party ! That's what you've said to me—me, who ought to be your head-girl ! I would *hate* to come ! And what is more, if you're going to hold it at night, Anna had better look out. You're second-formers now, not first-formers, and if you're caught, Anna will soon find *she* isn't head-girl any more, either.'

' You're impossible, Elsie,' said Carlotta, in disgust at Elsie's tone of voice. ' Well, if you don't want to come, don't. I for one am pleased.'

' So are we all ! ' cried Pat, Isabel and a few others, who had listened in indignation to Elsie's stinging speech. ' Keep away, Elsie. The party will be better without you ! '

Elsie went on with her sewing, pursing up her thin lips scornfully. She badly wanted to go to the party, for she loved good things as much as anyone else. But her spitefulness and obstinacy made it impossible for her to climb down and accept. She sat sewing, thinking that if she could possibly prevent the party from being held, she would.

' If I could find out when and where Carlotta is going to hold it, I could drop a hint to Miss Jenks,' she thought. ' Miss Jenks doesn't look kindly on things like that. I've only got to say a word—or write an anonymous note— and the feast would be stopped before it had begun. That would be fine ! '

But the others did not mean to let Elsie know when the feast was to be held! They felt certain she would try to spoil it in some way. They had decided to hold it on the night of Carlotta's birthday, in the common room itself. If they drew the blinds, and shut the door, they were reasonably safe. The common room was a good way away from any Mistresses' room, and yet fairly near their own dormitories.

They talked about it with excitement whenever Elsie was not in the room. As soon as she appeared they dropped the subject at once. Not one girl, not even silly little Alison, mentioned the subject when Elsie was there, much as they sometimes wanted to.

Carlotta had been down to the shop in the town and ordered what she wanted. The cake was to be a magnificent affair, with fifteen coloured candles. It was to have pink icing, with roses round the edge, and silver balls and sugared violets for decoration. The candles were to be fixed in roses made of sugar. Every one was very excited about it.

'The ginger-pop has come,' announced Carlotta, gleefully. 'I got the boy who brought it, to put it at the back of the bicycle shed. I was afraid Miss Jenks would have a fit if she saw all those bottles of ginger-beer and lemonade arriving for me. We'll each have to bring in a bottle or two when it's safe.'

'It will be fun,' said Mirabel. She looked at Gladys, who was beaming too. 'I'm glad I stayed on. Fancy missing Carlotta's feast! I would have been an idiot.'

'You would,' said Gladys. The mouse-like girl was no longer the Misery-girl. She laughed and smiled with the rest, and followed Mirabel about like a shadow. The bigger girl was very fond of her, and the two were quite inseparable. St. Clare's had already done a good deal for both of them!

'We'd better not cook anything at all,' said Pat. 'I remember when we fried sausages once in the middle of the night, they made a terrific smell. We'd better just be content with cold things. We'll borrow some plates from the dining-room cupboard. There are heaps of old ones on the top shelves that won't be missed for a day or two.'

It was fun to plan everything—fun to smuggle glasses and mugs, plates and dishes and spoons and forks into the common room. Carlotta's birthday was coming nearer and nearer. The birthday cake was made and the girls went down to the shop to inspect it. It was marvellous.

'I wish your birthday night would come, Carlotta!' said Pat. 'What sport we'll have! And *what* a feast!'

16   CARLOTTA'S BIRTHDAY PARTY

THE girls were gathered in their common room, the day before Carlotta's birthday. Alison took a quick look round the room. Elsie was not there.

'What time's the feast tomorrow night?' she asked. 'Exactly at midnight? Let's make it *exactly*! It's much more thrilling. Miss Quentin calls it the " witching midnight hour ", and somehow . . .'

'I suppose you'd like to ask your beloved Miss Quentin?' said Isabel, pulling Alison's curly hair. 'Can you see her sitting here in our common room, her hair done up in curl-papers, her face shining with grease, eating pine-apple chunks and sardines? I can't.'

' She *doesn't* do her hair in curl-papers,' said Alison,
indignantly. ' She's got beautiful, naturally wavy hair.
Why are you always so unkind about her ?   I wish she
could come to the feast.   I'm sure she'd love it.'

' Well, *we* shouldn't,' said Pat, who had no great liking
for the rather affected teacher of Drama.   ' You make
me sick the way you go mooning round after Miss Quentin.
She's not so marvellous as you think she is.   I think it
was pretty mean of her to take the credit to herself for
Gladys's acting at our concert the other night.'

' Whatever do you mean ? ' cried Alison, indignantly.

' Well, Alison, you know when Gladys put up that
grand performance of Shakespeare's characters the other
night,' said Pat, who thought it was about time that
Alison was cured of her senseless admiration for Miss
Quentin.

' Yes,' said Alison.

' Well, at the end of it, Miss Theobald leaned across
to Miss Quentin and congratulated her on Gladys's performance and said she was sure she herself had coached
her for it,' said Pat, mercilessly.   ' And your wonderful
Miss Quentin just nodded and smiled and looked pleased—
and didn't say that she knew nothing about Gladys
Hillman's acting powers at all !   We all think that was
pretty mean.'

' I don't believe it ! ' cried Alison, quick to defend the
mistress she so much admired.

' Well, Pam Boardman was sitting near, and she heard
it all,' said Pat.   ' She told us.   So now just stop thinking
Miss Quentin is the world's greatest wonder.'

Alison changed the subject quickly.   It really hurt her
to hear such things of Miss Quentin.   She was always
one to shut her ears to possibly unpleasant things.

' To come back to what I was saying,' she said, ' what
time's the feast tomorrow night ? '

'Well, as you so badly want it at exactly midnight, we'll have it then,' said Carlotta. 'I've got a dear little alarm clock I'll set for the time—and one of you in the other dormitory can stick it under your pillow so that it'll wake you without rousing every one in the building. I daren't put it under *my* pillow because Miss Catty Elsie sleeps near me and would wake too. We want to be sure she doesn't know the time.'

'All right then—midnight exactly, tomorrow night,' said Doris, in her clear voice.

At that moment the door opened, and Hilary came in. She had been to the school library to choose a book. She looked round at the others.

'I hope you haven't been talking about anything that matters,' she said, 'because dear sweet-natured, honest-souled Elsie was outside the door, listening for all she was worth ! '

The others stared at her in dismay.

'Blow ! ' said Carlotta. 'We *have* been talking—about the feast—and we said a good many times it was to be midnight tomorrow. Blow, blow, blow ! '

'Well, Elsie will certainly do her best to spoil it for us tomorrow night,' said Pat. 'She's sure to split on us somehow—absolutely sure to.'

'I'm not *going* to have our feast spoilt.' said Carlotta, in a determined voice. 'Pat, go to the door and see if Elsie's anywhere about now. Stay by the door and warn us if she comes.'

Pat looked outside the door. There was no one there. Elsie had got the information she wanted, and was content !

'Now listen,' said Carlotta, 'the feast is off for tomorrow night—but it's ON for tonight instead ! '

'Goody, goody ! ' said every one, pleased.

'We must make sure Elsie doesn't hear us creeping out of the room,' said Bobby.

' She sleeps very soundly,' said Carlotta. ' I think we can manage it all right. Now, not a word, any one ! We'll hold the feast tonight—and Elsie will get a frightful shock tomorrow when she finds it's all over, and she hasn't been able to spoil it ! '

Elsie had no idea that the time of the feast was altered. She hugged her secret all day long, pondering how she could spoil the feast without any one guessing it was she who had done so.

Should she tell Miss Jenks ? That would certainly stop the feast, but Miss Jenks did not like tale-bearers. Should she write a note to Miss Jenks, informing her of the feast, but not sign her name ? This seemed quite a good idea—but then Miss Jenks might throw the note into the fire and take no notice of it. Elsie had once heard her say that no one should ever take notice of anonymous letters—they were too despicable even to read.

' It's no good writing a note that Miss Jenks won't read or take notice of,' thought the girl. ' I wish I knew the best way to spoil the feast.'

She thought about it earnestly—so earnestly that Mam'zelle nearly ' went up in smoke ', as Bobby put it, because Elsie paid so little attention in the French class.

' Elsie ! This is the third time I have asked you to come out and write on the blackboard,' said Mam'zelle, exasperated. ' Ah, I have the patience of a donkey or I would not put up with you.'

' You mean, the " patience of an *ox*," Mam'zelle,' chuckled Bobby.

' A donkey is patient too,' said Mam'zelle. ' I need the patience of cows, donkeys, sheep and oxen too, when I deal with such a person as this Elsie. You will either depart from this room, Elsie, or pay attention to what I say. I will not have inattention in my class.'

Elsie had to give her thoughts to the French lesson after that—but during prep. time that evening she suddenly made up her mind what she would do.

' I'll wait till they're all out of the room tomorrow night—then I'll slip along to Miss Jenks's room and say I'm very worried because all the others have vanished,' thought Elsie. ' She'll come back to see—and will then go and hunt around, and find every one feasting in the common room. I can say I am afraid they've been kidnapped or something. After all, that American girl, Sadie, was nearly kidnapped last term—so I can pretend to be afraid it's happened again ! '

This seemed to Elsie a good idea. If she really pretended to be frightened that the others had been kidnapped, Miss Jenks would not think she was telling tales—and the others would not know she had given them away, because it would be Miss Jenks who suddenly came along and found them !

Elsie had no idea that the feast was for that night not the next. The second-formers kept their secret well. In fact, Carlotta and Bobby went a bit further, and whispered loudly together, in Elsie's hearing, about all that was to happen the night following ! Elsie took it all in, and grinned to herself. Just wait, you second-formers, and see what happens to your wonderful feast tomorrow night !

That night Carlotta wound up and set her tiny alarm clock. She gave it to Kathleen, who slept in the next room with the others. ' Put it under your pillow,' she said. ' When it goes off, wake the others quietly. Then come and wake me in the next dormitory. I'll wake our lot and we'll all go to the common room as quiet as mice.'

Kathleen put the clock under her pillow. She felt sure she would not need it, because she was too excited to sleep. But sleep overtook one tired girl after another, and soon both dormitories were peacefully dreaming.

Elsie was fast asleep too. She was a heavy sleeper, and sometimes snored. Tonight she was huddled up beneath her blankets, because it was cold. She meant to sleep well that night so that she would be well-rested, and able to keep awake the following night.

Every one was asleep at midnight. The alarm clock under Kathleen's pillow suddenly went off with a tiny ringing noise. Kathleen woke with a jump. She put her hand under the pillow and stopped the alarm from ringing. No one else had waked up. Kathleen sat up in bed, hugging herself in joy. The midnight feast was about to begin !

She sprang out of bed and put on her slippers and dressing-gown. Then she went softly from one bed to another, shaking the sleepers, and whispering the magic words into their ears ; ' Midnight feast ! Midnight feast ! '

Every one sat up at once. Dressing-gowns and slippers were groped for in the dark. Excited whispering rose.

' I can't find my slippers ! '

' Blow this dressing-gown ! The girdle's all tied in a knot ! '

' Sh ! ' warned Kathleen. ' We've got to be careful not to wake dear Elsie, you know.'

She slipped into the next dormitory and made her way quietly to Carlotta's bed. Carlotta was under sheets and blankets, curled up like a little animal. Kathleen shook her gently. Carlotta shot upright in bed and Kathleen pressed her shoulder warningly.

' Midnight,' she whispered in Carlotta's ear. Carlotta's heart jumped for joy. Her birthday feast, of course ! She padded round the dormitory as quietly as a cat, waking every one but Elsie.

There was no whispering in that room, and not a single giggle! Each girl took slippers and dressing-gown and crept quietly to the door. Elsie snored a little, much to every one's relief. Carlotta shut the door quietly—and locked it! She took out the key, and put it into her dressing-gown pocket. Now, if Elsie *did* wake up, she couldn't get out and spoil the feast!

Everyone went to the common room. Not until the door was fast-shut and cushions put along the bottom to hide the crack of light, was the light switched on. Then what a whispering and giggling there was!

'Elsie snored as we went out!' giggled Carlotta. 'Such a nice, gentle little snore! Now—come on—set out the plates and things!'

Everything was taken from the hiding-places—from the bottom of cupboards, and the back of shelves, from tuck-boxes and tins, and from behind books in bookcases. Soon the common room tables were set with the empty plates and dishes. The largest plate of all was put in the middle. That was for the lovely birthday cake.

'Now for a real, proper Feast!' said Carlotta, happily. She and the others set out the goodies they had—the cakes and the buns, the biscuits and the sweets. They opened the tins and emptied the contents on to dishes—sardines, fruit salad, pine-apple, prawns—the most wonderful selection of things imaginable!

Carlotta opened a dozen ginger-beer bottles. At each pop there was a giggle.

'Here's to our dear, sleeping-beauty, Elsie!' said Bobby, with a laugh, and drank the fizzy ginger-beer. 'Come on, every one—let's really enjoy ourselves!'

A TRICK

THE second-formers certainly *did* enjoy themselves.
After a bit they forgot to whisper, and began to speak
in their normal voices. It didn't matter, really. They
were too far from any sleeping mistress to be heard.
They giggled at everything, and laughed till the tears
came at Doris and her idiotic antics with empty ginger-
beer bottles.

They ate everything. Carlotta even ate sardines and
pine-apple together. Alison tried prawns dipped in
ginger-beer, which Pat and Isabel said were 'simply
super', but they made her feel sick taken that way.
However, the others didn't mind, and mixed all the food
together with surprising results.

'Nobody would dream that sardines pressed into ginger-
bread cake would taste so nice,' said Janet. 'My brother
told me that and I didn't believe him. But it's true.'

The birthday cake was marvellous. It melted in the
mouth ! The candles were lighted very soon and the light
turned off. All the girls sat munching happily, watching the fifteen candles flicker and glow. It was lovely.

'A happy year to you, Carlotta !' said Pat, holding
up her mug of ginger-beer. 'It's your birthday now,
because it's past midnight. Many happy returns of the
day !'

'Thanks,' said Carlotta, her vivid little face radiant.
Her dark eyes sparkled as she looked round at her friends.
It was lovely to give people pleasure. She would tell
her grandmother all about it.

'Happy returns !' said one voice after another.
'Happy birthday ! Good old Carlotta !'

Carlotta cut second slices of her big birthday cake for every one. There was a fairly big piece left, enough for two extra slices.

'Two more bits,' said Carlotta, slicing the piece in half. 'Who shall we give them to?'

'One to Miss Jenks!' said Pat. 'You needn't say we had the cake at midnight!'

'And one to Miss Quentin,' said Alison eagerly.

'Don't be silly,' said Carlotta. 'Do you think I'm going to waste my birthday cake on Miss Quentin! I'd rather give a slice to Elsie!'

'Well, let's,' said Anna, unexpectedly. 'It's supposed to be good for people to heap coals of fire on their head— you know, return good for evil—and anyway, what a shock for Elsie when we give her a bit—and she realizes we've had the party!'

'We'll give it to her after the next night then,' said Carlotta, grinning. 'Let her try and spoil the feast this coming night—and then the next day we'll present her with a bit of cake. That really would be funny.'

Everyone agreed to that—not that they wanted to make Elsie a present at all—they just wanted to see her face when she saw the piece of cake, and realized that the feast had been held in peace without her, and hadn't been spoilt.

'Well, one bit for Miss Jenks, and the other for darling Elsie,' said Carlotta, and put them away in a tin. 'Now, girls, is there anything else left to eat?'

There wasn't—and very little to drink either. 'It's a good thing,' said Anna. 'I simply couldn't eat another crumb!'

'Fancy *you* saying that, Anna!' said Pat, with a laugh, looking at the plump, round-faced girl. 'I should have thought you could have gone on eating till breakfast-time!'

' Don't be rude to your head-girl,' said Anna, lazily.
Nothing ever ruffled her good temper. ' Carlotta,
we'd better clear up and get back. We've been here
ages ! '

' What a pity ! ' said Alison, with a sigh. She never
liked clearing up. The girls set to work and stacked the
dishes and plates neatly at the back of a cupboard, hoping
they would be able to wash them and put them back into
their proper places in the morning.

They swept up the crumbs and threw them out of the
window. They put the ginger-beer and lemonade bottles
into a cupboard outside in the passage. Then they
looked round the common room. There was not a single
sign of the lovely feast they had had.

' Good girls,' said Anna. ' Now come along—as
quietly as you can, so as not to wake Elsie.'

The second-formers crept quietly back to their rooms.
Carlotta unlocked her dormitory door. The first sound
that greeted her was the light snoring of the sleeping
Elsie ! She had not even stirred.

' Good,' thought Carlotta, cuddling into bed. ' Everything went off marvellously. Oh, I wish we could have
it all over again tomorrow night ! '

The second-formers were very sleepy the next morning.
They found it difficult to get up. Alison said she felt
sick, and so did Kathleen.

' Well, never mind, it was worth it, wasn't it ? ' said
Pat. ' Do you want to go to Matron ? '

' No,' said Alison and Kathleen together. Matron
would only give them a large dose of nasty-tasting medicine. She had an unfailing way of knowing when a
midnight feast had been held, and kept special medicine
for girls who complained of feeling sick the next day !

Elsie did not for one moment suspect that the feast
had been held. Nobody said a word about it in front of

her.   The common room had been so well-cleared up that
there was not a crumb left to give the secret away.

Elsie looked at the second-formers as they worked in
Miss Jenks's geography class.   ' You may think you are
going to have a lovely time tonight ! ' she thought, ' but
you won't !   Miss Jenks will come and spoil it all—and
that will serve you right for being so mean to me ! '

Neither Alison nor Kathleen were sick after all, but
because they would eat no breakfast and no dinner, Miss
Jenks sent them to Matron.   Matron took their temperatures, and found they had none.

' H'mmmm ! ' she said, thoughtfully.   ' Any one had
a birthday in the second form ? '

' It's Carlotta's today,' said Kathleen.

' I thought so,' said Matron.   ' You are both suffering
from Too-Much-To-Eat.   A dose of medicine will soon
put you right ! '

That night the second form went to bed with giggles
and nudges.   They felt quite certain Elsie was going to
give them away—or was hoping to.   They had made a
lovely plan.

' We'll all wake up at midnight and creep out of the
room,' planned Bobby.   ' Then, as soon as we're gone, I
bet Elsie will go off to tell Miss Jenks, or even Miss
Theobald!   You never know !   When we see her go,
we'll all creep back into bed and be there, pretending to be
sound asleep, when Miss Jenks comes.   What a sell for
dear Elsie ! '

Every one approved of this plan.   Elsie saw them
whispering and giggling, and felt certain it was about
the feast that night !   She made up her mind to keep
awake, whatever happened.

Carlotta set her alarm clock for midnight once more—
this time under her own pillow, as she wanted to make
sure of waking Elsie up that night !   It went off at twelve

o'clock, and Carlotta sat up. She grinned to herself in
the darkness.

She went from bed to bed, waking every one up,
making rather a noise. Elsie woke up too, for she had
fallen asleep after all. She pretended to lie fast asleep,
and did not stir until all the girls had crept out of the
dormitory. Then she sat up and pulled on her own
dressing-gown.

' The beasts ! Enjoying themselves without me ! ' she
thought maliciously, forgetting that she could have
joined in the party if she had said she would behave
sensibly. ' Well, now I'll go and wake Miss Jenks—and
pretend I'm frightened because the others have all
disappeared ! '

She slipped out of the dormitory. Carlotta, who was
hiding round a corner, saw her going down the passage
in the opposite direction, on her way to Miss Jenks's
room.

' Come along,' she whispered to the second-formers,
who were giggling nearby. ' She's gone ! I bet Miss
Jenks will be along in half a minute ! What will she say
to Elsie when she sees us all safe and sound in our warm
beds ! '

The girls took off dressing-gowns and slippers, and
hurried back into their beds, which were still nice and
warm. They cuddled down and waited, giggling every
now and again when someone made a silly remark.

Meanwhile Elsie was knocking on Miss Jenks's door.
There was no answer. She knocked more loudly. There
was a creak from the bed and then Miss Jenks's voice.
' Who's there ? What's the matter ? '

Elsie opened the door. Miss Jenks switched on the
light beside her bed. She saw Elsie, who had put on a
very frightened expression indeed.

' Is somebody ill ? ' asked Miss Jenks, springing out of

bed and dragging her dressing-gown on. 'Quick, tell me!'

'Oh, Miss Jenks—I'm so frightened,' stammered Elsie, filling Miss Jenks with foreboding, she looked so scared. 'All the girls out of my dormitory have disappeared— every one of them. Oh Miss Jenks—do you think they can have been kidnapped? I feel so scared.'

Miss Jenks snorted. She had a wonderful snort which was often faithfully copied by Doris.

'My dear Elsie, don't be a ninny! As if seven or eight girls could be kidnapped in your room and you hear nothing! Use your common sense, for pity's sake!'

'Miss Jenks, they really aren't there,' said Elsie, looking more wide-eyed than ever. 'Not one of them. Where can they be?'

'It's Carlotta's birthday, isn't it?' said Miss Jenks, crossly. 'I suppose it's a feast. Just like you to try and spoil it!'

'Oh, Miss Jenks, I never thought of that!' cried Elsie, pretending to be astonished and hurt. 'Oh, so long as they aren't kidnapped!'

'You really make me cross, Elsie,' said Miss Jenks, who, having had Elsie for more than a year in her form, knew her very well indeed. 'Well, come along—I suppose I'll have to look into this—but you'll just come along with me too, my girl—and the second form can see who's spoilt things for them!'

This was not what Elsie had planned at all! But it was no use, she could not draw back now. She had to go with Miss Jenks.

They went along to the dormitory where Elsie slept. The girls heard them coming and cuddled closer into bed, shutting their eyes tightly, hoping they would not giggle and give everything away. Doris gave one or two beautiful little snores, so real that Carlotta wondered if she

could possibly have gone to sleep ! Miss Jenks heard the
snores. She switched on the dormitory light.

She stared in silence at the beds, all except Elsie's
occupied by apparently sleeping girls. Doris gave
another marvellous little snore, and then, with a realistic
grunt, turned over in bed and settled down again. Miss
Jenks watched her. She felt certain Doris was awake.

Elsie stared in the utmost astonishment and horror at
the occupied beds. She simply could not understand it.
She had not been more than three minutes away, surely—
and yet here were all the girls asleep in bed. Could she
have dreamt it all ? Had the girls not stirred from their
beds at all ? What had happened ?

' Well, Elsie,' said Miss Jenks, not troubling to lower
her voice, for she felt certain every girl was awake, ' you
appear to have brought me out on a wild-goose chase.
We shall have to have a talk about this tomorrow, I
think. I don't feel at all pleased to be waked up with a
story of wholesale kidnappings, and then to find that the
only girl out of bed is yourself. Not a very creditable
performance on your part, I feel.'

Elsie got into bed without a word. Miss Jenks snapped
off the light and went back to bed, shutting her ears to
the giggling and whispering that immediately broke out.
No one said a word to the cowering Elsie. Let her try
to puzzle out what had happened ! After ten minutes
giggling the room went to sleep again—all but Elsie, who
lay awake worrying about what was to happen to her the
next day !

The first thing that happened had its funny side.
Carlotta solemnly approached her and offered her a piece
of the birthday cake. ' You weren't there, so we saved
it for you,' she said, a very goody-goody expression on her
glowing little face.

Elsie was startled out of her silence. She stared at the

cake and said, ' So you *did* have the feast after all ?
When did you ? '

' We had it when we were kidnapped,' said Carlotta,
solemnly. ' Oooh Elsie—it was thrilling ! Somebody
came in the middle of the night—and kidnapped us all—
and took us away—but we offered them a bit of the birthday cake and they were so pleased with it that they set
us free ! '

' Don't tell such untruths ! ' said Elsie, angrily. There
were squeals of laughter at this.

' Untruths ! Why, who was it went and told Miss Jenks
we had been kidnapped ? *You* can't talk about untruths !'

Elsie turned away. She would not take the cake. She
was sick at heart, and longed for a friendly look or a
friendly word. Now she had to go and face Miss Jenks.
That would be awful too. She had to go just before
morning school, at ten minutes to nine in the classroom.

She went. Miss Jenks was there, busy as usual
correcting piles of exercise books. On the desk in front
of her was a most surprising sight—a large piece of birthday cake ! It had been offered to her by Carlotta with a
merry twinkle—and had been accepted with a merry
twinkle also ! Elsie stared at it and bit her lip. To
think that Miss Jenks had accepted the cake ! Why,
she must have guessed about the feast—and here she was
accepting a bit of the cake ! It was too bad.

' Elsie, there is something seriously wrong with you
this term,' began Miss Jenks. ' You had a great chance
as head-girl, and both Miss Theobald and I hoped you
would take it. Apparently you haven't. None of the
girls will accept you. Instead of standing up to things
and realizing you had to do better and change your
attitude, you chose to do stupid things like coming to
me last night with a cock-and-bull tale, in order to spite
the others. They were too smart for you, I am pleased

to see. Now what is to be done ? Are you going to go
on like this for the rest of the term ? Your report will
not make pleasant reading if so. Or are you going to
show that you really have a little courage and common
sense in you, and try to make up for your silly behaviour
before it is too late ? '

Plain speaking was Miss Jenks's strong point. Elsie
listened in silence. She looked at the calm eyes of her
form-mistress. There was absolutely nothing else to be
done now but admit herself to be in the wrong, and say
she had courage to do better. That was hard—but the
alternative was harder—getting a thoroughly bad report,
and having to bear the sneers of the girls for the rest of
the term.

'I'll try to make up for being silly," said Elsie, in a
half-sulky tone.

' You've been more than silly,' said Miss Jenks. ' Pull
yourself together. You know that St. Clare's only keeps
the girls it can do something with. The second-formers
are decent. If they see you showing a little courage and
common sense, they will help you.'

' All right,' said Elsie, ungraciously. ' But, Miss
Jenks—don't make me tell them I'm sorry or anything.
I can't do that. I really can't.'

' My dear Elsie, I haven't had you in my form for over
a year without knowing that I can't expect you to have
either the good feeling or the courage to say you're sorry,"
said Miss Jenks, impatiently. ' Now here come the
others. Go and get my books for me out of the mistresses' common room, and put on a little brighter face.
I simply cannot bear to see you looking like a hen left
out in the rain any longer ! '

Elsie went to fetch Miss Jenks's books as the second-
formers crowded into the room. They sat down at once,
surprised to see their form-mistress there before them.

' I want to say a word to you this morning,' said Miss
Jenks. ' About Elsie. She has agreed to try and have
a little courage and do better from now on—rather
unwillingly, I must admit. She tells me she cannot
possibly say she is sorry to you for her stupid conduct—
and in any case, I don't think she *is* sorry—but try to act
towards her in a way to help her efforts, not hinder them,
will you ? After all—you played a wonderful trick on
her last night, didn't you ? '

This unexpected ending made all the girls smile
delightedly. So Miss Jenks guessed everything—and
there was the birthday cake, sitting waiting to be eaten !
Good old Miss Jenks ! The girls were ready to do anything she asked them.

' All right, Miss Jenks—we'll put up with Elsie as
graciously as we can,' said Hilary, smiling. ' We got
our own back last night—so we can afford to be generous ! '

Elsie came back into the room. She had tried to make
her face pleasanter. She placed the books on the desk.
' Thank you, Elsie,' said Miss Jenks, in a pleasant tone,
and gave her a smile. The girls saw it and approved.
What Miss Jenks could do, they could do also. Things
would be easier for Elsie than she deserved !

18   AN EXCITING MATCH

THE term went on its way, happy and busy with lessons,
games and fun. Lacrosse matches were played, and the
whole school turned out to watch and cheer at the home
matches.

The second form were very proud of Gladys. Anna had told Miss Wilton, the games-mistress, that she thought Gladys would be worth trying in some other position than goal-keeper, and Miss Wilton rather doubtfully agreed to try her.

'She has never shown any aptitude for running, catching or tackling,' she said. 'However—we will see.'

So Gladys, to her delight, was put in a position where running and catching would count, and after once or twice the girl proved herself to be very good. She was small, but very wiry and agile, and she was amazingly good at dodging the enemy and passing the ball quickly to some one else.

'Good, Gladys, good!' Miss Wilton said, time after time, one Monday afternoon. 'You *are* coming on!'

Gladys flushed with pleasure. She looked very happy these days. Miss Quentin was taking a good deal of notice of her in the Drama class, and now Miss Wilton was praising her at lacrosse—the two things she liked most. She was writing very happy letters to her mother now, and although she still had no reply, she had had a letter from Mirabel's mother that had delighted her.

DEAR GLADYS [the letter had said],

I thought you might like to know that I was able to go today to the hospital your mother is in. The nurse actually allowed me to see her for two minutes, as it was one of her good days. I told her about you, and how you and my Mirabel were friends. She could not say much, but she did say how delighted she was to hear what a success you were at the concert. Perhaps you will be able to see her in the holidays. It is early days to say yet whether she is really making progress, but I think you may be hopeful. I will go to see her again if I can.

Give my love to Mirabel, and say I hope she is treating you properly! You are such a little mouse and Mirabel is just the opposite!

Love from

ELISE UNWIN

This letter Gladys treasured greatly. She thought with intense gratitude of Mrs. Unwin. She began to hope that her mother really might get better. She knew that when she was well enough she had to have a serious operation, and this thought worried her greatly —but now that she was happier things did not seem so bad.

Meantime there was lacrosse, and the excitement of the next match, which was to be a home one, against St. Christopher's. Belinda Towers had let it be known that she would like to choose one girl from the second form for the team. No one in the first form was good enough as yet—but the second form were on the whole not at all bad at the game.

'*You* might be chosen, Gladys!' said Mirabel, half-teasingly. She did not seriously think that the shy girl would be picked out, for although she certainly was very good at the game now, she was not half the size of some of the other girls in the form.

'I wish I could!' said Gladys. 'But I know who will be—Hilary! She's terribly good, I think.'

Hilary certainly was very good—very sure and very swift. Her catching was graceful to watch, and it seemed certain she would be chosen for the match.

But two days before the match Hilary went down with a cold again. Matron popped her into bed, in spite of her wails about lacrosse.

'Belinda said I could play in the match!' she said. 'Can't I get up tomorrow for certain?'

'Nothing is certain with bad colds,' said Matron. 'So don't count on anything.'

Thus it came about that Hilary, although chosen by Belinda, could not play—and Belinda, running her pencil down the list of names in the second form, suddenly came to a stop by Gladys Hillman's name. She sat and thought.

'That kid's good,' thought the head-girl. 'I watched her yesterday. She's fast—and jolly good at tackling, although she is small. I've a good mind to try her.'

So, when the list of names was put up on the big notice-board, showing the girls chosen for the next match, Gladys Hillman's appeared at the bottom—the only one chosen from the second form ! Mirabel saw it and went hurriedly in search of Gladys.

'Gladys ! What do you think ? You're down for the match ! '

'Really ? ' said Gladys, her face flushing brightly. 'Oh—how marvellous ! Golly, I *shall* be nervous, though ! '

'No, you won't. You'll just remember that your mother is longing to hear that you've shot twelve goals for St. Clare's, and that you've won the match for the school ! ' said Mirabel, laughing. 'Oh, I say—I *am* pleased. Good for you ! '

Gladys was happy to see Mirabel's real pleasure. That was the best of friends—they shared your troubles with you, and they doubled your joys. It was good to have a friend.

The school turned out as usual to watch the match. The St. Christopher girls came in a big coach, their lacrosse sticks beside them. The St. Clare's girls gave them a cheer.

The game began. Belinda was referee, and blew her whistle sharply. There was the click of lacrosse sticks

as the two girls in the centre of the field began the game.
Then the ball was flicked quickly away, and Margery
Fenworthy, of the third form, picked it up in her lacrosse
net and flew down the field with it. She passed to Lucy
Oriell, her friend, and then when Lucy was tackled,
cleverly caught the ball once more and passed to Gladys,
who was hopping about in excitement, ready for any
chance.

Click! Gladys caught the ball, dodged a tackling
enemy, and threw to Lucy. From one to another went
the ball, and Lucy tried to throw a goal, which was
deftly stopped by the St. Christopher's goal-keeper.

The game was very even. The St. Clare girls were
better runners and catchers, but the St. Christopher goal-
keeper was marvellous. She had a quick eye, a firm
wrist, and a real talent for stopping the ball every time
the St. Clare girls threw at the goal.

St. Christopher's threw a goal first, and the St. Clare
girls clapped, though their faces were rather anxious.
This was going to be a stiffer match than they thought.
Thank goodness both Margery Fenworthy and Lucy Oriell
were playing today—they were always first-class. Some
of the St. Clare girls looked doubtfully at Gladys Hillman.
She seemed very small in comparison with the others.
Margery Fenworthy, for instance, was a big strapping
girl who over-topped Gladys by a head and a half!

'Play up, Gladys!' yelled Mirabel, every time her
friend came near her. 'Go on—play up!'

And the whole second form would yell in chorus.
'Play UP, Gladys! What about a goal from you?'

Half-time—and no goals for the St. Clare girls! One–
love! The St. Clare girls who were watching crowded
round their team, trying to buck them up and spur
them on.

'You are doing well, Margery and Lucy,' said Belinda

Towers, approvingly. Her eye caught the flushed face
of Gladys Hillman, and she gave her one of her sudden
wide smiles. ' You're not doing too badly either, kid !
But keep a bit closer to Margery, will you ? You might
be able to score a goal off one of her passes to you.'

' Yes, Belinda,' said Gladys, happily. ' I'll try.' She
kept her word. She hovered closer to Margery, and
caught the ball slickly each time. Twice she was tackled
and had to pass before she could shoot at the goal—
but the third time she threw the ball with all her might
at the net in the distance.

' Goal, goal ! ' yelled the St. Clare girls. But no, the
St. Christopher goal-keeper deftly flicked the ball away.
No goal—but a jolly good try !

' Go it, Gladys, go it ! ' yelled the second form, dancing
about in excitement. ' Try again ! '

Gladys did her best. She was everywhere, in and out,
running, tackling, passing. Time slipped on, and still
no goals were scored by St. Clare's. On the other hand
no more were scored by St. Christopher's, either. It
was the closest match the schools had ever played.

' Oh golly, it's almost time ! ' groaned Mirabel, glancing
at her watch. ' Gladys ! Play up. There's only four
minutes more ! '

Gladys heard, and ran to tackle an enormous St.
Christopher girl. The girl dodged, and Gladys tripped.
She wrenched her ankle, and gave a groan. It was
going to be painful to run now. But she couldn't possibly
give up !

The ball rolled near her. She nipped it up into her
lacrosse net, and ran, limping, down the field. She
passed to Margery, who at once passed back again when
she was tackled. Gladys didn't catch the ball. It was
neatly caught by a much taller girl, who leapt into the
air. The ball fell into her net, and she turned to run

Gladys raced after the ball

down the field. But quick as thought Gladys hit her lacrosse stick upwards, and the ball flew into the air. Gladys caught it, and ran again. She shot for the goal.

It was not such a good shot as before—but the ball bounced over a tuft as it rolled towards the goal, and avoided the waiting lacrosse net of the goal-keeper. In the greatest dismay she saw it roll into the goal !

The St. Clare girls nearly went mad with joy. The second form thumped each other on the back and yelled " Good old Gladys " at the tops of their voices. It was all very thrilling.

The match was a draw—one all. The St. Christopher girls went back to tea with St. Clare's, and discussed the match at the tops of their voices. The second form treated Gladys to a special cake for making the score even.

'Good for you, kid ! ' said Belinda, as she passed. That was Gladys's biggest reward ! Words of praise from the great head-girl were words of praise indeed !

19   ALISON AND MISS QUENTIN

THE term hurried on its way. The girls began to talk about Christmas holidays and what they were going to do—pantomimes, parties and theatres were discussed. Gladys looked a little bleak when the girls began to talk excitedly about the coming holidays.

' Will your mother be well enough to leave the hospital and have you home with her ? ' asked Mirabel.

'No.   I'm staying at school for the hols.,' said Gladys.
'Matron will still be here, you know, and two girls from
the third and fourth form, whose parents are in India.
But I shall be very lonely without you, Mirabel.'

'Poor Gladys!' said Mirabel in dismay. 'I should
hate to stay at school for the hols. I must say. After
all, most of the fun of being at boarding-school is being
with crowds of others, day and night—it won't be any
fun for you being with one or two! Won't your mother
really be better?'

'She's going to have a serious operation soon,' said
Gladys. 'So I know quite well she won't be able to
leave the hospital, Mirabel. But the operation may
make her well again, so I'm just hoping for the best—
and I'm quite willing to stay on at school for the hols.
if only I hear that Mother is getting better after the
operation.'

Mrs. Unwin had written to Mirabel about Gladys's
mother. She had told Mirabel not to show the letter
to Gladys.

'I feel rather worried about Gladys's mother,' she
wrote. 'She is to have the operation soon—and I can't
help wondering if she really will get over it, because she
is very weak. If there is bad news, you must comfort
Gladys all you can. She will be very glad to have a
friend if sadness comes to her. I will let her know at
once if the news is good.'

Mirabel said nothing to her friend about the letter—
but she was extra warm and friendly towards Gladys.
It was unusual for the rather selfish, thick-skinned
Mirabel to think of some one else unselfishly and tenderly.
It softened her domineering nature and made her a much
nicer girl.

Gladys was pleased to be able to tell her mother about
the match. She wished she had shot a winning goal—

but it was something to shoot the goal that made a draw !

' *I* shall write and tell your mother too,' said Mirabel, who could not do enough for her friend just then.

' Oh Mirabel—you are good ! ' said Gladys, delighted. ' You wrote to Mother after the concert, and I guess she was pleased to hear all you said. My word—what a silly I was at the beginning of the term, all mopey and miserable, couldn't take an interest in anything. I should think you hated me.'

' Well, I didn't like you very much,' said Mirabel, honestly. ' But I guess you didn't like *me* much, either ! '

Gladys was not only shining at lacrosse but in the Drama class as well ! Miss Quentin, who had been really amazed at Gladys's performance on the night of the concert, was making a great fuss of her and her talent. Alison didn't like it at all. She was jealous, and there were some days when she could hardly speak to Gladys.

The play was to be performed at the end of the term. Miss Quentin had tried out Alison, Doris, Carlotta, and now Gladys in the principal feminine part. There was no doubt that Alison looked the prettiest and the most graceful, and that she was quite word-perfect and had rehearsed continually. But Gladys was by far the best actress.

Miss Quentin had given Alison to understand that she would have the chief part. She had not actually said so in so many words, but the class as a whole took it for granted that Alison would take the part. They found it quite natural too, for they knew how hard the girl had worked at learning the words, a task always difficult for her.

Alison was really silly about Miss Quentin. She waited round corners for her, hoping for a smile. She hung on every word the teacher said. She was worse than she had been with Sadie Greene the term before—for one thing Sadie had had a little common sense and often laughed at Alison, but Miss Quentin had no common sense at all ! So Alison became worse instead of better, and the second-formers became quite exasperated with her.

Then Alison heard some news that gave her a great blow—Miss Quentin was not coming back the next term !

' Are you sure ? ' asked Alison, looking with wide eyes at Hilary, who had come in with the news.

' Well, I heard Mam'zelle say to Miss Quentin, " Well, well—so you will be on the stage next term, whilst we are all struggling with our tiresome girls ! " Apparently Miss Quentin had only just heard the news herself—she had a letter in her hand. I think she must only have been engaged for a term—it's the first time we've had a proper Drama class. Perhaps Miss Theobald was trying out the idea.' Hilary looked at Alison, who had tears in her eyes. ' Cheer up, Alison—the world won't come to an end because your beloved Miss Quentin isn't here next term ! You'll find some one else to moon round, don't fret ! '

It was a great shock to Alison. She had dreamed of term after term in Miss Quentin's Drama classes, with herself taking all the chief parts in every play, hearing honeyed words of praise dropping daily from the teacher's lips. She went away by herself and cried very bitterly. The silly girl gave her heart far too easily to anyone who attracted her, or made a fuss of her.

' What's come over Alison ? ' asked Pat, in surprise, when her cousin appeared with swollen eyes. ' Been in a row, Alison ? '

' She's only sorrowing because her beloved Miss Quentin won't be here next term to pat her on her back and tell her she is very very good ! ' said Janet.

' Alison, don't be an idiot ! ' said Isabel. ' You know

perfectly well Miss Quentin won't be much loss.   We all
think she's too soft for words !   And think how mean
she was in taking the credit for Gladys's performance at
the concert.'

' I have never believed that,' said Alison, tears coming
into her eyes again.   ' You don't know Miss Quentin
as I do—she's the truest, honestest, most loyal person !
I've never met any one like her.'

' Nor have I ! ' said Pat.   ' And thank goodness I
haven't.   Alison, why must you go and choose the wrong
people to moon round ?   Sadie Greene was amusing but
she hadn't anything in her at all—and neither has Miss
Quentin.   Now, take Miss Jenks for instance . . .'

' Miss Jenks ! ' said Alison, with an angry sniff.   ' Who
would want to moon round Miss Jenks, with her snappy
tongue and cold eyes ? '

' Well, I think she's pretty decent,' said Pat.   ' Not
that I should want to moon round her or any one, for
that matter.   I'm only just saying you will keep on
choosing the wrong people to lavish your affections on !
Sadie has never even written to you—and I bet Miss
Quentin won't, either ! '

' She will !   She's very fond of me,' said Alison.

The others gave it up.   Alison would never learn
sense !   ' It's a pity she can't find out how silly her
Miss Quentin really is—how undependable,' said Hilary.
' Your feather-headed cousin, Pat, wants to learn common
sense—it's a pity she can't find out that all her ideas
about Miss Quentin are only dreams—the real Miss
Quentin isn't a bit as Alison pictures her ! '

' Well, we can't teach her,' said Pat.   ' She'll make
herself miserable for the rest of the term now, and for
all the hols. too, I expect ! '

Alison was really unhappy to hear that her favourite
teacher was leaving.   She thought she would hang about

near the common room of the Junior mistresses, and watch for Miss Quentin to come out. Then she would tell her how upset she was.

So she went to a little lobby near the common room, and pretended to be hunting for something there. She could hear Miss Quentin's voice talking to Mam'zelle, behind the closed door of the common room, but she could not hear anything that was said.

Then some one opened the door and came out. It was Miss Lewis, the history teacher. ' Leave the door open ! ' cried Mam'zelle, ' it is stuffy in here ! '

So Miss Lewis left the door open, and went off towards the school library. Alison stood in the little lobby, her heart beating fast, waiting for Miss Quentin to come out. Surely she would come soon !

The mistresses went on talking. Some of them had clear, distinct voices, and some spoke too low for Alison to hear anything. She did not mean to listen, she was only waiting for Miss Quentin—but suddenly she heard her own name, spoken by Miss Quentin herself. Alison stiffened, and her heart thumped. Was Miss Quentin going to praise her to the others ? It would be just like her to say something nice !

' Alison O'Sullivan is going to get a shock,' said Miss Quentin, in the low, clear voice that Alison thought so beautiful. ' The silly girl thinks she's good enough to play the lead in the second-form play ! She's been wearing herself out rehearsing—it will do her good to find she's not going to have the part ! '

' Who's going to have it, then ? ' asked Miss Jenks.

' Gladys Hillman,' answered Miss Quentin, promptly. ' I've had my eye on that child ever since the beginning of the term. She's three times as good as any one else. She will be marvellous as the Countess Jeannette.'

' I wish Alison worked as hard in my classes as she does in yours,' remarked Mam'zelle, in her rather harsh, loud voice. ' Ah, her French exercises ! But I think, Miss Quentin, she really does work at Drama.'

' Oh well, she simply adores me,' said Miss Quentin, easily. ' I can always make her type work. She'll do anything for a smile or a kind word from me—like a dear little pet-dog. But give me somebody like that wild Carlotta—somebody with something in them ! Alison bores me to tears with her breathless ' Yes, Miss Quentin ! No, Miss Quentin ! Oh, *can* I, Miss Quentin ! ' It will be good for her to have a shock and find she has to take back place to Gladys Hillman.'

' I'm not so sure,' said Miss Jenks, in her cool voice. ' Shocks are not always good for rather weak characters, Miss Quentin. I hope you will break your news kindly to poor Alison—otherwise she will weep all day, and as exams. are coming on tomorrow, I don't want bad work from her because of you ! '

' Oh don't worry ! I'll just pat her curly head and say a few kind words,' said Miss Quentin. ' She'll eat out of my hand. She always does.'

Miss Lewis came back and shut the door. Not a word more could be heard. Alison sat on a bench in the lobby, sick at heart, shocked and hurt beyond measure. Her mind was in a whirl. She had not been able to help hearing—and once she had grasped that her idol, Miss Quentin, was poking fun at her, she had not even been able to get up and go. She had had to sit there, hearing every cruel word.

She was not to have the leading part in the play. Miss Quentin wasn't fond of her—only amused with her, thinking her a little pet-dog, some one to pat and laugh at ! Miss Quentin had told a lie—she had not noticed

Gladys Hillman at all until the night of the concert !
Miss Quentin was bored with her !

Alison was too shocked even to cry. She sat in the
lobby quietly, looking straight in front of her. What
was it that Miss Jenks had said ? ' Shocks are not
always good for weak characters ! ' Was she, Alison,
such a weak character then ? The girl rubbed her hand
across her forehead, which was wet and clammy.

' I have to think all this out,' said Alison to herself.
' I can't tell any one. I'm too ashamed. But I must
think things out. Oh, Miss Quentin, how could you say
all that ? '

Poor Alison ! This was the greatest shock she had
ever had in her easy-going life ! All her admiration and
love for Miss Quentin vanished at once—passed like a
dream in the night. There was nothing of it left, except
an ache. She saw the Drama teacher as the others saw
her—someone pleasant and amiable, but undependable,
disloyal, shallow.

Alison was a silly girl, as changeable as a weather-
vane, swinging now this way and now that, easily upset
and easily pleased. As the others often said, ' she hadn't
much in her ! ' But in this hour of horror—for it *was*
horror to her—she found something in herself that she
hardly knew she possessed. And that something was a
sense of dignity !

She wasn't going to go under because of some one
like Miss Quentin ! She wasn't going to be a pet-dog,
eating out of her hand ! She had too much dignity for
that. She would show Miss Quentin that she was wrong.
Hurt and shocked though she was, Alison had a glimmer-
ing of common sense all at once, and she held up her
head, blinked away the tears, and made up her mind
what she was going to do.

So it came about that when Miss Quentin broke the

news to the Drama class that Gladys was to have the leading part, and not Alison, the girl gave no sign at all of being disappointed. Her face was pale, for she had slept badly that night, but it had a calmness and dignity that astonished the watching girls.

' So Gladys is to have the part, you see,' finished Miss Quentin. She lightly touched Alison's curly head. ' I'm afraid my Alison will be disappointed ! '

' Of course not, Miss Quentin,' said Alison, moving away from the teacher's hand. ' I think Gladys *should* have the part ! She is the best of us all—and I am very glad.'

The girls stared at Alison in the greatest amazement. They had expected tears—even sulks—but not this cool acceptance of an unpleasant fact.

' Who would have thought Alison would take it like that ? ' said Janet. ' Well—good for her ! All the same, I think it's a shame. Miss Quentin made us all think Alison would have the part.'

Alison would not meet Miss Quentin's eye. She played the part she was given very well, but seemed quite unmoved when Miss Quentin praised her. Miss Quentin was puzzled and a little hurt.

' Girls, I have something to tell you,' she said at the end of the lesson. ' I shall not be here next term. I shall miss you all very much—especially one or two of you who have worked extremely hard ! '

She looked hard at Alison, expecting to see tears, and to hear cries of ' Oh, Miss Quentin ! We *shall* miss you ! '

But Alison did not look at the teacher. She gazed out of the window as if she had not heard. Hilary cleared her throat and spoke politely. ' I am sure we are all sorry to hear that, Miss Quentin. We hope you will be happy wherever you go.'

Miss Quentin was hurt and disappointed. She spoke directly to Alison.

'Alison, I know you worked specially hard for me,' she said.

'I worked hard because I like Drama,' said Alison, in a cool voice, looking Miss Quentin in the eyes for the first time. This was a direct snub and the girls gasped in surprise. Whatever made Alison behave like that? They gazed at her in admiration. So Alison had seen through her beloved Miss Quentin at last—and instead of moaning and wailing, had put on a cloak of dignity and coolness. One up to Alison!

Miss Quentin retired gracefully to her next class, very much puzzled. The girls crowded round Alison.

'Alison! What's happened? Has your beloved Miss Quentin offended you?'

'Shut up,' said Alison, pushing her way between the girls. 'I can't tell you anything. I don't want to discuss it. Let me alone.'

They let her go, puzzled, but respecting her request. 'Something's happened,' said Hilary, watching the white-faced girl going out of the room. 'But whatever it is, is for the best. Alison seems suddenly more grown-up.'

'Time she was,' said Pat. 'Anyway—if she stops mooning round somebody different each term—or at any rate chooses somebody worth-while—it will be a blessing!'

Nobody ever knew what had made Alison 'grow up' so suddenly Only Alison herself knew, and out of her hurt came something worth-while, that was to help her in many years to come.

EXAMS. were being held, and girls were groaning daily
over them. Mam'zelle was in a state of trepidation in
case any of the girls fell short of pass-marks. The girls
were in a far greater state, feeling quite certain that
nobody at all would pass in French ! Mam'zelle always
threatened to give them such difficult papers—but when
the time came, they were not so bad after all !

Gladys found the exams. difficult because her mother
was to have her operation that week. She was very
anxious indeed. Mirabel did all she could to help her to
prepare each evening. It was good to see the patience
and kindliness of the bigger girl. The others warmed
greatly to Mirabel because of it.

Even Elsie felt sorry for the anxious girl. ' I hope
you'll hear good news soon,' she said. Gladys looked at
her in surprised gratitude. Fancy Elsie saying anything
kind ! The others heard the low words, and looked at
one another with raised eyebrows. They had kept their
promise to Miss Jenks, and had not hindered Elsie in any
way, in her efforts to behave more reasonably.

But, on the other hand, no girl had been able to show
any liking for Elsie. It was impossible. The girl had
been too spiteful, too exasperating altogether to be liked
now. She would be tolerated, but nothing else. Miss
Jenks watched every one's behaviour, and came to the
conclusion that it was hopeless to expect any happiness
or real help for Elsie from the second-formers. On the
other hand, the lazy Anna had been a great success as
head-girl of the form. She had thrown aside her laziness,
and had come to the fore, taking responsibility and making

decisions capably and quickly. Miss Jenks was pleased
with her. She was now ready to go up into the third
form, and take her part with the older girls there. Hilary
Wentworth could be head-girl next term.

Miss Jenks spoke to Miss Theobald about it and the
Head agreed. ' But what are we to do with Elsie ? ' she
said. ' I will have a talk with her.'

So Elsie was sent for, and sat rather sullenly in Miss
Theobald's drawing-room, expecting to be scolded, or
something even worse—she might be told that St. Clare's
didn't want her any more !

' Elsie,' said Miss Theobald, ' I know you have found
things difficult this term—mostly your own fault, as I
think you will admit.'

Elsie looked at Miss Theobald's solemn face. ' Yes,'
she said at last. ' I suppose things *were* mostly my own
fault. The second form don't like me at all. They will
never have me as head-girl. They just tolerate me, that's
all. It makes things hard for me. I feel I can never do
anything to alter their opinion, and so I can't very well
take any pleasure in being there.'

' You see, Elsie, one of the hardest things in the world
to forget and forgive is spitefulness,' said Miss Theobald.
' Malice and spite rouse such bitter feelings in others.
Other faults, such as greed, irresponsibility, silliness—
these arouse disgust, but are forgotten and forgiven.
Spite always rankles, and is never forgotten. I can see
you will never do any good either to yourself or to others
in the second form.'

Elsie waited, her heart sinking. This meant that she
was to be asked to leave. She didn't want to do that.
She did like St. Clare's. She stared at Miss Theobald
miserably. The Head guessed what the girl was thinking.

' I'm not going to say you must leave St. Clare's,' she
said quickly. ' I think the school can do a lot for you,

Elsie, and you may be able to do something for St. Clare's too. No—you shan't leave ! I think you must go up into the third form instead—leave behind the second-formers who have seen such a bad side of your character—and go into the third form, which, next term, will have five or six new girls. You will have a chance then to show a different side of your character ! You are not really ready to go up, either in your work, or in your behaviour—but I will send you up if you will tell me that you will take this chance, and work hard, and, more important still, try to get the " cattiness " out of your nature that every schoolgirl detests ! '

Elsie's heart lifted in relief. Go up into the third form—and leave behind the girls who would always dislike her ! Wouldn't she work hard ! Wouldn't she be kind and friendly and helpful to the new girls who didn't know anything about her ! She smiled gladly.

' What about Anna ? ' she asked. ' Is she going up too ? '

" Yes—but you can trust Anna not to give you away at all,' said Miss Theobald. ' She's a good girl—she really has turned out well as head-girl. Now, Elsie—take this chance and make good ! '

' I will,' said Elsie. ' Thank you, Miss Theobald. I never thought of going up into the third form ! It makes all the difference in the world ! '

The girl went out, pleased and hopeful. She saw Gladys Hillman in the passage and went up to her with a warm gesture of friendliness.

' Any news of your mother, old thing ? ' she asked.

' Not yet,' said Gladys, wondering whatever could have made Elsie look so friendly and glad. Elsie went on her way and met Bobby.

' I say,' she said, ' I saw poor old Gladys just now.

Can't we do something to take her out of herself a bit ?
She's moping again.'

'Good idea ! ' said Bobby at once. 'I'll play that
trick on Mam'zelle—you know, the trick that makes plates
jump about ! Mam'zelle is taking lunch today at our
table, because Miss Jenks is going out. It will be sport ! '

So the second-formers were told that a trick was about
to be played, and they all cheered up, forgot about exams.,
and looked at Bobby with bright eyes. The first trick
that term ! It was time one was played !

Mam'zelle was in a good temper. The first form had
done unexpectedly well in their French exam. She
beamed at everybody. The second-formers beamed back,
and Doris gave a deep chuckle, exactly like Mam'zelle's.

'Ah, this bad Doris ! ' said Mam'zelle, clapping Doris
on the shoulder. 'She can imitate me perr-r-rfectly—
but she cannot roll her r's yet in the true French way !
Now—let us go to the dining-room. The bell for luncheon
has gone. Today I take you for the meal, because the
good Miss Jenks is out ! '

The second form seated themselves at their table.
Mam'zelle was at the head. Bobby was three places
away from her. The others looked at her, grinning.
They hoped she had been able to slip into the dining-room
and lay her plans !

Bobby had prepared everything carefully. There was
a pile of plates at Mam'zelle's place, ready for her to serve
the stew for each girl. Bobby had removed the plates,
and had deftly placed the long rubber tubing under the
table-cloth, so that it ran from where the plates were to
Bobby's own seat, and hung down under the cloth. The
bladder-end was where the plates were, and the bulb to
press was by Bobby's place. Bobby replaced the pile of
plates over the bladder-end. The plates were too heavy
to move when the bulb was pressed—but when all the girls

were served and only Mam'zelle's plate was there, it
would tip up beautifully as soon as Bobby pressed the
bulb which filled the bladder-end with air !

Mam'zelle served out the stew rapidly. The girls
began their meal hungrily, one eye on Mam'zelle's plate.
It was the only one left now. Mam'zelle filled it with
stew and gravy. She was very fond of gravy.

' At first,' said Mam'zelle conversationally, taking up
her knife and fork, ' at first when I came to England I
did not like this stew of yours ! But now—ah, it is
wonderful ! '

Bobby pressed the rubber bulb she was holding under
the cloth. The bladder-end under Mam'zelle's plate filled
with air and became fat and big. Mam'zelle's plate tilted
up on one side, gave a little wobble and subsided again as
Bobby let go the bulb she was pressing.

Mam'zelle was overcome with astonishment. She felt
her nose to see if her glasses were there. Yes, they were.
But could she have seen aright ? Her plate had moved !

She took a quick look round at the girls. They seemed
to have noticed nothing—though actually all the girls had
seen the plate lift and wobble, and were fighting hard
to keep from giggling.

Mam'zelle dismissed the matter from her mind. She
had imagined it ! She began to make conversation
again.

' Tomorrow you second-formers will have your French
tests,' she said, smiling round. Then she tried to cut
a piece of meat with her knife—whilst Bobby at the same
moment pressed the rubber bulb. Air ran through to the
bladder, and Mam'zelle's plate lifted itself up very suddenly, and spilt some gravy over one side.

Mam'zelle looked at her plate in alarm. It had done
it again. It was alive ! It had spilt its gravy on the
cloth.

' *Tiens !* ' said Mam'zelle, very much startled.   ' What is this ! '

' What is what, Mam'zelle ? ' asked Janet, with a solemn face.

' Nothing, nothing ! ' said Mam'zelle, hastily, not liking to say that she feared her plate was alive.   But something certainly was the matter with it.   She looked down at it, hardly daring to eat her meal.

Bobby gave the plate a rest.   Mam'zelle looked at it warily for a little while, and then plucked up her courage to eat her meal once more.   The plate seemed to be behaving itself.   Then it suddenly went mad again !

It tipped up and down slowly and solemnly three times, then jerked from side to side spilling some more gravy. Mam'zelle grew really alarmed.   She glanced at the girls. How strange that they did not seem to see what was happening !   She must be going mad !

' Don't you like your stew, Mam'zelle ? ' asked Pat, solemnly.   ' I thought you said it was wonderful.'

Mam'zelle looked suspiciously at her plate which was now quiet.   Doris made a silly joke in order to let the girls laugh loudly, for two or three of them were almost hysterical by now, and would certainly have given the game away if they had not been able to laugh loudly.

The rest of the school looked in amazement at the bellowing girls.   Miss Theobald, who sat at the head of the sixth-form table, was displeased.

' Quiet, please,' she called to the second-formers. They choked and became quiet.   Doris was purple in the face with trying not to laugh again.   Mam'zelle looked round with a frown.

' Such a noise ! ' she said, reprovingly.   But her attention was soon drawn to her plate again when it solemnly rose up and down twice, and then became quite still.

Mam'zelle frowned.   This could not really be happen-

ing ! Plates could not behave like that. It was nonsense.
She would eat her dinner and not think about it.

' Don't do it again till the pudding comes,' whispered
Carlotta to Bobby. ' We can't help squealing with
laughter now. We shall get into a row. Give us a
rest ! '

So for the rest of the first course the plate behaved
itself, and Mam'zelle was much relieved. But when the
pudding arrived, and she had served it out, leaving only
her own plate in its place, the fun began again. The
pudding-plate leapt quite wildly, and Mam'zelle pushed
her chair back with a scream. The girls choked and the
tears ran down their cheeks.

' Ah ! This plate ! ' cried Mam'zelle. ' It is as bad as
the other one. See how it jumps ! '

Bobby kept the plate quite still. Doris exploded into
laughter and two or three joined her helplessly. Miss
Theobald began to look really vexed. The rest of the
school craned their necks to see whatever could be
happening at the second-form table.

The plate moved again, and Mam'zelle backed away
still farther. Miss Theobald, amazed and puzzled, left
her place and walked over to the second-form table.
Every girl was rocking in helpless laughter. Not even
the presence of the Head Mistress could stop them.
This was the funniest thing they had ever seen.

' Mam'zelle ! What *is* the matter ? ' asked Miss
Theobald, really annoyed. Mam'zelle turned to her
wildly.

' My plate ! ' she said. ' My plate ! '

' Well, what is wrong with it ? ' asked Miss Theobald,
impatiently, thinking that Mam'zelle must really have
gone mad. ' It seems all right to me.'

' Miss Theobald, it jumps, it dances, it leaps around the
table,' said Mam'zelle, earnestly, exaggerating in the hope

that Miss Theobald would be impressed. 'It is a mad
plate. I cannot bear it.'

The Head Mistress looked at the plate of pudding. It
lay quite still on the table, perfectly ordinary. She
glanced round at the giggling girls. She supposed they
were laughing at Mam'zelle's behaviour. Well, it certainly
was extraordinary.

'You had better go and lie down, Mam'zelle,' she said
at last. 'I think you can't be well.'

'*I* am well,' said poor Mam'zelle. 'It is the plate that
is mad. You should see it jump, Miss Theobald.'

Miss Theobald looked doubtfully at the plate—and
Bobby had a tremendous urge to make it jump again.
She pressed the bulb hard, and the plate jumped up at
once, wobbled and fell back again. Miss Theobald looked
astonished and Mam'zelle gave another squeal. The girls
screamed with laughter.

Miss Theobald lifted up the plate, and pushed back
the table-cloth. There, underneath, was the little rubber
bladder attached to the tubing that led to Bobby's place.
Mam'zelle's eyes nearly fell out of her head when she
saw it.

'I think, Mam'zelle, one of the girls is playing a trick
on you,' said Miss Theobald. 'I will leave you to deal
with it. I daresay Roberta can explain how it was done.'

The girls stopped laughing. They stared at Miss
Theobald walking back to her seat. They looked at
Mam'zelle, who glared at poor Bobby.

'What is this horrible trick?' she inquired in a loud
voice.

Bobby explained, and Mam'zelle listened carefully.
She removed the whole thing and looked at it. Then
she put back the table-cloth and her plate and began to
eat her pudding, looking straight in front of her with her
sloe-black eyes.

The girls felt uncomfortable. Was Mam'zelle really offended, really angry? The trick was quite a harmless one. They finished their pudding and sat still.

Suddenly there came a snort from Mam'zelle and all the second-formers looked up in surprise. Mam'zelle threw back her head. She roared, she bellowed! She laughed so much that the relieved second-formers couldn't help laughing again too.

'It was a good trick,' said Mam'zelle at last, wiping her eyes. 'Yes, a good trick. I shall make my sister laugh till she cries when I tell her. When I think of that plate jumping at me like that—ah, *magnifique*!'

'I'll lend you the whole trick, if you like,' said Janet. 'It belongs to my brother. You can play the trick on your sister.'

Mam'zelle stared at her in delight. 'What a good idea!' she exclaimed, beaming. 'This will cheer my good sister immensely. You shall show me how it works.'

Miss Theobald smiled as she left the room. It really had been funny. What a good thing Mam'zelle had seen the funny side—but she could generally be trusted to. Poor Mam'zelle—the hundreds of tricks that had been played on her during her years at St. Clare's! She would never learn to be suspicious of the girls!

'Marvellous!' said Janet, when the second-formers were in their common room again, discussing the affair. 'Simply super. Bobby, you did it awfully well. I thought I should have died, trying to keep in my laughter. Oh, dear—when I think of that plate jumping about—and Mam'zelle's horrified face—I want to scream all over again!'

Every one was amused, and Gladys, who had seen few tricks played in her life, laughed as much as any one. She forgot her worry for a while, and Mirabel was glad to see her smiling face as she listened to the talk.

The next day Mam'zelle gave out the French papers.
They were much easier than the class expected and every
one gave a sigh of relief.   Even Doris hoped she might
get enough marks for a pass !

In the middle of the exam., when everything was
perfectly quiet, some one flashed by the window on a
bicycle.   Mirabel glanced up.   It was a telegraph boy !
She looked across at Gladys.   Gladys had seen him too
and had gone white.   She wondered if the telegram held
any news for her.

After a few minutes the door opened and a maid looked
in.   ' Please could Miss Gladys Hillman go to Miss
Theobald,' she said.   Gladys stood up, her knees shaking.
She was sure the telegram said that her mother was dead.
She went out of the room as if she was walking in a dream.
Mirabel stared after her, miserable.   She feared the
worst too.

But in two minutes Gladys was back !   The door was
flung open, and she burst into the room, her face beaming,
and her eyes shining.   She rushed to Mirabel.

' Mirabel !   Mother's had the operation, and she's come
through it wonderfully !   She's going to get better !
I'm to see her soon, just for an hour !   Perhaps next
week, Mirabel !   Isn't it marvellous ! '

Mirabel was as glad as if it had been her own mother.
She forgot about the class, and put her arm round the
happy girl.

' Oh, Gladys ! ' she said.   ' It's marvellous !   I *am*
glad ! '

' Hurrah ! ' yelled Bobby, as delighted as any one.
' Good old Gladys ! '

' I too am glad,' beamed Mam'zelle, forgetting all about
the French exam., for a wonder.   ' Such a surprise for
you !   Now you will be able to smile again ! '

Gladys glanced round the room, suddenly remembering

where she was. She had forgotten everything for the moment except that she must tell Mirabel, her friend, the great news. She went back to her seat, so happy that she felt she might cry with gladness at any moment.

' And now, we must look at our exam. papers again,' said Mam'zelle, in a kindly voice. ' Gladys, you should do a wonderful paper, with such good news to help you ! '

Every one was glad. The term had only two more days to go, and the girls were pleased to think that Gladys had something to look forward to. They were as nice to her as they could be, even Elsie !

The last day came, and packing was begun. Gladys couldn't help feeling a little sad as she saw every one preparing to go away for the holidays. She would have to stay at school—but, never mind, she would be able to see her mother soon. What a pity she was so far away— it would be difficult to see her more than once.

Just as the second form were in a complete muddle over their packing, Miss Theobald came into the room with a letter in her hand. She had just received it. The girls stood up and listened.

' Oh, Mirabel,' said Miss Theobald in her clear voice, ' I have just received a letter from your mother. She says you can take Gladys home with you for the holidays if I will give my permission, as then she can go to see her mother twice a week quite easily from your home, which is not very far from the hospital.'

Mirabel gave a shriek of delight. Gladys turned as red as a beetroot.

' Miss Theobald ! How marvellous ! Isn't mother a brick ? Can Gladys come with me ? '

' Of course,' said the Head Mistress, smiling at the bewildered, radiant Gladys. ' But she will have to pack very quickly. Hurry up, Gladys, and see if you can be ready by the time the school-coaches arrive ! '

Ready! Of course she could be ready! Helped by willing hands Gladys flew here and there, cramming everything in, her heart singing with joy. To go home with Mirabel—see her friend's brother and sister—visit her own mother twice a week! What wonderful luck!

'And if I hadn't tackled Mirabel that time, and got her to change her mind and stay on, nothing like this would have happened!' thought the girl, packing her jerseys. 'It just shows you've got to have courage and go straight for things. Oh, it's too good to be true!'

But it was true, and Gladys went off in the school-coach with Mirabel beside her, singing heartily with the others as they rolled down to the station. Alison clapped her on the back. 'Happy holidays, Gladys!' she said.

'Same to you,' said Gladys. Alison was changed. 'Not so silly,' thought Gladys. 'I like her better now. I like lots of people better—but most of all Mirabel!'

'Good-bye, everybody!' yelled the twins. 'Merry Christmas and Happy New Year when they come!'

'Good-bye! Don't eat too much Christmas-pudding, Anna!'

'Good-bye, Elsie! Happy hols.!'

'Good-bye, Bobby! Think out a few more tricks. I say, *do* you remember Mam'zelle's face when the plate jumped?'

'Good-bye, Hilary. See you next term. Nice to think you'll be our head-girl again!'

'Good-bye, everybody! Good-bye!'

CLAUDINE
AT ST CLARE'S

CONTENTS

PAT and Isabel O'Sullivan walked into the fourth form-room at St. Clare's, and looked round.

'Fourth form,' said Pat. 'Golly, we're getting on, aren't we, Isabel!'

'Yes—fourth form seems a long way from the first form,' said Isabel. 'I say—do you remember when we were in the first form—ages ago? We were called the Stuck-up Twins then, because we hated St. Clare's, and didn't want to belong to it.'

The twins thought back to the days when they had been first-formers. They remembered how they had settled down at St. Clare's, their first dislike of it turning to pride and admiration, and now here they were, fourth-formers at the beginning of the summer term!

'Don't the first-formers seem babies now?' said Pat. 'We thought we were quite big when we first came, but when I see the first-formers now they seem very young to me! I shall enjoy being in the fourth form, won't you, Isabel?'

'I shall,' said Isabel. 'I hope we shall stay on at St. Clare's until we are in the top form—and I hope our friends do too.'

'Well, some of them have left already,' said Pat. 'Pam isn't coming back, nor is Sheila. Lucy Oriell has gone too—to an Art School. She was going to stay on here, but she's too brilliant at her art, and she's won a scholarship to the best art school in the country.'

'Good for Lucy!' said Isabel. 'We shall miss her though. I wonder if there are any new girls this term?'

'Sure to be,' said Pat. She looked round the big form-room. 'I say, this is a fine room, isn't it?—the nicest classroom we've had so far. There's a wonderful view out of the window.'

So there was. The twins could see miles of beautiful country. It was country they knew well now, and loved very much. Down below, in the school grounds, were the tennis-courts, the games fields, and the big swimming-pool. The girls could see the school gardens too, and the big kitchen garden full of fresh vegetables.

'Bags I sit by the window,' said Pat. 'Hallo, there's Bobby, and Janet!'

Roberta and Janet walked into the classroom, grinning. Bobby's freckled face had a very boyish look, and she was very like a boy in her ways, full of fun and tricks.

'Hallo!' she said. 'Come to look at our new home? Nice room, isn't it?'

'What's our new form-mistress like?' said Pat. 'Miss Ellis—she's supposed to be quite nice, isn't she?'

'Oh yes—very calm and unruffled and dignified,' said Bobby. 'She'll be all right.'

'Got any new tricks to play, Janet?' asked Isabel. Janet always had a stock of tricks each term, most of them from her school-boy brother, who seemed to be a real scamp. Janet grinned.

'Wait and see,' she said. 'Anyway, I suppose I'd better go carefully now I'm a fourth-former. Can't rag about so much when you get high up the school. And I'm going to work for my matric. exam. too, so I guess I won't have much time for tricks.'

'I guess you will, all the same,' said Pat. 'Any new girls, do you know?'

'Two or three,' said Bobby. 'Hallo, Hilary! Had good hols.?'

Hilary Wentworth came into the room, dark and smiling. She had been at St. Clare's even longer than the twins.

'Hallo!' she said. 'Yes, I had fine hols. I rode every

day, and I played tennis on our hard court every day
too. I say, who's the angel? '

' What do you mean ? ' asked the twins and Bobby.

' Oh, haven't you seen her ? ' said Hilary. ' She's just
arrived, complete with posh new trunk, three tennis
rackets, and a handbag with gold initials on. What do
you bet your Cousin Alison will think she's one of the
world's seven wonders ? She's got pale golden hair,
bobbed like angels in pictures, and a pointed face like a
pixie, and a voice like a princess.'

' Golly ! Where is she ? ' said the others, with interest.
' Will she be in our form ? '

' She's down in the hall,' said Hilary. ' She arrived in
the biggest car I've ever seen, with a crest on the panels,
and two chauffeurs.'

' Let's go and see her,' said Pat. So the five of them
went into the corridor, and hung over the stair banisters
to see the newcomer.

She was still there—and it was quite true, she did look
a bit like an angel, if an angel could be imagined dressed
in school uniform, carrying three beautiful tennis rackets !

' She's lovely, isn't she ? ' said Bobby, who not being at
all lovely herself, always admired beauty in others. ' Yes
—I bet Alison will follow her round like a dog. Alison
isn't happy unless she's thinking some one is just too
wonderful for words ! '

Alison came up at that moment. She was the twins'
cousin, a pretty, feather-headed little thing, with not
many brains. ' Hallo ! ' she said. ' Did I hear you
talking about me ? '

' Yes,' said Hilary. ' We were just saying that you'd
be sure to like that school-girl angel down there. Did
you ever see anything like her ? '

Alison leaned over the banisters—and, just as the others
had guessed, she immediately lost her heart to the new
girl.

'She looks like a princess from a fairy-tale,' said Alison.
I'll go down and ask her if she wants to be shown round
a bit.'

Alison sped downstairs. The others grinned at one
another. 'Alison has lost her heart already,' said Pat.
'Poor old Alison—the wonderful friends she's made and
lost ! Do you remember Sadie, the American girl, and
how Alison was for ever saying, "Well, Sadie says so and
so ", and we made a song about it and sang it ? Wasn't
Alison cross ? '

'Yes, and when she was in the second form she thought
the drama mistress was simply wonderful, and when she
was in the third form she lost her heart to the head-girl
and made herself a perfect nuisance to her,' said Janet.
'Really, the times Alison has lost her heart to people, and
they never think anything of her for it.'

'Funny old feather-head,' said Pat. 'Look at her,
taking the angel's arm and going off with her, all over
her already ! '

'There's another new girl down there too,' said Bobby.
'She looks rather forlorn. Well, I do think Alison might
take her round as well. Hie, Alison ! '

But Alison had disappeared with the golden-haired
angel. The twins went down the stairs and spoke to the
other new girl.

'Hallo ! You're new, aren't you ? You'd better come
and see Matron. We'll take you.'

'What's your name ? ' said Pat, looking at the new
girl, who was trying not to show that she felt new and
lost.

'Pauline Bingham-Jones,' said the new girl in rather an
affected voice. 'Yes, I'd be glad if you'd tell me what
to do.'

'Well, Matron is usually here to see to all the new
girls,' said Hilary, a little puzzled. 'I wonder where
she is ? '

' I haven't seen her at all,' said Pat. ' She wasn't here when we came, either.'

' Funny,' said Isabel. ' Let's go to her room and find her. We've got to see her, anyway.'

They went to Matron's room, taking Pauline with them. They banged on the door. They liked Matron, though they were very much in awe of her. She had been at St. Clare's for years and years, and some of the girls' mothers, who had also been at St. Clare's, had known her too.

A voice called out. ' Come in ! '

' That's not Matron's voice,' said Pat, puzzled. She opened the door and went in, the others following. A woman in Matron's uniform sat sewing by the window. It wasn't the Matron they knew so well. The girls stared at her in surprise.

' Oh,' said Pat. ' We were looking for Matron.'

' I am Matron this term,' said the new Matron. ' Your old Matron fell ill during the holidays, so I have come to take her place. I am sure we shall all get on very well together.'

The girls stared at her. They didn't feel so sure about that. Their old Matron was fat and round and jolly, with a strong and comforting kind of face. This Matron was thin and sour-looking. She had very thin lips that met together in a straight line. She smiled at the girls, but her smile stayed at her mouth and did not reach her eyes.

' We came to find you,' said Bobby. ' Usually Matron meets the new girls. This is one of them. She has to give you her list of clothes and towels and things.'

' I know that, thank you,' said Matron, biting off the thread she was using. ' Send all the new girls to me, will you ? How many have arrived ? '

The girls didn't know. They thought it was Matron's business to find out, not theirs. They thought of their old Matron, bustling about looking after the newcomers, making them welcome, taking them to their form-mistresses, or finding girls to take care of them.

' Well—this is Pauline Bingham-Jones,' said Pat, at last. ' There's another new girl somewhere. We saw her. Our Cousin Alison seems to be looking after her.'

The girls disappeared from the room, leaving Pauline to the new Matron. They looked at one another and screwed up their noses. ' Don't like her,' said Isabel. ' Looks like a bottle of vinegar ! '

The others laughed. ' I hope our old Matron will come back,' said Bobby. ' St. Clare's will seem funny without her. I wonder where Alison has gone with the angel.'

Alison appeared at that moment, looking flushed and radiant. It was quite plain that she had made a friend already. With her was the ' angel '.

' Oh,' said Alison, ' Pat, Isabel, Bobby, Hilary—this is the Honourable Angela Favorleigh.'

The Honourable Angela bent her head a little as if she was bowing to her subjects. Bobby grinned.

' I had a doll called Angela once,' she said. ' She was a bit like you ! Well—I hope you'll like St. Clare's. Alison, take her to Matron.'

' Where *is* Matron ? ' said Alison. ' I've been looking for her.'

' There's a new Matron this term,' said Bobby. ' You won't like her.'

The Honourable Angela Favorleigh didn't like Bobby. She gazed at her as if she was something that smelt rather nasty. She turned to Alison and spoke in a pretty, high little voice.

'' Well—let's go to Matron. I want to take my things off.'

They went off together. Hilary laughed. ' Well, we shall all know where Alison will be most of this term,' she said, ' In the Honourable's pocket ! '

'LOOK,' said Bobby, 'there's another new girl. She's got her things off, too. She looks as if she'd be a fourth-former, I should think.'

The new girl came up, walking quickly as if she had somewhere to go. 'Hallo,' said Bobby. 'You're new, aren't you? What form will you be in, do you know?'

'Fourth,' said the girl. 'My name's Eileen Paterson.'

'We're fourth form too,' said Pat, and she introduced herself and the others. 'Do you want to be shown round a bit? Usually Matron is here to welcome people, but there is a new one this term who doesn't know the ropes yet.'

The girl looked suddenly annoyed. 'I know my way about, thank you,' she said stiffly. 'I've been here a week already.'

Without saying any more she swung off. The others stared after her. 'What's bitten *her*?' said Bobby. 'No need to be rude like that. And what did she mean—that she's been here a week? Nobody comes back before the first day of term.'

Mirabel came up, with her friend Gladys. 'Hallo, hallo!' said the others. 'Nice to see you again. I say, have you spoken to that girl who's just gone—new girl called Eileen Paterson. Seems to think the whole school belongs to her!'

"No, I haven't spoken to her yet,' said Mirabel. 'But I know her mother is the Matron now—our old one is ill you know. Eileen is the new Matron's daughter, and she's going to be educated here. She came with her mother a week ago, when her mother came to take over the job and see to the linen and things.'

Bobby whistled. 'Oh! No wonder she was annoyed when we said the new Matron ought to be welcoming the new girls, and didn't know the ropes yet!' she said. 'And no wonder she knows her way about if she's already been here a week. I didn't like her much.'

'Give her a chance,' said Hilary. 'You know how you feel sort of on the defensive when you come to anywhere new, and meet girls who've been here ages. You feel a kind of outsider at first.'

There were new girls in the other, lower forms, but these did not interest the fourth-formers much. They were glad to see one another again—the twins, Bobby, Hilary, Kathleen, Doris, Carlotta, and the rest. They had all come up together into the fourth form. There were a few old girls left in the fourth form, most of whom the twins liked. Susan Howes was head of the form, a pleasant, kindly girl with a good sense of responsibility and fairness.

The fourth form settled down under Miss Ellis. She was firm and calm, seldom raised her voice, expected good work and saw that she got it. She was interested in the girls and fond of them, and they, in return, liked her very much.

The Honourable Angela Favorleigh looked more like an angel than ever in class, with her bobbed golden hair falling to her shoulders, the ends curling underneath most beautifully. All her school clothes, though cut to the same pattern as those of the others, were really beautiful.

'Do you know, she has every single pair of shoes especially made for her?' said Alison, in a hushed voice to the twins. 'And she has a handbag to match every single frock she wears, all with gold initials on.'

'Shut up,' said Pat. 'Who cares about things like that? Your darling Angela is a snob.'

'Well, why shouldn't she be?' said Alison, ready to defend her new friend at once. 'Her family is one of the oldest in the country, she's got a third cousin who is a prince, and goodness knows how many titled relations ! '

' You're a snob too, Alison,' said Isabel, in disgust. ' Why must you always suck up to people like that ? Don't you know that it's what you *are* that matters, not what you have ? '

' I'm not a snob,' said Alison. ' I'm pleased that Angela has chosen me for her friend, of course. I think she's lovely.'

' Pity she hasn't got more brains,' said Bobby. ' Honestly, I don't believe she really knows her twelve times table ! '

Angela Favorleigh certainly was a snob. She was intensely proud of her family, of its wealth, its cars, and her own well-bred looks. She was very particular about making friends. She liked Alison because the girl was pretty and dainty, had beautiful manners and quite plainly adored the lovely Angela from the bottom of her foolish little heart.

Angela liked very few of her form. Bobby she detested because she had said she was like a doll. Carlotta she would have nothing to do with at all.

Carlotta didn't mind in the least. The dark-eyed, dark-haired girl had once been a little circus-girl, and she was not at all ashamed of it. Her mother had been a circus-rider, but her father was a gentleman, and now Carlotta lived with her father and grandmother in the holidays, for her mother was dead. She had learnt to be lady-like, to have good manners, and was very popular indeed—but she had never forgotten the exciting days of the circus, and she often amused the others by turning cart-wheels, or going completely mad in a foreign, Spanish way that the girls enjoyed very much.

Alison had told Angela the histories of all the girls, Carlotta included, and Angela had turned up her delicate little nose when she heard that Carlotta had actually ridden horses in a circus.

' How *can* they have her here, in a school like this ? ' she said. ' I am sure my people wouldn't have sent me here if they had known that.'

' Why did you come to St. Clare's ? ' asked Alison, curiously. ' It's supposed to be a sensible, no-nonsense school, you know—not a swanky one.'

' I didn't want to come,' said Angela. ' My mother wanted to send me to a much nicer school, but my father has funny ideas. He said I wanted my corners rubbed off.'

' Oh, Angela ! You haven't any corners ! ' said Alison. ' Honestly, I don't think you've any faults at all.'

This was the kind of thing that Angela loved hearing, and was one reason why she liked Alison for a friend. She looked at Alison out of innocent blue eyes, and smiled an angelic smile.

' You do say nice things, Alison,' she said. ' You are far and away the nicest girl in the form. I can't bear that common Eileen, nor that awful Carlotta, nor that dreadful Pauline Bingham-Jones.'

Pauline certainly wasn't much of a success. In her way she seemed as much of a snob as Angela, but she could not carry it off so well, because her clothes were not beautifully made, and she had no marvellous possessions such as Angela had. But she too turned up her nose at Carlotta, and disliked the ready-witted Bobby. As for Eileen, she would hardly speak to her at all.

' I don't see why Eileen should be allowed to join the school just because her mother is here as Matron,' said Pauline, in her rather affected voice. ' Good gracious me—we shall have the cook's daughter here next, and the gardener's too ! It's bad enough to have Carlotta. She always looks so wild and don't-carish.'

Carlotta always did look a little wild at the beginning

of term, partly because she was no longer under the rather strict eye of her grandmother. But nobody minded Carlotta's untidiness and wildness. It was all part of the vivacious, amusing girl. Carlotta knew that Angela and Pauline didn't like her, and she took a real pleasure in talking slang, making rude faces, and unexpectedly walking on her hands in front of them.

Miss Ellis, however, did not encourage things of this sort in the fourth form. Her form was a kind of half-way house, where girls had to learn to shed their irresponsible ways, and to become more serious, reliable members of the school. As soon as they moved up into the fifth and sixth, they had studies of their own, instead of common rooms, and were expected to take a good deal of responsibility.

So Carlotta was often called to order by Miss Ellis, in her low, firm voice, and then Angela and Pauline looked down their noses at the one-time circus-girl, and whispered mocking things to the girl next to them.

Pauline and Angela vied with each other in their boasting. The girls sometimes giggled to hear them.

'My third cousin—the one who is a prince,' Angela would say, 'he has an aeroplane of his own, and has promised to take me up in it.'

'Haven't you *been* up in an aeroplane yet ? ' Pauline would say, with affected surprise. 'Good gracious ! I've been up three times already. That was when I was staying with the Lacy-Wrights. Fancy, they had sixteen bathrooms in their house—well, it was really a mansion, of course. . . .'

'I bet you haven't more than one bathroom in your own home,' said Angela, spitefully. 'We've got seven.'

'We've got nine, if you count the two in the servants' quarters,' said Pauline, at once. The other girls stared at her in surprise. They could well believe that Angela had scores of bathrooms, for wealth was written all over

the little snob—but somehow Pauline didn't fit in with a
number of bathrooms, a fleet of expensive cars and things
like that.

' Well,' said Bobby, ' let me count *my* bathrooms.
Three for myself—four for Mother—five for Daddy—two
for visitors—er, how many's that ? '

' Idiot I ' said Pat, giggling. Angela and Pauline
scowled.

' I can't remember whether we've got a bathroom at
home or not,' said Hilary, entering into the fun. ' Let
me think hard I '

But no amount of teasing would make either Angela or
Pauline stop their vieing with each other. If it wasn't
bathrooms, it was cars ; if it wasn't cars, it was their
beautiful, expensively-dressed mothers ; if it wasn't
mothers, it was clothes. The others really got very tired
of it.

Eileen Paterson did not seem to mind very much being
cold-shouldered by Angela and Pauline. She only spoke
with eagerness of one thing—her elder brother. He was
at work somewhere in the next big town, and it was quite
plain that Eileen adored him.

' His name is Edgar,' she said. ' We call him Eddie.'

' You would,' said Angela, cattily. ' And if he was
called Alfred, you'd call him Alf. And if he was called
Herbert, you'd call him Herb—or Erb perhaps.'

Eileen flushed. ' You're a beast, Angela,' she said.
' You wait till you see Eddie—Edgar, I mean. He's
marvellous I His hair's curly, and he's got the loveliest
smile. He's the best brother in the world. He's working
terribly hard at his job. You see, Mother lost a lot of
money, so that's why she had to take a job as Matron,
and why Eddie—Edgar—had to go to work.'

' Your family history doesn't interest me, Eileen,' said
Angela, coldly, and went off with Alison. Eileen shrugged
her shoulders.

'Little snob!' she said, loudly. 'She wants a good spanking.'

Carlotta agreed with her. 'Yes—sometimes my hand tingles because it wants to slap Angela hard,' she said. 'But now I'm a fourth-former—what a pity! I shall quite forget how to give a slap to any one who needs it!'

'Oh no you won't,' said Bobby, laughing at the solemn Carlotta. 'When you fly into a temper, you'll forget all about being a fourth-former—you'll just be the same wild Carlotta you've always been!'

3   THE ARRIVAL OF CLAUDINE

BEFORE a week had gone by, a fourth new girl arrived. Mam'zelle herself announced her coming.

'I have a surprise for you,' she beamed one morning, coming in to give a French lesson. 'We shall soon have another companion in the fourth form. She arrives today.'

'Why is she so late in coming?' asked Pat, in surprise.

'She has just recovered from the measle,' said Mam'zelle, who always spoke of this illness in the singular and not in the plural. 'The measle is a most tiresome disease. Claudine had a very bad measle, and she could not come back any sooner.'

'Claudine?' said Isabel. 'What a pretty name! I like it.'

'Ah, and you will like the little Claudine too!' said Mam'zelle. 'For she is French. She is my niece!'

This was news to the girls. They hadn't even known that Mam'zelle had a niece. One coming to St. Clare's too!

' I hope she will be happy at St. Clare's,' said Hilary, feeling that some one ought to say the right thing.

' Ah, she will be very happy,' said Mam'zelle. ' She would be happy anywhere, the little Claudine. There never was such a child for happiness. Always she smiles and laughs, and always she plays the trick and the joke.'

This sounded good. The girls began to look forward to Claudine's coming. They looked at Mam'zelle expectantly, hoping to hear more.

Then Mam'zelle's face grew solemn. She pinched her glasses more firmly on her nose and gazed at the listening girls with her short-sighted, much-magnified eyes.

' I have especially asked for Claudine to come here,' she said. ' Before, she has been to a Convent School, but it was too strict for her, and always they found fault with the poor little Claudine. They said she cared nothing for any one, nor for any rules or customs. And I thought to myself, " Ah, the good, hard-working Bobby was once like that—and see what St. Clare's has done for her ! Now she works for her Matric. and she is as good as gold ! Maybe the same thing will happen to my little Claudine." '

Bobby looked uncomfortable as Mam'zelle made this speech. She wasn't at all sure that she wanted to be referred to as ' good as gold '. But Mam'zelle was so much in earnest that Bobby made no protest. It wouldn't have been any good, anyway ! Mam'zelle swept on with her speech.

' And so the little Claudine comes today, well-recovered from the measle, and you will all give her a grand welcome, will you not ? For your old Mam'zelle's sake ? '

' Of course we'll make her welcome,' said Susan Howes, and most of the others murmured the same, except Angela, Alison and Pauline, who all put on a bored look, as if a niece belonging to Mam'zelle wasn't worth giving a thought to.

' Ah, you are good kind girls,' said Mam'zelle. ' I will

introduce Claudine to you as soon as she comes. She will love you all. She is a good girl though she seems to care nothing for what is good and proper. But you will change all that, *n'est-ce pas* ? '

The girls thought that Claudine sounded distinctly amusing. It would be fun to have a French girl in the class ! They glanced at one another, thinking that of all the new girls, this latest one sounded the most promising.

About five minutes before the lesson finished the door was opened, and a strange girl appeared. She was small, dark and smart. She had a very cheeky look and she gave a quick sidelong glance at the girls before advancing to Mam'zelle.

Mam'zelle gave a shriek, and then flung herself on the new girl. She kissed her several times on both cheeks, she stroked her dark hair, and poured out such a torrent of French that no one could follow it.

The girl replied in smooth, polite French, and kissed Mam'zelle on each cheek. She did not seem to mind her aunt's outburst in the least.

' Ah, ma petite Claudine, here you are at last ! ' cried Mam'zelle. She swung the girl round to face the class. ' Now see, here is the little Claudine,' said Mam'zelle, her glasses falling off her nose in her violent delight. ' Greet your new friends, Claudine.'

' Hallo, buddies ! ' said Claudine, amiably. The girls stared in surprise and then giggled. It was funny to hear such an American expression from the little French girl.

' What did you say ? ' said Mam'zelle, who was not well up in American slang. ' Did you say " hello, bodies " ? That is not correct, Claudine. You should say, " Hallo, everybody." '

The class roared. Claudine grinned. Mam'zelle beamed. She was plainly very proud of Claudine and very fond of her.

The bell rang for the end of class. Mam'zelle picked out Hilary. 'Hilary, you will take the little Claudine with you, please, and show her everything. She will feel strange and shy, poor little one.'

Mam'zelle was quite mistaken about that, however. Claudine didn't feel shy, and certainly didn't seem to feel strange. In fact she acted as if she had known the girls all her life ! She spoke easily and naturally to them. Her English was good, though like Mam'zelle, she sometimes put things in an unusual way.

She had been to school in France, and then had spent a term or two at a Convent School in England. It seemed that Claudine did not want to remain at her last school and they did not want to keep her.

'You see—it was most unfortunate—the Science Mistress went up a ladder into a tree to collect some curious fungus that grew there,' explained Claudine, in her little French voice. 'And I came along and borrowed the ladder. So we did not have a Science lesson that day.'

'Golly ! Do you mean to say that you left the teacher stranded up the tree ? ' said Bobby. 'Well, you have got a nerve ! No wonder Mam'zelle thinks St. Clare's will be good for you. You can't do that sort of thing here.'

'No ? ' said Claudine. 'What a pity. Still, maybe you have good fun. I am sorry I did not come back to school on the first day. But I had caught a measle.'

The girls giggled. Every one liked Claudine, except Angela. Even Pauline listened to the new girl, and Alison was much amused by her. But Angela as usual looked down her nose.

'What did I tell you ? ' she said to Alison. 'First we have to have Matron's daughter, and now we have to have Mam'zelle's niece ! I can't see what you find to be amused at in Claudine, Alison. I'm surprised at you.'

'Well, I like her voice and her manners,' said Alison.

' I like the way she uses her hands when she talks—just like Mam'zelle does. She's really quite amusing, Angela.'

Angela did not like Alison to disagree with her about anything. She looked coldly at her friend and then turned away sulkily. That was always the way she punished any one—by withdrawing from them and sulking. Alison couldn't bear it.

Alison tried to make it up. She went after Angela, and took her hand. She praised her and flattered her, and at last Angela condescended to smile again on her willing slave.

Then Alison was happy. ' You needn't think I shall bother about Claudine at all,' she said to Angela. ' She's a common little thing, really.'

' Not so common as Carlotta,' said Angela, spitefully. Alison looked uncomfortable. She sincerely liked Carlotta, who was absolutely honest, truthful and straight, besides being amusing company. Even her hot temper was likeable. Alison thought that Carlotta was more completely herself, more natural than any of the other girls. And to be natural was to be very likeable.

Claudine settled in at once. She took a desk at the back of the room, and bagged a locker in the common room. She arranged her belongings in the locker, and put a photograph of her mother on top. She had brought a fine big cake with her and shared it generously all round, though Angela refused a slice. Alison did too, after hesitating. She was afraid that Angela might go into a sulk again if she saw her sharing the cake.

At first the girls were very much amused with Claudine, but they soon discovered that she had very un-English ways. For instance, she thought nothing of copying from some one else's book! She had a quick brain, but she was often lazy—and then she would simply copy the answers set down by the girl next to her. This was Mirabel, whose brains were not of the highest order. So,

more often than not, Claudine copied down mistakes.
But she did not seem to mind at all.

'Look here—we oughtn't to let Claudine cheat like
this,' said Pat. 'She keeps *on* copying from Mirabel.
Mirabel says Claudine didn't bother to do a single sum—
she copied the answers of all hers!'

'The funny thing is, she does it so openly,' said Isabel.
'I mean—I really don't believe she thinks it's wrong!'

Claudine was very astonished when Susan Howes, the
head girl of the form, spoke to her about the copying.

'It's cheating, Claudine; surely you can see that!'
said Susan, her honest face glowing scarlet, for she did
not like accusing any one of cheating.

'No, I do not see it at all,' said Claudine. 'You all
see me do it. Cheating is a secret thing.'

'No, it isn't,' said Susan. 'Cheating is cheating
whether you do it in front of any one, or on the sly.
Besides, it's so silly of you to copy from Mirabel. She
gets so many answers wrong. Miss Ellis will find out and
then you'll get into a row.'

'You think then it would be better to copy from
Hilary?' asked Claudine, seriously. Susan sighed.

'Claudine, you mustn't copy from *any* one. I know
French people have different ideas from ours—Mam'zelle
has, for instance—but you'll have to try and get into our
ways if you're going to be happy here.'

'I am happy anywhere,' said Claudine at once. 'Well,
Susan, I will perhaps not copy again—only if I have not
done any of my prep at all.'

Another thing that the girls found irritating about
Claudine was the way she borrowed things. She borrowed pencils, rubbers, rulers, books—anything she happened to want at the moment. And nine times out of
ten she didn't give them back.

'I forget,' she explained. 'I borrow a pencil and I use
it, and I am most grateful for it—and then I forget about

it, and poor Hilary, she says, " Where is my pencil, I have lost my pencil "—and there it is on my desk all the time, not at all lost.'

' Well, you might *try* and remember to give back things you borrow,' said Hilary. ' After all, it was a silver pencil of mine you borrowed, one I like very much. And you might ask permission before you borrow things.'

' Oh, you English ! ' sighed Claudine. ' Well, I will be good, and always I will say " Dear Hilary, please, please lend me your so-beautiful silver pencil." '

Hilary laughed. No one could help being amused by Claudine. She rolled her expressive black eyes round and used her hands in the same way that Mam'zelle did. After all, she hadn't been in England very long—she would learn English ways before the term was over !

4   BEWARE OF MATRON!

THE first few weeks passed, and soon the fourth-formers, those who had come up from the third form, felt as if they had always been in the fourth form ! They looked down on the third-formers, and as for the second- and first-form girls, well, they were very small fry indeed. No fourth-former would have dreamed of taking any notice of them.

The summer term was always a nice one. There was tennis, and there was swimming. Angela proved to be an unexpectedly good swimmer, deft and swift. Alison, who disliked the water, did her best to shine in it in order to try and keep up with her beloved Angela.

Claudine frankly hated the water. She entirely refused to go in, much to the games-mistress's annoyance.

' Claudine ! What is the use of coming to an English

school if you do not learn the good things in it ? ' she said.

' Swimming is not a good thing,' said Claudine.   ' It is a horrible thing, wet and cold and shivery.   And I do not like your habit of playing so many games.   Tennis is also silly.'

As no one could undress Claudine by force, she did not go into the water.   The others teased her by splashing her as much as they could.   The games-mistress saw that sooner or later Claudine would be pushed in, fully-dressed, and she sent her back to the school.

Claudine's tennis was even worse than Carlotta's. Carlotta had never managed to play properly.   She was still very wild and uncontrolled in games, and the tennis ball was quite as likely to drop into the middle of the distant swimming-pool as over the tennis net !   But Claudine did not even attempt to hit the ball !

' This is a so-silly game,' she would say, and put down her racket and go off by herself.

' But Claudine, it's your tennis-practice time.   You *must* come,' Hilary would say.

' I must not,' was Claudine's reply, and that was that.

Angela played a neat and deft game.   She always brought her three beautiful rackets out with her, in spite of every one's teasing.   Pauline was jealous of them. She tried to pay Angela out by being spiteful.

' I've two or three more rackets at home,' she said in a loud voice.   ' But it isn't good manners to bring more than one to school.   My mother says that would be showing off.   No well-bred person shows off.'

Nobody liked Angela's conceit, but nobody liked Pauline's spite, either.   In fact, few people liked Pauline for, rich and grand as she made out her people and her home to be, she was a plain and unattractive girl—unlike Angela, who was really lovely.   Nobody could help looking at the angel-faced Angela without admiration and pleasure. Alison thought she was the prettiest girl she had ever seen.

Eileen was moderately good at both tennis and swimming. She was moderately good at her lessons too. She took a liking to Alison, for some reason or other, and was very upset when Alison showed her far too plainly that she had no time for her.

'*Why* can't you sometimes walk with me when we go out in the afternoons?' Eileen said to Alison. 'You can't *always* walk with Angela. And *why* do you always refuse when I offer you sweets? They won't poison you!'

'I know,' said Alison, coldly. 'I just don't want them, that's all. And I don't particularly want to walk with you, either.'

'I suppose Angela told you not to!' said Eileen, angrily. 'You haven't got any mind of your own, have you? Whatever Angela thinks, *you* think! Whatever Angela does, *you* do! You're even trying to grow your hair the way she grows hers—down to your shoulders and curled under. Well, you look a perfect fright like that!'

Alison was very offended. She looked coldly at Eileen.

'Well, if you want to know, Angela doesn't approve of you, and as she is my friend, I respect her wishes. Anyway, I don't approve of you, either. You're a tell-tale!'

Eileen walked away, her face scarlet with rage. Alison's last hit had gone home. Eileen ran to her mother with tales, and there was nothing the fourth form did that the new Matron did not know about.

Worse than that, if Eileen told her mother that some one had been horrid to her, the Matron soon saw to it that that some one was called to her room, and shown a huge rent in one of her bed-sheets to mend, or holes in her games stockings, or buttons off vests.

'I believe she makes the holes on purpose and pulls the buttons off herself!' raged Angela, who had been given three stockings to darn in her spare-time. ' I've never darned a stocking in my life. What's a matron for if she doesn't keep our things mended ? '

' Well, it is the rule at St. Clare's that we do some of our own mending,' said Pat. ' But I must say, Angela, I can't think that you made all those enormous holes in your stockings ! I've never seen you with a hole yet.'

' Oh, I *know* I didn't make them,' said Angela, trying in vain to thread a needle with wool. ' *How* do you make the wool go through the needle's eye ? I've been trying to thread this for ages.'

The girls laughed. Angela had no idea how to double over the end of the wool and thread the darning-needle in the right way. Alison took the needle and stocking away from her.

' I'll do your darning, Angela,' she said. ' Don't worry. I bet it's that tell-tale Eileen that ran to her mother about something you said or did—and so Matron gave you this work to do out of spite.'

Alison darned the three stockings—not very well, it is true, because darning was not one of Alison's gifts. But Angela was grateful, and was so sweet to Alison that the girl was in the seventh heaven of delight.

Pauline was the next to get into trouble with Matron. She, like Angela, turned up her nose at Eileen, and would have no more to do with her than she could help. When she told Bobby one morning that she had a sore throat, Eileen overheard. She went off out of the room, and in a short while Pauline was sent for.

' I hear you have a sore throat, Pauline,' said Matron, with a thin-lipped smile. ' You should report to me at once. Eileen felt worried about you, and told me. It was very kind of her. I have a gargle for you here, and some medicine.'

' Oh, my throat is much better now,' said Pauline in alarm. And it was—but Matron was not going to let her

off. She made poor Pauline gargle for ten minutes with
a horrible concoction, and then gave her some equally
nasty medicine to drink.

Pauline went back to the others, angry and afraid.
She glanced round the room to make sure that Eileen was
not there.

' Eileen's been telling tales again,' she said. ' She told
her mother I'd got a sore throat—and I've just been
having an awful time. I feel quite sick. I know Eileen
told Matron she didn't like me, and that's why Matron
gave me such a beastly time.'

' We'll have to be careful what we say and do to Eileen,'
said Alison, scared, for she hated medicine of any sort.
' Perhaps we'd better be friendlier.'

' I shall not be friendlier,' said Claudine. ' That is a
girl I do not like.'

And, far from being friendlier, Claudine really seemed
to go out of her way to be rude to Eileen ! The result
was that Matron came down heavily on Claudine, and
gave her a whole basketful of mending to do !

' You have torn the hem of both your sheets,' she told
Claudine. ' And you have holes in all your stockings,
and you need a patch in one of your vests. You are a
very naughty, careless girl. You will do most of this
mending yourself, as a punishment.'

Claudine said nothing. She took the basket of mending
and put it on top of her locker. At first the girls thought
she would simply forget all about it, and refuse to do it,
as she refused to do other things. But, to their surprise,
Claudine took down the mending and settled herself in a
corner of the common room to do it.

Bobby watched her needle flying in and out. ' I say—
you do sew beautifully ! ' she said. ' You really do ! And
your darning is as good as embroidery. It's beautiful.'

' I like sewing and darning,' said Claudine. ' We are
always taught that well in France. You English girls are

clumsy with your needles. You can bang all kinds of silly balls about, but you cannot make a beautiful darn ! '

' Claudine, put that mending away now, and come out and swim,' said Susan. ' It's such a nice sunny day.'

But nice sunny days did not appeal to Claudine at all. ' I can see the sun out of the window,' she said, sewing away hard. ' Leave me. I like sewing.'

Bobby stared hard at the bent head of the little French girl. Then she gave a chuckle.

' Claudine, you like sewing a whole lot better than you like swimming and games, don't you ? ' she said.

' Yes,' said Claudine. ' Sewing is very okay, I think.'

The others laughed. Claudine always sounded funny when she brought American slang into her speech.

' I believe this is all a little trick of Claudine's,' said Bobby. ' She wants to have a real excuse for getting out of games ! We all know we have to give up games time if we have mending to do—and Claudine has made Matron give her a punishment that will get her out of games, and give her something to do instead that she really likes ! '

Miss Ellis came into the room. ' Hurry up and go out, girls,' she said. ' Don't waste a minute of this nice fine day. Claudine, put away your sewing.'

' I'm sorry, Miss Ellis, but Matron said I was to do my darning and mending before I could go to play with the others,' said Claudine, looking up with big innocent dark eyes. ' It is very sad—but I suppose I must do this, Miss Ellis ? '

' Hmm,' said Miss Ellis, not at all taken in by the wide-open eyes. ' I'll have a word with Matron.'

But Matron was quite insistent that Claudine had been careless, and must mend her things, so Miss Ellis left the girl to her sewing. And Claudine had a very nice time, sewing away happily in a corner of the sunny room, hearing the shouts of the girls in the swimming-pool. She had no wish whatever to join them!

'Horrible wet cold water!' she thought to herself, and then looked up as she heard footsteps coming into the room. It was her aunt, Mam'zelle.

'Ah, *ma petite*!' said Mam'zelle, beaming. 'So you are here. Let me see your sewing. It is beautiful! Why cannot these English girls sew? Where are the others?'

'In the water,' said Claudine, in French. 'Always they are in the water, or hitting a ball, these English girls. Me, I prefer to sew, *ma tante*!'

'Quite right, little Claudine!' said Mam'zelle, who, for all her years in England had never been able to understand why English girls liked cold water, hitting balls, and running madly about. 'You are happy, my little one?'

'Yes, thank you, *ma tante*,' answered Claudine demurely. 'But I am a little dull. Does nothing ever happen in these English schools?'

'Nothing,' said Mam'zelle. But she was wrong. Things did happen—and they were just about to!

5   ANGELA GETS A SURPRISE

ABOUT the third week of the term, when every one had settled down, and got into their work, Angela had a surprise.

She had been playing tennis, and one of the balls had been lost. 'Don't let's bother to look for it now,' said Bobby, who hated to stop in the middle of a game. 'It's sure to turn up. Tennis balls always do. If it doesn't we'll look for it afterwards.'

The ball hadn't turned up, and Angela had offered to look for it. The others had music-lessons to go to, or elocution practice. Angela was the only one free.

' All right,' said Hilary. ' Thanks, Angela. You look for the ball, and pop it back into the box with the others if you find it.'

The other three girls ran back to the school, and Angela began to look for the lost ball. It was nowhere to be seen. The court they had been playing on backed on to a high wall, and Angela wondered if the ball could possibly have gone over it.

' I remember Bobby sending a pretty high ball once,' she thought to herself. ' Well, it doesn't seem to be *this* side of the wall—so I'll just slip out of the garden gate here and look in the lane.'

The girl opened the gate and went out into the narrow green lane. She looked about for the ball, and at last saw it. As she went to get it, she gave a start of surprise. A tall, rather thin youth was behind the bush near the ball.

Angela picked up the ball and was about to go back into the school grounds, when the boy spoke to her.

' I say—do you belong to St. Clare's ? '

Angela looked at him and didn't like him. He had hair that was curly, and much too long. His eyes were small and puffy underneath, and he was very pale.

' What business is it of yours whether I belong to St. Clare's or not ? ' said Angela, in her haughtiest voice.

' Now look here—don't go all stuffy and stupid,' said the boy, coming out from behind the bush. ' I just want a word with you.'

' Well, I don't want a word with *you*,' said Angela, and she opened the garden gate. The boy tried to stop her going through.

' Wait a bit,' he said, and his voice sounded so urgent that Angela turned round in surprise. ' I want you to take a message to one of the girls for me,' he said.

The boy tried to stop Angela

'Of course I shan't do that,' said Angela, 'Let me pass, please. You deserve to be reported for this.'

'Listen. You tell Eileen that Eddie wants to see her,' said the boy. 'Wait—I've got a note for her. Will you give it to her?'

'Oh—so you're Eileen's brother, are you?' said Angela. 'All right—I'll give her the note. But I can't think why you don't come right in and see your mother and Eileen too, if you want to. Your mother is Matron here, isn't she?'

'Yes,' said Eddie. 'But for goodness' sake don't go and tell my mother you've seen me. She doesn't know I'm here. I'd get into an awful row with her if she knew I was.'

'Your mother gets lots of people into rows besides you!' said Angela, taking the note.

The girl went through the gate and shut it. Then she stuffed the note into the pocket of her blazer, meaning to give it to Eileen when she saw her.

Eileen was not about when Angela went back to the cloakroom to change her shoes. The girl saw Alison there and began to tell her what had happened.

'I say, Alison!' she said, 'A funny thing happened just now. I went out into the lane to look for a tennis ball, and there was a boy there, hiding.'

'Gracious!' said Alison, startled. 'What did you do?'

'He was an awful creature,' said Angela, beginning to exaggerate, as she usually did when she had a tale to tell. 'Honestly, he looked like the boy who brings the fish here every day—you know, that awful boy with the too-long hair and the piercing whistle! I half expected him to say "I've brought the 'addock and 'ake and 'alibut, miss!" like the fish-boy said to Matron the other day, thinking she was the cook.'

Alison laughed. So did one or two other girls in the

cloakroom. Angela loved an admiring audience. She
went on with her tale, not seeing that Eileen had come
in to put away gym. shoes.

' Well, he asked me if I belonged to St. Clare's, and I
put him properly in his place, you may be sure ! And
then he told me who he was. You'll never guess ! '

The girls crowded round her in interest. ' Who ? '
said Alison. ' How should we know who it was ? '

' Well, it was dear, darling wonderful Eddie, Eileen's
big brother ! ' said Angela. ' As common as could be !
I nearly asked him why he didn't get his hair cut ! '

Some one elbowed her way roughly through the group
round Angela. It was Eileen, her cheeks scarlet. She
glared at Angela.

' You frightful fibber ! ' she said. ' My brother's nowhere near St. Clare's ! How dare you make up a story
like that ? I shall go and tell my mother at once—you
hateful, horrid little snob ! '

She burst into tears and went out of the door. The
girls stared after her.

' I say ! ' said Alison, ' she really *will* go to Matron—
and there's sure to be a row. You didn't make it up,
did you, Angela ? '

Angela raised her voice and shouted after Eileen.
' Well, go and tell if you like—but your darling Eddie
begged and begged me *not* to let your mother know he
was here. So you are just as likely to get *him* into a
row, as me ! '

Eileen turned round, looking scared. It was plain that
she now believed what Angela said. It *had* been Eddie !

' What did he say to you ? ' she asked Angela, in a
strangled voice. ' Did he want to see me ? '

' Shan't tell you,' said Angela, in an irritating voice, ' I
was going to do you a good turn and give you his message
—but if you behave like this I'm jolly well not going to
be a go-between for you and dear, darling Eddie ! '

Just at that very thrilling moment Miss Ellis put her head in at the door, looking most annoyed.

'Girls! Didn't you hear the bell? What in the world are you doing, chattering here in the cloakroom? You know that isn't allowed. Really, I do wish you fourth-formers would realize that you are half-way up the school and not in the first form! I am most annoyed at having to come and fetch you.'

'Sorry, Miss Ellis,' said every one, and hurried to go out of the cloakroom back to the classroom, where they had prep to do. Certainly they had heard the bell—but who could tear themselves away when a first-class quarrel was going on between the angelic Angela, and the unpopular Eileen?

Angela felt delighted when she sat down at her desk. Now she had Eileen exactly where she wanted her—under her thumb! And if Eileen ever told tales of her again and got Matron to give her heaps of mending to do, she, Angela, would threaten to tell Matron about dear Eddie! Angela smiled a secret smile to herself, which made her look more like an angel than ever. It was extraordinary how Angela could look so innocently beautiful when she was thinking spiteful thoughts!

Eileen saw the secret smile. She pursed her lips together and ground her teeth. She hated Angela bitterly in that moment, with as deep a hatred as the love she had for Eddie. How dared Angela call Eddie common? How dared she say he was like that horrid little fishmonger's boy, with his long, greasy hair and shrill whistle?

To Eileen her brother Edgar was the most wonderful being in the world. Their father had died when they were both very young, and their mother was a hard and stern woman. The little girl had turned to her big brother for love and companionship, and the boy had guarded and cherished his sister tenderly.

' As soon as I grow up, I'll get a fine job, and make heaps of money for you and Mother,' he told Eileen. ' Then Mother won't need to work so hard and be so tired and cross, and you shall have lots of nice presents. You'll see what wonderful things I'll do ! '

And now Angela had poured scorn on to darling, kind Eddie. Eileen felt as if she must burst with anger and tears. She was very anxious too. Why had Eddie left Woolaton, where he worked, and come to see her secretly ? What had happened ? Oh, if only that beast of an Angela would tell her !

Eileen thought of Eddie out there in the lane. She had not seen him for some weeks, and she was longing to talk to him and tell him everything. Perhaps he felt the same and had got some time off to slip along and see her. Perhaps he didn't want to come up to the school, because then he would have to see Mother too, and that would spoil the heart-to-heart talk they might have together.

Eileen looked at Angela. The girl was studying her French book, looking serene and lovely. Eileen gritted her teeth again, knowing that she would soon have to do something very difficult, something she would hate, and which yet would have to be done gracefully.

' I'll have to go and beg Angela's pardon and ask her to tell me what Eddie said,' thought Eileen. ' Beast ! I do hate her ! '

She gave a loud sigh. Miss Ellis looked up. She had already seen that Eileen was making no attempt at all to do her prep.

' Eileen, don't you feel well ? ' she inquired. ' As far as I can see you haven't done any work at all.'

' I'm all right, thank you, Miss Ellis,' said Eileen hurriedly. ' This—this French is a bit difficult today, that's all.'

' I should think it must be *very* difficult to learn your French out of your geography book,' said Miss Ellis in her calm voice. Eileen looked hurriedly down at her book—dash—it was her geography book she was holding ! Trust the sharp eyes of Miss Ellis to spot that !

She said nothing, but got out her French book. Angela looked round and gave a scornful little smile. She knew quite well why it was that Eileen muddled her books just then—she was worried about dear darling Eddie. Well—let her worry !

Alison sat next to Eileen, and she couldn't help feeling a little sorry for her. Although she was such a little scatter-brain, Alison was sensitive to the feelings of others, and she knew that Eileen was desperately longing to know about Eddie. So, after prep was over she went to Angela and spoke to her.

' I say, Angela—hadn't you better tell Eileen her brother's message ? She's in an awful state. She sighed so hard in prep that she almost blew my papers off the desk ! '

Angela was not amused at Alison's feeble little joke, neither did she like her giving her advice of any sort. She turned away, and Alison's heart sank. Now Angela was going to go all cold and sulky again. The beautiful little face was hard and haughty, and Alison knew it would be ages before she could get a smile out of her again.

She was just going after her when Eileen came up, a forced smile on her face. ' Angela ! Can I speak to you for a minute ? Alone, please ? '

6   ANGELA AND EILEEN

' I'M busy,' said Angela, curtly.

' No, you're not,' said Eileen, trying to speak calmly and smilingly. ' It's important, Angela.'

'I hope you're going to apologize for your rudeness to me,' said Angela, haughtily. 'I certainly shan't speak to you unless you do. I'm not going to let people like you call me a hateful horrid snob.'

Eileen swallowed hard and forced herself to speak, though the words almost choked her.

'I beg your pardon, Angela. I—I just lost my temper!'

Carlotta overheard this conversation and unexpectedly came to Eileen's help. 'Well, if you ask *my* opinion I think Angela ought to apologize to *you*, Eileen, for some of *her* remarks!' said Carlotta, in her fresh, candid voice. 'I'm jolly certain I wouldn't apologize to *her*—little cat!'

Angela turned on Carlotta in a fury, her blue eyes gleaming with spite.

'You don't suppose we care what circus-folk think, do you?' she said. But instead of being crushed, Carlotta gave one of her hearty laughs.

'If I wasn't in the fourth form I'd give you the hardest slap you've ever had in your life, Angela,' she said, amiably. 'A good spanking would be the best thing you could have.'

'Nobody has ever laid a finger on me in my life,' said Angela, feeling an intense desire to smack Carlotta's vivid little face.

'I can tell that,' said Carlotta. 'You'd be a lot nicer if they had. Come on, Eileen, leave Angela to her haughty ways and come and play cards with me in the common room.'

Eileen felt very grateful to Carlotta for her unexpected help, but she shook her head. She had simply *got* to find out about Eddie. How unfortunate it was that it should be Angela, of all people, that he had spoken to. Any of the others would have been decent about it—except Pauline perhaps.

Carlotta shrugged her shoulders and went off to find Bobby and the twins. She didn't like Eileen very much, because she thought, as the others did, that she was a tell-tale—but all the same Angela was behaving like a little cat to her, putting out those claws of hers and giving as deep a scratch as she could !

Angela turned to Eileen. 'Well,' she said, 'you've apologized and I accept your apology. What do you want to say to me ? '

' Angela, *please* tell me what Eddie said,' begged Eileen. ' Did he give you a message for me ? '

' Yes. He gave me a letter,' said Angela. Eileen went red with excitement and stared at Angela eagerly.

' Please give it to me,' she said.

' I don't see why I should,' said Angela. ' I don't think I *ought* to take notes and deliver them, like this.'

Eileen knew that Angela was saying this to irritate her. She felt intensely angry, but she kept her temper.

' You'll never have to do it again,' she said. ' I'll tell Edgar he mustn't send in notes this way. He must post a letter. Please give me the note.'

' Now, listen,' said Angela, suddenly getting down to business, ' if I give you this note and don't tell your mother I saw her precious Eddie, you've got to promise *me* something.'

' What ? ' asked Eileen, in surprise. ' I'll promise you anything ! '

' All right,' said Angela. ' You've jolly well got to promise me that you'll never run sneaking to your mother about *me*, see ? I'm not going to have shoals of mending to do any more—I hate sewing and darning ! I know you complained to Matron about me before, and that's why she presented me with stockings that had holes in *I* never made ! '

' You're not to say things like that about my mother,' said Eileen.

' Well, I shall,' said Angela. ' We all know you sneak to her about us. Sneak about the others all you like—but don't you sneak about *me* any more. You'll be sorry if you do.'

There was nothing for it but to promise. So Eileen promised. ' I won't sneak about you,' she said in a trembling voice. ' I don't sneak. If Mother hands out sewing and mending, it's not my fault.'

' Hmm,' said Angela, disbelievingly, ' well, all I can say is—it's a funny thing that as soon as any one dares to say anything about you, Matron heaps a beastly lot of mending on to them, so that they have to miss games and swimming. Anyway, Eileen, I warn you—you've got to tell your mother nice things about me, or I'll tell tales of *you*, and say I've seen Eddie and he didn't want his mother to know ! '

Eileen bit her lip. It was very hard to keep her temper during this long speech. But she knew she had to, for Eddie's sake.

' I've apologized to you, Angela, and I've promised you what you want,' she said, in a low voice. ' Please give me the note now.'

Angela fished in her pocket for the note. She was a long time about it, pretending she had lost it, feeling in her blouse for it as well as in her pockets. Eileen hated her for this petty meanness, but she stood waiting patiently whilst Angela looked.

At last Angela produced the note. Eileen snatched it from her and without another word went off by herself to read it. It was very short.

DARLING SIS, [said the note]

I must see you. Don't say a word to Mother. We simply must have a talk. Can you meet me outside the garden-door in the wall, any time this evening ? I'll wait behind a bush till you come.

Your loving brother,
EDDIE.

Eileen read the note three times and then tore it up.

She was afraid her mother might find it, and then she would be angry with Eddie. Mother wasn't very sympathetic, somehow. She didn't seem to think much of Eddie, and was always telling him what a fine man his father had been and how curious it was that Eddie hadn't done much good at school, or won any scholarships, or made her really proud of him.

' I'll slip down to the garden-door and see Eddie as soon as all the others are safely in the common room,' thought Eileen. ' Poor old Eddie—he must have been waiting a long time. He couldn't send a letter through the post, because Mother would have been sure to see it, and would have asked to read it.'

The girl waited until she saw that all the fourth-formers were in their common room. She sat by the door and watched them. Doris and Carlotta were fooling about and the others were watching them, laughing. Claudine got up to join the two who were clowning, and Eileen saw that now was her chance. She slipped out.

But one person saw her go. That was Angela, who had been expecting Eileen to slip away down to the lane. It was forbidden for the girls to go out of the school grounds without permission after evening prep, and Angela smiled spitefully to herself.

' If Eileen makes a habit of meeting dear brother Eddie out of hours, I shall be able to hold that over her, too,' thought Angela. She went out of the room and walked into a little music-room that overlooked the school grounds. It was difficult to see any one in the trees and bushes, but because she knew exactly where to look, Angela was able to catch a glimpse of Eileen now and again, hurrying through the trees to the little gate in the wall.

She went back to the common room. Doris, Carlotta and Claudine were still fooling about, keeping every one in fits of laughter. Doris was a wonderful mimic, Carlotta could do extraordinary tricks, and Claudine could imitate Mam'zelle, her aunt, to perfection.

Angela could not see anything to laugh at at all. ' Do they really think it's funny, to pull faces and make themselves ugly and stupid-looking ? ' she thought to herself, as she watched Doris imitating an old charwoman, and Claudine playing up to her as a French maid. She patted her beautiful pale gold hair, comparing it with Carlotta's wild mop. A smug little smile came on her lovely face. She knew she was more beautiful than any other girl in the school ! What did brains and gifts matter ? Every one stared at her in the street, every one thought she must be a princess at least. And perhaps one day she would marry a prince and be a real princess ! Angela dreamed away, not listening to the chatter around her at all.

Two people watched her, one with envy and the other with devoted admiration. The first was Pauline, who, plain and unattractive, envied Angela her beauty, and longed with all her heart to look like her. But her own perfectly straight hair, well-brushed as it was, would never shine like Angela's, nor would it curl under at the ends, as Angela's did, so prettily. Angela's eyes were a brilliant, startling blue—Pauline's were pale. Angela's cheeks were a beautiful rosy pink. Pauline's seldom had any colour. It was too bad that Angela had so much and she, Pauline, had so little in the way of looks !

The other person watching Angela, was, of course, her devoted slave, Alison. She wondered if Angela had forgiven her for offering advice about Eileen. She tried to catch Angela's eye, but Angela was lost in beautiful day-dreams.

' You do look so lovely, Angela,' whispered Alison, at last. Angela heard and smiled prettily. She had forgotten that she was offended with Alison She spoke to her in a low voice, boasting of her conquest of Eileen.

' I ticked Eileen off properly for being a sneak,' she said to Alison. ' I forbade her ever to sneak again, and she promised she wouldn't.'

' Oh, Angela—did you really make her promise thát ? ' said Alison. ' You're wonderful, you really are ! ' She looked round the common room. ' I say—where *is* Eileen ? '

' Would you like to know ? ' said Angela, looking at the expensive gold watch on her wrist, and seeing that there were only five minutes to go before bed-time. ' Well, come with me and I'll see if I can show you where our dear Eileen is ! '

She took Alison into the little music-room. ' See the school wall, right down there ? ' she said. ' You know the little door let into it there, behind the tennis-courts ? Well, I think Eileen has gone through there into the lane to talk to dear, darling Eddie ! '

' Look—is that Eileen coming back ? ' said Alison. ' Golly, she'll get into a row if she's caught ! '

' Yes—it's Eileen all right,' said Angela, as a figure came into view between the trees and then disappeared again. ' Let's wait outside the common-room door and catch her as she comes in ! '

So the two waited there. Eileen came quickly up the passage to the room, and Angela spoke to her.

' Well—how's dear darling Eddie ? '

Eileen stared at her, hardly seeming to see her. She looked pale and worried. She pushed at the shut door of the common room, meaning to go and fetch her night-dress, which she had been mending. But Angela stopped her.

' You didn't answer my question,' she said, in a smooth little voice. ' How's dear darling Eddie ? '

Eileen faced the spiteful girl. ' Eddie's all right,' she said, in a trembling voice. ' Eddie's fine. He had lots of good news to tell me. He's getting on well.'

She went into the common room. Alison felt uncomfortable again. She didn't like this teasing, there was something spiteful in it—but how could she dare to find fault with the Honourable Angela?

7 CLAUDINE GETS HER OWN WAY

'THIS is a jolly nice term,' said Pat to Isabel, as they dried themselves after swimming in the big bathing-pool. 'I simply adore all this open-air life—tennis and swimming and riding and gardening—and today we even had lessons out-of-doors, it was so hot!'

Isabel grinned. 'Poor old Claudine doesn't like the open air as much as we do!' she said. 'Wasn't she funny in maths?'

Claudine had indeed been funny. To begin with she had been quite horrified to hear that Miss Ellis proposed to take lessons out-of-doors under the trees. Apparently no school she had ever been to had ever thought of doing such a thing.

'Lessons out-of-doors!' said the little French girl. 'But why? What is the matter with indoors? I do not like this out-of-doors—the sun is too hot, it burns me.'

'Pity it doesn't burn you a bit more,' grinned Bobby, who was as brown as an acorn. 'Look at us, all brown and tanned—and you are like a lily, pale and white.'

Claudine looked down at her lily-white hands with great satisfaction. 'That is another thing I do not understand about you so-jolly English girls,' she said. 'It is not pretty to get burnt, it is ugly to grow freckles—and yet you try to grow as brown as you can, all day long! Me, I like to be white-skinned. It is more natural, more becoming. And now—what can Miss Ellis be thinking of to say lessons out-of-doors! I shall take a sunshade with me, for I will not grow one single freckle.'

But Miss Ellis did not approve of sunshades being brought out in a maths lesson. She looked at Claudine with disapproval. ' I don't know if you are merely being funny, Claudine, or if you seriously think that you need a sunshade under the trees, where there is no sun—but whatever your reason, the sunshade must go back to the school at once. I can't imagine where you got it!'

The sunshade had been used in a play, and was simply enormous. Claudine was quite lost under it. She looked at Miss Ellis pathetically.

' Please, *chère* Miss Ellis, I am not making a joke, it is because I do not wish to grow a freckle on my nose,' she said, beseechingly. ' A freckle is not for a French girl. Freckles are English, Miss Ellis, and I do not want to grow them.'

' Oh, freckles can be French as much as English!' said Miss Ellis. ' It will do your pale face good to have a few nice brown freckles here and there, Claudine. Take the sunshade back, please, and don't bring it out again.'

' Oh please, Miss Ellis, couldn't Claudine and I share the sunshade ? ' said Angela, who also had a fear of freckles. Her face was tanned a rosy-brown, and she had no freckles at all—she was careful not to get too sun-burnt, for she knew that would spoil her delicate beauty. She gave Bobby's face a scornful glance. It was absolutely covered with little brown freckles, right to the tip of the up-turned nose. ' I couldn't bear to get freckled like poor Bobby,' went on Angela, no spite showing in her smooth little voice. ' This sun is so hot, Miss Ellis—just see how it has treated Bobby!'

' Don't you believe it,' said Bobby, not standing any nonsense of that sort. ' My face is freckled winter and summer alike. Nothing to do with the summer sun! I was born with freckles!'

The class giggled, and Bobby opened her mouth to continue. But Miss Ellis knew Bobby's speeches, and spoke first !

'That will do, Bobby. I don't want any more of the maths lesson wasted on freckles. Claudine, take the sunshade back. Angela, don't look as if you are going to faint away—it would do both you and Claudine good to get a few freckles—Claudine because she sits too much indoors, and you because you think too much of your looks. It would be better if you thought a little more about your work. You may think it is amusing to be bottom each week, as you have been so far, but I must say I can't see the joke.'

Angela flushed. How horrid Miss Ellis could be ! She caught a satisfied smile on Pauline's face. Pauline was cleverer than Angela—that was one way in which she was better than Angela, anyhow ! Angela scowled and glanced at Alison for comfort. Alison gave it, smiling adoringly, and making a face at Miss Ellis.

Lessons out-of-doors were not a success at all, with Claudine in the class. She screamed whenever an insect flew near, and if a bird dared to fly suddenly out of a bush, she made every one jump by her yells. Miss Ellis got very tired of her.

' *Now* what's the matter, Claudine ? ' she said, when a bee flew near the girl and hummed in her ear. Claudine had squealed, jumped up and run to the other end of the long table on which every one was working.

' It is an animal that goes " Zzzz " and carries a sting, Miss Ellis,' said Claudine, looking genuinely frightened.

' A bee,' said Miss Ellis, in disgust. ' It won't sting you. Sit down. You are disturbing all the others.'

The next thing that upset Claudine was an ant. It crawled up her leg and she suddenly felt it. She gave such an agonized yell that every one jumped violently.

'CLAUDINE! I shall send you indoors if you squeal again!' said Miss Ellis in exasperation. 'What's the matter now?'

Claudine was undoing her suspender with trembling hands, giving little squeals and French exclamations all the time. The ant had explored the inside of the top of her stocking. The girls went into fits of laughter, and Miss Ellis rapped angrily on her table.

'Claudine, what are you doing? Surely you are not taking off your stockings!'

Claudine was deaf to anything that Miss Ellis said. When she at last saw the ant, inside her stocking, she did not dare to touch it, and gazed round with such an agonized expression on her face that Bobby took pity on her, and flicked the ant deftly on to the grass.

'Ah!' said Claudine. '*Merci bien*, Bobbee! What a terrible thing to happen to me!'

'Much more terrible things will happen to you if I have any more disturbance,' said Miss Ellis, in such a grim tone that Claudine was much astonished. She sat down again, doing up her suspender.

'One more squeal from you and you go indoors,' said Miss Ellis. Claudine gazed at her thoughtfully. If there was one thing more than another that Claudine wanted at that moment it was to go indoors, where creatures that flew and crawled did not molest her.

She waited until Miss Ellis had bent her head to correct Hilary's book, and then she let out a piercing yell that made her neighbour, Pauline, jump so violently that she upset the ink over the table. Miss Ellis leapt to her feet, her usual calmness quite deserting her.

'Claudine! This behaviour is intolerable. Go indoors at once and find the Mistress in the teachers' common room who is free at the moment. Tell her I sent you in in disgrace and ask her to let her sit with you, whilst you do your maths. And if there is a single mistake in your

Everyone jumped as Claudine gave an agonized yell

paper I shall have a great deal to say about it. I am thoroughly displeased with you.'

With the greatest cheerfulness and alacrity Claudine obeyed Miss Ellis, scurrying indoors with her books before the mistress could change her mind. Doris exploded into one of her giggles. Miss Ellis glanced at her sharply, and Doris subsided. It then occurred to Miss Ellis that Claudine, as usual, had got exactly what she wanted, in her usual unscrupulous way !

Miss Ellis wondered who the mistress was who would be in the teachers' common room just then. She thought it would be Miss Rollins. That was good. Miss Rollins was very strict, and would make Claudine feel very small and humble before she had done with her.

But it was not Miss Rollins, much to Claudine's delight. When she knocked timidly on the mistress's common-room door, she ran over in her mind what mistress was likely to be there. She hoped it would be the art mistress—she had a sense of fun and was very jolly.

She opened the door and went in—and she saw that it was Mam'zelle ! Mam'zelle was having a cosy time by herself. She had taken off her big, flat-heeled shoes and had opened the collar of her high-necked blouse. It was such a hot day ! She was half-asleep over her exercise books when the small neat figure of Claudine appeared. They stared at each other.

' Why are you here, Claudine ? ' asked Mam'zelle severely, in French. Claudine at once poured out a voluble and heart-rending explanation—how all the insects and winged beasts of that horrible English out-of-doors had molested her, yes, and bitten her and stung her, and altogether made life not worth living. And the sun had burnt her and she was sure she had dozens of those so-ugly freckles coming, and what would her dear mother say to that ? Ah, life was very very hard at this so-sporting English school, with its love for the cold,

cold water, and for striking at balls so many times a week, and for its detestable nature-walks, and . . .

Mam'zelle sympathized whole-heartedly. She too detested too much sun, and insects and reptiles of any kind filled her with fear and disgust. She forgot to inquire whether Claudine had come in of her own accord, or had been sent in in disgrace. Soon the two were talking nineteen to the dozen, going back in their thoughts to their beloved France, where girls were proper girls, and studied and did sewing and embroidery, and did not rush about in the mad way that all English girls did.

So, later on, when Miss Ellis asked Mam'zelle if she had scolded Claudine properly for being sent indoors in disgrace, Mam'zelle got a shock. She stared at Miss Ellis in dismay.

' Ah, the poor little Claudine ! ' she said at last. ' You must not be too hard on her, Miss Ellis. It is so difficult for a poor little foreign girl to learn your English ways.'

Miss Ellis snorted. ' I suppose that means that you and Claudine patted each other on the back, and that you believed everything the naughty little girl said—and I should think it is very likely that you helped her to do her maths too ! She has never got all her sums right before.'

Mam'zelle felt extremely uncomfortable. She *had* helped Claudine with her work—and certainly she had believed every word she said. Would Claudine deceive her own good aunt ? No, no—impossible !

But when Mam'zelle thought things over she knew that the clever little Claudine could and would deceive her if she felt inclined to. Mam'zelle loved Claudine very much, and thought the world of her—but all the same sometimes a doubt came into her mind—wasn't Claudine just a little *too* clever ? Didn't she get her own way just a little *too* often ? The trouble was—you never knew what Claudine wanted until she had got it, and then it was too late to do anything about it.

'My word,' said Bobby, when the maths lesson came to an end and the girls packed up their books. 'That little monkey of a Claudine can do anything she likes and get away with it I I bet she's had a perfectly lovely time indoors.'

So she had. She came beaming to meet Miss Ellis at the end of the morning, with a prettily-worded apology.

'Ah, Miss Ellis I I am so, so ashamed of myself. You English, you are not frightened of anything, you keep the hairs on your head always, always you are calm—but me, I am a silly little French girl, so please excuse me and I will do better in future. My aunt was veiy, very angry with me, she caused me to cry bitterly, see how red my eyes are I '

Miss Ellis saw no signs of red eyes, and felt quite certain that Mam'zelle had not been angry at all. All the same, she found it difficult to hide a smile. Claudine was so very, very earnest and apologetic I

'I'll forgive you *this* time, Claudine,' she said. ' But you be careful *next* time I '

8   THE TERM GOES ON

ALTHOUGH the girls knew quite well that Claudine told fibs when it suited her, borrowed without asking and still copied answers from other people's books if she wanted to, they couldn't help liking her. She was very funny, generous in her own way, and never took offence whatever was said to her.

She might easily have taken offence at things that Angela said, or Pauline. Angela looked down on her in the same way that she looked down on Eileen—because she was a pupil who was probably not paying the school fees.

'Charity-girls, both of them!' she said to Alison, scornfully. 'I must say I didn't think we'd get them at schools like this.'

If Bobby, Hilary or the twins overheard things like this they ticked Angela off unmercifully.

'Look here,' Pat said once, 'we don't like Eileen any more than you do—but you've got to realize, Angela, that if Eileen's mother gets Eileen here for nothing, it's because of the work she does herself as Matron, and it doesn't matter tuppence if you pay for things in work or in money, it's good payment just the same, and Eileen isn't kept by "charity" as you call it. You're a disgusting little snob.'

Angela hated to be called a snob. She shut her book with a bang. 'Snob!' she said. 'That's a favourite word of yours for some one who happens to be out of the top drawer. Think of something more original to say.'

'Right,' said Bobby, at once. 'You think that Claudine is a charity-girl too—well, instead of saying that to us, what about saying it to Mam'zelle—or even to Claudine herself? You're too cowardly to do that. You'll hit at Eileen because you've got some hold over her and she can't hit back—but you daren't hit at Claudine openly, because she's quite likely to fly at you and scratch your angelic face, or put Mam'zelle on the war-path after you!'

'Oh, you're impossible!' said Angela, angrily. 'I shall ask my mother to take me away at half-term. In fact, when she comes here and sees what kind of girls I have to live with I'm certain she'll take me away with her, then and there!'

'Golly! If only your mother would be sensible enough to *do* that!' sighed Bobby. 'But she won't. I know mothers. She'll leave you here to be a pest to us for the rest of the term.'

Tears of anger came into Angela's eyes. In all her spoilt, petted life she had never been spoken to like this. She was angry, hurt, and miserable. She blinked back her tears, because a tear-stained face spoilt her beauty. She went to find Alison.

Alison could always put soothing ointment on to Angela's wounds. In her usual feather-headed way she made herself quite blind to Angela's grave faults, and saw only the loveliness of Angela's face, and the beauty of her clothes and possessions. Poor Alison always seemed to attach herself to the wrong kind of people.

' She'll never learn ! ' said Hilary. ' I did think once, when she was in the second form, and was so keen on that awful drama mistress, Miss Quentin, that she had learnt a pretty sharp lesson—you remember how Miss Quentin let her down, don't you ? She pretended to be awfully fond of Alison, and then laughed at her behind her back.'

The twins nodded. ' Yes,' said Pat. ' It's really a pity that Alison isn't happy unless she is worshipping someone. She's awfully bad for Angela. As soon as we get a bit of sense into Angela's head, Alison gets it out, by saying she's wonderful, too lovely for words, and all the rest of it.'

' I must say she's not a bit like you two,' said Bobby. ' You've got plenty of common sense. It's funny you should have a cousin like Alison ! '

The weather went on being hot and sunny, with blue skies every day. The girls swam and played games to their hearts' content. They all got very brown, except Claudine who managed to remain pale as a lily in spite of everything. She worried very much one week because she felt sure she had a freckle coming on her nose. The girls teased her unmercifully.

' Golly ! Isn't Claudine's freckle getting pronounced ? ' said Hilary, staring at Claudine's dainty little nose.

'Yes. It's going to be a real beauty,' said Pat.

'Big as a threepenny bit,' said Isabel.

Claudine gave a squeal of horror and fished out the little mirror she always carried with her. She and Angela and Alison always carried small mirrors about with them, and were for ever examining their faces for something or other.

'I have no freckle,' she announced indignantly. 'You talk under your hats !'

The girls laughed. 'Claudine, you talk *through* your hat, not under it,' said Bobby. 'But if you want to keep a secret you keep it *under* your hat ! See ? '

Claudine sighed. 'Ah, your English sayings are so difficult. I will remember—to talk *through* your hat means to be silly—to keep something *under* your hat means to keep a secret. Ah—there goes one who keeps something under her hat !'

The girls turned to see who Claudine meant. It was Eileen Paterson.

'Yes—Eileen does seem to be all bottled up, somehow,' said Hilary, rather worried. 'As if she's got a secret and is afraid some one will get to know it. She's been looking rather miserable sometimes.'

'Well, she's got her mother here to tell anything to,' said Pat. The others made scornful noises.

'Pooh !' said Bobby, 'would *you* tell Matron anything if she were *your* mother ? I know I wouldn't. She's as hard as nails ! I hope to goodness I'm never ill whilst she's here as Matron. I shouldn't fancy being looked after by her !'

The girls were all rather careful in the way they treated Eileen now, because they felt certain that any slight, intended or otherwise, that they showed Eileen, was reported to Matron, and then Matron landed them with all kinds of unexpected mending to do. All except Angela. Angela could say and do what she liked to

Eileen. Matron always seemed to look on Angela with a favourable eye. Eileen did not dare to tell tales of her.

'I think Eileen misses that dear brother of hers,' said Bobby. 'You know what Angela told us—how he came to see her, but didn't want to see his mother. I get he's in some kind of trouble, and Eileen's worried about it.

'Poor Eileen!' said Hilary. 'I'll just pump her a bit and see.'

So Hilary kindly and tactfully 'pumped' Eileen, but she learnt very little.

'How old is your brother, Eileen?' she said. 'Is he like you at all?'

Eileen fetched a snapshot and showed it to Hilary. She seemed glad of the chance of talking about Eddie.

'Eddie's eighteen,' she said. 'Two years older than I am. He's fine, Hilary. But he's never had much chance. You see, my father died when we were so little. Eddie ought to be at college now, but he's got to earn his living.'

Hilary looked at the snap of the rather weak-looking boy in the picture. He looked kind but that was about all one could say.

'What work is he doing?' she asked.

'He's in engineering works,' she said. 'He's doing awfully well. He'll make a lot of money one day.'

'You're not worried about him, are you?' said Hilary, kindly, looking at the flushed face of the girl beside her.

Eileen answered at once. 'Worried about him. 'Of course not! Why should I be? I wish I saw him more often, that's all. You see, until this term, when Mother took this job, we all lived together. Now he's in lodgings and I do miss him a lot.'

Hilary said no more. She still thought that Eileen looked worried, and certainly she did not pay as much attention to her lessons as Miss Ellis expected—but after all, thought Hilary, it was enough to make any one look worried if they had to listen to Matron's grumbles in their spare-time!

Eileen had to help her mother with the school linen every week, and sometimes when the girls passed Matron's room they could hear her grumbling away at Eileen. True, Eileen answered back sometimes, but usually she listened in silence. Some of the girls felt sorry for Eileen, others were glad, because they knew she was a tale-teller when it suited her to pass on things she had heard in the fourth form.

Another week or two went by, and half-term began to come near. Three or four fourth-form birthdays came along too, and there was a good deal of present-buying.

Angela had unlimited pocket-money and bought most extravagant presents. Pauline tried to vie with her and to buy marvellous gifts too. But it was impossible to spend as much as Angela did! She thought nothing of spending ten shillings on a bottle of bath salts or a lace-edged handkerchief.

Eileen gave no presents at all. 'Sorry,' she said to Hilary, whose birthday it was. 'I'd like to give you something—but I've no money at the moment. Many happy returns of the day, anyway!'

'Thanks,' said Hilary, thinking that Eileen could be very straightforward and honest, and liking her at that moment for being courageous enough to own up to having no money at all.

Angela presented Hilary with a magnificent blotter, made of real leather, and decorated very beautifully at the corners. Hilary liked it very much. Then Pauline presented her with a purse on which were Hilary's initials, H.W.W.

'Oh, Pauline—how beautiful!' said Hilary. 'But I wish you wouldn't spend so much money on me! I'm sure you can't afford it!'

This was an unfortunate remark to make to Pauline.

who was very touchy about money, and was always trying to compete with Angela. She flushed and answered stiffly.

' You know that my family, the Bingham-Joneses, are wealthy,' she said, putting on the affected voice that Hilary detested. ' I have as much money as I wish. It's true I don't splash it about in the vulgar way that Angela does—I hope I am better-bred than that. But I have all I ask for, Hilary, so please accept this purse with my best wishes, and don't think it cost any more than I could afford I '

' What with the Bingham-Joneses and the Honourable Favorleighs we're just overwhelmed with high-and-mightiness I ' said Pat to Isabel, with a giggle. ' Well—I think I prefer Pauline of the two—Angela is really too spiteful for words, sometimes—and she says the cattiest things with the most angelic smile on her face I '

' I can't say I think a great deal of any of the four new girls, considering everything,' said Isabel, wrinkling her forehead and thinking. ' Angela's a spiteful snob. Pauline is an envious snob. Claudine is amusing but quite unscrupulous—hasn't any sense of honour at all, as far as I can see—and Eileen is a sneak and a bit of a bore I '

' Golly—you sound pretty catty yourself, Isabel I ' said Pat.

' No, I'm not,' said Isabel, earnestly. ' I'm only just sizing them all up. I'm not like Alison, unable to see beyond a pretty face. And though I don't think much of any of those four, you know jolly well I'd help every one of them if they were in trouble. And if you're really catty, you don't feel like that, do you ? '

' No, you don't,' said Pat. ' You're quite right, old thing—it doesn't matter seeing people for what they are, and even disliking them—so long as you're willing to help if necessary I '

HALF-TERM came along very shortly, and the girls were excited because their parents were coming to see them. There were to be tennis-matches and swimming-matches for the parents to watch. Hilary, Bobby, the twins and one or two others were excited about these, because they hoped to be in the teams.

'I'd like my mother to see me swim under water for the whole length of the bath,' said Bobby. 'She was a very good swimmer herself when she was young. Hope I'm chosen for the swimming-competitions.'

The twins hoped to be in one of the tennis-matches. They were both good at tennis, and it would be lovely for their mother to see them play together and win a match. Both girls were intensely proud of St. Clare's, and badly wanted to show off their school, and their own prowess to the best advantage.

Hilary was to play in a singles match with one of the fifth-formers. She had been chosen for her very graceful style, and it was to be an exhibition match more than a battle. Both girls had a beautiful natural style and the games-mistress was proud of them.

Mirabel was hoping to win the one-length race in the swimming-bath. She was very fast and very strong. Her smaller friend, the mouse-like Gladys, was also in the swimming competitions, for, although she was small, she was a beautiful little swimmer. She was longing for her mother to see her. She had no father and no brother or sister, so her mother was everything to her.

'Half-term will be fun,' said Hilary. 'Is your mother coming, Angela?'

'Of course,' said Angela. 'And Daddy too. I'm

longing to see their new car. It's a Rolls-Bentley, black with a green line, and . . .'

' I bet you're looking forward to seeing the new car more than to seeing your people ! ' said Bobby, with a chuckle. ' You never talk of your parents except in terms of the wealth they own, Angela. Did you know that ? '

Angela looked sulky. ' I don't know what you mean,' she said. ' I guess you'd talk about cars and things if your parents had the same as mine. And you just see my mother when she comes ! She will stand out above every one else. She's absolutely beautiful—golden hair like mine—and the bluest eyes—and she wears the most marvellous clothes . . .'

' And even the safety-pins she uses are made of pure gold set with diamonds,' finished Pat.

' That's not funny,' said Angela, as the others shouted with laughter. ' I tell you, you just wait and see my mother ! She's the most beautiful person you'll ever see.'

' *What* a pity you don't take after her, Angela ! ' said Bobby, sorrowfully. ' Isn't your mother sorry to have a daughter like you ? You must be a terrible disappointment.'

Angela flushed with anger. She could never bear this kind of teasing. ' All right,' she said, in a bitter voice. ' All right. But just wait till you see my mother—and then tell me if she isn't the most wonderful person you ever saw in your lives. I hope she wears her double-string of pearls. They are worth five thousand pounds.'

' Well,' said the soft voice of Gladys, who rarely butted in on any conversation of this sort, ' well, I don't care if *my* mother wears her very oldest clothes, I don't care if she's got a ladder in her stockings, I don't care if she hasn't even powdered her nose—so long as my mother comes to see me and I can be with her for a few hours, she can be the untidiest, ugliest, poorest-dressed there—

but I shall still be proud of her, and think she's the best
of all ! '

This was a long speech for the timid Gladys to make.
Every one was silent when she stopped. Pat found that
she suddenly had tears in her eyes. There was such love
in Gladys's voice—and what she said was fine. That was
the way to love some one—not to care how they looked or
what they did—but just to welcome them all the same !

Even Angela was taken aback. She stared at Gladys
in surprise. She was about to make a sneering remark
but Bobby stopped her.

' Now you shut up,' said Bobby, in a warning voice.
' Gladys has said the last word about mothers, and she's
right. Good for you, Gladys.'

After that Angela said no more, but privately she
rejoiced when she thought of her own beautifully-dressed
mother, and how the girls would have to admire her and
her clothes when she came.

' Are *your* parents coming ? ' said Hilary to Pauline.

' Oh yes,' said Pauline, in a bright voice, and she began
to talk eagerly of them. ' My Father is such a good-
looking man, and Mother is sweet. I do hope she wears
the dress she bought in the holidays—it's really beautiful.
It makes her look so young and pretty.'

Pauline chattered away about her parents, in her way
as much of a snob as Angela, though, far more than
Angela, she talked of them as real people, generous, kind,
amusing, instead of people cluttered up with great
possessions.

' Pauline's people sound rather nice,' said Pat. ' I
shall take a good look at Angela's family—I sort of feel
that her father will wear diamond buttons on his coat
and her mother will wear five or six furs at once ! '

Isabel giggled. ' Well, I'm rather glad that our mother
is just ordinary,' she said, ' pretty and kind and sensible,
just an ordinary nice mother ! '

The girls all practised hard for half-term, swimming and playing tennis as much as they could, so that their parents might be proud of them. There was to be an exhibition of pictures too, done by the girls themselves, and a show of needlework. Here Claudine expected to shine. She had done a really beautiful cushion-cover, on which was embroidered a peacock spreading its lovely tail.

Mam'zelle was intensely proud of this. She bored every one by talking about it. 'It is exquisite!' she said. 'Ah, the clever little Claudine! Miss Ellis, do you not think that Claudine has done the tail most perfectly?'

'I do,' said Miss Ellis. 'Much better than she does her maths or her history, or her geography or her literature, or her . . .'

'Come, come!' said Mam'zelle, hurt. 'It is not given to us to have great gifts at everything. Now, the little Claudine, she . . .'

'I don't expect Claudine to have great gifts at anything but needlework,' said Miss Ellis. 'All I ask is a *little* attention in class, and a *little* thought in prep time! You spoil Claudine, Mam'zelle.'

'I! I spoil Claudine!' cried Mam'zelle, her glasses falling off her nose in rage. 'I have never spoilt any girl, never. Always I am strict, always I am fair, always I am . . .'

'All right, Mam'zelle,' said Miss Ellis, hastily, seeing that Mam'zelle was going to make one of her long and impassioned speeches, 'all right. I must go. You can tell it all to me when you see me next.'

Mam'zelle sought out Claudine. She fell upon her and hugged her, much to Claudine's surprise. But it had suddenly occurred to Mam'zelle that 'the poor little Claudine' would not have parents visiting her at half-term, for they were in France. So, immediately on thinking this, she had gone to comfort Claudine, who, however, was not in any need of comfort at all. She liked her parents, but as she was one of a very large family, and had only got a small share of their love and attention, she had not missed them very much.

' Ah, my little Claudine ! ' said Mam'zelle, flinging her arms round the astonished Claudine. ' Do not be sad, do not be discouraged ! Do not fret yourself—you shall not be alone at half-term.'

Claudine wondered if her aunt had gone mad. ' I am not sad, *ma tante*,' she said. ' What is the matter ? Has anything happened ? '

' No, no,' said Mam'zelle, still full of tender thoughts for her little Claudine, ' nothing has happened. It is only that I feel for you because your parents will not be with you at half-term. When every one else has their handsome fathers and their so-beautiful mothers, you will have no one—no one but your loving Aunt Mathilde ! '

' Well, that's okay,' said Claudine in English. Mam'zelle wrinkled up her nose and her glasses fell off.

' Do not use these expressions ! ' she said. ' They are vulgar. Ah, my little Claudine, you will not have any parents to admire your so-fine cushion-case with its magnificent peacock—but I will be there, my little one, I will stand by your cushion-cover all the time, not one minute will I go away, and I will say to every one ! " See ! See the beautiful cover made by the clever Claudine ! Ah, it needs a French girl to do such work as this ! Regard the tail, regard each feather so finely-done in silk, regard the priceless cushion-cover, the most beautiful thing in this school today ! '

' Oh, Aunt Mathilde, I wish you wouldn't think of saying anything like that,' said Claudine in alarm. ' The girls would laugh like anything. They would tease me terribly. Please don't. I shan't be lonely. I shan't mind not having any one there.'

' Ah, the brave little one ! ' sighed Mam'zelle, wiping

away a tear from her eye. ' I see your courage. You will not show others that you suffer.'

' I *shan't* suffer,' said Claudine, getting impatient. ' I shan't really, Aunt Mathilde. Please don't make a fuss like this. It would be dreadful if you stood by my cushion-cover all the afternoon and made remarks like that.'

The idea of Mam'zelle standing like a bull-dog on guard, telling surprised parents of her poor lonely little Claudine, and praising to the skies the little cushion-cover filled Claudine with horror. She began to wish that half-term was safely over.

But it hadn't even come ! Four days away—three days—two days—the night before. Ah, now it really *was* near ! The girls went to bed very excited that night and talked in whispers long after lights were out. Susan Howes, the head-girl of the form, pretended to be asleep. She could not bear to be a spoil-sport on the night before half-term, strict as she was on all other nights.

Angela was thinking of the wonderful impression her mother would make, and how she would bask in her reflected glory. She hoped her mother would wear her famous pearls—and that wonderful fox fur.

Eileen was thinking about her own mother. She would be there as Matron, not all dressed up and pretty as other people's mothers would be. She wished that Eddie could be there—not because she was going to do anything in the swimming or tennis matches, or had anything in the art or needle work exhibition—but because it would have been lovely to have seen him looking for her—her own darling big brother !

Alison was looking forward to seeing her own pretty mother, and also to seeing Angela's mother too. She hoped the two would be friends. It would be lovely if they liked one another, and what fun if Angela's mother asked her, Alison, to stay with them in the holidays. That *would* be fine !

Pauline was thinking of her parents too. So was
Bobby. It seemed a long time since the last holidays.
School was fun—but your own home and people were
something very solid and real and lovely. It would be
nice to get a bit of them tomorrow.

One by one the girls fell asleep. Bobby was the first
to wake up. She sat up and spoke loudly. 'Wake up,
you sleepy-heads ! It's half-term !'

10   HALF-TERM AT LAST!

HALF-TERM Saturday was a perfectly beautiful day.
The sun shone down from a blue sky that hadn't a single
cloud in it.

'Gorgeous, isn't it, Claudine ? ' said Doris happily to
the little French girl. 'Couldn't be better.'

Claudine groaned. 'To think we shall all have to be
out-of-doors in this terrible sun ! ' she said. 'I know I
shall get a freckle. I wish it had rained.'

'You spoil-sport ! ' said Bobby, grinning. 'You would
like to huddle indoors even on a day like this. Come on,
cheer up and smile—it's really a heavenly day.'

The art exhibition was all ready for the parents to
admire. There were some really good pictures there.
Miss Walker, the art mistress, was proud of them. She
had a water-colour class which went out regularly to
paint country scenes with her, and some of them were
very good.

'Good enough to sell ! ' said Claudine. 'Do we sell
our work ? How much would you get for this so-
beautiful picture, Hilary ? '

Hilary laughed. 'You have got funny ideas, Claudine,'
she said. 'Of course we don't sell our work. As if our

proud parents would let us! No, they will take our pictures home, and our pottery, and place them in conspicuous places on the walls, or mantel-piece, so that all their friends can admire them, and say, " How clever your daughter must be, Mrs. So-and-So!"'

' I bet your mother will be pleased if you send her that lovely cushion-cover of yours for her birthday,' said Pat. Claudine laughed.

' I have three sisters who do much more beautiful work than I do,' she said. ' My mother would look at my cover and say, " Ah! The little Claudine is improving! This is not bad for a beginning."'

' Mam'zelle thinks it's wonderful, anyhow,' said Bobby, grinning. ' There's one thing about you, Claudine— you're not in the least conceited. With all the fuss that every one has made of your embroidery, you might quite well have begun to swank about it. But you don't.'

' Ah, I know that it is good compared with the sewing of you English girls,' said Claudine, seriously, ' but, you see, I know that it would be quite ordinary in France. I have a different standard to compare that so-beautiful cover with, and I cannot think it is as wonderful as you do.'

Claudine was a very funny mixture of honesty, sincerity and deceitfulness. Even her deceitfulness was queer, because she did not attempt to hide it. She often tried to deceive Miss Ellis, for instance, and if Miss Ellis saw through it, Claudine would at once admit to her attempted deceit without any shame. It was almost as if she were playing a game with the teachers, trying to get the better of them, but not trying to hide the fact that she *was* trying to get the better of them. The girls could not quite make her out.

Pat and Isabel were playing together in a school-match, and they were delighted. They looked out their white skirts and blouses, their red socks and white shoes,

and took the clothes to Matron for the school-maid to
iron. Every one had to look their best when parents
came!

Pauline looked a little miserable at breakfast-time,
and the girls wondered why. Hilary spoke to her in
her usual kindly way.

'What's up, Pauline? You're looking glum. You're
not upset because you haven't been chosen to play in
the school-matches, are you?'

'Oh no,' said Pauline. 'I've had a great disappointment, that's all.'

'What?' asked Hilary, and the other girls came round
to hear.

'Well, you see,' said Pauline, 'it's most unfortunate—
Mother is ill, and my Father doesn't like to leave her—so
they won't be coming today!' And I was *so* looking
forward to them being here and seeing everything.'

'Bad luck, Pauline!' said the twins, sympathetically.
A disappointment of that kind was awful at the last
minute. Every one was very sorry.

'I hope your Mother isn't really ill,' said Susan
Howes.

'No, not seriously,' said Pauline. 'But she can't
possibly come. Oh dear—and I did so badly want you
all to see my good-looking Father and my pretty Mother.
I even wrote to ask her if she would wear the pretty new
frock I liked so much, and she said she would.'

'Well, never mind,' said Isabel, feeling very sorry
indeed. 'You can come out with us and our people, if
you like, Pauline. Then you won't feel so lonely.'

'Oh, thank you,' said Pauline, and after that she
seemed to cheer up a good deal, and entered into everything with enthusiasm.

Mam'zelle had displayed Claudine's beautiful cushion-
cover in a very prominent place. She still seemed
inclined to fall on Claudine's neck, and tell her she must

not feel lonely, and the little French girl kept out of her
way as much as possible, slipping deftly round the corner
whenever she saw her aunt approaching.

'Sort of hide-and-seek you're playing, Claudine!'
said Bobby. 'You'll have to have a word with Mam'-
zelle soon, or she'll burst. She's longing to show you
how beautifully she has arranged your so-marvellous
cushion-cover!'

Lunch was a very scrappy affair that day because the
maids were concerned with the strawberry tea that the
parents were to have in the afternoon, and scores of
pounds of strawberries were being prepared in big glass
dishes. The cooks had made the most lovely cakes and
biscuits, and there were sandwiches of every kind. The
girls kept peeping into the big dining-room, where the
dishes were all set out.

Claudine slipped in and sampled some of the strawberries. She was the only one who dared to do this.

'You'll get into a row if any one catches you,' said
Bobby.

'You go and taste them,' said Claudine, running her
little pink tongue round her crimson lips. 'They are so
sweet and juicy!'

'No,' said Bobby. 'We've been put on our honour
not to sample this afternoon's tea, and I wouldn't dream
of breaking my honour.'

'This honour of yours, it is a funny thing,' said
Claudine. 'It is a most uncomfortable thing. It stops
you from doing what you want to do. I have no honour
to worry me. I will never have this honour of yours. I
do not like it.'

'You're awful, Claudine,' said Angela, screwing up her
nose. 'You do exactly as you like. I'm glad I'm not
as dishonourable as you are.'

The tone was very unpleasant, but Claudine only
laughed. She hardly ever took offence. 'Ah, Angela!'

she said, ' you think it is worse to take a few strawberries than to tell untruths about another girl behind her back ? Me, I think it is really dishonourable to speak lies against another girl as you do. To me you are dishonourable, a worth-nothing girl, not because of a few strawberries but because of your evil tongue ! '

The listening girls laughed at this. It was said in a pleasant voice, but there was such truth in it, and the tables had been turned so cleverly on Angela that the girls couldn't help being amused. Only Angela was angry. But there was little time to quarrel on half-term day. There were so many jobs to do, and every one had her own allotted task.

Some had to do the flowers all over the school, and this took a long time. The vases had to be washed, old flowers thrown away, new ones picked, and then arranged to the best advantage in all kinds of bowls, jars and vases. The twins were especially good at this, and were very busy all the morning.

After lunch every one changed into either sports frocks or school uniform. The summer uniform was a brightly-coloured tunic. The girls could choose any colour they liked, so every girl was able to wear the one that suited her best. Dark girls, like Carlotta, chose reds and oranges, fair girls like Angela chose pale colours, blues and pinks. They looked like flowers, moving about against the green lawns of the school grounds, on that hot summer day.

' The parents are arriving ! ' squealed Alison, as she heard the sound of wheels coming up the drive. ' The first lot are here. Who are they ? '

The fourth-formers looked out of their windows, but nobody knew the people in the car. ' They must belong to some of the lower school,' said Bobby. ' Here come some more ! '

' They're mine ! ' cried Janet. ' Oh goody-goody ! I

hoped they'd come early. I say, doesn't my mother look nice and brown. I'm going to greet them.'

She sped off happily. More and more cars drove up the drive, and soon the lawns were crowded with fathers and mothers and aunts, and with younger or older brothers and sisters. How Eileen wished that Eddie could be there!

Eileen's mother was very trim and starched in her Matron's uniform and white apron. Some of the parents went to talk to her about the health of their children. Eileen was glad that her mother was sought out by so many parents—but she could not help wishing that she had on a pretty frock and looked as sweet and attractive as many of the other girls' mothers.

' Mother ought to smile more,' thought Eileen. ' She looks so strict and hard. Look at the twins' mother over there—she's really sweet. And I do like the way she's got her arm round both Pat and Isabel. Mother never puts her arm round me or Eddie.'

An enormous car rolled up the drive, with a smartly-uniformed chauffeur in front. It was a beautiful new Rolls-Bentley, black with a small green line. It came to a stop and the chauffeur got out. Angela gave a loud squeal.

' That's our new car! Look, every one, isn't it a beauty! And do you like the chauffeur's uniform, black with green piping to match the car? The cushions are black too, with green edges and green monograms.'

' I should have thought you would have been so excited to see your parents that you wouldn't even have noticed the car!' said Janet's cool voice. But Angela took no notice. She was very pleased indeed that so many of the fourth-formers were near when her grand new car drove up!

The chauffeur opened the car-door. Angela's mother stepped out. Certainly she was a vision of beauty!

She looked very young, was extraordinarily like Angela, and she was dressed in a most exquisite fashion.

The girls stared at her. She looked round with brilliant blue eyes, also very like Angela's. After her came her husband, a tall, soldierly-looking man, with rather a serious face. Angela gave another squeal.

She ran to her parents and flung her arms round her mother as she had seen the others do, purposely exaggerating everything because she knew they were watching.

'Angela dear! Be careful of my dress!' said her mother. 'Let me see how you are looking.'

Her father gave Angela a good hug, and then pushed her a little way away so that he could have a good look at her.

'She looks very well indeed,' said her father.

'But this awful school uniform spoils her,' said her mother. 'I do think it is most unbecoming. And I can't bear those terrible school shoes, with their flat heels.'

'Well, all the girls wear the same,' said Angela's father, reasonably. 'I think Angela looks very nice.'

'If only the school had a prettier uniform!' said Angela's mother, in a complaining voice. 'That was one reason why I didn't want to send her here—the dress was *so* ugly!'

11 ANGELA'S 'WONDERFUL' MOTHER

THE complaining voice of Angela's mother could be heard very often indeed that afternoon. Beautiful as she was, attractive and exquisite in her dress and looks, the lovely face was spoilt by an expression of discontent and boredom.

She complained of so many things, and her voice was

unfortunately harsh and too loud ! She complained of
the hard bench that she had to sit on to watch the tennis-
matches. She found fault with the cup of tea that
Angela brought her. ' What terrible tea ! They might
at least provide China tea. You know I can't drink
Indian tea, Angela.'

She complained of the cake she took. ' Awfully dry,'
she said. ' I can hardly eat it.'

' Leave it then,' said Angela's father. And to Angela's
horror her mother dropped the cake on the ground, where
it could be trodden underfoot. The sharp eyes of the
other girls noted all these things, and Angela began to
feel rather uncomfortable.

' Isn't my mother lovely ? ' she whispered to Alison.
' Don't you think those pearls are marvellous ? Hasn't
she got beautiful hair ? '

Alison agreed. Privately she thought that Angela's
mother acted like a spoilt child, complaining and grumbling all the time. She did not praise the pictures in the
art exhibition, neither did she show any enthusiasm for
the pottery work. She was forced to express a good
opinion on Claudine's cushion-cover, because Mam'zelle
stood there like a dragon, looking so fierce that every one
felt they must praise her niece's handiwork.

' Ah ! So this is your mother, Angela ? ' said Mam'zelle,
in a most amiable voice. ' We will show her the work
of the little Claudine ! Is it not beautiful ? See the
exquisite stitches ! Regard the fine tail, spreading so
well over the cover ! '

Angela's mother looked as if she was going to pass the
cover by without saying anything, but Mam'zelle was
certainly not going to let that happen. She took hold
of the visitor's arm and almost forced her to bend over
Claudine's cushion-cover. ' You have not seen it ! It is
a work of art ! It is the finest thing in the exhibition ! '
said Mam'zelle, getting excited.

' Very nice,' said Angela's mother, in a tone that seemed to say ' Very nasty ! ' She took her arm away from Mam'zelle's hand, brushed her sleeve as if it had some dust left on it, and turned away impatiently.

' Who is that awful old woman ? ' she asked Angela, in much too loud a voice. ' Surely *she* doesn't teach you, my dear ? Did you ever see any one look so dowdy ? '

The girls were very fond of Mam'zelle, and they were angry to hear this remark. Bobby felt certain that Mam'zelle herself had caught some of it. The French-woman was standing looking after Angela and her parents with a puzzled and hurt expression in her eyes.

' Well—I always thought Angela was pretty beastly,' said Bobby to Pat, in a low tone, ' and now I see where she gets her cattiness from ! How ashamed I'd be of *my* mother if she walked round like that, criticizing things and people at the top of her voice. Poor old Mam'zelle ! It's a shame to hurt her.'

Claudine had overheard the remarks made by Angela's mother, and she too was hurt and angry. She was fond of her Aunt Mathilde, and though she was cross with her for standing by her cushion-cover and behaving in such an exaggerated way about it, she saw that it was the intense love and pride she had for Claudine herself that made her do it.

She looked at Angela's beautiful mother. She noted her discontented face, and the petulant droop of the mouth that at times quite spoilt its loveliness. She thought of all the hurts and insults that that beautiful mouth must have uttered through the years. And Claudine longed to punish Angela's mother in some dramatic way for the cruel words she had spoken about her Aunt Mathilde !

Angela took her parents to the swimming-pool. St. Clare's was proud of this, for it was one of the finest and biggest swimming-pools owned by any school in the kingdom. The water lapped against the sides, a beautiful blue-green colour.

But even here Angela's mother had fault to find. ' I suppose they change the water every day, Angela ? ' she said.

' No, Mother, twice a week, sometimes three times,' said Angela. Her mother gave a little disgusted squeal.

' Good gracious ! To think they can't even change the water every day ! What a school ! I really must make a complaint about it. Angela, you are not to bathe in the pool unless the water has just been changed. I forbid it.'

' But Mother,' began Angela, uncomfortably, ' I have to do what the others do—and really, the water *is* quite clean, even when it's two days old, or three.'

' I shall complain,' said Angela's mother. ' I never did like the idea of sending you here. It's a second-rate school, I think. I wanted to send you to High Towers School. *Such* a nice school ! I can't think why your father wanted to send you here. Perhaps now he has seen it he will think again.'

' Pamela, don't talk so loudly,' said Angela's father. ' People here don't like to listen to what you are saying. You are in a minority—it is plain that all the other parents here think as *I* do—that St. Clare's is splendid in every way ! '

' Oh, *you*,' said Angela's mother, as if what her husband thought was of simply no account at all. She shut up her scarlet lips, and looked just as sulky as Angela always did when anybody ticked her off.

No—Angela's mother was certainly not a success ! Beautiful she might be, expensive she certainly was—but she had none of the graciousness of the twins' mother, or the common sense of Bobby's jolly-looking mother, or the affection of Gladys's plainly-dressed but sweet-faced mother.

' I'm jolly glad I haven't got a mother like Angela's ! '
said Janet to Alison.   ' Isn't she perfectly awful ? '

Loyal though Alison wanted to be to Angela, she
couldn't help nodding her head.   She had overheard
many of Angela's mother's rude remarks, and she had
not liked them, because even feather-headed Alison felt
a deep sense of loyalty to St. Clare's and all it stood for.
She was not at all eager to be introduced to Angela's
mother now—but the time came when she had to be, for
Angela sought her out and took her off.

' Mother, this is Alison, the friend I told you about in
my letters,' said Angela.   Her mother looked at the
pretty, dainty girl with approval.   Alison was like Angela,
and could wear the school uniform well.

' Oh, so this is Alison,' said Angela's mother.   ' How do
you do ?   I must say you look a little more attractive
than some of the girls here.   One or two that Angela
has introduced me to have been perfect frights ! '

Bobby had been introduced to Angela's mother and
was presumably one of the ' frights '.   Her frank freckled
face was not at all attractive to any one as exquisite as
Angela's mother.

' Where is your mother ? ' asked Angela.   ' We must
introduce her to mine.   Mother wants to ask if you can
spend some of the summer hols. with me.'

But, rather to Alison's relief, when the introduction
had been made, and the two mothers had greeted one
another, the invitation was quite firmly declined by
Alison's own mother !

' Thank you,' she said, ' but I am afraid I have other
plans for Alison.'

She did not explain what these were.   She did not say
that she had watched Angela's mother, and had heard
some of her insolent remarks and detested them.   She
did not say that Angela's mother was the sort of person
she would hate Alison to spend even a day with !   But

Alison knew what her mother was thinking, and silly girl as she was, she knew that her mother was right.

Angela's mother sensed that the other mother was snubbing her, and she was surprised and annoyed. She was about to say something more, when a bell rang loudly

' Oh I   Must they ring bells like that I ' said Angela's mother, putting her hands to her ears. ' How crude I '

' But sensible, don't you think so ? ' said Alison's mother drily, and left her.

' That's the bell to tell us to go and watch the swimming,' said Alison, slipping her hand into her mother's arm. ' Come on, Mummy. You'll see Bobby swimming there—you know, the freckled girl you liked. And Mirabel too—she's awfully fast.'

The hot sun blazed down as the company took its place round the swimming-pool. The parents sat at the edge of the baths, but the girls were in the big gallery above, watching eagerly.

Many of them were not taking part in the swimming, but they were all keen to see the performers diving, somersaulting and swimming. It was fun to hear the continual splashes, and to see the rippling of the blue water.

' Isn't it a gorgeous afternoon,' said Janet, happily. ' I *am* enjoying myself I   I feel so glad that it's a fine day so that we can show off St. Clare's at its very best.'

' All our parents seem to think it's a great success,' said Bobby. ' Well—except *one* parent I '

She meant Angela's mother.   Angela heard this remark and flushed. She had been so pleased to show off her beautiful mother—but somehow everything had been spoilt now. She couldn't help wishing that her mother had made nice remarks like the others had made. But then, Mother wasn't usually very pleased with things, no matter what they were.

Claudine, Alison, Angela and many others not in the

swimming, got front places in the big gallery above the
water. Claudine leaned over rather far, not so much to
look at the swimmers, in their navy-blue swim-suits, but
to see the rows of parents.

' Look out, Claudine, you'll fall in ! ' said Alison, in
alarm, trying to pull her back.

' I shall not fall,' said Claudine. ' I am just looking at
that so-discontented person below, with the voice that
makes loud and rude remarks ! '

' Sh,' said Alison. ' Angela will hear you.'

' I do not care,' said Claudine. ' Why should Angela
expect us to praise a mother who is beautiful only in
appearance, and whose character is ugly ? '

' Do be quiet,' said Alison, afraid that Angela would
hear. ' I'm sorry Angela's mother said that about your
aunt, Claudine. I heard it, and I'm sure poor Mam'zelle
was hurt.'

The swimming began. Angela's mother looked disgusted when a drop of water splashed on to her beautiful
frock. She shook it daintily and tried to move backwards a little—but other people were behind her and she
couldn't.

It was an exciting hour, for the swimmers were fast
and good, and the divers graceful and plucky. But the
most exciting bit of the whole afternoon was not the
swimming or the diving, or the backward somersaulting
done so cleverly by Bobby.

It was an unexpected and highly dramatic performance,
quite unrehearsed, given by Claudine !

She was leaning well over the gallery balcony. She
suddenly gave a piercing shriek that made every one jump
in alarm—and then to the horror of all the lookers-on,
the little French girl fell headlong from the gallery into
the water below !

SHE made a most terrific splash.   The water rose up and
fell all over Angela's mother, soaking her from head to
foot !

'Good gracious !' said Miss Theobald, the Head
Mistress, startled out of her usual calm dignity. 'Who
has fallen into the water ?   Get her out, quickly !'

Claudine could not swim.   She sank under the water,
and then rose to the surface, gasping.   Bobby and
Mirabel who were in the water, too, at once swam over
to her.   They got hold of her and helped her to the
steps.

'Claudine !   Whatever happened ? ' said Bobby.   'You
are an idiot !'

Claudine was gasping and spluttering.   She cast an eye
towards Angela's mother, and saw, to her delight, that
she was drenched.   Miss Theobald was by her, apologizing, and saying that she must come at once to the school,
and allow her, Miss Theobald, to lend her some clothes
whilst hers were drying.

Angrily Angela's mother followed the Head Mistress
from the swimming-pool.   She looked a dreadful sight,
with her dress soaked and clinging tightly to her, and her
beautiful hat dripping with water.   Angela looked very
distressed.

'You too, Claudine, you must go with Matron and get
into dry clothes,' said Miss Ellis to the soaking wet
fourth-former.   'Get into another tunic, quickly, or
you'll catch cold.   Hurry, now.'

Claudine, out of the tail of her eye, saw Mam'zelle
bearing down upon her, alarm and anxiety written all
over her.   The little French girl at once fled off up to the

Claudine cast an eye towards Angela's mother

school. She felt she could not bear to be enwrapped in
Mam'zelle's overwhelming affection just then.

'Wait, wait, Claudine,' called Matron, who was annoyed
that Claudine had caused her to leave the company and
go back to the school. But Claudine did not wait.
Better to face Matron's annoyance rather than Mam'-
zelle's loud exclamations of dismay and sympathy !

'How exactly like Claudine to cause such a disturbance !' said Pat to Isabel. 'Oh Isabel—I can't help
feeling delighted that the person who got soaked was
Angela's tiresome mother !'

'I suppose Claudine couldn't possibly have done it on
purpose, could she ?' said Isabel, doubtfully. 'You
know, she doesn't care in the least what she does, if she
wants to get a result she has set her heart on. I bet she
wanted to punish Angela's mother for her rudeness to
Mam'zelle !'

'But Claudine simply hates and detests the water !'
said Pat. 'Nothing will make her undress and have a
swim. And to let herself fall from the gallery into the
water would be a very brave thing to do, considering she
can't swim.'

Claudine soon returned, in dry clothes, looking demure
and innocent. She could look just as innocent as Angela
when she liked—and now that the girls knew her better,
they were certain that the more innocent Claudine looked,
the worse mischief she had done or was about to do !

Angela's mother also returned, after a while—dressed
in Miss Theobald's clothes ! Miss Theobald was about
the same size as Angela's mother, but a little taller, and
although she always looked nice, her clothes were very
simple, plain and dignified.

They did not suit Angela's mother at all. In fact she
looked very extraordinary in them and she knew it. She
was angry and she showed it. It was bad enough to be
drenched like that by some silly, careless girl, but much

worse to be made to wear clothes too long for her, and so dowdy and frumpish after her own !

But somehow Angela's mother could not be rude to Miss Theobald. The Head Mistress was extremely kind and apologetic, but she was also calm and dignified, and she acted as if she expected Angela's mother to be calm and dignified also. And, much to her surprise, the spoilt woman found herself guarding her tongue and behaving quite well, whilst she changed into Miss Theobald's clothes.

The rest of the time went quickly. The matches and competitions were all over. Parents went off with their children, taking them out to dinner in the various hotels round about, for a treat.

Pauline went with Mrs. O'Sullivan, the twins' mother. The twins had told their mother about the girl's great disappointment, and she had at once said that Pauline must come with them.

Alison's mother spoke to Alison. ' Is there any one you would like to bring with you this evening ? I hope you don't want to go with Angela and her people, because your father and I would rather be on our own with you.'

Alison understood that her mother had no wish to become at all friendly with Angela's mother. If she could choose some one to go with her, it would be easy to refuse Angela, if she asked for the two families to have dinner together. Alison wondered whom she could ask.

She took a look round at the girls. Most of them were clustered around their parents, chattering gaily, waiting for the various cars to come along. Eileen stood alone, watching. Her mother had disappeared—gone to see to some of the younger children, probably. The girl had such a forlorn look on her face that Alison was touched.

' I'll ask Eileen, Mother,' she said. ' I don't like her much—or her mother, who is Matron—but she would so enjoy coming! And oh, Mother—could I ask some one else too?'

'Who?' said her mother, in surprise.

'Could I ask Claudine, the little French girl who fell into the water?' said Alison. 'Her parents are in France. She's only got her aunt here, Mam'zelle. I know she would simply love to come! She adores going out.'

'All right, dear. Ask them both,' said her mother, pleased. Anything rather than having that spoilt little Angela and her equally spoilt mother with them!

Alison tore off to Eileen. 'Eileen. Go and ask your mother if you can come out to dinner with my people. Hurry up.'

'Oh!' said Eileen, her eyes suddenly shining like stars. 'Oh, Alison—do you really mean it? You *are* decent!'

She rushed off to find her mother. Alison went up to Claudine. 'Claudine, will you come out with me and my people? Mother said I could ask you. Eileen is coming too.'

'Thank you,' said Claudine, all her pretty manners coming into play. 'It is indeed very kind of you, Alison, and of your mother too. I will go to ask my aunt.'

Mam'zelle was delighted. She liked Alison, although she despaired over her French. 'Yes, you go, my little Claudine,' she beamed. 'You need a treat after your so-terrible shock this afternoon. Poor little one—to fall into the water like that, to be nearly drowned, to . . .'

'Well, I wasn't nearly drowned really, you know,' said Claudine, a twinkle coming into her eye. 'I knew I *shouldn't* be drowned, Aunt Mathilde, because Bobby and Mirabel were both in the water—and oh, wasn't it grand when I splashed that hateful woman from head to foot? I never guessed I would drench her like that!'

Mam'zelle's mouth fell open, and she stared at Claudine as if she could not believe what she heard.

' Claudine I Claudine I What is this that you are
saying ? Surely, no it is not possible—you could not
have fallen on purpose I You would not be such a bad
girl I ' Poor Mam'zelle could hardly get the words out.

Claudine answered demurely. ' On purpose, Aunt
Mathilde I Why, how could you think of such a thing ?
Do you suppose that your niece could do a so-shocking
thing as that ? But how wonderful that it should happen
just by Angela's mother I Ah, truly, that was a miracle I '

With a wicked twinkle in her eye, the unscrupulous
Claudine walked off to get herself ready for going out.
Mam'zelle stared after her. Ah, this Claudine—she was
a bad, bad girl—and yet what a good, good girl she was
too, to throw herself into the water in order to splash and
punish an unkind woman, some one who had hurt and
puzzled her aunt I Mam'zelle sat down on a hall-seat,
feeling quite breathless. Which *was* Claudine—a bad
girl or a good one ? For the life of her Mam'zelle could
not decide.

Meanwhile all the girls and their parents had gone off
in their different cars. Angela had rolled away in her
magnificent car—but a very quiet and subdued Angela.
Somehow things had not turned out quite as she had
planned. She hadn't shone in the reflected glory of her
beautiful mother. She had only felt the scorn of the
other girls because her mother had criticized their school
in loud and complaining tones.

Angela looked out of the car-window and saw the
happy faces of the twins, and saw Pauline walking with
Mr. and Mrs. O'Sullivan. They were all going off together,
chattering gaily.

' You all did *mar*vellously I ' she heard Mrs. O'Sullivan
say, in clear, happy tones.

Then she saw her friend Alison—and to Angela's enormous surprise, Eileen and Claudine were with her, all
getting into a car together I Oh I How mean of Alison I

The excited girls made their way towards the pool

Why hadn't she asked Angela to join up with her and her people ? Fancy asking that common little sneak, Eileen, and that awful outspoken niece of Mam'zelle's, Claudine ! How *could* Alison do such a thing !

Angela did not think of what the real reason might be—a real feeling of kindness on Alison's part. She was angry and annoyed. She would show Alison exactly what she thought of her when she saw her next ! If Alison wanted to make friends with charity-girls, let her—but she wouldn't have Angela Favorleigh, the Honourable Angela Favorleigh for her friend too !

There were two or three fairly big towns within easy reach of the school by car, and the different families chose their own town and hotel, and drove off. To Eileen's intense joy, Alison's mother chose to go to the town where Eddie lived !

'Oh,' she said, as the car slid into the town. 'This is where my brother lives. I wonder if I shall see him.'

'Would you like to ask him to come and have dinner with us ? ' said Alison's mother.

Eileen shook her head. 'Oh no, thank you. It's kind enough of you to ask *me* without asking *him* as well ! But—if you wouldn't mind—I would love to slip along and see him after we've had dinner. His lodgings aren't very far from the hotel. He'd love to see me.'

'Just as you like, dear,' said Alison's mother. So they had their dinner, and a very good one it was, and then Eileen slipped off to see Edgar.

Claudine proved a great success with Alison's people. The French girl had naturally good manners, she was vivacious and amusing, and she was extremely pleased to have such a treat. Alison's parents really enjoyed the girl's company.

'Alison, I wish that French girl was your friend, and not Angela,' said her mother. 'She really is nice. Don't you like her ? '

' Yes, Mother, I do.' said Alison.   ' She's quite different
from us English girls, though—I mean, she hasn't our
sense of honour—and honestly, she simply doesn't care
what she does.   But she's fun, quite sincere, and awfully
kind.'

' Here comes Eileen back again,' said Alison's mother.
' She must be very fond of her brother.   She really looks
happy now ! '

Eileen did.   Eddie had been delighted to see her.   She
beamed at Alison and Claudine in an unusually friendly
manner.   What a lovely day it had been !

13   JANET AND THE 'STINK-BALLS'

AFTER the excitements of half-term the girls felt flat and
dull.   There didn't seem anything to look forward to
now.   Lessons were boring.   The weather was too hot.
It seemed a long time till the summer holidays.

' Janet !   Bobby !   Can't you think up some trick or
other ? ' said Pat, with a yawn.   ' I wish you would.   I
shall die of boredom this week if something doesn't
happen.'

Janet grinned.   ' I've got rather an awful trick from
my brother,' she said.   ' I don't really know if we ought
to play it, now we're fourth-formers.'

' Oh, don't be an idiot ! ' said Doris.   ' Why can't we
have a few jokes, even if we *are* fourth-formers !   What's
the trick ? '

' Well—it's a perfectly frightful Smell,' said Janet.
' Wait a bit—I'll get the things.'

She went up to her dormitory, rummaged about in one
of her drawers and then came down again with a small box.

The others crowded round her.   The box was full of

what looked like tiny round glass balls, full of some sort of clear liquid.

'What are they ? ' said Pat, puzzled. ' I've never seen them before.'

' They are smell-balls,' said Janet. ' Stink-balls my brother calls them. When you break one and let out the liquid, it dries up at once—but leaves the most frightful smell behind.'

' What sort of smell ? ' asked Doris, with great interest. ' Like drains or something ? '

' Well—like very bad eggs,' said Janet. ' My brother— he's simply awful, you know—he broke one of these balls at a very solemn meeting once, in our drawing-room at home—and in less than a minute the room was empty ! You simply can't imagine what it was like ! '

Bobby chuckled. ' Let's break one in French class tomorrow,' she said. ' It's going to be terribly dull— translating pages and pages of that book Mam'zelle is so keen on—that French play. This trick is absolutely *sent* for things like that. Will you break one of these balls tomorrow, Janet, or shall I ? '

' Well, you take one and I'll take one,' said Janet. ' Then if mine doesn't work—my brother says they are sometimes disappointing—you can use yours. See ? '

The whole class were thrilled about the ' stink-balls '. Every one but Eileen knew about them. The girls were afraid of telling Eileen in case she sneaked to Matron, and the secret was found out. So Eileen was not told a word. She was astonished to find that so many of the girls hurriedly stopped talking when she came up, and then began chattering very loudly about quite silly things. She was sure they had been talking about her, and she felt hurt.

' If they're going to be beastly to me, I shall tell Mother, and they'll all get dozens of stockings to mend ! ' thought Eileen, spitefully.

Janet and Bobby went into the French class the next day with the little ' stink-balls ' in their pockets. The lesson was just before Break.

' We'd better not choose any lesson except one just before Break,' Janet had said, ' because if the smell goes on too long, it might still be there in Miss Ellis's class, and I bet she'd smell a rat.'

' She'd smell much worse than a rat once she sniffs one of your " stink-balls ",' said Bobby, with a grin.

' You see, we can open all the windows and doors and let the smell out well during Break,' said Pat. ' There won't be anything of it left by the time Maths. lesson comes afterwards with Miss Ellis.'

The class were standing politely and silently when Mam'zelle came in. She beamed at the girls.

' Sit ! Now today we will go on with this play of ours. I will allot the parts. You, Janet, can take the part of the old servant ; you, Alison . . .'

The girls opened their books, hiding their grins as best they could. A trick performed by Janet or Bobby was always fun, great fun ! The girls remembered the many other tricks the two had played, and chuckled. This would liven up a dull French lesson very considerably.

' Janet, will you please begin ? ' said Mam'zelle, aimiably. She liked this fourth form. They were good, hard-working girls—and her dear little Claudine was there too, her face buried in her book—the good, good little girl !

Janet began reading in French. Her hand stole to her pocket. The girls behind her saw it, and tried to choke back their giggles. That was the worst of playing a trick —you always wanted to begin giggling far too soon, and it was terribly difficult to stop real giggles. Doris gave one of her sudden snorts, and Mam'zelle looked up in surprise.

Doris turned it into a long cough, which set Mirabel off into giggles too. Mam'zelle glared at Mirabel.

' Is it so funny that the poor Doris has a bad cough ? ' she inquired.

This seemed funnier still to Mirabel and she went off into more helpless giggles which began to infect the others. Janet turned round and frowned. She didn't want Mam'zelle to suspect too soon that she was playing a trick. The others caught her warning look, and became as serious as they could again.

The lesson went on. Janet slid the little glass ball out of her pocket. Her hand was behind her, and the girls saw her press firmly on the tiny glass ball. The thin glass covering broke, and the liquid ran out, drying almost as soon as the air touched it. The liquid disappeared, and the tiny fragments of thin glass dropped unheeded to the floor.

After a few moments a curious smell drifted all round. Doris coughed. Alison sniffed loudly and said ' Pooh ! '

It was a horrid smell, there was no doubt about that. It smelt of bad eggs, drains, dead rats, old cats' meat . . . all that was horrid !

Mam'zelle did not smell the smell at first. She was astonished at the sudden outburst of sniffing and coughing. She looked up. She saw expressions of disgust on every one's face, mixed with the desire to giggle.

' What is the matter ? ' demanded Mam'zelle, suspiciously. ' Why do you pull these faces ? Alison, stop saying " Pooh ! " Janet, why do you look so disgusted ? '

' Oh, Mam'zelle—can't you smell it ? ' said Janet, an agonized expression on her face.

' Smell *what* ? ' said Mam'zelle, exasperated. The smell had not drifted her way as yet.

' Oh, Mam'zelle—the *smell* ! ' chorused half a dozen voices.

Mam'zelle looked puzzled and angry. She took a few enormous sniffs of the air, which made Doris explode into laughter.

'I smell no smell,' said Mam'zelle. 'This is a silly trick, yes. Stop sniffing, Janet. If you say " Pooh " again, Alison, I will send you out of the room. Claudine, do not look like a duck that is dying.'

'But, Aunt Mathilde, the smell, the smell! *C'est abominable!*' cried Claudine, who detested bad smells, and looked as if she was about to faint.

'Claudine! You too!' rapped out Mam'zelle, who, safely away at the end of the room, had not even got so much as a sniff of the evil smell yet. 'Now listen, *mes enfants*—one more mention of a smell, and I fetch Miss Theobald herself here to smell it! It is all pretence. You are bad children.'

This was a truly terrible threat! Miss Theobald would certainly be able to smell the smell as soon as she got into the room, and then there would be a big row. The girls looked at one another in dismay. They put their handkerchiefs to their noses and tried not to sniff up the ghastly odour.

Mam'zelle began to read out loud from the French play. After a few lines, she stopped. Strange! She felt as if she too now could smell something. She took a cautious sniff. Was it a smell, or was it not? Nonsense! Strange and horrible smells do not invade classrooms all of a sudden. Mam'zelle took another breath and went on reading.

The smell stole round her. Mam'zelle could smell it quite distinctly now. She stopped reading again and sniffed wildly. Yes, there was no doubt about it, a perfectly horrible smell was in the room! The poor, poor girls—they had smelt it first—and she had not believed them.

Mam'zelle gave a gulp and a choke as the smell really took hold of her. She fished about for her handkerchief. The girls, divided between disgust at the smell and an intense desire to giggle at Mam'zelle's horrified face,

stuffed their hankies into their mouths, making all kinds
of most peculiar noises.

' Girls,' said Mam'zelle, in a choking kind of voice,
' girls, you are right. There is a terrible smell in here.
What can it be ? '

' A dead rat under the floor-boards ? ' said Doris,
obligingly, removing her hanky from her mouth for a
moment.

Mam'zelle gave a small shriek. Rats, dead or alive,
gave her shivers all down her back.

' Perhaps a drain has burst outside the window,' said
Pat, speaking in a muffled voice. ' I'll look.'

She went to the open window and leaned out, taking
in deep breaths of the pure air there. One or two others
joined her, thinking it was a very good idea.

' Perhaps it will go away,' said Mam'zelle, hopefully.

' Open the door, Janet, and maybe it will help to clear
the room of this evil odour.'

Janet thankfully opened the door. This was an
amusing trick to play—but it had its drawbacks !

The draught of air took a good strong dose of the smell
over to Mam'zelle's desk. She gave a loud exclamation.
' Tiens ! This is terrible ! We shall all be ill. Pick up
your books quickly and we will finish our lesson in the
garden. I will tell Miss Theobald and maybe she will
have the boards up to seek for a rat that is quite dead.'

All but Claudine were delighted to go out into the
garden. Claudine did not know which was worse—the
smell in the classroom, or the insects out-of-doors. She
thought there was very little to choose between them !

Soon the girls were sitting in a nice shady part of the
garden, giggling whenever they thought of the awful smell
drifting round their classroom. The lesson was no longer
boring or dull ! The smell had made it a great success.

Mam'zelle kept her word and reported the smell to Miss
Theobald. ' Ah, Miss Theobald ! ' she said, ' it is a smell

truly unbelievable ! Of dead rats and mice, of eggs that are bad, of drains that are broken ! It came into our classroom whilst the girls were reciting their French lesson, and it spoilt the whole hour. We had to leave the room and go into the garden.'

Miss Theobald was surprised to hear of such a very strong and disgusting smell. In all her experience of schools, she had never yet come across a smell that had driven a class from the room.

' I will go and smell it,' she said to Mam'zelle. ' If it is a dead rat, or bad drains, then, of course, we must have the smell seen to at once, this very afternoon. The smell will remain there, if those are the causes.'

But, to Mam'zelle's great astonishment and to Miss Theobald's mild astonishment, not a trace of the smell remained. The two of them sniffed all round the room, but it smelt fresh and clean.

' Extraordinary,' said Miss Theobald, gazing at Mam'-zelle. ' You are quite sure, Mam'zelle, that it *was* a strong smell, a really bad one ? '

Mam'zelle was most indignant. What, the Head Mistress was doubting her word ? Mam'zelle at once began to describe the smell all over again, this time making it a smell ten times worse than before. Miss Theobald smiled to herself. She knew Mam'zelle's indignant exaggerations by this time.

' Well,' she said, ' I won't have the floorboards up, or the drains inspected today—maybe the smell will not return. If it does, Mam'zelle, kindly report it to me at once, please, so that I may smell it myself before it goes away.'

' Yes, Miss Theobald,' said Mam'zelle, and went to the mistress's common room, full of the Smell and of its power in sending her class into the garden. Every one listened in astonishment. It didn't occur to any one but the first form mistress, Miss Roberts, that it might

be a trick. But Miss Roberts had had much experience
of Janet's jokes, and it did cross her mind to wonder if
this could be one of them.

' Let me see, Mam'zelle,' she said, thoughtfully, ' Janet
is in the fourth form, isn't she ? '

' Yes,' said Mam'zelle, ' but what has that got to do
with my smell ? '

' Oh—nothing I expect,' said Miss Roberts. ' But—if
I were you, Mam'zelle, if that smell appears again, you
trot down to Miss Theobald AT ONCE. I think she may
be able to find the cause of it without taking up any
floor-boards and examining any drains ! '

' Of course I shall report to the Head at once,' said
Mam'zelle, with dignity.

And the time came when she did !

14   MISS ELLIS PLAYS A TRICK TOO

THE girls had been really delighted with the success of
Janet's ' stink-ball '. Whenever Eileen had not been in
the room, they had chattered and laughed about Mam'-
zelle's disgust and astonishment.

' All the same, we'd better not do it again,' said Janet.
' I have a sort of feeling that once would be a success,
but that twice would be a failure ! You can pull Mam'-
zelle's leg beautifully once in a while, but not all the
time.'

' If you do the smell again, I shall be sick and go out
of the room,' said Claudine. ' It is the worst smell I
have ever sniffed.'

' We won't do the smell again,' promised Bobby. ' But
I tell you what we *will* do—we'll pre*tend* there is a smell,
shall we—and get old Mam'zelle all hot and bothered

expecting one—she'll sniff and snuff, and we shall die of
laughing ! '

' Oh yes—that's a good idea,' said Janet.   ' Doris, you
can start off about the smell again in tomorrow's French
Grammar class.'

Doris grinned. She could act that kind of thing very
well. So the next day, when Mam'zelle was ensconced
safely in her desk at the end of the room, Doris began her
act.

There was a very nice smell in the room, for Alison, the
girl doing the flowers for the classroom that week, had
filled a big vase with white pinks, and they scented the
room beautifully. The girls could smell them as they
worked.

Doris began to sniff. At first she gave very little
sniffs. Then she gave two or three bigger ones.

' Doris ! Have you a cold ? ' said Mam'zelle, impatiently.   ' Are you a first-former, come to class without
a handkerchief ? '

' I've got a hanky, thank you, Mam'zelle,' said Doris,
humbly, and took it out.

Then Janet began to sniff. She screwed up her nose,
sniffed, and looked all round. Bobby gave a chuckle and
turned it into a long cough. Mam'zelle frowned. She
did not like behaviour of this sort ; it made her angry.

Then Pat began to sniff, and pulled out her hanky too.
Soon the whole class, all except Eileen, who was not in
the joke, were sniffing as if they had bad colds.

Mam'zelle gazed at the sniffing girls, exasperated.
' What is all this noise ? Sniff-sniff-sniff ! I cannot
bear it.'

Doris put on an expression of disgust. Mam'zelle saw
it, and an alarming thought came into her head. Could
it be that terrible Smell again ?

' Doris,' she said, urgently, ' what is the matter ? '

' I can smell something,' murmured Doris.   ' Distinctly.

It's very strong just here. Can't you smell anything, Mam'zelle ? '

Mam'zelle couldn't, which was not at all surprising. But she remembered that before she could not smell the smell until after the girls. She looked anxiously at the class. They all seemed to be smelling it.

' I will report it at once,' said Mam'zelle, and she left the room in a hurry.

' Crumbs ! ' said Bobby. ' I don't know that we wanted her to go to the Head about it ! I say—she shot off so quickly we couldn't stop her ! '

Unluckily for Mam'zelle the head was out. Mam'zelle was annoyed and upset. Here was the Smell again, and no Miss Theobald to smell it, and to know that she, Mam'zelle had not exaggerated last time !

Mam'zelle popped her head in at the mistress's common room as she hurried back to the classroom. Miss Ellis was there, correcting exercise books belonging to the fourth form.

' Miss Ellis—I regret to say that that terrible Smell is back again,' said Mam'zelle. ' It is abominable ! I do not think you will be able to take the fourth form in your room next lesson.'

She withdrew her head and hurried back to the fourth form. She went in, expecting to be greeted by a wave of the terrible Smell. But there seemed to be no smell at all. Very strange !

' Miss Theobald is out,' said Mam'zelle. ' Alas, she cannot smell our Smell. Neither do I smell it yet ! '

It was good news that Miss Theobald was out ! The girls felt cheerful about that. Doris spoke up at once.

' Don't worry, Mam'zelle. We know what the smell was this time—quite different from last time. It was only these pinks ! '

Doris picked up the big bowl of pinks, walked jauntily to Mam'zelle and thrust them under her big nose. Mam'zelle took a sniff and the strong and delicious scent went up her nose.

'So !' she said to Doris. 'It was the pinks you smelt. Well, it is a good thing Miss Theobald was not in. She would have come to smell for nothing !'

There were a few giggles—and then, as the door opened, the girls fell silent, and looked to see if it was Miss Theobald coming in after all.

But it wasn't. It was Miss Ellis, who, curious to smell this extraordinary smell that Mam'zelle seemed continually to get excited about, had come to smell it herself. She stood at the door, sniffing.

'I can't smell anything, Mam'zelle,' she said, surprised. Mam'zelle hastened to explain.

'I smelt nothing, either, Miss Ellis. It was the pinks the girls smelt. Doris has just told me.'

Miss Ellis was surprised and most disbelieving. 'I don't see how the girls could mistake a smell of pinks for the kind of awful smell you described to me last time,' she said. 'I am not at all sure I believe in that Smell at all.'

She gave her form a glare, and went out.

Mam'zelle was indignant. Had she not smelt the smell herself last time ? For the rest of the lesson the class had a very peaceful time, discussing smells, past and present, with their indignant French mistress.

After Break came geography, taught by Miss Ellis. She came into the room looking rather stern.

'I just want to say,' she said, 'that I shall regard any mention of smells, bad or good, as a sign that you want a little extra work given to you.'

The class knew what that meant. 'A little extra work' from Miss Ellis meant a good two hours extra prep. So every one immediately made up their minds not to mention the word smell at all.

But a terrible thing happened in ten minutes' time.

Bobby had quite forgotten that she still had her 'stink-ball' in her pocket, left over from the day before. And, in sitting down rather violently, after going with her book to Miss Ellis, she broke the thin glass surrounding the liquid. Then, in a trice, the perfectly awful Smell came creeping round the classroom once more !

Doris smelt it. Janet smelt it. Bobby smelt it and put her hand at once into her pocket, desperately feeling about to see if she had accidentally broken the little 'stink-ball'. When she found she had, she gazed round, winking and nodding at the others, to tell them of the awful accident. Miss Ellis's sharp eyes caught Bobby's signs. So she was not really very surprised when she smelt the smell coming towards her. What a terrible smell it was !

Miss Ellis thought things out quietly. Evidently yesterday's Smell had been this same horrible one—and the one Mam'zelle had reported today, and which Doris had said was pinks after all, was nothing to do with the real Smell—just a silly joke played on Mam'zelle.

'But this awful Smell is the real thing again,' thought Miss Ellis, 'and, judging by Bobby's signs to the others, was a mistake. I don't think the girls would dare to play a trick like this on me. Well—I will just play a little trick on *them* !'

Quietly Miss Ellis wrote a few directions on the board. Then she turned and left the room, closing the door after her. The girls stared at the board.

'Page 72. Write down the answers.

'Page 73. Read the first two paragraphs and then rewrite them in your own words.

'Page 74. Copy the map there.'

'I say !' exploded Doris. 'She's gone—and we've got to stay here in this awful Smell and do that work. Bobby, you absolute idiot, why did you break that stink-ball ?'

' It was an accident,' said Bobby, most apologetically.
' I sat on it. I quite forgot it was there. Isn't this
frightful ? Miss Ellis has smelt it, of course, guesses it's
a trick, and for punishment we've got to sit through the
smell and work at our geography—and we simply daren't
complain ! '

' I am not going to sit in the Smell,' announced
Claudine, emphatically. She got up. ' I feel sick. I go
to be sick.'

She went off, and she made such wonderful sick-noises
as she passed Miss Ellis in the passage outside, that Miss
Ellis said nothing, but let her go to the bathroom. Trust
Claudine for doing what she wanted ! Not one of the
others dared to leave the room.

They sat there, choking into their handkerchiefs,
moaning over their fate, but not daring to scamp their
work. At the end of the hour, when the smell had some-
what lessened, Miss Ellis opened the door.

She left it open. ' You may go for a short run round
the garden and back,' she said. ' Bobby, remain behind,
please.'

With a wry face Bobby remained behind whilst the
others fled out gladly into the fresh air.

' I was the one who caused that terrible smell this time,'
said Bobby, at once. It was never any good beating
round the bush with Miss Ellis—not that Bobby was
given to that, anyway. She was a straightforward and
truthful girl. ' But it was an accident, Miss Ellis, really
it was. Please believe me.'

' I do,' said Miss Ellis. ' But it is an accident that is
on no account to happen again. You have all had your
punishment, so I shall say no more about it. But I want
you to warn the fourth-formers that any future smells
will result in quite a lot of punishment ! '

'ISN'T it gorgeous weather?' said Isabel to Pat. 'Day after day we get nothing but sun and blue sky. I wish we could have lessons sitting in the swimming-pool!'

'The coolest part of the day is the night!' said Doris. 'I should like to sleep all day and work all night in the cool night breeze.'

'Last night I woke up and saw the moon shining in at the window,' said Hilary. 'I got up and looked out—I simply can't tell you how beautiful the country looked, all lit up by moonlight. I wished I could go for a walk—have a moonlight picnic all by myself!'

'I *say*!' said Bobby, at once, 'a moonlight picnic! What an absolutely marvellous idea! Let's!'

'Oooh,' said the others, staring at Bobby, really impressed by the unusual idea. 'Golly—what fun!'

'Yes, it would be,' said Hilary, 'but—now that we're fourth-formers, do you think we *ought* to?'

'Oh, Hilary—don't be so pious!' said Janet.

'I'm *not*,' said Hilary, indignantly. 'That's a thing I've never been. Well—perhaps it wouldn't matter. We could picnic in the school grounds. Oh I *say*—let's picnic by the swimming-pool, and have a moonlight swim!'

'Better and better!' said Bobby, giving a whoop of delight. 'Golly—that would be super! Look here— let's wait till full-moon night—that's two nights from now—and have it then. The pool would be brilliantly lit and we could have a gorgeous time.'

'It's my birthday then,' said Mirabel. 'That *very* day. Oh, let's make it then, and I'd feel it was a birthday treat too!'

'Right,' said Janet. 'Now we'd better make plans quickly, because we haven't much time to get anything.' She turned to the quiet and responsible head-girl of the form, Susan Howes. 'Susan, you'll come, won't you?'

Susan nodded. She was a good and trustworthy girl, but she loved a bit of fun, and she could not see that there was any harm in a moonlight picnic.

'I'll go down to the town today with Hilary, and buy a few things,' she said. 'I'll leave word at the grocer's and the baker's that you will all go in at different times and fetch one or two things. Then no one will suspect anything—we shall just quietly return to school with small parcels!'

'Shall we tell Eileen or not?' said Janet.

'No, of course not,' said Bobby. 'I bet she'd split on us and tell her mother—and then we'd all get caught and everything would be spoilt.'

'Well—it's a pity to leave Eileen out of everything like this really,' said Pat, 'but we can't risk being found out. And these midnight affairs *are* such fun!'

Mirabel was thrilled that it was her birthday that day! It would make it all the nicer. She and Gladys, her quiet little friend, talked and talked about it.

'I'll take my birthday cake, of course,' said Mirabel. 'I'll save it up till then. Mother said she would send sixteen candles separately, and we'll stick them on the cake in their holders, and light them in the moonlight!'

Eileen was by now used to the others planning things without her. She knew that the tricks they whispered about together were not told her beforehand because she was known as a sneak. So she did not prick up her ears at all when she saw the girls talking together in low tones.

'What do I care for their silly tricks?' she thought. 'If they want to act like that, let them!'

So she did not try to overhear or find out their fresh secret. She went her own way, looking rather pale and unhappy. She rarely smiled now, kept herself quite to herself, and did not try to make friends with any one. She had been nice to Alison after the half-term treat, and Alison had benefited by her kindness by having no mending of her own at all to do ever since ! But she still struggled with Angela's darning, though Angela was never very grateful.

Mirabel's birthday came. As usual her form gave presents. Some were small presents, if the girls had little money left, some were extravagant, like Angela's.

Angela gave Mirabel a book of very expensive music that she wanted. It cost twenty-one shillings and Mirabel was really quite overcome. ' You shouldn't spend so much money on a birthday ! '

' Why not ? ' said Angela. ' My grandfather sent me five pounds last week. What's the good of having money if you don't spend it ? '

Pauline, not to be outdone, gave Mirabel a music-case of fine leather. Mirabel was amazed. It was not usual to have such beautiful presents for a school birthday. She had not even known that Pauline had noticed that her own old music-case had a broken strap and was almost worn out.

' Oh, Pauline—this is beautiful ! ' said Mirabel, red with surprise and delight. ' But you shouldn't do it. It's bad enough for Angela to do it—and for you to give me something so extravagant too, well really, I feel quite overwhelmed ! '

' If Angela can do it, I can as well,' said Pauline, a little stiffly. That took the pleasure out of the gift somehow, thought Mirabel. If Pauline only gave her something fine just because she didn't want to be outdone by Angela, well, there wasn't much kindness or affection behind the gift !

Claudine surprisingly gave Mirabel a very pretty bag. Claudine was one of the girls who had very little money, and said so—so Mirabel was really touched to have such a nice gift from her.

'Oh, thank you, Claudine,' she said. 'It is really lovely. But it's too extravagant of you ! I know you don't have much pocket-money.'

But Claudine seemed to have plenty that week ! She bought eight pounds of cherries as her share of the picnic's goodies, and they came to ten shillings. Every one thought it was decent of her.

'Ah, when I have a little money, I like to spend it,' said Claudine. 'It is nice to spend. I wish I could spend always. That would be fine, to be like Angela and to say, " I will have this, I will have that ! " '

'Yes—but it does mean you don't have many treats, real *treats*,' said Gladys. 'I mean—if Mother and I save up for ages to go a good holiday together, it means much more to us and is a greater treat than any holiday could possibly be to Angela—who can have expensive holidays whenever she likes. To have a lot of money doesn't mean that you get more enjoyment than those who haven't much.'

'Quite right as usual,' said Isabel, giving the quiet Gladys a little pat. 'Well, I wish I and Pat could buy more for this picnic, but it was our Granny's birthday last week and we spent most of our money on that mauve silk scarf we sent her. So we're cleaned out for a bit. I hope you won't turn up your nose at our birthday offering, Mirabel—it's only two drawing pencils with your name on ! '

'That's very decent of you,' said Mirabel, who really did not mind whether gifts cost ten shillings or ten pence. 'I think you're all decent to me, every one of you. Everybody has given me a present.'

Even Eileen had, though with many apologies for the poorness of her gift. 'It's only a little hanky,' she said to Mirabel. 'And I'm afraid it's not even new. It's one of my own, but please take it, Mirabel, with my birthday wishes. I don't want to be the only one not giving you anything! You know I have hardly any pocket-money, and it's Eddie's birthday soon and I'm saving every penny for that.'

Every one knew that Eileen had less money than any girl in the school. Her mother was mean over pocket-money. Certainly she had to work hard for her own money, but she seemed to think that the sixteen-year-old Eileen could manage on a penny or two a week, just as she had managed when she was a small six-year-old.

' I wish we could ask Eileen to go with us tonight,' said Mirabel. She was usually a thick-skinned girl, who had little feeling for any one else, except for her friend Gladys—but she had been touched by Eileen's little gift, and her honest confession of having no money.

' Well, we can't ' said Bobby, decidedly. ' I know she told her mother that Janet said that there seemed to be more torn sheets in the fourth-form dormitories than in the whole of the rest of the school put together—and poor Janet has done oceans of mending this week. But who can help thinking our sheets are torn on purpose? On purpose to give us work to do! They were never torn like this before. Why, I could go a whole term without having to mend a pillow-case or sheet at all when our old Matron was here!'

' All right. We won't ask Eileen,' said Mirabel. ' I don't really care. She *is* a dreadful sneak, I suppose.'

Everything was prepared in readiness for the moonlight picnic and swim. The sky was clear when the girls went to bed that night. They went to bed in the daylight, for the evenings were very long just then.

' There won't be any darkness at all, I should think,' said Bobby, looking out of the window. ' When daylight begins to go, the full moon will come swimming up the sky, and then everything will be almost as bright as day

again. Golly, isn't it hot ? I shall adore being in the
water at midnight ! '

Luckily for the girls, Eileen was a very sound sleeper.
Once she was asleep, nothing ever seemed to wake her,
and even when the fire-practice alarm had gone once in
the middle of the night, she had not awakened. So the
girls felt sure she would know nothing.

It was too hot to sleep ! Some of the girls dozed off,
and Eileen and Mirabel slept soundly. But the others
tossed and turned, half-asleep and half-awake. So, when
the big clock in one of the towers struck half-past eleven,
there was only Mirabel to wake !

Eileen slept in a bed by the door of one of the fourth-
form dormitories, and the girls had to tip-toe past her.
But she did not stir. She had looked rather pale and
tired lately, and now she slept very deeply. The girls
had on bathing-suits under their dressing-gowns, and
rubber shoes on their feet. They made no sound as they
stole down the corridors, went down the stairs, and came
to the big cupboard where they had hidden their food
and drink.

With giggles and whispers they loaded themselves with
the goodies, and then undid the garden door as quietly
as they could. They left it a little open so that they
could get in easily when they returned. There was no
wind to bang it shut.

Keeping in the cover of the trees, the line of excited
girls made its way towards the swimming-pool. How
gorgeous the still water looked, lying calm and deep in
the brilliant moonlight. The moon was now up, and was
flooding the grounds with cold, silver light. Everything
could be plainly seen. Only the warm colours of daylight
were missing.

' We mustn't make too much noise,' said Janet. ' Our
voices would carry a good way on a still night like this.
I only hope no one will hear the splashing of the water

when we go in! Let's go in first, before we eat. I'm so hot.'

Off came the dressing-gowns. Bare long legs gleamed in the moonlight. One after another the girls dived in or jumped in—all but Claudine, who had steadfastly refused to come in a bathing-suit, but had on her night-gown under her dressing-gown. The little French girl liked the excitement of the midnight picnic, but, hot though it was, nothing would persuade her to go into the water! She would throw herself in to punish a spiteful-tongued woman—but she certainly would not go in for pleasure!

She stood and watched the girls, laughing. She glanced away from the pool—and suddenly saw a figure slipping silently between the trees. Whoever could it be?

16   CLAUDINE DEALS WITH MATRON

CLAUDINE ran quietly in her rubber shoes to see who was out in the grounds that night, besides the fourth-formers. It was Eileen! Eileen, whom the girls had left sound asleep in bed.

' The sneak!' said Claudine to herself. ' She comes to peep and pry at us, and then she goes back to her so-severe mother to tell a tale! I will follow her back.'

But somehow she missed Eileen, and could not see where she had gone. Claudine rushed back to the pool and almost fell into the water in her excitement at telling the others what she had seen.

' Oh blow!' said Bobby, climbing out, the moonlight shining on the silvery drops running down her legs. ' I suppose that sneak of an Eileen will go straight off to Matron—and before we can have anything to eat, she'll be here scolding us and rowing us and sending us back in disgrace.'

' I will go back to the school, and keep watch,' said Claudine, eagerly. ' I know where Matron sleeps. I will go outside her door and stand there till I know for certain that either she is coming here, or that Eileen has not told tales after all.'

' Right,' said Bobby. ' Hurry ! And be sure to race back and warn us if you hear Matron dressing or wandering about. We simply mustn't be caught. But oh, what a shame if we can't have the moonlight picnic. And I bet Matron will confiscate Mirabel's lovely cake ! '

Claudine sped off in her rubber shoes. She did not see Eileen at all. She went in at the open garden door and ran quietly up the stairs to the corridor at the end of which Matron slept.

She stood outside Matron's door and listened. There was not a single sound from inside. She could not hear either Eileen's voice or Matron's. On the other hand, she could not hear slight snores or heavy breathing. Claudine stood there, wondering what to do. *Had* Eileen seen the picnickers ? *Did* she mean to tell tales ? Where had she gone ?

Then Claudine's quick ears caught a sound from inside Matron's room. The bed was creaking ! Plainly Matron was awake. The bed creaked a little more, and then there came the sound of some one shuffling into slippers.

' Now she puts on a dressing-gown,' thought Claudine. ' Now she ties the girdle. But why is she getting up just now, if Eileen has not been to tell her ? '

The little French girl squeezed herself into a dark corner as Matron's door suddenly opened. The thin narrow-shouldered figure appeared framed in the door-way, full in the moonlight. Matron looked rather grim.

She set off silently down the passage and turned off in

the direction of the dormitory belonging to the fourth-formers. Claudine followed her like a moving black shadow, keeping cleverly in the dark corners. Matron went into the dormitory where Eileen always slept.

' Eileen ! ' said Matron, in a whisper. But there was no answer. Then Matron evidently patted the bed and found no one there. There came an exclamation, and Matron switched on the light. In a moment she saw the empty beds !

She went into the next dormitory, where the fourth-formers also slept, and again switched on the light. No girls there !

' Where are they ? ' said Matron, angrily. ' I will not have this sort of thing ! Why didn't Eileen warn me of this ? She ought to know better than to join in tricks of this sort ! '

Claudine heard these muttered words, and was surprised. So Eileen *hadn't* warned her mother ! She had followed the others out, and must be hiding somewhere in the grounds, watching the fun.

And now Matron was going to spoil everything. Why should she ? Claudine felt a sudden and intense dislike for the severe and spiteful Matron. There was no harm in a moonlight swim and picnic ! Quite likely if the girls had asked Miss Theobald's permission, she would have laughed and granted it, just for once ! And now Matron was going to interfere.

Matron went down the stairs. She came to the cup-board where the girls had stored their picnic food and drink. They had left the door open. Matron gave an angry exclamation and went to shut it.

And it was then that the Great Idea came to Claudine ! It was an idea that might have occurred to any angry girl, but only Claudine would have carried it out.

Matron suddenly got the shock of her life ! Some one gave her a violent push so that she landed inside the cupboard, among old lacrosse sticks and tennis-rackets. Then the door was shut—and locked !

Matron was a prisoner ! Claudine took the key out of the cupboard and put it into her dressing-gown pocket. Choking with laughter she ran out of the garden door and made her way to the swimming-pool. She could hear Matron hammering on the door. But the little back-hall beyond the garden-door, near the cupboard, was seldom used, and far from any sleeping-quarters. It was quite likely that no one would hear Matron at all.

' Now we are safe ! ' thought Claudine, triumphantly. ' What a fine joke ! But will these English girls think it is a joke ? '

For the first time a doubt came into her mind. She, Claudine, knew it to be a grand, grand joke to lock that so-detestable Matron up in a dark cupboard, to stop her from spoiling the fun—but would the others think like Claudine ? Might not this curious ' honour ' they were always talking about prevent them from thinking it a joke? Might not Susan Howes, fourth-form head-girl, think it her duty to go and rescue Matron ? One could never tell what the English would think to be right or wrong !

' Then I shall not tell them what I have done ! ' thought Claudine, as she sped along to the pool. ' If they do not know, they cannot worry. Now I will only tell them that it is all right, Eileen has not told tales, and that Matron is quite, quite safe.'

The girls climbed out of the pool and surrounded Claudine when she came running back.

' It's all right,' said Claudine. ' Very much okay. Eileen has not told tales. She is not back at the school. And Matron is quite, quite safe ! '

' Oh *good* ! ' said all the girls, and shook the water from themselves. ' What about some eats now ? '

' Where's Eileen then, if she isn't in bed and didn't go back to school ? ' said Bobby, puzzled.

But nobody knew and nobody cared. Let Eileen wander where she liked so long as she didn't spoil their fun. And how good that Matron was safe too!

The girls were very hungry after their swim. They sat down to enjoy the food. There was bread, butter, potted meat, tins of sardines, marmalade, apricot jam, cherries, biscuits and Mirabel's big birthday cake. The candles did not show up very well in the bright moonlight, but still, it was fun to light them.

The girls had their picnic by the edge of the water, dangling their legs in the pool. The water was lukewarm, for the sun had warmed it thoroughly. It was simply lovely. There had never been such midnight fun as this!

'This cake is gorgeous,' said Bobby, eating an enormous slice. 'My word—I don't ever remember feeling so hungry. Are those sardine sandwiches? Pass them along, Susan.'

Claudine enjoyed her meal more than any one. True, she was not so hungry as the others, for she had not been in for a swim—but she could not help thinking of Matron shut up in the dark cupboard, quite unable to spoil the fun of the fourth-formers! And that gave a very keen edge to her enjoyment of the picnic. She felt no anxiety as to what would happen when Matron was let out. Claudine never let things like that worry her at all!

The meal was over at last. Every scrap was finished. Even Angela said she had enjoyed it. Alison had not enjoyed it quite so much as the others because she had fallen into the water in her dressing-gown, and was worried as to how to dry it before Matron saw it. Mirabel said she had never enjoyed a birthday so much in all her life.

'It's been a great success,' said Janet, pleased. 'Now we'd better go back. Hark—there's one o'clock striking —Dong! Golly, I'm tired now.'

Every one was tired. The swim had been rather

strenuous, for there had been a lot of good-humoured racing and teasing. The girls cleared up crumbs, cartons, and paper-bags, and put empty ginger-beer bottles into a locker up in the gallery, meaning to collect them when it was safe.

'That's all, I think,' said Susan, looking round. 'Isn't the water lovely, gleaming in the moonlight. I just hate to leave it!'

But they had to leave the gleaming pool. They made their way back through the trees, whispering together. They came to the garden door, which was still open.

And then they heard a most peculiar noise. Bang, bang, bang, knock, knock, knock!

'Crumbs! What's that!' said Susan, startled.

'Let me out, let me out!' cried a muffled voice, and somebody kicked against a wooden door.

Alison and Angela were terrified. 'It's a burglar!' said Alison, and tore up the stairs as fast as ever she could. Angela followed her, trembling.

Claudine pushed the others towards the stairs quickly. 'Don't stop,' she whispered. 'Get back to the dormitories as quickly as you can. Don't stop. I will explain everything.'

In the greatest astonishment the girls went upstairs to their dormitories. They crowded into the one in which Claudine slept, and demanded to know what the explanation of the curious noises was.

'It's Matron,' said Claudine. 'She's locked in that cupboard.'

There was an amazed silence.

'*Who* locked her in?' said Bobby at last.

'I did,' said Claudine. 'She came into our dormitories and saw we weren't there. I did not want her to spoil your fun—so I pushed her into the cupboard and locked her in. Was I not quick and clever?'

FOR a minute or two no one said anything at all. The girls found it simply unbelievable that Claudine should have done such a thing. Locked Matron into a games cupboard! Left her there, shouting and hammering! Really, the French girl must be completely mad.

'No, I am not mad,' said Claudine, reading their thoughts. 'It was the only thing to do, wasn't it? She would have spoilt your fun, and I could stop her. So I stopped her.'

'But Claudine—you'll get into the most fearful row!' said Janet at last.

'That matters nothing,' replied Claudine, and certainly she acted as if she did not mind what happened! She was not in the least excited or upset. The girls went on staring at her, hardly able to take in the fact that Matron had been, and still was, a prisoner downstairs.

Then an awful thought came to Bobby. 'Who's going to let her out?'

Nobody said anything. Not even Claudine wanted to set free a woman who would be sure to be violently and spitefully angry. But certainly she could not be left in the cupboard till the morning.

'Where's the key?' said Janet. Claudine produced it from her dressing-gown pocket. It was a large key. Claudine put her finger in the hole at the top of it and swung it thoughtfully to and fro.

'As I was the one who locked her in, I will also be the one to let her out,' she said at last. 'But I shall unlock the door very, very quietly, then open it a tiny way, and then I shall fly up the stairs, taking my heels with me.'

The girls couldn't help smiling. 'You mean, you will

take to your heels and fly upstairs ! ' said Bobby.   ' You
do say ridiculous things, Claudine.   Honestly, I can't
imagine how you dared to do such a thing—locking
Matron into a cupboard—golly, it's unheard of !   Why
didn't you tell us what you had done, when you came
back to the pool and joined the picnic ? '

' I thought you would say, " Ah, it is not honourable
to do such a thing," ' explained Claudine.   ' I thought
maybe Susan would feel she ought to go and set Matron
free.   So I said nothing.'

' I never met any one quite like you before,' said **Pat.**
' You do the most awful things for perfectly good reasons !
I mean—you throw yourself into the pool when you *hate*
the water, just to punish some one who's been unkind to
your aunt—and you go and lock Matron up into a cupboard just so that we shan't have our picnic spoilt !   I
must say you do the most dramatic things—we never
know what you're going to do next ! '

' Well—what are we going to do about Matron ? '
demanded Susan, who was getting worried.   ' Shall **we**
let Claudine let her out ? '

' I go,' said Claudine, and got up with much dignity.
She loved moments like this, when she took the stage and
every one looked at her.   She was not at all conceited,
but there was to her a very satisfying feeling in doing
something unusual and dramatic.

She went.   The girls scrambled into bed, feeling that
very shortly Matron would come bursting into the
dormitories like an angry bull !

Claudine crept downstairs to the little back-hall by
the garden-door.   Matron was still shouting and hammering.   Claudine slipped along to the door and put the key
quietly into the key-hole—but just as she was about to
turn it and unlock the door, she heard the sound of quiet
footsteps on the gravel path outside !

She darted up the stairs at once, without turning the

key. Let whoever it was coming by unlock the door! They would be sure to hear Matron, and set her free. Then she, Claudine, could get away in safety!

The footsteps came to the garden-door, and then some one slipped inside. It was Eileen! She stood still in the greatest astonishment as she heard the muffled cries and the banging on the door of the games cupboard.

'Why—it's Mother's voice!' said Eileen out loud, in the very greatest amazement. 'Where is she? She can't be in that cupboard!'

But she was, as Eileen very soon realized. The girl turned the key at once and opened the door. Matron stumbled out, almost beside herself with rage. She caught hold of Eileen in a fierce grip, not seeing what girl it was. Eileen cried out in pain.

'Mother! Don't! It's me, Eileen. However did you get into that cupboard?'

'*You!*' cried Matron, and let go Eileen's arm. 'What are *you* doing here? Where have you been? How dare you go out at night like this? Tell me what you have been doing, at once!'

Eileen said nothing at all. Her mother gave her a shake. 'You've been out somewhere with the fourth form. They are all out of their beds! What have you been doing? I shall report you all to Miss Theobald. Why didn't you tell me what was happening?'

'I can't say anything, Mother,' said Eileen, in a frightened voice. It was news to her that the fourth form had been out that night. She had not noticed any empty beds when she had slipped out herself. She had not heard any noise from the swimming-pool either. She had been out to meet Eddie her brother in the lane, and she was not going to tell her mother this. She no longer dared to meet him in the daytime, for she felt that any one might see her, and report her. So she had been meeting him once a week in the middle of the night, when all her dormitory was sound asleep.

Nobody knew this. And certainly she must not let her mother know, or Eddie would get into trouble too. What had the fourth-formers been doing ? How mean of them to go off on a spree at night and leave her out ! Somehow or other she must make her mother think she had been with them.

'You won't say anything ? ' said her mother in a threatening voice. ' Well, tell me this—who locked me in here ? I can't imagine that *you* would dare to ! '

' Of course I didn't,' said Eileen. ' And I don't know who did, either. Carlotta might have. It's the kind of thing she would do. I really don't know, Mother. Please let me go back to bed ! '

But Matron was far too angry and humiliated to let the matter drop. She swept up the stairs to the fourth-form dormitories, and switched on the lights. The girls all pretended to be asleep. Matron walked into the dormitory where Eileen slept, and spoke in a loud and angry voice.

' It's no good your pretending to be asleep. I know you're not. I've come to find out who locked me into that cupboard ! I insist on knowing, here and now. That girl will be expelled from St. Clare's ! '

Susan Howes sat up and looked at the angry Matron. ' We all take the blame for that,' she said, quietly. ' We are very sorry, Matron, and we hope you will accept our apologies.'

Matron made a fierce explosive noise. ' Accept your apologies ! Of course I don't ! You won't get out of this as easily as that ! I insist on knowing who locked me in. Otherwise I shall go straight to Miss Theobald, here and now, in the middle of the night.'

Claudine sat up in bed, ready to speak. She did not in the least mind owning up. But Bobby laid a warning hand on her shoulder, and pulled her over towards her, to whisper into her ear.

' Don't own up to Matron ! She will go to your aunt too, and make a fearful fuss, and there's no reason why Mam'zelle should be brought into this. You can tell Miss Theobald yourself tomorrow if you want to.'

' *Bien !* ' said Claudine, snuggling down into bed again. ' Very good ! I do as you say, Bobbee.'

Matron stood glaring round the room. Then she stamped heavily with her foot and almost shouted. ' All right ! I shall go to Miss Theobald. You will all have to explain what you were doing in the middle of the night, leaving your beds like that—and I warn you, I shall show no mercy on the person who has not owned up to locking me in. Eileen, get into bed. I am absolutely ashamed to think that a daughter of mine should have joined in midnight wrong-doing, and should refuse to tell me anything about it ! '

She went off down the corridor, walking angrily. The girls sat up.

' Whew ! ' said Bobby, ' what a volcano ! I say, Eileen, where were you ? Does your mother really think you were with us ? '

' Yes,' said Eileen, in a low voice. ' Please don't give me away. I was only meeting Eddie, my brother. I was afraid to tell my mother that, so I let her think I was with you. I didn't know what you had been doing, so I couldn't possibly tell her, of course, and that has made her very wild with me. We're all going to get into a most fearful row.'

' I bet Miss Theobald won't be too pleased at being wakened up at this time of night,' said Janet, looking at her watch. ' It's half-past one ! We'd better try and get some sleep—though I expect the next thing will be Miss Theobald coming in and demanding explanations too ! '

The girls tried to settle down and go to sleep. Mirabel fell asleep first, and then one by one the others did . . . all except Eileen, who lay awake, staring into the dark, worried and unhappy. Everything was going wrong! Everything was getting worse! Oh dear, she did hope the girls wouldn't give her away and say she had not been with them that night. They might quite well sneak about her. She had done plenty of sneaking that term, and it would not be at all surprising if they got a bit of their own back!

Matron walked down the corridor and made her way to the separate wing in which the Head Mistress, Miss Theobald, had her set of rooms. She knocked loudly on the bedroom door.

' Come in! ' said a startled voice, and there was the sound of a light being switched on. Matron opened the door. Miss Theobald was sitting up in bed, eyes heavy with sleep.

' What is the matter? ' she said anxiously. ' Is some one ill, Matron? '

' No,' said Matron, her thin face still purple with rage. ' Something much worse than that! '

' Good gracious, what? ' asked Miss Theobald, hurriedly getting out of bed and reaching for her dressing-gown. ' Quick, tell me! '

' It's the fourth form,' said Matron, in a grim voice. ' All out of their beds, every one. Even my Eileen. Goodness knows what they were doing! '

Miss Theobald sat down on her bed in relief. ' Oh! ' she said, ' a midnight feast, I suppose? I thought you had come to report something really serious! Couldn't this have waited till the morning, Matron? '

' Indeed it couldn't,' said Matron, ' and for a very good reason, too. Somebody locked me for hours into the games cupboard in the back-hall by the garden-door! '

Miss Theobald stared at Matron as if she really could

not believe her ears. 'Locked you into the cupboard?'
she said at last. 'Are you quite sure? I mean—I
really cannot imagine any of the fourth-formers doing
that.'

'You don't know half that goes on in the school,'
answered Matron in a grim and righteous tone. 'Not
half! My Eileen tells me most things, and you'd be
surprised if I told you some of them.'

'I don't think I want to hear,' said Miss Theobald,
'and I can't help thinking it is a mistake, Matron, to
encourage Eileen to tell tales to you. Also I think you
need not worry whether I know all that goes on or not.
That is my concern.'

Matron sensed the rebuke in Miss Theobald's words,
and she began to feel angry that the Head had not
expressed more anger and concern over her imprisonment
in the cupboard. She looked grimmer than ever.

'Eileen set me free,' she said. 'Otherwise I might
have been in the cupboard till the morning. A fine thing
to happen to the Matron of a school like this! I went
up to the fourth-form dormitories at once, and there
were all the girls pretending to be asleep. Little
hypocrites!'

'Oh, Matron, don't be quite so vindictive!' said Miss
Theobald, feeling rather shocked at the Matron's tone.
'You have never been Matron in a girls' school before,
and you are not yet used to the mischievous ways of the
various forms. But as a rule there is little harm in
them. Who locked you in?'

'The girls won't say,' said Matron, angrily. 'But I
demand that whoever locked me in should be expelled,
Miss Theobald. A girl that does a thing like that is a
very bad influence on the others!'

'Well, I expect they were all in it,' said Miss Theobald.
'I should never expel a girl without a much stronger
reason than mere mischief, Matron. I am certain that

the whole form shared in the fun, and you would not
expect me to expel the whole lot, would you ?   Do try
and see things in a reasonable light.   You are angry and
annoyed now—you will not be so inclined to want girls
expelled in the morning.'

' Aren't you coming back to the dormitories with me
to demand who it was that locked me in ? ' demanded
Matron, furiously, as she saw Miss Theobald taking off
her dressing-gown and slippers.

' The girls will, I hope, be asleep by now,' said the
Head, getting into bed.   ' I see no reason for waking
them all up again.   This can easily wait till the morning.'

Matron was infuriated.   She had planned a most
dramatic return to the dormitories with Miss Theobald,
and had gone so far as to hope that the Head would
demand to know the culprit and announce her expulsion
there and then.   She bit her thin lips and glared at
Miss Theobald so angrily that the headmistress began to
feel annoyed.

' Please go now, Matron,' she said.   ' We will continue
this rather complicated conversation in the morning.'

Matron took a step forward, and her face took on a
malicious look.   ' Well,' she said, ' I wasn't going to tell
you till I'd found out the thief—but there's somebody in
the fourth form who's been stealing, Miss Theobald !
I've missed money—yes, and stamps too—and all kinds
of things like notepaper and envelopes.   You've got a
nasty little thief in the fourth form, and I shall want
that matter cleared up too !   Otherwise, I am afraid—I
shall go to the police ! '

MISS THEOBALD disliked Matron intensely at that
moment.   It was quite plain that she took a real pleasure
in saying these poisonous things.

'I think all these things must wait till the morning
Matron,' said the Head.   'I will go into them thoroughly
then.   We can do nothing satisfactory tonight.   Good
night.'

Matron walked out of the room without answering.
She hoped she had given Miss Theobald a shock.   She
had not meant to talk about her missing money, for she
was taking a great pleasure in trying to track down the
thief herself—and then she had meant to take her by
the shoulder and lead her triumphantly to Miss Theobald.
Matron hoped that the thief and the one who had locked
her into the cupboard were one and the same.   She felt
certain they were.   Surely only a very bad character
could lock her into a cupboard!

'We shall perhaps get to the bottom of things tomorrow!' she thought, as she got into bed.   'I'll make
Eileen tell me all that the fourth form did.   I shan't say
anything about my missing money to her, though, in case
she warns the fourth form and the thief isn't caught.'

The fourth-form girls woke up tired and sleepy and
rather fearful the next morning.   Had Matron been to
Miss Theobald?   What was going to happen?

Matron appeared at breakfast, grim and stern.   Eileen
had tear-stained eyes.   Her mother had scolded her and
demanded to know what the fourth form had been doing
the night before.   But Eileen had not told.

Bobby had spoken seriously to her.   'Look here,
Eileen—we didn't ask you to our picnic last night because

we were afraid you'd sneak to your mother, as you often do. But we'll make a bargain with you. We will say nothing at all about your not being with us—Matron can go on thinking you *were* with us—but you in your turn aren't to give us away any more at all. See? And if you do, the bargain is automatically broken, and we shall tell of you. It's the only way to teach you that sneaking doesn't pay.'

Eileen, looking pale and unhappy, had nodded. ' Thank you,' she said. ' I couldn't bear Mother to know I go and meet Eddie. She would be so angry with him. I won't split on any of you any more. I've sneaked, I know—but it's so difficult not to answer Mother's questions sometimes.'

Bobby guessed it was. Eileen had her own problems—but they wouldn't be solved by being weak and telling-tales! She had to find that out sooner or later.

But this morning Eileen had been determined and strong, for once, and had not answered Matron's insistent questions. Her mother had been very angry, and had even boxed her ears hard. Matron had a fierce temper when she let herself go, and poor Eileen had had to bear the brunt of it.

' Claudine,' said Susan, in a low voice at breakfast-time, ' if you want to own up to Miss Theobald about locking Matron up, you'd better go immediately after breakfast. But if you don't want to own up, you needn't. We'll all stick by you, and ask Miss Theobald to hand out a punishment to the whole form. After all, we had a good time, because of you, and we none of us want you to be punished for something we would all dearly like to have done ourselves.'

' Thank you, Susan,' said Claudine, thinking that these English girls could be very nice and fair and generous. ' But I shall go to Miss Theobald. I am not ashamed of what I did. She is a nasty woman, the Matron, and I shall tell Miss Theobald that it filled me with pleasure to punish her for some of the unkind things she has done this term.'

' Well—do and say what you like,' said Susan, thinking that Claudine would, all her life, quite probably do and say exactly what she liked ! ' And good luck to you ! '

So Claudine went to the Head, knocked firmly at the door and went in.

She began without any beating about the bush, ' Please, Miss Theobald, I have come to say that it was I who locked Matron in last night. I suppose it is not a thing that any English girl would have done, with their so-fine sense of honour, but I am French, and I did not like Matron, and I wanted the fourth form to have a good time. We went for a moonlight picnic, Miss Theobald, and swam in the pool. At least, I did not swim, but the others did, and they said it was magnificent.'

Miss Theobald found it difficult not to smile at the frank confession. Claudine always had such a very disarming and innocent air, even when she was doing, or owning up to the most extraordinary things. The Head looked keenly at the intelligent French girl.

' Why do you dislike Matron ? '

' You wish me to say the truth to you ? ' asked Claudine. ' Well, then, I will say this. Matron can find out, through Eileen, all the little stupidities and mischiefs of the fourth-formers, and then, see what happens ! Miraculously our sheets get torn and we spend hours mending them. Suddenly stockings are full of holes, vests are without buttons. Alas, Miss Theobald, we do not all like Eileen, and if we show it, then these unhappy things happen, and we sit indoors mending, whilst others play games.'

' I see,' said Miss Theobald. She had suspected this. ' Claudine, you cannot go about locking people into cupboards.　I am certain that even French schoolgirls do not do this ! '

' Ah, Miss Theobald, I do not go about always locking people up ! ' said Claudine, beginning to launch herself on to one of her long and involved speeches. ' No, no—only those people who deserve it should be imprisoned into cupboards. Me, I would never . . .'

Miss Theobald thought that Claudine had many of Mam'zelle's own ways.　She smiled to herself and stopped the voluble explanation.

' That will do, Claudine.　You will please apologize to Matron this morning, and you will accept what punishment she gives you.　There is one thing more . . .'

She stopped and looked keenly at Claudine.　The little French girl listened intently, for she had a great liking and respect for the wise and kindly Head Mistress.

' That one thing more is about the English sense of honour,' said Miss Theobald.　' You speak lightly of it, even mockingly—but I think, Claudine, in your heart of hearts you see it for the good and fine thing it really is. When you go back to France, Claudine, take one thing with you—the English sense of honour.'

Claudine looked solemn.　She was very much moved. ' Miss Theobald,' she said, ' believe me when I say that I do not really mock at it.　First I did not understand it. Then I thought it was tiresome in others and even more tiresome to have oneself.　But now I begin to learn it, and it is good, very good.'

There came a knock at the door and Matron came in, looking grimmer than ever.　She meant to have things out with Miss Theobald at once.　Claudine was simply delighted to see her.　' Now,' thought the clever girl, ' now I will apologize to Matron in front of Miss Theobald, and she will not dare to be too spiteful to me nor to give me too great a punishment ! '

So Claudine went meekly up to Matron, cast her

eyes down to the ground, and spoke in a very timid voice.

'Matron, it was I who locked you in last night. I apologize to you and beg your forgiveness. I will gladly bear what punishment you give me!'

Miss Theobald looked on with much amusement. She knew that Claudine was acting a part, and had cleverly taken advantage of Matron's coming, to apologize at once, in front of the headmistress herself.

Matron went purple in the face. She glared at Claudine and scolded her severely.

'You're a very naughty girl! You deserve to be expelled! And what is more, I *would* have you expelled if it was not that your aunt is the French mistress here, and it would break her heart to have a thing like that happen.'

Actually Matron was afraid of Mam'zelle, who was apt to fly off into even more violent tempers than Matron herself. Matron even felt that Mam'zelle might come and scratch her face and pull her hair out if she dared to try and get Claudine expelled.

'It is good of you to consider my kind aunt,' replied Claudine, still in a very meek voice. 'What is my punishment to be?'

'You will spend every hour of your spare-time this week helping me to mend the school linen,' said Matron. She did not see the flash of joy in Claudine's downcast eyes. Ah, now she would be able to get out of games and walks for a whole week! 'Very well, Matron,' she said, putting on a most miserable voice, that did not deceive the listening Miss Theobald in the least. She turned to the Head.

'I will return now to my class,' she said, and gave Miss Theobald a brilliant and grateful smile. She went out of the room, shutting the door quietly. Miss Theobald thought that no one could help liking the naughty

little girl, clever as she was at always getting her own
way !

'Well, Miss Theobald,' said Matron, in a war-like tone,
' can we get down to this business of stealing ?   I can't
have it happening any longer.   It's got beyond me.   Day
after day it happens.   And what's more, some more of
my money has gone since last night !   Only two shillings,
it is true—but stealing two shillings is as bad as stealing
two pounds.   It's thieving, right down bad thieving.
And I think the girl who does it ought to be expelled.
You wouldn't agree to expelling the girl who locked me
in last night—but maybe you'll have to, Miss Theobald !
Yes, maybe you'll have to ! '

' What do you mean ? ' asked Miss Theobald in surprise.

' I mean this,' said Matron, ' I think it's that little
French girl who's taking things !   She's always in and
out of my room with mending—and I hear she's been
throwing a lot of money about lately—and *I* know she
hasn't much, because Mam'zelle herself told me.   So
maybe, Miss Theobald, you will find that it's best to get
rid of a girl of that sort, and will agree with me that it
would be a good thing to expel her ! '

19   PAULINE'S MOTHER

BEFORE Miss Theobald could make up her mind that
day what would be the best way to tackle the Matron
and her accusations, a nasty accident happened in the
gym.

It happened to Pauline.   She was climbing one of the
ropes, and somehow slipped and fell to the ground.   She
fell with one leg doubled up under her, and there was a
sickening crack.

Pauline crumpled up on the floor, went very white, and then quietly fainted. The games-mistress hurried to her in alarm, and Matron was at once called and the doctor telephoned for.

'Broken her leg,' he said. 'Clean break. Nothing to worry about.'

He set it, and Pauline was put to bed, still white from the shock. Miss Theobald went to see her, and Pauline looked beseechingly up at her.

'Don't tell my mother,' she said. 'I don't want to worry her. Please don't tell her.'

'My dear child, I have already telephoned to her,' said Miss Theobald in surprise. 'Why shouldn't she be told?'

'I don't want to worry her,' said Pauline, faintly. 'Please ring her up again, Miss Theobald, and say she is not to worry, and of course she is not to bother to come and see me. Say I will write to her today.'

'You can't write today,' said Miss Theobald gently. 'You must keep absolutely quiet today. I will ring your mother up again this evening, and tell her not to bother to come and see you if she cannot do so.'

'Tell her *not* to,' said Pauline. 'She—she hasn't been well, you see. I don't want her to be worried.'

Every one was sorry about Pauline. The girls were not allowed to go and see her that day, but they sent her in little gifts of flowers and fruit and books.

'Everything seems to be happening at once,' said Bobby. 'I say—wasn't that a perfectly awful talk that Miss Theobald had with us this morning?'

It had been a very serious and solemn talk indeed, and had happened just before dinner that morning. All the fourth-formers, except Pauline, who was in the sanatorium, under Matron's care, had been called to Miss Theobald's drawing-room.

The Head had lightly touched on the night before,

telling them that Claudine had confessed, and had apologized to Matron and received a punishment for her extraordinary behaviour. She said that she would have given permission herself for a moonlight picnic and swim if she had been asked, but she realized that girls as young as the fourth still thought it was more fun to do things with*out* permission, than with.

This made the more responsible ones squirm a bit. They did not like being considered young and silly. Then Miss Theobald passed on to Matron's other complaint. This was very much more serious, of course, and the fourth form listened in great discomfort as the Head told them that a thief was in their midst, and must be found out, or must come and confess.

'You must realize that what would be a small thing, comparatively speaking, in the lower school, among the younger children, is a much more serious thing among you older girls,' said the Head, 'and Matron is quite rightly concerned about the matter. Whoever is taking things from her room is doing it deliberately and continually—it is not something done in a moment of urgency and perhaps regretted bitterly afterwards—it is, apparently, quite cold-blooded, frequent and deliberate.'

The girls talked about it all afterwards, the affair of Matron being locked up in the cupboard taking second-place to this much more serious accusation. Who in the wide world could it be?

'Matron is certain it's some one in the fourth form because our common room is the only one near to her room,' said Bobby. 'It would be easy for some one to slip out now and then, see if the coast was clear, and then pop into Matron's room and sneak something.'

'Such queer things have been stolen besides money,' said Janet, puzzled. 'Stamps—and notepaper and envelopes. Why those? Matron says that biscuits and sweets have been taken too. It almost looks as if somebody has been taking anything they could, just out of spite.'

'Well, we none of us love Matron!' said Bobby, grinning. 'If it was just a question of paying her out for her meannesses, any one of us might be the culprit!'

'I am glad such things happen to her,' said Claudine. 'She deserves to have unhappiness, because she gives so much sadness to others. The poor Eileen has red eyes all day long today!'

'Yes, I can't help feeling sorry for her,' said Doris. 'It's bad enough to have Matron as Matron, but to have her as mother as well must be pretty awful!'

Pat, Isabel, Janet, Bobby and Hilary discussed the matter between themselves on the tennis-court that day.

'Who *could* it be?' said Bobby.

'Has any one suddenly been having more money than usual?' wondered Pat. The same thought at once came into every one's mind.

'Yes—Claudine has! She's been splashing it about like anything!'

'And she has plenty of chance of going into Matron's room because she is always taking mending there!'

'But it *can't* be Claudine! It's true she hasn't our sense of honour—but she wouldn't do a thing like that!'

'You know she doesn't care *what* she does when she dislikes somebody or wants to get even with them. She wouldn't think it was wrong, even.'

The five looked at one another, suddenly feeling extremely uncomfortable. They knew Claudine had very little money indeed—and yet she had given Angela that lovely bag—and had spent ten whole shillings on cherries for the picnic. It did really seem as if it might be Claudine.

The bell rang for tea-time and the girls sped into the school. After tea Angela and Alison went off together down to the town to get something they wanted. On the way back they overtook an elderly woman, dressed in sober black clothes, sensible flat-heeled shoes, and a plain hat. She wore glasses, and her face was thin and worn, but kindly.

'I bet that's a cook come after the job at St. Clare's,' said Angela to Alison. The girls passed her and she turned and spoke to them.

'Could you tell me if I am on the right road for St. Clare's? You are St. Clare girls, aren't you?'

'Yes,' said Alison. 'Keep straight on.'

The girls made as if to go on, but the woman stopped them with a question that astonished them very much.

'How is my girl Pauline now? The Head Mistress telephoned me to say she had broken her leg this morning, and I caught the first train I could. I'm Mrs. Jones.'

Angela and Alison stopped dead in the road and stared open-mouthed at the little elderly woman. They remembered Pauline's wonderful stories of Mrs. Bingham-Jones, her beautiful and wealthy mother. They simply could not understand this plain, tired-looking woman, almost old, being Pauline's supposedly wonderful mother.

Scorn welled up at once in Angela's heart. So Pauline, who was always trying to out-do and out-boast Angela herself, had, for a mother, a woman who looked like a worn-out cook. She tried to pull Alison up the road quickly.

But something in Mrs. Jones's tired face had touched Alison. Alison had many faults, but she was sensitive to other people's feelings, and she could sense Mrs. Jones's worry and anxiety. She shook her arm away from Angela's.

'Pauline is all right,' she said, kindly. 'We couldn't see her today but we've all sent her something—you know, flowers and books and things—just to cheer her up. Are you better now? Pauline was *so* disappointed

that you and her father couldn't come and see her at
half-term, because you were ill.'

Mrs. Jones looked extremely surprised. ' I haven't
been ill,' she said. ' I wanted to come at half-term, but
Pauline wrote to say there was a case of scarlet fever at
the school, and the half-term matches had been put off,
so would I not come.'

Alison was horrified. In a flash she saw that Pauline,
afraid that her mother would not shine among the other
mothers, knowing that she had told all kinds of lies that
would be found out when the girls saw her elderly, tired
mother, had actually made up the lie about scarlet fever
to stop her people from coming at half-term—and had
pretended to be bitterly disappointed because they
weren't coming !

Angela, of course, heard what was said, and an expression of scorn and contempt came over her face.

' *Well !* ' she said, ' there was no case of . . .' But
Alison was not going to let Angela interfere in the matter.
She gave her friend a sharp nudge that made her squeal
in surprise. Then she gave her such a fierce look that
Angela said no more, but thought in surprise that Alison
must be mad to treat her, Angela, like that.

' I hope Pauline is happy at St. Clare's ? ' said Mrs.
Jones. ' She has always wanted to go there, ever since
she heard about it. I didn't see that I could afford to
send her, but I managed to scrape enough together. Her
poor father is an invalid, you know—has been for years—
but I expect she's told you all that. We haven't a lot
of money, but I did want Pauline to have a good time at
a nice school. I said to her, " Well, my dear, you won't
have as much pocket-money as the others, and you won't
have as many treats, but there you are, if you like to go
under those conditions, I won't stop you." '

Mrs. Jones talked to Alison, not to Angela. She liked
Alison's pretty, kindly little face, and was glad to have

some one to talk to. Angela gave a snort of contempt, and went quickly on, up the hill towards St. Clare's.

' It's quite a way, isn't it ? ' said Mrs. Jones, beginning to pant. ' I didn't take a taxi, because taxis are expensive and I thought I could easily walk. Poor little Pauline—it is terribly bad luck to have broken her leg like this. I thought she would be so pleased to see me, if I can hurry along at once.'

Alison didn't feel so certain. She thought that if Pauline had kept her mother away by lies at half-term she would certainly not want her at St. Clare's now, with all her lies exposed for what they were.

' Pauline is disgusting,' thought Alison. ' She really is. She takes everything from this poor little mother of hers, who probably goes without a lot of things she wants in order to pay for Pauline here—and then keeps her away from the school because she is ashamed of her ! Beast ! '

Alison took Mrs. Jones to the school door and left her there in charge of a maid. She went to take off her hat and blazer and joined the rest of her form in the common room.

' I hope Angela doesn't go and hold forth about Pauline's poor old mother,' thought Alison uncomfortably. ' I feel sorry for the old thing. She looked so tired and worn.'

She heard Angela's voice as she opened the common-room door.

' And my dear, *I* know who it was that took Matron's beastly money and everything ! There's not a doubt of it. It was Pauline ! '

' Pauline ! What do you mean ? Why do you say that ? ' came Janet's voice at once.

' I'll tell you why,' said Angela, and paused dramatically. ' I and Alison walked up the road with Pauline's mother today—and from what she said to us it's pretty certain that our dear Pauline is a frightful story-teller and quite likely a horrid little thief!'

20 ANGELA—AND CLAUDINE

'YOU'LL have to tell us why you say all this,' said Bobby. The whole of the fourth form crowded round to hear. Only Claudine was not there, and neither, of course, was Pauline.

'Well, listen,' said Angela, spitefully, 'I and Alison were walking up the road and we saw an ugly little elderly woman, awfully plain, dressed in black in front of us. I thought she must be a cook coming to try for the job going here. And it turned out to be Mrs. Jones, Pauline's mother—not Mrs. *Bingham*-Jones, if you please, but just plain Mrs. Jones.'

'She's a nice little woman,' said Alison, not liking the contempt in Angela's voice.

'*Nice* little woman!' said Angela, rounding on Alison scornfully. 'Common as dirt, you mean! And when I think of Pauline's airs and graces—trying to make out her mother was as good as mine—trying to pretend that her family were as grand as mine really are—swanking about her cars and things—and they're as poor as church mice, and can only just afford to send Pauline here! Golly, won't I tell Pauline what I think of her when I see her! *I'll* tell her what I think of dear Mrs. Jones, dressed up like a cook, moaning about her poor little Pauline.'

Before any one else could speak, Alison stood up. She was rather white, and there was a queer look on her face.

'You won't tell Pauline anything of the sort,' she said. 'You won't tell Pauline *any*thing that's going to make her ashamed of that poor old mother of hers. Don't you realize how you'll make her hate her mother, if she knows you saw her and are saying this kind of thing about her ? I think Pauline has behaved disgustingly about things, but I'm not going to have you making matters worse for Mrs. Jones by saying horrible things about her to Pauline.'

Angela was amazed. Could this be her friend Alison talking to her like this ? She stared at her, unable to say a word. Then she found her tongue.

' Well, if you stick up for people like Pauline's awful mother, I'm jolly glad you're not coming to stay with me for the holidays,' she said, spitefully. ' I'm going l I shan't stay here to be insulted by somebody I thought was my best friend.'

Poor Alison was now trembling, for she hated rows. Angela moved towards the door. But to her intense surprise and annoyance, two girls caught firmly hold of her arms and sat her down violently, almost jerking the breath out of her body.

' You may not want to listen to Alison, but you're jolly well going to listen to *us* l ' said Carlotta, her gypsy eyes flashing fire. ' Now *we* will say a few things l '

' Let me go, you beasts,' said Angela, between her teeth.

' You seem to be talking a lot about mothers,' said Carlotta, bending over the angry Angela, and talking in such a fierce tone that Angela drew back, afraid. ' Well, we *will* talk about mothers—*your* mother l We would not talk about her if it was not necessary—but it is very necessary now, in order to get some sense into your thick head l '

' I'll scream if you don't let me go,' said Angela, in a rage.

' Every time you scream I shall slap you hard, like that,' said Carlotta, and gave Angela such a smack on her plump shoulder that she squealed in pain.

' You're jolly well going to listen to us! ' said Carlotta

'Shut up, Carlotta,' said Bobby. 'You can't act like that.'

'Yes, I can,' said Carlotta, coolly. And Angela knew she could, so she made no further sound.

'Pauline's mother may be tired and old and plain and poor,' said Carlotta, ' but that's no reason to despise her. Now there *is* reason to despise *your* mother, Angela ! She is a spoilt, rude, discontented, horrible little snob— just like you are ! And will you please tell her on no account to come here again, turning up her nose at every-thing, because we don't want to see her, we dislike her and despise her, and we want her to take you away as soon as ever she will ! '

'Hear hear ! ' said Bobby, Janet and the twins. Angela went very pale. These were terrible things to hear, but she had brought them on herself. She, too, had been ashamed of her spoilt mother when she had come at half-term—but she had not guessed how bitterly the girls had resented her contemptuous attitude towards the school and all it stood for.

'That's enough, Carlotta,' said Susan Howes, uncom-fortably. And it was enough. Angela looked as if she was about to faint. She wanted to sink through the floor. She, who had boasted and bragged of herself and her family, who had set herself up as better than any of them, was being spoken to as if she were dirt. She gave an enormous sob, and fled from the room.

'Well, thank goodness she's gone,' said Pat. 'Cheer up, Alison. I was proud of you when you spoke up like that. Perhaps now you will see Angela as clearly as *we* see her.'

'Yes—I do,' said poor Alison, really distressed. 'I think she's awful. I did feel so sorry for that poor Mrs. Jones—and Angela had nothing but scorn for her. There's no kindness in her ! '

'None at all,' said Janet. 'Well—she's got to learn

that kindness breeds kindness, and spite breeds spite. She'll have an awful time if she doesn't.'

' Do you think it's right, what Angela said, that Pauline might be the thief ? ' said Doris. ' She *has* splashed money about very much lately—and if she's really poor—where did it come from ? '

' We half thought it might be Claudine,' said Isabe'. ' You know, she's poor too—hardly ever has a penny—and then, quite suddenly she had lots of money. And you know how unscrupulous Claudine is ! I like her—but she simply has no sense of honour at all ! We did wonder if it could be her.'

' Sh ! Sh ! ' said some one. But too late—for Claudine, who had come in unnoticed, had heard what Isabel had said !

The little French girl at once pushed her way to the front of the crowd of girls. Isabel saw her coming, and was horrified. Not for the world would she have had Claudine hear what she had said !

' Claudine ! ' she said, ' I'm sorry you heard. Don't be angry. We only thought it because you seem so different from us in your ideas of honour. And it did seem to us that if you disliked Matron, you might pay her out in that way.'

Claudine looked round the little group, intense anger in her small face. She saw Isabel's earnest face, Pat's scared one, Bobby's watchful one—and then, to the enormous astonishment of the listening girls, the anger in her face melted away—and Claudine threw back her head and laughed !

The girls stared at her in surprise. Honestly, thought Doris, you simply never know what Claudine will do !

Bobby thought how like Mam'zelle she was, in her swift changes from anger to laughter. But what a blessing that Claudine could see any humour in Isabel's words !

'I am not angry,' said Claudine, at last, wiping away the tears of laughter. 'No, I am not angry. You English girls, you are so serious and solemn and so very, very honourable. I too have my own honour, and although it is not quite like yours yet, perhaps, one day it will be. The good Miss Theobald, she said to me this morning that one thing I must take back to France with me, one only—the English sense of honour.'

'Just like Miss Theobald to say a thing like that,' said Janet. 'But why did you laugh just now, Claudine?'

'I laugh because I was thinking so suddenly of the reason why I have so much money now to spend,' said Claudine, smiling her infectious smile. 'But first, if I tell you, you must promise, on your English honour, that never, never will you tell my Aunt Mathilde what I have done!'

'Oh, Claudine—*what* have you done?' said Pat, imagining the most awful things.

'You remember my so-beautiful cushion-cover that my aunt loved so much?' said Claudine. 'Well, I sold it to one of your mothers for quite a lot of money! You see, I needed money—there were birthdays coming, and I do not like to have so little. And one of your mothers, she was so nice to me, and she bought my so-beautiful cover, and I sent it to her by post. I explained to her that it was my own, and I lacked for money, and she was so, so kind to me.'

'Was that *my* mother?' asked Alison, suspiciously. 'I saw you talking nineteen to the dozen to her at half-term. Mother *would* do a nice thing like that, and never say a word about it. I hope she puts the cushion-cover in my bedroom, that's all!'

'Well,' said Claudine, grinning all over her little monkey-face, 'it *might* have been your so-nice mother, Alison. My sense of honour forbids me to say. And now I appeal to *your* sense of honour also, not to tell my

aunt what has happened to my cushion-cover. I told
her I had sent it to my mother.'

'You *are* an awful story-teller, Claudine,' said Gladys,
shocked. 'You deceive people right and left! I just
can't understand you. Why couldn't you tell Mam'zelle
you had sold the cover, instead of telling lies and keeping
it a secret?'

'Ah, me, I adore secrets!' said Claudine, her eyes
dancing. 'And Aunt Mathilde would have written to
the so-kind mother and got the cover back and repaid
the money, and I should have been so, so sad, for it is
nice to earn money, do you not think so?'

'I think you're a puzzle,' said Janet. 'I'll never make
you out, Claudine. You go and tell lies in order to sell
your cushion-cover and get money for somebody's birthday—you shut Matron up to give us a good time—
you . . .'

'Ah, say no more of my badness,' said Claudine,
earnestly. 'One day I may become good. Yes, certainly I shall become good if I stay at this so-fine school
for another term!'

'Well, you're jolly decent not to have taken offence at
what I said,' said Isabel, warmly. 'I'm glad you told
us where you got the money from. I'm afraid now it
means that Pauline must have taken it. She's had such
a lot of money lately. Blow! I wish beastly things like
this wouldn't happen! What do you think we ought to
do about it?'

'Hilary and I will go to Miss Theobald and tell her
everything,' said Susan. 'We can't tackle Pauline now,
she won't be fit enough. But Miss Theobald ought to
know what we think and why. Come on, Hilary. Let's
get it over!'

HILARY and Susan went to Miss Theobald's room and knocked on the door. She called out to them to come in. Fortunately she was alone. She looked up with a pleasant smile as the two girls came in.

' Well ? ' she said, ' what do you fourth-formers want ? You haven't been getting into any more trouble I hope ? '

' No, Miss Theobald,' said Susan. ' But we are rather worried about this stealing business—and we have an idea who it is.'

' Why doesn't the girl herself come to me, then ? ' said Miss Theobald, looking very serious.

' Well—she can't,' said Susan. ' You see—we think it's Pauline—and you know she's in the San. with a broken leg.'

' *Pauline !* ' said Miss Theobald, astonishment showing in her face. ' I can't think it is Pauline. She isn't the type. No—surely it cannot be Pauline.'

' We thought it might be Claudine at first,' said Hilary. ' But it isn't.'

' Ah, I am glad of that,' said Miss Theobald. ' I still cannot think it is Pauline. She is not altogether sensible in some ways—but she did not seem to be at all a dishonest girl.'

' Well, Miss Theobald, we have something else to tell you about Pauline, which will show you that she is really peculiar in some ways, and not at all truthful,' said Susan, gravely. ' We are not, of course, telling tales to you— but we know we can't deal with this ourselves, so we have come to you.'

' Quite rightly,' said Miss Theobald, also very gravely. ' Well—what is there to say about Pauline ? Her mother

is with her now, and possibly I might be able to have a
talk with her about Pauline before she goes.'

Hilary and Susan together told Miss Theobald of
Pauline's ridiculous boasting and lying—of how she had
put off her mother coming at half-term, by telling an
absurd story about a scarlet-fever case—how she had
pretended to be bitterly disappointed—how she had
always seemed to have plenty of money, and yet her
mother had told Alison she was afraid that Pauline would
always be short of pocket-money.

'So, you see,' said Hilary, ' putting everything together,
and knowing what an awful fibber Pauline was, we felt it
was probably she who stole from Matron.'

'I see,' said Miss Theobald. 'Curiously enough, people
who tell lies for the reason that Pauline tells them, are
rarely dishonest in other ways. You see, Pauline lies
because she longs to be thought better than she is—that
is the *only* reason she lies. Now, if she stole, she would
know herself to be despicable, and that others would
despise her too. So she would not steal. But from all
you tell me I am afraid that she does steal. Having so
much money when it is clear that her mother cannot
supply her with much, is very curious.'

'Yes, it is,' said Susan. 'Well, Miss Theobald, we
have told you all we know and think. We would all like
this stealing business to be cleared up—the fourth form
hate it, as you can imagine—and we are glad to leave it
in your hands to settle.'

There came a knock at the door. Miss Theobald called
' Come in '. Before any one entered she nodded to the
two fourth-formers to dismiss them.

'I will see to everything,' she said. 'I will talk to
Pauline—possibly tomorrow or the day after—as soon as
she has recovered from the shock of her broken leg. The
doctor is to put it into plaster, and then she will return
to school to do lessons, whilst it is healing. It is essential

that I should have this matter cleared up before she returns to the fourth form.'

A maid had entered the room and waited until Miss Theobald had finished speaking. ' Please, Madam,' she said, ' Mrs. Jones would like a word with you before she goes.'

' Tell her to come in,' said Miss Theobald. Mrs. Jones came in. Hilary and Susan glanced at her curiously as they went out. So this poor, tired, worried-looking little woman, so plainly dressed, was Pauline's marvellous, pretty, beautifully dressed wealthy mother! What an idiot Pauline was !

Mrs. Jones plunged into her worries as soon as the door shut. ' Oh, Miss Theobald, I'm really bothered about Pauline. She didn't seem at all pleased to see me. She cried her heart out when I told her I'd met some of her school-fellows on the way up, and had talked to them. I just can't understand her. I thought she'd be so pleased to see me. She even blamed me for coming— said I was making a fuss—and after all she's my only child, and very precious to me.'

Miss Theobald looked at the distressed woman and was very sorry for her. She wondered whether or not to say anything about Pauline's stupid boasting, and to explain that Pauline's unkindness was because she was ashamed of having her lies exposed for what they were—she was ashamed of her mother, ashamed of not having enough money, ashamed of everything, so that she had forced herself to make up a whole new family and home of her own.

Then she decided not to say anything. It would only hurt and worry the poor little woman even more. She must have a serious talk with Pauline first, and perhaps she could persuade Pauline herself to put matters right.

So she listened, and tried to comfort Mrs. Jones as best she could. ' Don't worry,' she said. ' Pauline has had

a shock, through falling like that. Don't take any notice
of what she says.'

Mrs. Jones went at last, only half-comforted, feeling
puzzled and hurt. Miss Theobald sighed. There suddenly seemed to be quite a lot of difficult problems to
solve. How upset poor Mrs. Jones would be if she had
to be told that her only child was a thief, as well as a
stupid boaster !

' I will have a talk to Pauline tomorrow or the next
day,' thought Miss Theobald. ' I only hope Matron does
not make any more fuss—really, she is a most unpleasant
woman.'

Matron did make plenty more fuss ! She went storming
into Miss Theobald's room the next morning, with another
complaint.

' Ten shillings gone this time ! A ten-shilling note !
Out of my purse too. And I had hidden it for safety in
my work-basket. But it's gone all the same. Miss
Theobald, that girl has got to be found and expelled ! '

Miss Theobald listened in astonishment. How could
Pauline be the thief if she was in the San. with a broken
leg ? But, as Matron went on complaining, it appeared
that her work-basket had been in the San. She had
taken it there to do her mending, as she had to sit with
Pauline.

So Pauline *might* have been able to take the note from
the purse. Other girls had popped in and out too, as
Pauline was allowed to see her form that day. It was
all very tiresome. Miss Theobald got rid of Matron as
soon as she could, thinking that a lot of trouble was
coming out of the fourth form that term !

The fourth-formers had been very cool towards Angela
since the row. Angela looked pinched and unhappy but
nobody felt sorry for her, not even Alison. At half-past
twelve Alison saw Angela putting on her hat to go out.

' Where are you going ? ' she asked. ' You know we

mustn't go down to the town alone—do you want me to
come with you ? '

' No,' said Angela, sulkily. ' If you want to know
what I'm going to do, I'll tell you. I'm going down to
the nearest telephone box to telephone to my mother and
tell her all the beastly things you've said about her, and
ask her to come today and take me away ! '

' No, don't do that,' said Alison, distressed. ' We only
said those things because you were so horrid about poor
old Mrs. Jones, Angela.'

But Angela's mind was made up and off she went.
Alison waited about miserably, not liking to tell the
others. She pictured Angela's mother sweeping down in
her Rolls-Bentley, spiteful and malicious, ready to say
all kinds of horrible things about St. Clare's and its girls.
It was not a pleasant thought.

Presently, about five minutes before the dinner-bell,
she saw Angela coming back. But what a miserable,
tear-stained Angela ! Alison went to meet her, unexpectedly liking this humble, unhappy Angela far more
than she had liked the bright and boastful one.

' What's the matter ? ' she said. Angela turned to
Alison, and began to weep bitterly.

' Oh, Alison ! Mother's away—and I got on to Daddy
instead. But instead of listening to me and comforting
me, he was very angry. And oh, he said Mother hadn't
any right to talk as she did at half-term—and he was
going to see *I* didn't grow up thinking I could say hurtful
things to people—and he's coming today to see Miss
Theobald about me ! '

' Oh, Angela ! ' said Alison, in dismay. ' How simply
awful ! He *must* have been angry. Miss Theobald won't
be at all pleased when she hears you've been telephoning
to your people and complaining. You'll get into a row
from every one ! '

' Oh, I know, I know,' wept Angela. ' I don't know

what to do. Oh, Alison, I know I've been beastly. But
please don't desert me now. I was awful yesterday
about Pauline's mother. I'm ashamed of it now. Do,
do be my friend again.'

' Angela,' said Alison, looking very serious all of a
sudden, ' I've been a very bad sort of friend to you.
I've praised you and flattered you and thought the world
of you, when all the time it would have been better to
have laughed at you and teased you, like the others do.
Bobby would have made you a much better friend, or
the twins. They would have been sensible with you.
I've spoilt you and been silly.'

' Well, never mind, go on being my friend,' begged
Angela, who, now that things were looking black, felt
that she simply *must* have some one who liked her.
' Please do, Alison. I'll try and be nicer, I really will.
But oh, what shall I say to Daddy when he comes this
afternoon ? I'm so afraid of him when he gets really
angry.'

' Listen,' said Alison, ' immediately after lunch we'll
go down to the telephone box again. You get on to your
father, and then say that you've been thinking things
over, and you've come to the conclusion you've been an
idiot but you'd like another chance. Then let me have
a word with him, and maybe between us we can stop
him coming.'

' Oh, Alison, you're a brick ! ' said Angela, drying her
eyes, and sniffing. ' Daddy liked you. He'll listen to
you. Oh thank you for your help.'

The dinner-bell had long since gone. The two girls
were late. Miss Ellis, taking a look at Angela's swollen
eyes, contented herself with a few sharp words and then
said no more.

Immediately after dinner the girls went off to the
telephone box. Angela got through to her annoyed
father, and made her little speech. ' I've been an idiot.

I see it now. Don't come down, Daddy. I'm going to try and do better. Here's my friend Alison to talk to you.'

The telephone receiver was passed to Alison, who, rather nervous, spoke the little speech she herself had prepared.

'Good afternoon! This is Alison speaking, Angela's friend. Angela is all right now. She was upset before, and rather silly. But I am sure she is going to settle down now and be a sport. So I don't think you need to leave your work and come to St. Clare's.'

'Oh,' said Angela's father, in a grim voice. 'Well, as I'm very busy, I won't today. But any more nonsense from Angela and I shall come down and make a Big Row. I put Angela into St. Clare's because it's the finest school I know. And there she is going to stay until she, too, thinks it's the finest school *she* knows. If you really are her friend, you'll help her to realize this. You've been there some time, I know.'

'Yes, I have,' said Alison, earnestly. 'And it is the very finest school in the kingdom! I'll teach Angela that, really I will, and so will the others.'

'Well, don't spoil her,' said the far-off voice, not sounding quite so grim. 'Shake her up a bit! She may look like a golden princess, or an angel, but she's not a bit like one inside. And I'd like her to be. Tell her to speak to me again.'

Angela took the receiver. What she heard comforted her. 'Thank you, Daddy,' she said. 'I'll try. I really will. Good-bye.'

She put the receiver back, looking much happier. 'Daddy said that although he is often angry with me, he will always love me,' she said to Alison. 'And he said if I loved him, I'd try to be a bit more like he wants me to be. So I shall try now. Thanks, Alison, for your advice!'

She squeezed her friend's arm. Alison took Angela's arm in hers and they walked back to the school. Alison was talking sternly to herself as they went.

'Now, no more telling Angela she is lovely ! No more flattering her ! No more praising her up to the skies because she looks like an angel ! It's no good looking like one if you're just the opposite inside. Tease her and laugh at her and scold her and point out her faults—that's what I've got to do if I'm to be a real friend to Angela.'

And, to the astonishment of all the fourth form, things between the two friends appeared now to be quite changed ! Angela was now the docile one, accepting teasing criticism, and Alison was the leader !

'Good for both of them !' said Bobby, with a grin. 'This will make Angela a nicer person altogether, and will end in giving Alison quite a lot of common sense !'

22   MATRON HAS A SHOCK

'I WONDER whether Miss Theobald has tackled Pauline about taking Matron's money and other things yet,' said Hilary to Susan, after tea that day.

Eileen looked up, startled. She had not been there the day before when the matter had been discussed, and Hilary and Susan had gone off to see Miss Theobald. She had been cross-examined continually by her mother, who had tried to find out exactly what the fourth-formers had done on Mirabel's birthday night—but Eileen had kept her word, and had not told her anything.

'Pauline—taking Mother's money ?' said Eileen, amazed. 'What's all this ? I haven't heard a word about it.'

'*Haven't* you ?' said Janet, surprised. 'Oh no—you

were with Matron when we discussed it yesterday—and today we haven't had a minute to say anything about it. Not that there's anything much to say, really, except that we all think it's Pauline who has taken the things belonging to your mother. You see, we know now that her people can hardly afford to send her here and that she hasn't much pocket-money—so, as she has been splashing money about lately, we felt sure she was the thief. She's such a fibber, she could quite well go a bit further and be a thief as well!'

'And Miss Theobald is going to tackle her about it,' said Susan. 'Hilary and I went and told her everything yesterday. I'm sorry Pauline broke her leg—but really, if she's a thief as well as a story-teller, I think it's a good punishment for her.'

Eileen sat and stared at the chattering girls. Bobby thought she looked rather strange.

'Do you feel all right?' she asked. 'You look a bit funny.'

'Of course I'm all right,' said Eileen. She got up and went out. To the girls' astonishment they saw her, a minute later, flying down the drive at top speed.

'What's up with Eileen?' said Hilary, in amazement. 'Has she forgotten we've got prep to do tonight?'

She apparently had. She did not turn up for prep at all, and Miss Ellis sent to ask Matron if she had kept Eileen with her for any reason. Matron appeared at the classroom door, looking annoyed.

'I can't imagine where Eileen is,' she said. 'I hope you will punish her, Miss Ellis. She has been such an obstinate, stubborn girl lately.'

Eileen did not even return for supper, and it was only when the fourth-formers were getting undressed that they saw her again. Doris looked out of her dormitory window and saw Eileen coming up one of the school-paths. With her was somebody else.

'It's Eddie!' said Alison. 'Gracious, won't Eileen get into a row! She must have shot off to see Eddie, and now he's come back with her.'

Eileen looked strung-up and tearful. Eddie looked much the same. They disappeared into the school. Instead of going up to their mother's room, they went straight to Miss Theobald's room.

'Cheer up!' whispered Eddie. 'I'm here! I'll take care of you, Eileen.'

The two went into Miss Theobald's room. The Head Mistress looked surprised to see Eileen with a boy. Eileen told her who Eddie was.

'This is my brother Edgar,' she said, and then she broke down, and began to sob bitterly and piteously. Miss Theobald was distressed. Eddie put his arm protectingly round his sister.

'Don't cry,' he said. 'I'll tell about everything.' Then he turned to Miss Theobald.

'Miss Theobald,' he said, 'today Eileen heard that another girl, Pauline, was going to be accused of stealing from Matron, our mother. Well—it was Eileen that took all the money and other things, not Pauline or any one else!'

'Well!' said Miss Theobald, thinking that surprises were coming thick and fast in the last few days. 'But why? What made her do such an extraordinary thing?'

'It was because of me,' said Eddie. 'You see, I got a job in an engineering works at the beginning of this term, and Mother was very pleased. Well, I hadn't been there long before I had an accident with a car, and they sacked me. I—I didn't dare to tell my mother, Miss Theobald.'

Miss Theobald looked at the weak, thin face of the lad in front of her, and was not surprised that he feared his bad-tempered, spiteful-tongued mother. How she would tear him and rend him with her tongue, if she knew he had failed in his job!

'Well,' went on Eddie, swallowing hard, and still holding his arm round Eileen, ' well, I thought maybe I'd be able to get another job fairly soon, and then Mother need only be told that I'd changed jobs. But, you see, I'd no money, and I had my lodgings and food to pay for—so I managed to hitch-hike over here one day and see Eileen without Mother knowing. And I asked her to give me what money she had.'

' I see,' said Miss Theobald, very grave. ' And Eileen stole from her mother to give to you.'

' I didn't know she was taking Mother's money,' said Eddie. 'I thought it was her own—out of her money-box or out of the post office savings. I knew she'd got a little. And she brought me biscuits too, and some notepaper and stamps to apply for other jobs. She's— she's been such a brick to me, Miss Theobald.'

' Oh, Eddie, I'd do anything for you, you know that,' sobbed poor Eileen. ' But Miss Theobald, when I knew Pauline was going to be accused of something *I'd* done— then I rushed out and went to Eddie, and told him every-thing. And he came back with me to tell you. Oh, Miss Theobald, we don't dare to tell Mother ! '

' What a mix-up ! ' said Miss Theobald, looking at the two scared, unhappy young faces before her. She could not help in her heart blaming Matron very much for all this. If she had been a kindly, loving mother, helping her children instead of expecting far too much of them, this would never have happened. They would have gone running to her for comfort and help, instead of hiding things from her, and stealing from her, too frightened to do anything else.

' You see,' said Eileen, drying her eyes, ' as Eddie is Mother's son, I didn't really think it was wrong to take her money and other things to help him.'

' I see,' said Miss Theobald. ' But it *was* wrong all the same. Eileen, I am glad to think that you had the courage to realize that you could not let another girl bear the blame for your own wrong-doing. That is a great point in your favour.'

There was a pause. Then Eddie spoke, rather nervously. 'Miss Theobald—do you think you could see Mother for us ? Please do. She might not be so terribly angry if you spoke to her first.'

Miss Theobald felt a little grim. 'Yes,' she said, 'I *will* see her. You two can wait in the next room until I have spoken to her.'

Eddie and Eileen retired to the next room, looking forlorn and frightened. Miss Theobald rang her bell and told the maid who answered it to ask Matron to come and speak to her.

Matron soon appeared, crackling in starched apron and uniform.

'Sit down, Matron,' said Miss Theobald. 'I have found out who has taken your money and I wanted to tell you about it.'

'I hope you will expel the girl,' said Matron, in a severe voice. 'After all, Miss Theobald, I've got a girl here myself, in the fourth form. It's not a very good influence for her, is it, to have a thief living side by side with her ! '

'Well, Matron,' said Miss Theobald, 'I have made up my mind that I myself will not decide whether to expel this poor little thief or not. You shall decide, and you alone.'

Matron's eyes sparkled. 'Thank you,' she said. 'You may consider that my decision is taken. The girl will go—and go tomorrow ! '

'Very well,' said Miss Theobald. 'Now listen to my story, please. This girl did not steal for herself, but for some one she loved, who was in trouble.'

'Stealing is always stealing,' said Matron, in a righteous voice.

'She was afraid to go to her mother for help, afraid to go to her for advice,' continued Miss Theobald.

'Then the mother is as much to blame as the girl,' said Matron. 'Mothers who have children so scared of them that they will steal have done a very bad job as mothers.'

'I thoroughly agree with you,' said Miss Theobald. 'Nevertheless, this girl had the courage to come and tell me, and she asked me to tell you.'

'Where *is* the little thief?' said Matron, fiercely. '*I* shall have a few words to say to her, I promise you! Out she goes tomorrow!'

Miss Theobald stood up and opened the door connecting her drawing-room with her study. 'You will find the little thief in here,' she said. 'With her brother.'

Matron walked firmly into the study, ready to lash out at the thief. She saw there her two children, Eileen and Eddie. They stared at her nervously.

'What's this?' said Matron, in a faint voice. 'Why is Eileen here—and Eddie?'

'Eileen is the thief, Matron—and Eddie is the one she stole for—and you are the hard mother they were too scared to come to for advice and help,' said Miss Theobald, in a grave and serious voice. 'And I think, knowing you as I do—that Eileen is not the one who should leave St. Clare's—but you!'

Matron's face suddenly crumpled up and her mouth began to tremble. She stared unbelievingly at Eileen and Eddie. Eileen was crying again.

'You are a hard and spiteful woman,' went on Miss Theobald's solemn voice. 'This boy and girl need help and comfort, but they would never get it from you!'

'I've got another job, got it today, Mother!' said Eddie. 'I shall pay back every penny Eileen took. You're not to scold her. She did it for me because she loved me. Soon I shall earn enough money to let her

live with me and keep house for me. Then you won't be
bothered by either of us. We've always disappointed
you. We weren't clever or gifted, though we did our
best. But I'll look after Eileen now.'

'Don't, Eddie, don't,' said his mother, in a choking voice.
'Don't talk like that. What have I done? Oh, what
have I done to have this punishment on my shoulders?'

Miss Theobald shut the door. They must sort things
out for themselves. Matron had made her own bed and
must lie on it. Those two children would probably be
all right because they loved each other and would always
stick together. They were weak-willed and not very
attractive characters—but their love for each other
would give them strength and courage.

Miss Theobald took up the telephone receiver. She
got through to the old Matron, who was now almost
recovered from her illness.

'Matron?' said Miss Theobald. 'Can you come back
tomorrow? You can have as easy a time as you want
to—but we can't do without you any longer! Yes—I
have a feeling that the present Matron will be gone by
tomorrow! Good—we *shall* be pleased to see you back!'

23   THINGS SETTLE DOWN AT LAST

AND now still one more thing remained to be done.
Pauline must be seen, and her affairs put right too. So
accordingly next day Pauline was astonished to see Miss
Theobald coming into the San. looking much more
serious than usual.

It was the second surprise Pauline had had that day.
The first was when quite a new Matron had appeared,
plump and jolly and twinkling. Pauline had stared at

her in astonishment, delighted not to see the other
Matron.

'Hallo!' said this new Matron. 'So you've broken
your leg! Very careless of you. Don't make a habit
of it, will you?'

'Where's the other Matron?' asked Pauline.

'She's had to leave in a hurry,' said Matron, putting
Pauline's bed-clothes straight. 'So I've come back.
And let me warn you I'm a Real Old Bear! I've been
here for years and years, I'm probably a hundred years
old, and I've scolded most of the girls' mothers as well
as the girls themselves!'

'Oh, you're the old Matron the girls have told me
about,' said Pauline, pleased. 'That's good! Why did
Matron leave in such a hurry? Has Eileen gone too?'

'Yes,' said Matron. 'They both had to leave in a
hurry. Not our business why, is it? Now then—what
about those pillows?'

Pauline had hardly got over her astonishment at seeing
a different Matron, when Miss Theobald came in. As
usual the Head went straight to the point, and soon the
horrified Pauline was realizing that Miss Theobald, and
the girls too, all knew what a stupid, untruthful boaster
she had been.

She lay back in bed, feeling ashamed and miserable.
Miss Theobald went relentlessly on, and finished by telling
her how unhappy and puzzled she had made her mother.

'She came rushing to see you,' said Miss Theobald.
'She panted up from the station because she could not
afford a taxi—and you know what sort of a welcome you
gave her!'

Pauline turned her face to the wall and a tear trickled
down her cheek.

'And there is yet another thing,' said Miss Theobald,
remembering. 'Some one has stolen money—and because
you seemed to have plenty, though the girls heard this

week you were supposed to have very little pocket-money,
you were suspected of being the thief! So you see,
Pauline, to what big and terrible suspicions bragging and
story-telling can lead us!'

'Oh! I've never stolen a thing in my life!' cried
Pauline. 'I had some money in the savings bank—and
without Mother knowing I took my savings book here
with me—and when I wanted money I took some out.
That's how I had plenty of pocket-money, Miss Theobald.
Please believe me!'

'I do believe you,' said Miss Theobald. 'But you
must hand over your book to me and not withdraw any
more money without your mother's permission. And, if
you stay here at St. Clare's, you will have to do what
some of the other girls do, who have very little money—
say so quite honestly! Nobody minds. We should
never judge people by the amount of money or possessions they have, but by what they *are*. You must
learn that, Pauline, or you will never know what real
happiness is.'

'I feel very miserable,' muttered Pauline, anxious for
a kind word. 'I—I don't know how I shall face all the
girls after this!'

'Tell Susan or Hilary or the twins that you have been
foolish,' said Miss Theobald, getting up. 'They are all
sorry you have broken your leg, and I think they will
see that you are treated kindly—but you will have to
earn their kindness and friendship now, Pauline—not try
to buy it with tales of wealth and great possessions!
Earn their friendship by being sincere and natural and
kindly. As for feeling very miserable—well, that is part
of the punishment you have brought on yourself, isn't it,
and you will have to bear it as bravely as you can!'

Miss Theobald turned to go. She smiled down at
Pauline, her smile kinder than her words, and the girl
felt a little comforted.

She did as Miss Theobald had advised and confided in Hilary, when she came to see her. Hilary was outspoken but helpful.

'You're a frightful idiot, really frightful. And I shall only help you, and make the others decent to you on one condition, Pauline.'

'What?' asked Pauline.

'That you write to your mother, and say you are sorry for being such a beast to her when she came to see you, and tell her you'll give her a great welcome next time she comes,' said Hilary. 'I'm not going round putting everything right for you, my girl, unless you first do a little putting-right yourself! And don't you dare to brag about a single thing more this term, or we'll all sit on you good and hard!'

And with that piece of advice, Hilary went off to tell the others that Pauline had come to her senses at last, and, as she had broken her leg, and was feeling pretty miserable, what about giving her a chance when she came back to class?

'Well, what with Eileen gone, and Angela reforming herself fast, and Pauline getting a little sense knocked into her, and Matron disappeared for good, we seem to be getting on nicely!' said Bobby, with one of her grins.

'It only remains for Claudine to get the English sense of honour,' put in Pat. 'Then we shall indeed be a form of saints!'

Alison had a letter from Eileen the following week. She read it to the others.

DEAR ALISON,

I don't know whether you were ever told, but I was the thief. You see, Eddie was out of a job (he's got a good one now) and hadn't any money, so he asked me to help him and I did. But I hadn't much money myself, so I took Mother's, and some other things too.

Well, it was a most frightful shock to Mother, and she said she couldn't bear to stay at St. Clare's another day. So we

packed and went. Miss Theobald was frightfully decent to
Eddie and me. I simply can't tell you how decent. She even
offered to keep me on at St. Clare's, when Mother went. But
I couldn't face you all, and anyway I don't fit in there. I know
I don't.

So I am going to study shorthand and typing, and then I am
going to get a job in the office where Eddie works, and we shall
be together. Mother is quite different now. I think it was an
awful shock to her to find out how bad I was—but it was for
Eddie, and I couldn't help it. Mother has been kinder and
gentler. Really, you would hardly know her. Eddie and I
think that when we are both earning money Mother won't need
to work, and then she can take a rest and perhaps feel happier.

I thought I had better let you know what happened to me,
because I left so suddenly. I left my silver thimble behind, in
the school work-box—the one in the fourth-form cupboard.
Will you please have it yourself in gratitude for taking me out
at half-term, as I can never repay that ?

I hope Pauline's leg is better. Please, Alison, don't always
think unkindly of me, will you ? I know I was a sneak, but
you can't imagine how difficult things were for me sometimes.

Yours with gratitude,

EILEEN PATERSON.

The girls were all rather touched by this letter. Alison
at once found the thimble and said she would wear it and
not think too badly of Eileen.

' It was mostly her mother's fault she was such a little
sneak and beast,' said Bobby. ' Golly, we're lucky to
have decent mothers, aren't we ? '

Angela went red at this remark but said nothing. She
had been so much nicer lately—and she had determined
that when she went home for the holidays, she was going
to praise St. Clare's night and day, and not allow her
mother to say a single word against it ! Mothers could
make bad or good children—' but,' thought Angela,
' maybe children could alter mothers sometimes too'.
She was going to have a good try to make her mother
change her mind about quite a lot of things. Miss
Theobald would have been very delighted if she had

known some of the thoughts that went through Angela's golden head those days.

'Hols. will soon be here now,' said Pat to Isabel. 'It's been an exciting term, hasn't it—and aren't you glad our old Matron is back? Hie, Bobby—what about a really good trick to round off the term? Can't you and Janet think of one?'

'I dare say we can,' grinned Bobby, her good-natured face looking tanned and even more freckled than usual.

'We could put a frog in Claudine's desk, or fill her pencil-box with earwigs,' suggested Janet with a wicked look at the horrified Claudine.

'If you do such a thing I take the train and the boat to France at once,' declared the French girl.

'She would too,' said Janet. 'Well—perhaps we'd better not try out anything of that sort on Claudine. It would be a pity if she went back to France before she had had time to get that "sense of honour" she is always talking about!'

Claudine threw a cushion at Janet's head. It knocked over Doris's work-basket. Doris leapt up and threw a heap of mending at Claudine. It scattered itself over Mirabel who was just coming into the room. The girls shrieked with laughter to see Mirabel standing in surprise with somebody's vest over her head.

In a trice there was a fine fight going on, with squeals and yells. Arms, legs, and heads stuck out in all directions.

The door opened again and Miss Theobald looked in with a visitor.

'And this,' she said, 'is the fourth-form common room. Girls, girls, what *are* you doing? What *will* you be like as six-formers, if you behave like kindergarten children now!'

What will they be like? Not very different I expect! We'll wait and see.

FIFTH FORMERS
OF ST CLARE'S

CONTENTS

ST. CLARE'S had stood silent and empty during eight weeks of the summer holiday. Except for the sound of mops and brushes, and a tradesman ringing at the bell, the place had been very quiet. The school cat missed the girls and wandered about miserably for the first week or two.

But now everything was different. The school coaches were rolling up the hill, full of chattering, laughing children—St. Clare's was beginning a new winter term!

'Who would think this was a winter term?' said Pat O'Sullivan, to her twin, Isabel. 'The sun is as hot as it was in the summer. We might be able to have a few games of tennis, still.'

'I shall certainly have a swim in the pool,' said Bobby Ellis, whose face seemed even more freckled than usual. 'I hope there's fresh water in today—I might have a swim after tea.'

'Ah, you Bobbee! Always you must play tennis or swim or run or jump!' said Claudine, the little French girl. 'And your freckles! Never did I see so many on one face. I have been careful in the hot sun these holidays—not one freckle did I catch!'

The girls laughed. Claudine was always terrified of getting freckles—but never did one appear on her pale face and white hands.

The girls poured into the school, running up the familiar steps, shouting to one another, dumping their lacrosse sticks everywhere.

'Hallo, Hilary! Hallo, Janet! Oh, there's Carlotta, looking more like a gypsy than ever. Hey, Carlotta, where did you go for your holidays? You look as dark as a gypsy."

'I have been to Spain,' said Carlotta. 'Some of my people live there, you know. I had a grand time.'

'There's Mirabel—golly, she's awfully tall now!' said Isabel. 'Gladys looks more like a mouse than ever beside her.'

'Hallo!' said the big, strapping Mirabel, coming up. 'How's every one?'

'Hallo, Mirabel, hallo Gladys,' said the girls. 'You've been spending the hols. together, haven't you? I bet you played tennis and swam all the time!'

Both Mirabel and Gladys were fond of games, and this term Mirabel was anxious to be sports captain at St. Clare's. She had been in the fifth form for two terms, and Annie Thomas, the sports captain, had let Mirabel help her. Now Annie had left, and there was a chance that Mirabel might be captain, for there was no one in the sixth form really fitted to have that post.

'Let's go and look at our classroom,' said Bobby Ellis. 'It was going to be re-decorated in the hols., I know. Let's see what it's like.'

They all trooped upstairs to the big fifth form-room. Certainly it looked very nice, painted a pale banana yellow. The light was clean and clear in the room, and the view from the windows a lovely one.

'We've only got this term here—and then we go up into the sixth form!' said Hilary. 'Fancy being at the top of the school! I remember when I first came to St. Clare's, I thought the fifth and sixth formers were almost grown-up. I hardly dared to speak to them.'

'I expect the young ones think the same thing of us,' said Janet. 'I know most of them scuttle out of my way when I come along—like frightened rabbits!'

'I have a young sister in the second form this term,' said Claudine, the French girl. 'She came over with me from France. Look—there she is, the little Antoinette.'

The girls looked out of the window. They saw a girl of about fourteen, very like the pale-faced, dark-haired

Claudine, standing watching the others. She looked very
self-possessed.

'Don't you want to go down and show Antoinette
round a bit ? ' said Pat. ' I bet she feels lonely and new.'

'Ah, Antoinette would never feel so,' said Claudine.
'She can stand on her own toes, like me.'

'Stand on her own feet, you mean,' said Bobby, with
a chuckle. 'You'll never get those English sayings right,
Claudine. Ah—there's old Mam'zelle ! '

The girls watched Mam'zelle going out into the garden,
an anxious look on her face.

'She is looking for the little Antoinette,' said Claudine.
'She has not seen her for two years. Ah, Antoinette will
now be swamped in love and affection ! My aunt will
think her little niece Antoinette is as wonderful as me,
her niece Claudine ! '

Mam'zelle was Claudine's aunt, and this fact was at
times useful to Claudine, and at other times, embarrassing.
For Antoinette just then it was most embarrassing. The
little French girl had been enjoying herself, watching the
excited English girls catching hold of one another's arms,
swinging each other round, chasing one another, and
generally behaving in the usual school-girl way—a way,
however, that the demure Antoinette had not been used
to.

Then, quite suddenly, an avalanche descended upon
her, two plump arms almost strangled her, and a loud and
excited voice poured out French endearments in first one
ear and then another. Loud kisses were smacked on
each cheek, and then another hug came which made
Antoinette gasp for breath.

'Ah, *la petite* Antoinette, *mon petit chou*,' cried Mam'-
zelle at the top of her voice. All the girls stopped
playing and stared at Antoinette and Mam'zelle. They
giggled. It was plain that Antoinette was not at all
pleased to be greeted in public in this way. She dis-
entangled herself as best she could.

She caught sight of her elder sister, Claudine, leaning

out of a high window, grinning in delight. She pointed up to her at once.

'Dear *Tante* Mathilde, there is my sister Claudine who looks for you. Now that she has seen you greet me, she will wish you to greet her too.'

Mam'zelle glanced up and saw Claudine. Still holding Antoinette, she waved frantically and blew kisses. 'Ah, there is the little Claudine too! Claudine, I come to embrace you.'

Antoinette wriggled away and lost herself in the nearby crowd of girls. Mam'zelle turned hér steps towards the door that led to the stairs. 'I come, I come!' she called to Claudine.

'And I go,' said Claudine, pushing away the giggling girls. 'Mam'zelle will be quite overcome this term with *two* nieces here.'

So, when poor Mam'zelle panted into the fifth-form classroom to embrace her second niece, Claudine was not to be found. 'I have missed her, but I will find her!' cried Mam'zelle, and she beamed round at the fifth formers there.

'Ah, Bobbee, you have come back—and you Angela —and Alison—all of you, the dear girls! And you are going to work hard for me this term, so hard—for is it not next term that you go up into the top form, the sixth form. That is indeed a solemn thought!'

The French teacher went out of the room, hunting for her dear Claudine. The girls laughed. 'Dear old Mam'-zelle,' said Hilary, 'I shall never forget her, if I live to be a hundred! The tricks we've played on her—do you remember those awful stink-balls you had, Janet, when we were in the fourth form? I laughed till I cried then, when I saw Mam'zelle's face as the smell reached her.'

'There's only one new girl this term,' said Janet 'in our form, I mean. I saw her name on the list downstairs. She's called Anne-Marie Longden. And Felicity Ray has come up from the fourth form.'

'About time too,' said Mirabel. 'She's older than most of the fifth already. I think she's a bit batty.'

' No, she's not—it's only that she's a real musical genius,' said Gladys. ' You've said yourself heaps of times that she is, Mirabel. She doesn't seem to care about anything but music—other lessons just roll off her, like water off a duck's back. She's always bottom of everything except music.'

' Well, Miss Cornwallis won't be very thrilled if Felicity takes no notice of anything but music,' said Bobby, who had reason to know that the fifth-form mistress was what the girls called among themselves ' a real slave-driver '. ' I bet Felicity will know more geography, history and maths. this term than she has ever known all the time she has been at school ! '

' Any other girls ? ' said Mirabel.

' Well, it's funny, Alma Pudden's name was down on the list of fifth formers,' said Janet. ' But she's sixth form, isn't she ? I mean, when she came last term, she was put into the sixth form—but now her name is down for our form. Perhaps she's been put back into the fifth for some reason.'

' Well, I wish she wasn't,' said Bobby. ' I can't say she thrills me. She's so like her name—puddeny ! She's a bit like a suet pudding, fat and stodgy and dull.'

' She's got a beastly temper,' said Hilary. ' I guess she won't be too pleased at coming down into the fifth form ! '

Matron appeared at the door of the classroom with a tall, slender, dark-eyed girl, whose pale blonde hair made her eyes seem very black indeed.

' Hallo, fifth formers ! ' she said, her cheerful smile beaming at every one. ' All back ? Good girls. Now don't any of you dare to go down with mumps or measles, chicken pox or anything else ! I've brought you the only new girl for your form—Anne-Marie Longden.'

Anne-Marie smiled nervously. She was not pretty, but her golden hair and dark eyes made her rather striking. '' Hallo,' she said, awkwardly, ' are you all fifth formers ? What are your names ? '

Hilary, who was head of the form, introduced every one quickly.

'These are the O'Sullivan twins, Pat and Isabel. You'll probably know t'other from which in a few terms ! This is Janet, and this is Roberta, commonly called Bobby. You'll always know her by her freckles ! Look out for these two, for they know more tricks than any one else.'

Anne-Marie smiled politely. Hilary went on, dragging first one girl forward and then another.

'This is Doris—she can mimic any one under the sun. She'll be mimicking *you* before long, Anne-Marie ! '

Anne-Marie did not look as if this thrilled her very much. She thought Doris looked a rather clumsy, stupid girl. She did not see the intelligent eyes and humorous mouth of the born actress that Doris was.

'Here's Carlotta, dark as a gypsy ! ' went on Hilary. Carlotta gave her usual cheeky grin.

'And please let me tell you, Anne-Marie, that I was once a circus-girl, and rode horses in a circus-ring,' said Carlotta. 'Angela is sure to tell you that sooner or later, so I may as well tell you now ! '

The golden-haired beautiful girl called Angela flushed with annoyance. It was quite true that she looked down on Carlotta and always had—but she had hoped that Carlotta had not thought of it the last term or two. Carlotta had a very sharp tongue, and lashed out unmercifully at any one she disliked.

Hilary hurried on, hoping to avert a quarrel between the hot-tempered Carlotta and the annoyed Angela. 'This is Angela,' she said. 'Our dream of beauty ! '

'You've forgotten the Honourable,' said a malicious voice—Carlotta's. 'The *Honourable* Angela Favorleigh ! Angela must have her label.'

'Shut up, Carlotta,' said Hilary. Angela scowled, making her lovely face quite ugly for a moment. Then she tossed her head and went out of the room. She had learnt by now that beauty and wealth were no match for a sharp wit like Carlotta's. Angela might be the most beautiful girl in the school and the richest, but Carlotta could always defeat her in a squabble.

'This is Pam, the brains of the form,' said Hilary, pulling a plain, undergrown girl forward, with great big glasses on her short-sighted eyes. 'She works much too hard, but nobody can stop her!'

Some one peeped in at the door. It was Claudine, come to see if her aunt was still there.

'It's all right. Mam'zelle is still looking for you, but not here,' said Carlotta. 'Anne-Marie, this is Claudine, the Bad Girl of the form—she only works at what she likes, she always gets what she wants—and she doesn't care how she does it. She has been here quite a long time already, trying to learn what she calls "the English sense of honour"—but she hasn't even smelt it yet!'

'Ah, you bad Carlotta,' said the good-humoured Claudine. 'Always you make fun of me. I am not so bad, and not so good.'

Mirabel and Gladys were pulled forward, and the plain, quiet Pauline, who had once been as big a boaster as Angela, but had learnt a bitter lesson, and was now a much nicer girl.

'There you are—that's the lot,' said Hilary, 'except Felicity, our musical genius, who is coming up from the fourth form, and hasn't arrived yet—and Alma Pudden who comes down from the sixth. I haven't seen her about yet, either.'

'I hope *you* don't do anything wonderful!' said Bobby, to Anne-Marie. 'What with Pam's brilliant brains, and Angela's film-star beauty, and Felicity's musical genius, the fifth form has got enough wonderful people in it! I hope you're a nice ordinary person, Anne-Marie.'

'Well—I'm not,' said Anne-Marie, flushing red. 'I'm —I'm a poet.'

There was a deep silence after this. A poet! What exactly did Anne-Marie mean by that?

'What do you mean—you write poetry, or something?' said Bobby. 'Oh, help!'

'You can't help being a poet, if you are one,' said Anne-Marie. 'You're born a poet. My grandfather was a famous poet, and my great-aunt was a great writer. It's in the family—and it's come out in me, I suppose. I'm always writing poetry. Mostly in the middle of the night.'

'Help!' said Bobby, again. 'We've had many queer things at St. Clare's—but not a poet, as far as I remember. You and Felicity will make a pair! She gets up in the middle of the night to write a tune—you get up to write poems! Well—you'll be able to keep each other company!'

Another girl put her head in at the door and the twins yelled to her. 'Alison! Where have you been? Come and be introduced to our poet.'

A pretty, dainty girl came into the room, smiling. It was the twins' cousin, Alison.

'This is Alison,' said Pat. 'Our little featherhead. Thinks of nothing but her hair and her complexion and whether she has a shiny nose, and . . .'

Alison would have scowled, or burst into tears a few terms before, at this candid introduction, but she was thicker-skinned now. She merely lunged out at Pat, and nodded amiably at Anne-Marie.

'You'd better look out, Claudine,' she said, 'your aunt is coming along the passage.'

'You can't escape now,' said Hilary. 'You've got to go through with it—go on, it pleases old Mam'zelle. She really is fond of you, goodness knows why!'

Mam'zelle swept into the room, saw Claudine and flung herself on her. '*Ma petite* Claudine! How are you? How are your dear father and mother, and all the family? I have seen the little Antoinette—ah, how lonely and shy the poor child looked. I have cakes and biscuits for you both in my room—you will come now, this very minute, and eat them with me!'

Claudine let herself be taken off. The others laughed. ' Funny to think of Claudine being a fifth-former ! Perhaps she will turn over a new leaf now she's so high up in the school.'

But that was the last thing Claudine meant to do. She went her own way, saying what she pleased, doing what she pleased, and always would. It was surprising that so many people liked her !

2   STUDIES OF THEIR OWN

IT was the rule at St. Clare's that as soon as any girl had been in the fifth form for two terms she should be allowed to have a small study of her own, which she shared with one other girl. These studies were tiny places, and the girls could, if they wished, furnish them themselves, though the school provided such things as a table, chairs and a carpet and shelves.

Most girls contented themselves with putting up a picture or two, bringing their own vases for flowers, a tablecloth or so, and a clock. A few were more ambitious and got a carpet from home, and maybe even an armchair.

The girls themselves chose the companion with whom they wanted to share a study. This was not usually difficult, because by the time they reached the top forms the girls had all more or less made their own friends, and, when they were in the fourth form, had planned with whom they were going to share the study.

It was fun arranging about the studies. The pairs had to go to Matron and tell her they were going to share a study, and then Matron would allot one to them.

' Fancy *you* having a study ! ' she would say. ' Dear

me—it seems no time at all since you were in the first form and I nearly gave you a spanking for not reporting your sore throats to me ! '

Pat and Isabel O'Sullivan were to share a study, of course. Mirabel and Gladys wanted to as well. Angela had asked Alison to share with her—both girls had the same dainty tastes.

' I bet there will be nothing but mirrors all the way round the walls of your study ! ' said Bobby to Alison. It was a standing joke that Alison always looked into any mirror she passed, or even in the glass of pictures, to see if her hair was all right.

Bobby and Janet were to share a study. Both were tomboys, with a love for practical jokes. What tricks would be hatched out, in their study !

One odd pair was Pam Boardman, the brainy one of the form, and Doris Edward, who was always near the bottom. For all her brilliance at mimicry and acting, Doris could not do ordinary lessons well, and admired Pam's brains deeply. Pam had tried to help the bigger girl at times, and a warm friendship had sprung up between them, which made Doris suggest sharing a study. Pam had left St. Clare's once, but had missed it so much that her parents had sent her back again some time later.

The lonely little Pam, who had never had a real friend, at once welcomed the idea of sharing a study with Doris. Doris made her laugh, she teased her and put on her big glasses and mimicked her. She was good for Pam.

' Whom is Carlotta going with ? ' wondered Pat. ' Hilary, perhaps. They like one another very much.'

But no—Hilary, as head-girl of the form, had the honour of a study all to herself. So Carlotta could not share with her. She chose Claudine !

Matron was openly doubtful about this.

' You'll have a mighty bad effect on each other,' she said. ' You're both as cheeky and don't-carish as can be. What you'll be like if you share a study, I can't think. But mind—any broken furniture or reports of rowdiness, and you'll go down to the common room of the fourth formers.'

'Oh, Matron—how can you think that we should be rowdy?' said Claudine, putting on her most innocent look. 'I shall keep our study beautifully, so beautifully. Did I not in the holidays embroider two table-cloths, and three cushion-covers for our study?'

Anne-Marie and Felicity were to share a study, although Felicity had not been two terms in the fifth form, and Anne-Marie was new. Matron did not want them to be the only two without a study.

'Two geniuses together,' said Bobby, with a laugh. 'They ought to use up the midnight oil all right, writing poems and tunes!'

No one had asked Pauline to share a study with them, and she had no friend to ask. She was not a girl that any one liked much, for she was envious, and had been very boastful till the others had found out that all her wonderful tales were made up. She had gone into her shell, and no one knew quite what the real Pauline was like.

'You had better share with Alma Pudden,' said Matron, ticking them off on the list. 'You're the only two left.'

'Oh,' said Pauline, dismally. She didn't like Alma very much. Nobody did. She was so fat and unwieldy and bad-tempered. But there was no one else to share with, so that was that.

'Well—that's the lot of you,' said Matron, shutting her book. 'You all know the study-rules, don't you? You can have your teas there by yourselves, if you don't want to go to the dining-room. You can get in some one from the first or second form to do any little job you want done. You can do your prep. there in the evenings, and you can go up to bed when you want to, providing it is not after ten o'clock.'

The girls felt free and independent, having little rooms of their own. The studies were cosy corners, dens, bits of home—they could be arranged how the girls liked, and the tiny fire-places could burn cosy fires to sit by.

Angela, of course, furnished hers like a miniature palace. She bundled out every bit of the school furniture there, and got her mother to send down things from her own bedroom. She went down to the town with Alison, and the two had a wonderful time choosing curtain material, cushion-covers and rugs.

They cost a lot of money. Alison hadn't very much, but Angela had had magnificent tips from wealthy uncles and aunts in the holidays, and had saved them up for her study. She spent lavishly, and would let no one into their room till it was finished.

Then she and Alison gave a ' house-warming ' as they called it. They had ordered in cakes and sandwiches from the local baker, and had bought lemonade and ginger-beer. The table was loaded with eatables, and a bright fire burnt in the grate, though the day was far too hot.

The girls crowded in curiously. They gasped at the polished furniture, beautiful mirrors and pictures, the two arm-chairs, and the lovely rugs. They fingered the silk curtains and looked at the brilliant chrysanthemums in the vases.

' *Well!* ' said Bobby, ' just wait till Matron sees all this ! She'll tell Miss Theobald you have too much money to spend, Angela ! '

' I don't see that it's anything to do with Matron,' said Angela, stiffly. ' Alison and I don't consider there is enough beauty or comfort at St. Clare's—not as much as *we* are used to at home, anyway—and now that we have a study of our own, we don't see why we can't fill it with our own ideas. Don't you like it, Bobby ? '

' Well—it's a bit too showy for me,' said Bobby. ' You know my simple tastes ! But you certainly have made a marvellous job of it, Angela—and this tea is super ! '

The other girls added what they wanted to their studies. Claudine put out her embroidered table-cloths and cushion-covers. Carlotta added a few things she had brought from Spain, one thing especially giving the little study colour and character—a deep red embroidered shawl from Seville.

The only people whose study was quite plain and without character was the one shared by Pauline and Alma. Neither of them had any taste or much money, and except for a blue vase contributed by Pauline and a tea-cosy as plump as Alma herself given by Alma, the little study was as bare as in the holidays.

Alma Pudden had a most unfortunate name. It would not have mattered a bit if she hadn't been so like a suet pudding to look at, but she was. Her school tunic always looked like a sack tied round in the middle. Her eyes were almost hidden in her round, pasty face.

It was the fifth formers who nicknamed her Pudding, and she hated it, which was not to be wondered at. If she had laughed, and said ' Yes, I *am* rather puddingy— but I shall thin out soon ! ' the others would probably have liked her, and called her Pudding more in affection than in derision. But Alma flew into one of her bad rages when she was teased.

She had queer tempers—not hot ones, quickly flaring up and down, like Carlotta's or Janet's—but cold, spiteful rages. Try as they would the others could not like anything about poor Alma.

Poor Pauline found sharing a study with Alma very dull indeed. Alma seldom had any intelligent remark to make, and though she pored over her prep. she rarely got good marks. She was selfish too, and always took the more comfortable chair, and helped herself to more cakes than Pauline.

Felicity and Anne-Marie found it rather trying to live together in the same study. Felicity thought there was nothing in the world but music, and she was always singing or trying out tunes on her violin, when Anne-Marie wanted to work or to write.

' Felicity ! *Must* you play that awful, gloomy tune again ? ' Anne-Marie would say. ' I'm trying to get the last verse of this poem right.'

'What poem? Is it the one you were doing last week?' Felicity would say. 'Well, it's a dreadful poem —all words and no meaning. You are no poet, Anne-Marie. Why should I stop my music in order that you should write third-rate poetry?'

Felicity did not mean to be rude or even hurtful. She was, as Bobby said, quite 'batty' about her music. She was working for a stiff exam., the L.R.A.M. and was very young indeed to take it. Miss Theobald, the Head Mistress, did not want her to work for it, and had already told Felicity's people that the girl must live an ordinary life, and take more interest in ordinary things.

'She is growing one-sided,' Miss Theobald explained to Felicity's parents, who came to see her one day. 'Sometimes I think she doesn't live in this world at all! That is bad for a young girl. She is already far too old for the fourth form, and yet is not fit to do the work of the fifth. But I think I had better put her up into the fifth, where the girls there of her own age will wake her up a bit. I wish you would say that Felicity must put off working for this difficult music exam. for a year or two. She has plenty of time before her!'

But Felicity's people were too proud of their brilliant daughter to put off any exam. It would be wonderful to have a girl who was the youngest to pass such an exam.!

'Put her up in the fifth form if you wish, Miss Theobald,' said Felicity's father. 'But don't let her slacken in any way in her music studies. We have been told she is a genius, and a genius must be helped and encouraged in every way.'

'Of course,' said the Head Mistress, 'but we must be sure that our ways of encouragement are the *right* ones, surely. I don't like all this hard, musical work for so young a girl, when it means that other, quite necessary work has to be scamped.'

But it was no use talking like that to Felicity's parents. Their girl was brilliant, and she must go on being even more brilliant! And so it was that Felicity was put up into the fifth form, to be with girls of her own age even though her work was far below the form's standard—and yet had to work even harder at her music than before.

She did not like or dislike Anne-Marie. She was there and had to be put up with, but so long as she did not interfere too much with her music, Felicity did not really notice her study companion.

But Anne-Marie was jealous of Felicity and her undoubted genius. Anne-Marie was convinced that she too was a genius. Her people were sure she was, as well. They had her best poems framed, they recited them to visitors, who were too polite to say what they really thought, and they tried to get publishers to print them

It was most annoying that the girls at St. Clare's didn't seem to think anything of her loveliest poems. There was that one beginning ı

> Down the long lanes of the Future
> My tear-bedimmed eyes are peering,

Only Angela and Alma had been impressed with it. Neither of them had enough brains to know a good poem from a bad one, and they could not see the would-be cleverness and insincerity of the long and ostentatious poem.

'What's it *mean*?' said Carlotta. 'I may be very stupid, but I don't understand a word of it. Why are your eyes tear-bedimmed, Anne-Marie? Are you so afraid of your future? Well, I'm not surprised, if that's the way you're going to earn your living! You won't get much money.'

'It's tosh,' said Bobby. 'You write something you really *feel*, Anne-Marie, and maybe you'll get something good out of your mind. This is all pretence—just trying to be awfully grown-up when you're not.'

So Anne-Marie was bitterly disappointed that *her* genius was not recognized, whilst every one apparently agreed that Felicity really was gifted.

Still, on the whole, the study companions got on fairly

well, some of them much better than others, of course. The twins rarely quarrelled, and had so much the same tastes and likings that sharing a study was, for them, a thing of delight. Bobby and Janet too were very happy together, and so were Mirabel and Gladys.

It was queer at first to get used to sending for the younger ones to do odd jobs. But on the whole that was quite a good idea too. Many of the first formers, for instance, had been head-girls, or at least in the top forms of their prep. schools, and it did them good to be at the bottom of another school, having, at times, to rush off to do the bidding of the older girls. The twins remembered how they had hated it at first.

'We thought it was beneath our dignity to light some-one's fire, do you remember?' said Pat to Isabel, as she poked up the fire that a first former had just been in to light for her. 'It was jolly good for us. We were so stuck up—thought such a lot of ourselves too! We got our corners rubbed off all right.'

'We get to know the younger ones too,' said Isabel. 'They chatter away to us when they come to do their jobs. I'm getting to like some of the little first formers very much. One or two of them will be very good at games—they are awfully keen.'

'Angela sends for the young ones far too much, though,' said Pat, frowning. 'She and Alison make them do too many jobs. They've got a bit of power, and they are using it badly.'

'Better get Hilary to tick them off,' said Isobel, yawning. 'Golly, it's five to ten. Come on, we'd better pack up and go to bed. Isn't it fun to go when we like?'

'So long as it's not after ten o'clock!' said Pat, imitating Matron's crisp voice. 'Hurry—or it *will* be after ten!'

3 THE NEW ENGLISH TEACHER

THAT term there were a great many more girls at St. Clare's in the younger forms, and Miss Theobald decided to engage an extra mistress, to take some of the work off the shoulders of the class-mistresses.

So, to the interest of all the girls, Miss Willcox appeared. She was present at Assembly the second day and looked round with vague, rather soulful eyes.

' Her name's Miss Willcox,' the girls whispered to one another. ' She's awfully clever. She's going to take English. She writes ! She has had a book of poetry published.'

The girls all gazed at Miss Willcox with awe. They thought that any one must indeed be clever to have written a book. Miss Willcox gazed back at the girls, her eyes dreamy and far away. What could she be thinking of ? Another book, perhaps ?

It was always exciting to have a new teacher. What would she be like in class ? Strict ? Humorous ? Lenient ? Dull ? Would she be a good one to play a few tricks on ?

' I think she looks most interesting,' said Alison. ' I do really. I think she looks as if all kinds of beautiful thoughts are passing through her mind.'

' She's probably wondering what there will be for lunch,' said Bobby. ' I always suspect those people that look dreamily into the distance. Anne-Marie does it sometimes, and I know jolly well that half the time she's wondering if Felicity has remembered to get the cakes for tea, or something like that, and the other half she's thinking of nothing at all.'

Anne-Marie wished she could think of something smart to say back, but she never could. Well—poets were always misunderstood, she knew that. People laughed at them, and jeered at their work—but then, years after they were dead, people said how wonderful they were.

'Perhaps Miss Willcox will know that I am a real poet,' she thought. 'It would be nice to have some one on my side. I daresay if Miss Willcox reads my poems and likes them she will make the others change their minds. I'll work awfully hard in her classes, and get on her good side.'

Miss Willcox's lessons were certainly interesting. They were filled with plays and poetry, and the girls were allowed to debate anything they liked, so long as it had to do with literature.

There was no doubt that Miss Willcox 'knew her stuff' as Bobby put it. She was very widely read, had an excellent memory, and really did know how to pick out things that would interest the girls, and make them think.

She was a strange woman to look at, though—untidy, vague and given to 'bits and pieces' as Janet said. A scarf wound round her neck, a brilliant belt, a very striking handkerchief. She wore gold-headed pins in her black hair, and her dresses all had a drapy look about them. They did not really fit her.

She had an affected voice which rather spoilt her reading of poetry, for she pitched it deep and low, when really it should have been quite ordinary. She had graceful, dramatic gestures, which filled Alison's romantic soul with delight.

Alison copied one or two of the gestures. She flung out her hand dramatically when she was telling Pat and Isabel something, and hit Bobby with the back of her fingers.

'Hey!' said Bobby. 'Our feather-head is copying Miss Willcox! Alison, you're not going to lose your heart to *her*, are you?'

Alison went red. She always blushed very easily, which annoyed her. 'I don't know what you mean,' she said. 'I admire Miss Willcox, I must say. Her knowledge of English literature is marvellous.'

'Oh, Alison!' groaned Bobby. 'Don't say you're going to worship Miss Willcox. Haven't you got over that silly habit yet? You never choose the right people to worship, either!'

'Why isn't Miss Willcox the right person?' said Alison trying to speak coldly, though she felt very hot and cross. 'She's clever—she's written a book of most marvellous poetry—she's got a lovely deep voice, and I think she's most picturesque-looking.'

'Untidy and messy, you mean,' said Bobby, in disgust. 'Picturesque-looking, indeed! What an idiot you are, Alison. I think Miss Willcox wants smartening up and making tidy. Gold-topped pins in her hair—gosh, it nearly made me sick to see them.'

Bobby was going to extremes and did not mean all she said. She was such a downright, boyish person, she so much hated nonsense and show, that people like Miss Willcox made her 'go off the deep end' and say more than she meant.

'Oh, Miss Willcox is not so bad as you make out, Bobby,' said Pat, seeing that Alison looked as if she was about to burst into tears. 'And she's not so wonderful as *you* make out, either, Alison. Anyway—for goodness' sake don't put on a worshipping act this term. You've been fairly sensible the last two terms or so.'

Alison turned away. 'Remember Miss Quentin,' said Bobby, warningly. 'Don't make the same mistake again!'

Miss Quentin had been worshipped by Alison when she was in a lower form, and Alison had been bitterly hurt by her, because she had found out that the mistress was laughing at her behind her back. She had learnt a hard lesson then and had been more careful whom she gave her heart to. But now it looked as if she was going to start all over again!

'It's no good trying to stop her,' said Pat, watching her cousin as she left the room, her head high in the air, and her cheeks burning. 'You only make her worse, Bobby. She goes all loyal and intense.'

'Well, I've said my say,' said Bobby. 'It wouldn't matter a bit if only Alison would choose somebody decent, but she never does.'

'If Miss Willcox was sensible she'd nip Alison in the bud,' said Pat. 'Miss Cornwallis soon nips any silliness in the bud! So do the other mistresses. I can see that Miss Willcox is going to encourage that awful Anne-Marie too.'

'Well—let her!' said Bobby. 'If she wants the Alisons and Anne-Maries of the world sitting at her feet, she's welcome to them. Come on—let's go and see if the court is hard enough for tennis.'

They passed Alma Pudden on the way out. The girl looked rather dull and miserable. Pat felt sorry for her.

'Come and have a game!' she called. 'Make up a four.'

'I can't run,' said Alma, in her usual dull voice. 'I'm too fat.'

'Well, it will get your fat down a bit,' said Isabel. 'Come on!'

But no—Alma was almost as obstinate at refusing any exercise as Claudine was. Claudine got out of all games if she could, and even out of the nature walks. At first she had arranged matters so that Matron piled mending on her, which had to be done in games time—but Matron had got wise to this little trick after a time, and Claudine suddenly found that she had not enough mending to make an excuse for missing out-door life.

But Claudine was not to be defeated in anything. If she did have to put on games clothes and shoes, and appear on the field or court, she would be taken with violent cramps, or would feel sick, and have to go off. It was simply amazing how she managed to slide out of the things she disliked.

She and Carlotta were a real pair in their study. Carlotta would not do things she disliked either, if she could get out of them but she used open and direct methods, whereas Claudine really enjoyed getting her way secretly, putting on an innocent face all the time.

They both made war against Mirabel, who, to her intense delight, had been made sports captain for the school that term, as she had hoped. Gladys had been made vice-captain, and this pleased them both. Gladys was small, but very quick and deft on the playing-field or tennis court, and a fine little swimmer. Also, she was very good at dealing with some of the shy, younger girls, who were a bit afraid of Mirabel's heartiness and drive.

Mirabel was a typical sports captain, loud-voiced, hearty in manner, strapping in figure, and not very sensitive to the feelings of others. She was always trying to make Alison, Claudine, Angela and Carlotta take more interest in the games, and they were just as determined not to. It annoyed her intensely when they would not turn up at practices she had arranged, or got bored on the field and talked.

' This Mirabel, she is a pest,' complained Claudine to her aunt, Mam'zelle. ' Always she wants me to go to the field and make myself hot and dirty and untidy. Can you not tell her my heart is weak, *ma tante* ? '

' Claudine ! Have you a weak heart, my child ? This you have never told me before ! ' cried Mam'zelle, in alarm. ' Have you a pain ? You must go to Matron.'

This was the last thing that Claudine wanted to do. Matron was the one person who consistently disbelieved all that Claudine said.

' No, I have no pain,' said Claudine, demurely. ' Only just a little flutter here—now and again when I run or go up the stairs.'

Mam'zelle looked at Claudine hard. She loved her dearly, but it did sometimes cross her mind that her niece might deceive her in order to gain her own ends. Claudine had pressed her hand over the place where she thought her heart was, to show where the flutter came—but unfortunately she wasn't indicating the right place.

'*Tiens!*' said Mam'zelle, half-alarmed still but a little angry. 'That is not your heart. That is your stomach. Maybe you need a dose of good medicine.'

Claudine disappeared at once. She was not going to have any of Matron's good medicine. She made up her mind to find out exactly where her heart was, so that another time she would not make a mistake.

After a few days the fifth form settled down into their usual familiar routine. They tackled their new work, grumbled and groused, laughed and talked, played games and went to bed tired out. It was a good life, an interesting, full and friendly one. Sometimes the fifth formers felt a little sad when they thought that they had only one more form to go into—and then St. Clare's would be left behind for ever.

There was to be a stiff exam. half-way through the term, which every one was to take, even Doris and Alma and Felicity, who felt absolutely certain they would not be able to pass it.

'But it won't do you any harm to work for it,' said Miss Cornwallis, in her crisp voice. 'If you could just get a Pass I should feel you had achieved something! I shall allow you to relax, all of you, after the exam. is over, but I must insist that you do your very best for the first half of the term, and really study hard.'

So there was some very hard work done in the little studies that term. Carlotta groaned over her maths and Claudine puzzled over grammar. Felicity tried to learn her English literature and to write essays which usually ended abruptly because she had suddenly thought of a new tune. Anne-Marie rushed through all her prep. except the English and then spent laborious hours over that, hoping to win approval from Miss Willcox.

Even Doris and Angela worked, though neither of them liked it. School was fun—but it *was* hard work too!

THE little first formers came and went at the bidding
of the fifth. They ran errands, they made toast for tea
and they chattered about their affairs to any one who
would listen.

Mirabel was always kindest to those who were good at
games. She encouraged them to practise well at catching
and running for lacrosse, she made up the teams for the
school, and coached them well in her spare time. The
younger girls thought she was wonderful.

'You know, that little Molly Williams is awfully good,'
said Mirabel to Gladys, when she was making up the
teams one day. 'I've a good mind to let her play in the
third team, Gladys. And Jane Teal is good too, if she
would practise running a bit more. She could be quite
fast.'

'Little Antoinette is just as bad as Claudine,' said
Gladys. 'I can't get her to practise at all, or to take any
interest in games. Claudine doesn't back us up there,
either. She is always telling Antoinette good excuses to
make.'

'I'm tired of Claudine and her silly ways,' said Mirabel,
impatiently. 'She's cunning. She'll get herself expelled
one day!'

'Oh, no—she isn't as bad as that,' said Gladys, quite
shocked. 'She's just different from us, that's all. She's
better than she was.'

'I should hope so, after all these terms at St. Clare's,'
said Mirabel, writing the list of girls for the third
team. 'Well—I've put Molly Williams down—she'll be
thrilled.'

'It's a pity Angela and Alison order the young ones
about so much,' said Gladys. 'They have always got one
or other of them in their study, doing something for

them.   Angela even got Jane Teal in to do some mending for her, and that's not allowed.'

' I'll speak to Jane about it,' said Mirabel, in her direct way.   ' I'll tell her she's not supposed to do Angela's mending, and she must use that time to get out on the practice field.'

' Well—wouldn't it be better to tell Angela that, not Jane ? ' said Gladys.   ' It would come better from Angela, if she told Jane to stop doing her mending, than it would from you.'

' I'll deal with Jane myself,' said Mirabel, very much the sports captain, rather over-bearing and arrogant that morning.

' Jane's fond of Angela,' said Gladys, as Mirabel went out of the roon.   Mirabel snorted.

' She looks up to *me* no end,' she said.   ' I'm pretty certain she'll do what *I* want, and not what Angela says. You really can leave these things to me, Gladys.'

Mirabel found Jane Teal and called to her.   ' Hie Jane ! Come here a minute ! '

The fourteen-year-old Jane, small, slight and quick, went to Mirabel, her face flushing.   She wondered if Mirabel was going to tell her she was to play in the third team with Molly.   What a thrill that would be !

' Jane,' said Mirabel, in her direct way, ' I want you to do a bit more practising in the field the next few weeks. You'll be good if you really do practice.   You ought to have been out this week.   I hear you've been doing Angela's mending instead, and you know you don't need to do that.'

' I like to,' said Jane, flushing again.   ' I'm good at sewing and Angela isn't.   I like doing things for her.'

' Well, you give that up and pay more attention to games,' said Mirabel.   ' I'm in charge of games and I want the good players doing their best.'

' I will do my best,' said Jane, proud to hear the great Mirabel say that she was one of the good players.   ' But I did promise Angela to do all her mending this term—at least I offered to, Mirabel.'

'Well, you must tell her you can't,' said Mirabel, who quite failed to see that anything mattered except what she wanted herself.

'But—she'll be very cross and upset—and I do like doing things for her,' said Jane, half-frightened, but obstinate. 'I—I think she's beautiful, Mirabel. Don't you ?'

'I don't see what that's got to do with it,' said Mirabel, impatiently. 'Anyway, I'm your sports captain and you've got to do as you're told. If you don't, I shan't let you play in even the fourth team, let alone the third.'

Mirabel's tone was sharp. She turned on her heel and went off. Jane looked after her, and tears smarted in her eyes. She admired Mirabel so much—and she did like Angela so much too. Angela had such a lovely smile and she said such nice things. The other girl she shared her study with was nice too—Alison.

Jane went to find her friend, Sally. She told her all that Mirabel had said and Sally listened.

'Well,' said Sally, 'you'll have to do what Mirabel tells you if you want to play in the third team and have some good matches. Why don't you go to Angela and tell her what Mirabel has said ? You know quite well that if she is as sweet and kind as you say she is, she'll say at once that of course you mustn't do her mending any more.'

'Oh—that's a good idea,' said Jane, looking happier. 'I couldn't bear to upset Angela, Sally. I do really think she's wonderful. I should be miserable if she was angry with me.'

'Tell her when you go and make toast for her tea today,' said Sally. So that afternoon, rather tremblingly, Jane began to tell Angela what Mirabel had said.

'Angela,' she began, putting a piece of bread on to the toasting-fork, 'Angela, I've brought your mending back. I've done everything, even that stocking that had a ladder all the way down the back of the leg.'

'Thanks, Jane,' said Angela and gave Jane a smile that thrilled her.

'But—I don't believe I'll be able to do it much more,' went on Jane.

'Why ever not ?' demanded Angela. 'You promised you would. I hate people who back out of things when they have promised to do them.'

'Well, you see—Mirabel spoke to me about it today,' said Jane, rather desperately. 'She said—she said——'

'Oh, I can guess what she said,' said Angela sneeringly. 'She said you were a wonderful player—and you must practise more—and you mustn't do odd jobs for that horrid Angela. And you meekly said you wouldn't. Little turn-coat.'

'Oh Angela, don't talk like that,' said poor Jane. 'It's not fair. Of course Mirabel didn't speak against you. But I have to do what she says, don't I ? She's sports captain.'

'I don't see why *any* one has to do what dear, hearty, loud-voiced Mirabel says !' said Angela. 'I don't see why because *she's* mad on something she should expect every one else to be mad on it too. This passion for games, games, games ! I agree with Claudine that it's silly.'

'Oh, but Angela,' said Jane, shocked, 'games are lovely. And they make you get the team-spirit too, and play for your side instead of yourself—and——'

'Don't preach at *me*,' said Angela, angrily. 'You're only a half-baked first former. I don't care what you do, anyway. Go and practise running and catching morning, noon, and night if you want to. I shall certainly not allow you to do anything for me in future. I don't like turn-coats. Leave that toast and go and find Violet Hill and send her to me. She can do my jobs instead of you.'

Jane was horrified at this outburst. She had given her heart to the beautiful, radiant Angela, and now it was treated as rubbish ! Angela didn't want her any more. She would have that silly Violet Hill, who adored Angela from afar and would do anything for a smile from her.

Jane gave a sob and rushed out of the room. In a few minutes Violet Hill came in, thrilled to be sent for. Angela gave her orders in a lazy voice, amused to see how the little first former almost trembled with excitement as she tidied up the room, and hung on Angela's lightest word.

Alison came in after a while and looked surprised to see Violet there instead of Jane. 'Where's our devoted Jane?' she asked.

Angela told her in a few words what had happened. Violet Hill listened eagerly. She was glad that Jane was in disgrace. She would show Angela how much nicer she, Violet, was!

When Violet went out Alison spoke rather shortly to Angela. 'You shouldn't have said all that in front of Violet. You know how keen Jane was on you—she'll have a fit if she knows all this will be passed round her form.'

'Serves her right,' said Angela, viciously.

'Angela, you make these kids awfully silly,' said Alison, after a pause. 'I don't really think you treat them properly. You oughtn't to let them think you're so wonderful. I bet poor Jane is crying her eyes out. You know Miss Theobald dislikes that kind of thing.'

Angela went pale with rage. She always hated being found fault with. She glared at Alison and tried to think of something really cutting. She found what she wanted at last.

'Really, Alison,' she said, in her lightest, most jeering voice, 'really, Alison—who are *you* to talk of thinking people wonderful! You're a perfect ninny over that wonderful Miss Willcox of yours, aren't you? Why, you're even trying to copy that deep voice of hers. It just makes me laugh.'

Alison was deeply hurt. When she was fond of any one she could not bear to hear a single word said against them.

'Miss Willcox is an absolutely sincere person,' she said,

with dignity. ' That's why I like her. You've no interest in English literature, or anything at all really, except yourself, Angela—so you can't understand my admiring any one with such an interesting character as Miss Willcox.'

' Tosh,' said Angela, rudely.

The two girls said no more to each other that evening. Angela fumed in silence and Alison wrote a long and, as she fondly hoped, intelligent essay for Miss Willcox. It was not a very happy evening.

Angela had her knife into Mirabel after that. She did not dare to go and tackle Mirabel openly about Jane, because she was afraid of Mirabel's rudeness. Mirabel was tasting power for the first time as sports captain, and she was rather arrogant and blunt in her speech. Also she was very thick-skinned and Angela despaired of being able to say anything that would hurt her.

So she had to content herself with looking at her sneeringly, and saying mocking things behind her back. But as sneering glances and words were typical of Angela when she was upset about something, no one took much notice, Mirabel least of all.

Angela made things up with Alison, not so much because she wanted to, but because she simply had to have some one to talk to and air her views to. Also, Alison genuinely admired her looks and her clothes, and it was always pleasant to bask in admiration of that sort.

Alison was not foolish with Angela as she had been when she first came. She no longer spoilt her and praised her and agreed with everything. But she could not hide her real admiration of the lovely girl with her shining golden hair, and brilliant blue eyes.

She was glad to make up the quarrel with Angela, for she wanted to talk about Miss Willcox—how wonderful she was in class, what beautiful poetry she wrote, how well she recited in that soulful voice of hers.

So, in return for admiration, Angela listened, rather

bored, to all that Alison wanted to say. They were friends again—but it would not take much to turn them into enemies once more !

5   HARD WORK—AND A LITTLE FUN

THE fifth form were certainly working very hard. Miss Cornwallis kept their noses to the grindstone, as Pat said, and piled prep. on to them. Miss Willcox expected a great deal of them too. Miss Theobald, the Head, took the form for one or two lessons and although she did not give them a great deal of prep. the girls felt that what she did give them must be specially well done.

When Mam'zelle piled prep. on them too, the girls grew indignant. ' Gracious ! What with all that maths. to do, and that map to draw, and those French poems to memorize, and that essay for Miss Willcox, we'll all have nervous breakdowns ! ' groaned Bobby

Only Pam Boardman did not seem to mind. She had an amazing memory, and had only to look at a page once to know it by heart. Doris envied her this gift from the bottom of her heart.

' I've no memory at all for lessons,' she sighed. ' What I learn in the morning I've forgotten in the evening.'

' Well, if you're going to be an actress, you'll have parts to learn, won't you ? ' said Pam.

' The funny thing is, when I act a part and say the words out loud, I can remember them quite easily,' said Doris. ' I never forget them then. It's sitting hunched up over a book, reading and re-reading the words that gets me down.'

' Well, Doris, stand up and recite the words out loud, and act them if you want to,' said Pam, a gleam of fun

coming into her solemn eyes. ' Here—take this French
poem—it's all about the so-beautiful country-side, as
Mam'zelle would say. Recite it out loud, act the cows
and the sheep, frisk when you come to the part where
the little lambs play, and waddle like a duck when you
get to them. You'll soon learn it.'

So, to the amazement of Pat and Isabel, who looked
in at Pam's study to borrow a book, Doris threw herself
heart, soul and body into the French pastoral poem.

She declaimed the poem loudly, with gestures of all
kinds. She frisked like a lamb, she chewed cud like a
cow, she waddled like a duck. It was perfect.

The girls shrieked with laughter. Doris had turned
the solemn and rather heavy French poem into a real
comedy.

' Now—do you know it ? ' said Pam, when Doris
finished, and sat down panting in a chair.

Doris screwed up her nose and thought hard. ' Let me
see,' she said, ' it begins like this . . .'

But until she got up and acted the poem as she had
done before, she could not remember a word. It was
evidently the acting that brought the words to her
mind.

' Well—you do know the poem,' said Pam, pleased.
' You won't forget it now. Mam'zelle will be pleased
with her *chère* Doris tomorrow ! '

Doris, however, was not in Mam'zelle's good books the
next day. Her French exercise was nothing but mistakes
and was slashed right across with Mam'zelle's thick blue
pencil. Mam'zelle never spared her blue pencil when she
was annoyed, and a page disapproved of by her was
always a terrible sight.

' Ah, you Doris ! ' began Mam'zelle, when she was going
through the work with her class. ' You ! Have I had
you on my thumb . . .'

' *Under* my thumb,' said Bobby, with a grin. Mam'-
zelle glared at her and resumed.

' Have I had you on my thumb for all these terms and

still you do not know that a table is she not he. Why
are you not in the kindergarten ? Why can you still not
pronounce the French R ? All the others can. You are
a great big stupid girl.'

'Yes, Mam'zelle,' said poor Doris, meekly. When
Mam'zelle flew into a rage, it was best to be meek. But
for some reason Doris's meekness irritated Mam'zelle
even more.

'Ah—you mock at me now ! " Yes, Mam'zelle " you
say, with your tongue in your mouth and butter melting
in your cheek ! ' cried Mam'zelle, getting things mixed up
as usual.

The girls giggled. 'You mean, with your tongue in
your cheek, and butter that won't melt in your mouth,'
suggested Bobby again.

'Do not tell me what I mean, Bobbee,' said Mam'zelle,
exasperated. 'Always you interrupt. Doris, stand up.'

Doris stood up, her humorous mouth twitching. She
would act this scene afterwards for the benefit of the
girls. How they would laugh !

'Your written work is very bad. Now let me hear your
oral work,' demanded Mam'zelle. 'You have learnt the
French poem ? Yes—then let me hear it. Begin ! '

Doris couldn't think of a single word. She stared into
the distance, racking her brains. She knew there were
all kinds of animals in it—but how did the words go ?

'She did learn it, Mam'zelle,' said Pam's voice,
earnestly. 'I heard her say it all through without
looking at the book once.'

'Then I too will hear it now,' said Mam'zelle. 'Begin,
Doris.'

Pam sat just behind Doris. She whispered the first
line to her. Doris began—and then she suddenly knew
that if only she could act the poem, she could say every
word—but not one line would come unless she acted it !
Oh dear—she couldn't possibly act it in front of Mam'-
zelle, who loved French poetry, and would think she was
making fun of it.

'Well, Doris, I wait.   I wait patiently,' said Mam'zelle, who was anything but patient at that moment. 'Can you or can you not say the poem to me?'

'Yes. I can,' said Doris. 'But—but only if I act it.'

'Then act it,' said Mam'zelle, losing the last of her patience. 'But if you are not telling me the truth, *ma chère* Doris, I complain to Miss Theobald. Act it—but say the poem through without mistake.'

So, in despair, Doris acted the French poem in her usual exaggerated, ridiculous manner, waggling herself, chewing the cud, waddling, frisking—and, of course, as soon as she acted the poem, she knew it all the way through without a single mistake. She certainly had a queer memory.

The girls were thrilled and amused at Doris's rendering of the solemn poem, but they felt certain that Mam'zelle would be exceedingly angry. It was Claudine that saved the situation.

She clapped her hands in delight. She threw back her head and laughed her infectious laugh. She held her sides and almost doubled herself up.

'Oh *ma tante, ma tante!*' she cried to her aunt. 'The clever Doris, the marvellous Doris! Such a poem she makes of it—and not one single mistake. Ah, never never shall I forget this poem now!'

Mam'zelle pushed her glasses on to her nose more firmly. Her face changed. She let out a roar of delighted laughter, and the class breathed loudly in relief. So long as Mam'zelle saw the joke it was all right.

Mam'zelle took off her glasses and wiped her streaming eyes. 'It is clever, very clever, Doris,' she said. 'It is not the right way to recite such a poem, no. But it is very clever and very amusing. I will forgive you this time for your bad work. It is true that you know the poem, and you have made it very funny. Is it not so, Claudine?'

Claudine agreed. 'We too will say the poem like

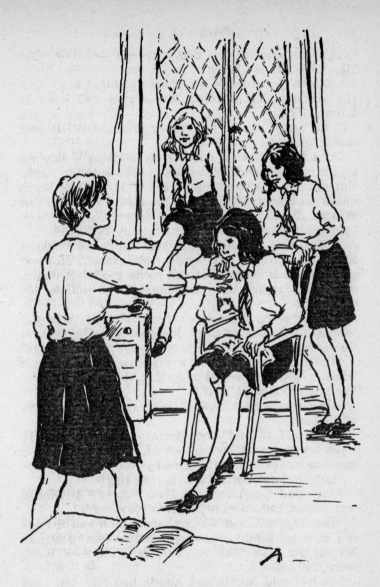

Doris declaimed the poem loudly

that,' she suggested, her eyes gleaming with fun. But Mam'zelle was not going so far as that.

' *Ah non !* ' she said. ' Doris has a gift that way. One girl is funny, but fourteen, fifteen girls would not be funny. *Tiens !* Look at the clock. We have wasted half the lesson on this bad, clever Doris. Get out your books, please.'

Doris found that she could learn anything if only she said it out loud and put ridiculous actions to the words. But so often she could not repeat what she had learnt unless she accompanied it with the absurd actions. Miss Willcox did not think this was funny. She called it ' playing the fool ' and said it was very bad taste.

As for doing such a thing in Miss Cornwallis's class or Miss Theobald's, it was quite unthinkable. However much the girls begged Doris to recite the latest maths. rules with appropriate—or inappropriate—actions she would not.

' I'm not going to get expelled just to make you laugh,' she said. ' I must go on plodding away, and get Pam's help as much as I can. I'll never be any good at lessons.'

' But you'll always be able to make people laugh ! ' said Isabel. ' I'd almost rather do that than anything, but I'm not much good at it.'

' I'd rather write a book or paint a beautiful picture,' said Alison.

' So would I,' said Anne-Marie. ' Much rather. To leave something of oneself behind, something one has made or created—now that's really worth-while.'

' Deirdre fans ! ' said Carlotta, mockingly.

Alison had found out that Miss Willcox's first initial was D. and had asked her what it stood for.

' Deirdre,' said Miss Willcox, and Alison had thought it a most beautiful name, almost picturesque enough for her darling Miss Willcox. Deirdre Willcox—a lovely name for a poet !

She had told Angela and Angela had told every one else. Both Anne-Marie and Alison were always round

Miss Willcox, and the girls now called them 'Deirdre fans'. It annoyed them very much. Alison was sorry now that she had told any one Miss Willcox's name—she would have liked to be the only one that knew it.

She and Anne-Marie both vied with each other for Miss Willcox's attentions. Alison was jealous of Anne-Marie because she could write poetry, and Miss Willcox encouraged her to bring her her poems. Anne-Marie was jealous of Alison because she felt sure that Miss Willcox liked Alison the better of the two, which was quite true. A little of Anne-Marie and her intenseness went a very long way.

'You're both silly,' said Bobby, who never could understand what she called 'sloppiness'. 'Can't you see that any one who encourages a couple of idiots like you can't be worth sucking up to?'

But this kind of remark only made Alison and Anne-Marie more devoted. It even brought them together a little in their common indignation, which amused the girls very much. The 'Deirdre fans' were the cause of a lot of fun that half-term!

6   ANGELA AND THE YOUNGER GIRLS

LITTLE Jane Teal turned up on the lacrosse field and practised zealously, much to Mirabel's satisfaction.

'There you are,' she said to Gladys, triumphantly. 'You see, a little plain talking has done Jane Teal a lot of good. I shall make her a very good player in no time.

Gladys had noticed that Jane had done exactly what Mirabel had told her, but she had also noticed too that Jane looked rather miserable.

'She doesn't seem very happy about it,' she said. 'And it doesn't seem to me that she puts much heart into all her practising. I bet Angela made things very unpleasant for her when she told her she couldn't do her mending any more.'

'Oh, well—it's a good thing if Jane gets that sort of nonsense knocked out of her,' said Mirabel. 'I can't bear these kids that go round worshipping people.'

'Well, a lot of them think no end of *you*,' said Gladys, 'and you like them to.'

'That's different,' said Mirabel at once. 'They look up to me because I'm sports captain, because I make them work hard, and because I don't stand any nonsense. I should tick them off if they got sloppy over me.'

'Well—all the same I think little Jane looks miserable,' said Gladys. 'Don't frown like that at me, Mirabel. After all, I'm your vice-captain, and I have a right to say what I think to you.'

Mirabel looked in surprise at Gladys, who was often called the Mouse, because she said so little and was so quiet. Mirabel was fond of Gladys—in fact she was the only girl in the school that she had any real affection for at all. All the same, she didn't think she could allow Gladys to find fault with her decisions—what was the sense of being captain if you didn't make your own decisions and stick to them? A little power had gone to Mirabel's head!

'You can say what you like to me, of course,' said Mirabel, stiffly, 'but that doesn't mean I shall pay attention to your suggestions, I'm afraid, Gladys. I shall *listen* to them, of course—but I am the one to decide everything.'

Gladys said no more. Mirabel was not going to be a very easy person to live with that term! Gladys wished she was bold like Carlotta, or downright like Bobby, or a strong character like Hilary—they always seemed able to cope with others in the right way, but Gladys was afraid of hurting them, or of making them angry.

Angela made a fuss of Violet Hill, in order to punish poor Jane. She gave her one of her best hair-slides and a book, which sent the foolish Violet into transports of delight. Violet showed them to Jane and Sally.

'Look,' she said, 'isn't Angela a dear? She's so generous. I think she's wonderful. I do think you were silly to quarrel with her, Jane. I think Angela is worth three of Mirabel!'

Jane looked miserably at the book and the hair-slide. Angela had never given *her* a present. She wished she could dislike Angela, but she couldn't. Every time she saw the golden-haired girl, with her starry eyes set in her oval face, she thought how wonderful she was.

Sally was sorry for Jane. 'Cheer up,' she said. 'Angela isn't worth worrying about. I believe she's only making up to Violet just to make you jealous. I think she's being beastly.'

But Jane would not hear a word against Angela, however much she had been hurt by her. Violet too was cross at Sally's remarks.

'As if Angela would give me presents just to make Jane jealous!' she said, sharply. 'If you ask *me*, I think she gave me them because I mended her blue jumper so neatly. It took me hours.'

'Do you do her mending then?' said Jane, jealously.

'Of course,' said Violet. 'I don't care what Mirabel says to *me*—if I prefer to do things for Angela, I shall do them.'

Violet told Angela how upset Jane was, and Angela was glad. She could be very spiteful when anything upset her. She was especially sweet to Violet and to the other first former who came when Violet could not come. The two of them thought she was the nicest girl in the whole school.

Antoinette, Claudine's little sister, also at times had to do jobs for the fifth and sixth formers. She did not like Angela, and always found excuses not to go to her study, even when an urgent message was sent.

'That young sister of yours is a perfect nuisance,' Angela complained to Claudine. 'Can't you knock some sense into her, Claudine? When I sent for her yesterday, she sent back to say that she was doing her practising—and now I hear that she doesn't even *learn* music!'

'She might have been practising something else,' suggested Claudine, politely. 'Maybe lacrosse.'

Angela snorted. 'Don't be silly! Antoinette gets out of games just like you do—the very idea of thinking she might put in a bit of practice is absurd. I believe you encourage her in these bad ways—slipping out of anything she doesn't like.'

Claudine looked shocked. 'Ah, but surely the little Antoinette loves everything at this so-English school?'

'Don't pretend to me,' said Angela, exasperated. 'I should have thought that in all the terms you have been here, Claudine, you would have got more English—you're just as French as ever you were!'

Claudine would not lose her temper at this ungracious speech. 'It is good to be French,' she said, in her light, amiable voice. 'If I were English I might have been *you*, Angela—and that I could not have borne. Better a hundred times to be a French Claudine than an English Angela!'

Angela could not think of any really good retort to this, and by the time she had found her tongue Claudine had gone over to speak to Mam'zelle. Angela knew she had gone to Mam'zelle on purpose—no one would dare to attack Claudine with Mam'zelle standing by! Mam'zelle was intensely loyal to her two nieces.

'All right,' thought Angela, spitefully. 'I'll just get that slippery sister of hers and make her do all kinds of things for me! I'll speak to Hilary about it, and she'll tell Antoinette she's jolly well got to come when I or Alison send for her.'

Hilary knew that Antoinette was being very naughty about coming when she was sent for—but she knew too that Angela used the younger girls far too much. She used her prettiness and charm to make them into little slaves. So she was not very helpful to Angela when the girl told her about Antoinette.

' I'll tell her she must obey the fifth and sixth formers,' she said. ' But Angela, don't go too far, please. Most of us know that you are using your power too much in that direction.'

' What about Mirabel ? ' said Angela, at once. ' Doesn't she throw *her* weight about too much ? She's unbearable this term, just because she's sports captain ! '

' There's no need to discuss Mirabel,' said Hilary. ' What we've all got to realize this term, the term before we go up into the sixth, is that this is the form where we first shoulder responsibilities, and first have a little power over others. You're not given power to play about with and get pleasure from, Angela, as *you* seem to think. You're given it to use in the right way.'

' Don't be so preachy,' said Angela. ' Really, are we never going to have any fun or good times again at St. Clare's ? Every one looks so serious and solemn nowadays. Bobby and Janet never play tricks in class. We never have a midnight feast. We never . . .'

' Remember that we are all working jolly hard,' said Hilary, walking off. ' You can't work hard and play the fool too. Wait till the exam. is over and then maybe we can have a bit of fun.'

Hilary spoke to Antoinette and the small, dark-eyed French girl listened with the utmost politeness.

' Yes, Hilary, I will go to Angela when she sends for me,' said Antoinette. ' But always she sends for me at so—busy a time ! '

' Well, make your excuses to me, not to Angela,' said Hilary, firmly. Antoinette looked at Hilary and sighed. She knew that Hilary would not believe in her excuses, and would insist, in that firm, polite way of hers, that Antoinette should do as she was told.

Angela saw Hilary speaking to Antoinette and was

pleased. She decided to give Antoinette a bad time—
she would teach her to 'toe the mark' properly.

'Violet, I shan't want you for a few days,' she told the
adoring Violet. 'Send me Antoinette instead.'

'Oh, but Angela—don't I do your jobs well enough for
you?' said Violet in dismay. 'Antoinette is such a mutt
—she can't do a thing! Really she can't. Let *me* do
everything.'

'Antoinette can sew and darn beautifully,' said Angela,
taking pleasure in hurting Violet, who had been very silly
that week. 'You made an awful darn in one of my
tennis socks.'

Violet's eyes filled with tears and she went out of the
room. Alison looked up from her work.

'Angela, stop it,' she said. 'I think you're beastly—
making the kids adore you and then being unkind to them.
Anyway—you'll have a hard nut to crack in Antoinette!
She won't adore you. She's got her head screwed on
all right.'

'She would adore me if I wanted her to,' boasted
Angela, who knew the power of her prettiness and smiles,
and who could turn on charm like water out of a tap.

'She wouldn't,' said Alison. 'She's like Claudine—
sees through every one at once, and sizes them up and
then goes her own way entirely, liking or disliking just as
she pleases.'

'I bet I'll make Antoinette like me as much as any of
those silly kids,' said Angela. 'You watch and see.
You'll be surprised, Alison.'

'I'll watch—but I shan't be surprised,' said Alison.
'I know little Antoinette better than you do!'

THE next time she was sent for, Antoinette arrived
promptly, all smiles. She was just as neat and chic as
Claudine, quick-witted and most innocent-looking. Miss
Jenks, the second form mistress, had already learnt that
Antoinette's innocent look was not to be trusted. The
more innocent she looked, the more likely it was that she
had misbehaved or was going to misbehave!

'You sent for me, Angela?' said Antoinette.

'Yes,' said Angela, putting on one of her flashing
smiles. 'I did. Antoinette, will you clean those brown
shoes over there, please? I'm sure you'll do it beautifully.'

Antoinette stared at Angela's beaming smile and smiled
back. Angela felt sure she could see intense admiration
in her eyes.

'The polish, please?' said Antoinette, politely.

'You'll find it in the cupboard, top shelf,' said Angela.
'How chic and smart you always look, Antoinette—just
like Claudine.'

'Ah, Claudine, is she not wonderful?' said Antoinette.
'Angela, I have five sisters, and I like them all, but
Claudine is my favourite. Ah, Claudine—I could tell you
things about Claudine that would make you marvel, that
would make you wish that you too had such a sister,
and . . .'

But Angela was not in the least interested to hear what
a wonderful sister Claudine was, and she was certain she
would never wish she had one like her. Angela preferred
being a spoilt only child. You had to share things with
sisters!

'Er—the polish is in the cupboard, top shelf,' she said,
her bright smile fading a little.

'The polish—ah yes,' said Antoinette, taking a step

towards the cupboard, but only a step. 'Now, Claudine is not the only wonderful sister I have—there is Louise. Ah, I wish I could tell you what Louise is like. Louise can do every embroidery stitch there is, and when she was nine, she won . . .'

'Better get on with my shoes, Antoinette,' said Angela, beginning to lose patience. A hurt look came into Antoinette's eyes, and Angela made haste to bestow her brilliant smile on her again. Antoinette at once cheered up and took another step towards the cupboard.

She opened her mouth, plainly to go on with her praise of Louise or some other sister, but Angela picked up a book and pretended to be absorbed in it.

'Don't talk for a bit,' she said to Antoinette. 'I've got to learn something.'

Antoinette went to the cupboard. She took a chair and stood on it to get the polish. Then she stepped down with a small pot in her hand, and a little secret smile on her mouth—the kind of smile that Claudine sometimes wore. Angela did not see it.

Antoinette found a brush and duster and set herself to her task. She squeezed cream on to the shoes and smeared it on well. Then she brushed it in and then rubbed hard with the soft duster. She held the pair of shoes away from her and looked at them with pride.

'Done?' said Angela, still not looking up in case Antoinette began talking again.

'They are finished,' said Antoinette. 'Shall I clean yet another pair, Angela? It is a pleasure to work for you.'

Angela was delighted to hear this. Aha—Alison would soon see that she could win the heart of Antoinette as easily as any one else's.

'Yes, Antoinette—clean all the shoes you like,' she said, smiling sweetly. 'How beautiful that pair look!'

'Do they not?' said Antoinette. 'Such beautiful shoes they are too! Ah, no girl in the school wears such fine clothes as you, Angela—so beautifully made, so carefully finished. You have more chic than any English girl—you might be a Parisian!'

'I've been to Paris and bought clothes there two or three times,' said Angela, and was just about to describe all the clothes when Antoinette started off again.

'Ah, clothes—now you should see my sister Jeanne! Such marvellous clothes she has, like those in the shops at Paris—but all of them she makes herself with her clever fingers. Such style, such chic, such . . .'

'You seem to have got a whole lot of very clever sisters,' said Angela, sarcastically, but Antoinette did not seem to realize that Angela was being cutting.

'It is true,' she said. 'I have not yet told you about Marie. Now Marie . . .'

'Antoinette, finish the shoes and let me get on with my work,' said Angela, who felt that she could not bear to hear about another sister of Antoinette's. 'There's a good girl!'

She used her most charming tone, and Antoinette beamed. 'Yes, Angela, yes. I am too much of a chatter-tin, am I not?'

'Box, not tin,' said Angela. 'Now, do get on, Antoinette. It's lovely to hear your chatter, but I really have got work to do.'

Antoinette said no more but busied herself with three more pairs of shoes. She stood them in the corner and put the empty pot of cream into the waste-paper basket. 'I have finished, Angela,' she said. 'I go now. Tomorrow you will want me, is it not so?'

'Yes, come tomorrow at the same time,' said Angela, switching on a charming smile again and shaking back her gleaming hair. 'You've done my shoes beautifully. Thank you.'

Antoinette slipped out of the room like a mouse. She met Claudine at the end of the passage and her sister raised her eyebrows. 'Where have you been, Antoinette? You are not supposed to be in the fifth form studies unless you have been sent for.'

'I have been cleaning all Angela's shoes,' said Antoinette, demurely. Then she glanced swiftly up and down the corridor to see that no one else was in sight, and shot out a few sentences in rapid French. Claudine laughed her infectious laugh, and pretended to box her sister's ears.

'*Tiens! Quelle méchante fille!* What will Angela say?'

Antoinette shrugged her shoulders, grinned and disappeared. Claudine went on her way, and paused outside Angela's study. She heard voices. Alison was there now too. Claudine opened the door.

'Hallo,' said Alison. 'Come for that book I promised you? Wait a minute—I've put it out for you somewhere.'

She caught sight of all Angela's shoes standing gleaming in a corner. 'I say! Did young Violet clean them like that for you? She doesn't usually get such a polish on!'

'No—Antoinette did them,' said Angela. 'She was telling me all about your sisters and hers, Claudine.'

'Ah yes,' said Claudine, 'there is my sister Louise, and my sister Marie and my sister . . .'

'Oh, don't *you* start on them, for goodness' sake,' said Angela. 'What's the matter, Alison, what are you staring at?'

'Have you used up all that lovely face-cream al*ready*?' said Alison, in a surprised voice, and she picked an empty pot out of the waste-paper basket. 'Angela, how extravagant of you! Why, there was hardly any out of it yesterday—and now it's all gone. What *have* you done with it?'

'Nothing,' said Angela, startled. 'I hardly ever use that, it's so terribly expensive and difficult to get. I keep it for very special occasions. Whatever can have happened to it? It really is empty!'

The two girls stared at each other, puzzled. Claudine sat on the side of the table, swinging her foot, her face quite impassive. Then Angela slapped the table hard and exclaimed in anger.

ANTOINETTE DEFEATS ANGELA

' It's that fool of an Antoinette ! She's cleaned my shoes with my best face-cream ! Oh, the idiot ! All that lovely cream gone—gone on my shoes too ! '

' But your shoes, they look so beautiful ! ' remarked Claudine. ' Maybe the little Antoinette thought that ordinary shoe-polish was not good enough for such fine shoes.'

' She's an idiot,' said Angela. ' I won't have her do any jobs again.'

' Perhaps that's why she did this,' said Alison, dryly. ' It's the kind of thing our dear Claudine would do, for ⁺he same kind of reason, isn't it, Claudine ? '

' Shall I tell Antoinette you will not need her again because you are very angry at her foolishness ? ' said Claudine. ' Ah, she will be so sad, the poor child ! '

Angela debated. She felt sure that Antoinette had made a real mistake. She was certain the girl liked her too much to play such a trick on her. How thrilled Antoinette had seemed when she had smiled at her ! No —the girl had made a genuine mistake. Angela would give her another chance.

' I'll try her again,' she said. ' I'll forgive her this time. We all make mistakes sometimes.'

' How true ! ' said Claudine. ' Now, my sister Marie, hardly ever does she make a mistake, but once . . .'

' Oh, get out,' said Angela, rudely. ' It's bad enough to have you and Antoinette here without having to hear about your dozens of sisters ! '

Claudine removed herself gracefully and went to find Antoinette to report the success of her trick. Antoinette grinned. ' C'est bien,' she said. ' Very good ! Another time I will again be foolish, oh so foolish ! '

Angela sent for her again the next day. Antoinette entered with drooping head and downcast eyes.

' Oh, Angela,' she said, in a low, meek voice, ' my sister Claudine has told me what a terrible mistake I made yesterday. How could I have been so foolish ? I pray you to forgive me.'

'All right,' said Angela. 'Don't look so miserable, Antoinette. By the way, I think I'll call you Toni—it's so much friendlier than Antoinette, isn't it?'

Antoinette appeared to greet this idea with rapture. Angela beamed. How easy it was to get round these young ones! Well—she would get all the work she could out of this silly French girl, she would wind her round her little finger—and then she would send her packing and teach her a good sharp lesson!

'What would you have me do today?' Antoinette asked, in her meek voice. 'More shoes?'

'No,' said Angela. 'No more shoes. Make me some anchovy toast, Toni.'

'Please?' said Antoinette, not understanding.

'Oh, dear—don't you know what anchovy toast is?' sighed Angela. 'Well, you make ordinary buttered toast —and for goodness' sake toast the bread before you put the butter on—then you spread it with anchovy paste. You'll find it in the cupboard. Make enough for three people. Anne-Marie is coming to tea, to read us her new poem.'

'Ah, the wonderful Anne-Marie!' said Antoinette, getting out the bread. 'Now one of my sisters, the one called Louise, once she wrote a poem and . . .'

'Toni, I've got to go and see some one,' said Angela, getting up hurriedly. 'Get on with the toast, and do it really carefully, to make up for your silly mistake yesterday.'

'Angela, believe me, your little Toni will give you such toast as never you have had before!' said Antoinette with fervour. She held a piece of bread to the fire.

Angela went out, determined not to come back till Antoinette had made the toast and was safely out of the way. Talk about a chatterbox! She seemed to have a never-ending flow of conversation about her family. She might start on her brothers next—if she had any!

As soon as Angela had gone out of the room, Antoinette put aside her artless ways and concentrated on her job.

She made six pieces of toast very rapidly and spread them with butter. Then she got a pot down from the cupboard shelf—but it was not anchovy. It was the pot of brown shoe polish that she should have used the day before!

It looked exactly like anchovy as she spread it on the toast. Carefully the little monkey spread the brown paste, piled the slices on a plate and set them beside the fire to keep warm. Then she slipped out of the room and made her way to the noisy common room of her own form.

Soon Alison came in and sat down by the fire. Then Angela popped her head round the door and saw to her relief that Antoinette was gone.

'I simply couldn't stay in the room with that awful chatterbox, drivelling on about her sisters,' said Angela. 'Ah, she's made a nice lot of toast, hasn't she? Hallo—here's Anne-Marie.'

Anne-Marie came in, her big eyes dark in her pale face. 'You look tired,' said Angela. 'Been burning the midnight oil? I wish I could write poems like you, Anne-Marie.'

'I worked on a poem till past twelve,' said Anne-Marie, in her intense voice. 'It's a good thing no one saw the light in my study. Ah—tea's ready, how lovely! Let's tuck in, and then I'll read my latest poem.'

8 THREE DISGUSTED GIRLS

ANGELA lifted the toast on to the table. 'I got Antoinette to make anchovy toast for us,' she said. 'It looks good, doesn't it? Take a slice, Anne-Marie.'

Anne-Marie took the top slice. It seemed to have

rather a peculiar smell. Anne-Marie looked rather doubtfully at it.

'It's all right,' said Alison, seeing her look. 'Anchovy always smells a bit funny, I think.'

She and Anne-Marie took a good bite out of their toast at the same second. The shoe-cream tasted abominable. Anne-Marie spat her mouthful out at once, all over the table. Alison, with better manners, spat hers into her handkerchief. Angela took a bite before she realized what the others were doing.

Then she too spat out at once, and clutched her mouth with her hands. 'Oh! Oh! What is it? I'm poisoned!'

She rushed to the nearest bathroom and the others followed, their tongues hanging out. Anne-Marie was promptly sick when she reached the bathroom. Tears poured from her eyes and she had to sit down.

'Angela! What filthy paste! How *could* you buy such stuff?' she said.

'Horrible!' said Alison, rinsing her mouth out over and over again. 'All that toast wasted too. It's wicked. Angela, whatever possessed you to get paste like that? I've never tasted anchovy like that before, and I hope I never shall again. Ugh!'

Angela was feeling ill and very angry. What in the world had that idiot Antoinette done? They went back to the study and Angela opened the door of the little cupboard. She took down the pot of anchovy. It was untouched. So Antoinette couldn't have used it. Then what *had* she used? There was only jam besides the paste.

Alison picked up the pot of brown shoe-cream and opened that. It was practically empty. 'Look,' said Alison, angrily. 'She used the shoe-cream—plastered all the toast with it! She deserves a good spanking.'

Angela was white with anger. She put her head out of the door and saw a first former passing. 'Hey, Molly,' she called, 'go and find Antoinette and tell her to come here at once.'

Anne-Marie rushed into the bathroom

'Yes, Angela,' said Molly, and went off. Very soon Antoinette appeared, her dark eyes wide with alarm, and her lips trembling as if with emotion.

'Antoinette! How *dare* you put shoe-cream on our toast?' almost screamed Angela. 'You might have poisoned us all. Can't you tell the difference between anchovy paste and shoe-polish, you absolute idiot? You've made us all ill. Matron will probably hear about it. You ought to be reported to Miss Jenks, you ought to . . .'

'Ah, ah, do not scold your little Toni so,' said Antoinette. 'You have been so kind to me, Angela, you have smiled, you have called me Toni! Do not scold me so! I will give up my tea-time, I will make you more toast, and this time I will spread it with the anchovy, there shall be no mistake this time.'

'If you think I'm ever going to trust you to do a single thing for me again, you're mistaken,' said Angela, still tasting the awful taste of shoe-cream in her mouth. 'I might have known a French girl would play the fool like this. I tell you, you've made us all ill. Anne-Marie was sick.'

'I am desolated,' wailed Antoinette. 'Ah, Angela, I pray you to let me come again tomorrow. Tomorrow I will be good, so good. Tomorrow you will call me Toni and smile at me again, tomorrow . . .'

'Tomorrow I'll get Violet Hill,' said Angela. 'Clear out, Antoinette, you're a perfect menace.'

Antoinette cleared out and there was peace. 'Well,' said Angela, 'she'll wish she'd been more sensible tomorrow. Serves her right! I was nice to her, and she thought the world of me—but I can't put up with idiots. She'll be jolly sorry when she sees I don't mean to give her another chance!'

'I don't feel like any tea now,' said Alison, looking at the remains of the toast with dislike. 'Do you, Anne-Marie?'

'No.' said Anne-Marie, and shuddered. 'I still feel

sick. I don't even know if I can read my poem. It doesn't go very well with shoe-polish.'

'Oh, do read it, Anne-Marie,' begged Angela, who really did admire her poems. 'What's it about?'

'It's all about the sadness of spring,' said Anne-Marie, reaching for her poem. 'It's a very sad poem, really.'

'All your poems are sad,' said Alison. 'Why are they, Anne-Marie? I like poems that make me feel happy.'

'I am not a very happy person,' said Anne-Marie, very solemnly, and looked intense. 'Poets aren't, you know.'

'But some must have been,' objected Alison. 'I know lots of very cheerful poems.'

'Shut up, Alison,' said Angela. 'Read your poem, Anne-Marie.'

Anne-Marie began her poem. It was very doleful, full of impressive words, and rather dull. Neither Alison nor Angela liked it very much, but they couldn't help feeling impressed. However could Anne-Marie write like that? She must indeed be a genius!

'It must be nice for you, sharing a study with Felicity, who thinks as much of music as you do of poetry,' said Alison. 'You ought to get Felicity to set some of your poems to music. That would be wonderful.'

'I've asked her. She won't,' said Anne-Marie, shortly. The truth was that Felicity would not admit that Anne-Marie's poems were worth tuppence. It was very humiliating to Anne-Marie.

'Write something real, and I'll put a tune to it,' Felicity had said. 'I'm not going to waste my music on second-rate stuff.'

The door opened suddenly and Matron looked in. 'I hear you poor girls have had a nasty dose of shoe-polish,' she said. 'I hope it wasn't anything very serious.'

Angela thought she would take the chance of getting Antoinette into trouble, so she exaggerated at once.

'Oh, Matron, it was awful! We had our mouths absolutely full of the beastly stuff. Anne-Marie must have swallowed a lot, because she was sick. I shouldn't be surprised if we are ill, seriously ill tonight,' said Angela.

'I'm sure I swallowed some,' said Anne-Marie, looking solemn. 'I expect we all did.'

'Then you must come and have a dose at once,' said Matron. 'That shoe-cream contains a poisonous ingredient which may irritate your insides for a week or more, unless I give you a dose to get rid of it. Come along with me straight-away.'

The three girls stared at her in alarm. They simply could not bear Matron's medicines. They were really so very nasty! Angela wished fervently that she had not exaggerated so much.

She tried to take back what she had said. 'Oh well, Matron,' she said, with a little laugh, 'it wasn't as bad as all that, you know. We spat out practically all of it— and we rinsed our mouths out at once. We're *per*fectly all right now.'

'I dare say,' said Matron. 'But I'd rather be on the safe side. I don't want you in bed for a week with a tummy upset of some sort. Come along. I've got something that will stop any trouble immediately.'

'But Matron,' began Alison.

It was no good. Nobody could reason with Matron once she had really decided to give any one a dose. The three girls had to get up and follow her. They looked very blue, and felt most humiliated. As a rule Matron left the fifth and sixth formers to look after themselves, and seldom came after them, suggesting medicine. They felt like first or second formers, trooping after her for a dose.

Matron took them to her room, and measured out the medicine into table-spoons, one for each of them. It tasted almost as nasty as the shoe-polish toast!

'Pooh!' said Alison, trying to get the taste out of her mouth. 'Why don't you get some nice-tasting medicines, Matron? I've never tasted any so beastly as yours.'

'Well, I've got a much worse one here,' said Matron.
'Would you just like to try it?'

'Of course not!' said Alison. Then a thought struck
her. 'Matron—how did you know we'd had shoe-polish on
our toast today? We hadn't told a soul. Who told you?'

'Why, the poor little Antoinette told me,' said Matron,
corking up the bottle. 'Poor child, she came to me in
a terrible state, saying she had poisoned you all by mistake, and what was she to do if you died in the night, and
couldn't I do something about it?'

The three girls listened to this with mixed feelings. So
it was Antoinette who not only provided them with
shoe-polish toast, but also with medicine from Matron!
The little horror!

'You've no idea how upset she was,' went on Matron,
briskly. 'Poor little soul, I felt really sorry for her. An
English girl might have been amused at the mistake she
had made, but Antoinette was so upset I had to comfort
her and give her some chocolate. It's wonderful what
chocolate will do to soothe the nerves of a first or second
former! Nothing but babies, really.'

The thought of Antoinette eating Matron's chocolate
was too much for Angela, Alison and Anne-Marie. They
felt that they simply *must* get hold of Antoinette and tell
her what they thought of her.

'Where is Antoinette, do you know, Matron?' asked
Angela, wishing she could get the combined tastes of shoe-
polish and medicine out of her mouth.

'I sent her to her aunt, Mam'zelle,' said Matron.
'I'm sure she would cheer her up and make her think
she hadn't done such a dreadful thing after all! Fancy
thinking she really had poisoned you!'

The three fifth-formers went back to the study. It
wouldn't be a bit of good going to fetch Antoinette now.
She would probably be having a nice cosy tea with
Mam'zelle, who would be fussing her up and telling her
everything was all right, a mistake was a mistake, and
not to worry, *pauvre petite* Antoinette!

'I'll send for her tomorrow and jolly well keep her nose to the grindstone,' said Angela, angrily. 'I told her she needn't do anything more for me—but I'll make her now. I'll make her sorry she ever played those tricks. Clever little beast—going off to Matron and play-acting like that. She's worse than Claudine!'

Alison was alarmed to hear that Angela was going to make Antoinette do some more jobs for them.

'For goodness' sake, don't be silly!' she said to Angela. 'Antoinette is far too clever for us to get even with. She'll only do something even worse than she has already done. I told you she wouldn't be like the others, silly and worshipping. I told you she would size you up! I told you. . . .'

'Shut up, Alison,' said Angela. 'I hate people who say "I told you, I told you!" I won't have Antoinette if you think she'll play worse tricks. She'd end in poisoning us, I should think. I wish I could pay her out, though.'

'It's partly your own fault, all this,' said Alison. 'If only you'd treat the younger ones like the others do, sensibly and properly, we shouldn't have all these upsets.'

Anne-Marie thought it was time to go. She always said that quarrels upset her poetic feelings. So she went, taking her mournful poem with her.

'We'd better not say a word about this to any one,' said Angela. 'Else the whole school will be laughing at us. We won't let it go any further.'

But alas for their plans—Antoinette told the story to everyone, and soon the whole school was enjoying the joke. It made Angela furious, for she hated being laughed at, it humiliated Alison too, for even Miss Willcox got to hear of it and teased her and Anne-Marie.

'What about a little essay on "Anchovy Sauce",' she said. 'Poor Alison, poor Anne-Marie, what a shame!'

MISS WILLCOX was in a bad temper. She had just had back from her publishers her second book of poems, with a polite note to say that they were not as good as the first ones, and they regretted they did not see their way to put them into book-form.

Miss Willcox had an excellent opinion of her own writings, just as Anne-Marie had of hers. Also she had boasted in advance of her second book of poems—and now it would not be published. She was disappointed, and, like many rather weak characters, her disappointment turned to resentment instead of to a determination to go on and do better.

So she went to her English class looking rather grim, and feeling that she could not stand any nonsense or bad work that morning.

As a whole, the class had been working really very well, for Miss Willcox's lessons were interesting. Alma Pudden had not been able to keep up with the class very well, and Doris could not learn by heart with any success unless she was allowed to act what she said. Felicity too was only really interested if the poems or plays aroused her sense of rhythm and music.

The girls were rather tired that morning. They had had a strenuous half-hour with the gym.-mistress, who, feeling rather brisk, had put them through a great many vigorous exercises. Then had come a very hard three-quarters of an hour over maths. and then the English lesson. The girls were feeling that they wanted to relax a little—but here was Miss Willcox demanding intense concentration and attention.

Carlotta let out an enormous yawn which drew Miss Willcox's wrath upon her. Then Claudine said she felt sick and please could she go out of the room?

' It is astonishing how many times you manage to feel
sick when you want to miss some part of a lesson,' said
Miss Willcox, irritated. ' Go straight to Matron, please,
and tell her.'

' I would rather not,' said Claudine, politely. ' I do
not feel sick enough for that. I can be sick in here if
you would rather I stayed for the lesson.'

It looked as if Miss Willcox was going to overwhelm
Claudine with her wrath, when Felicity made them all
jump. She began to tattoo on her desk, swaying to and
fro in ecstasy.

' La-di-la-di-la ! ' she sang, ' oh, la-la-la-di-la ! '

' Felicity ! What in the world are you doing ? ' cried
Miss Willcox, incensed with rage. Felicity took not the
slightest notice. With eyes still closed, she continued her
swaying, and her singing, at times thumping the desk to
accent the rhythm.

' *Felicity !* ' almost shouted Miss Willcox, one of her
gold-topped pins falling out of her hair on to the desk.
She didn't notice it. ' Do you hear what I say ? What
has come over this class this morning ? '

Bobby gave Felicity a bang on the shoulder. Felicity
opened her eyes with a start, and gazed round the room.
She did not in the least seem to take in the fact that
she was in class and that Miss Willcox was furious
with her. She shut her eyes again and began swaying.

' She's music-mad,' said Bobby. ' She's in a kind of
music-dream, Miss Willcox. I don't believe she can help
it. Hie, Felicity ! '

' She goes like this in our study at night, very often,'
said Anne-Marie. ' I often think she does it on purpose.
She always does it when I want to read one of my poems
out loud.'

' Jolly sensible of her,' remarked Pat.

' La-di-la-di-la ! ' hummed Felicity. Miss Willcox
stared at her very hard. She simply could not make out
if the girl's actions were genuine or put on.

' Boom-di-boom, di-boom,' finished Felicity and banged the desk hard. ' Ah, I've got it at last ! '

The girls laughed. Acting or not, it was very funny. Felicity beamed round. ' I have it ! ' she said. ' The melody I've had in my mind for the last two weeks. It goes like this—la-di-la-di-la . . .'

Now it was Miss Willcox's turn to bang on the desk. It was seldom that she really did lose her temper, for she considered that meant a loss of dignity, and Miss Willcox always liked to appear dignified and self-controlled. But really, Felicity was too much for any one !

' Leave the room,' commanded Miss Willcox, her voice trembling with anger. ' I won't have any one in my class playing the fool like this. You shouldn't have come up into the fifth form—you should have gone down into the third ! '

' Go out of the room ? ' said Felicity, puzzled. ' Why must I ? I didn't mean to interrupt the lesson—I didn't do it on purpose. It came over me suddenly. Now I am quite all right.'

' Leave the room,' ordered Miss Willcox again. The girls were silent. It was almost unheard-of for a fifth form girl to be sent from the room. If Miss Theobald heard of it there would be serious trouble for Felicity.

Felicity got up and walked out of the room as if she was in a dream. She looked puzzled and shocked. She stood outside the door and leaned against the wall. Her head ached. Then the new melody came back again into it and she began to sing it quietly. The sound came into the silent classroom.

' Anne-Marie, tell Felicity to go to her study, and to write out the whole of the act of the play she is now missing,' said Miss Willcox. ' I will not have this behaviour.'

' Felicity thinks she's a genius,' said Anne-Marie. ' She's always acting like this.'

' I didn't ask for any comment,' said Miss Willcox. She always forgot to put on her deep, rather drawling voice, when she was in a temper, and her voice now sounded rather harsh and unpleasant.

Almost every one got into trouble that morning. Doris was scolded for not knowing her part in the play they were reading. Alma was hauled up for eating sweets, 'like any silly little first former,' said Miss Willcox in disgust, taking the bag away from the fat, unhappy Alma.

'Poor old Pudding!' whispered Pat to Isabel. 'I believe eating is her only pleasure in life!'

'Pat! What did you say?' demanded Miss Willcox. Pat went red.

'Well—I can't very well tell you,' she said, not wishing to repeat what she had said, and hurt Alma.

Miss Willcox at once felt certain that Pat had been saying something rude about *her*. 'Miss games this afternoon and write out your part in the play instead,' she snapped. Pat looked upset, but did not dare to argue with Miss Willcox in her present mood.

The girls grew nervous. Pauline dropped her books on the floor and made Miss Willcox jump. She got a few sharp words that made her squirm and look at the mistress with resentment. Bobby debated whether or not to cheer things up by making Miss Willcox and the class laugh but decided that nothing on earth would get a smile out of the mistress that morning. Whatever could be wrong with her? She was not usually like this.

Only Alison and Anne-Marie gazed at her with admiration that morning. They both thought that their beloved Miss Willcox looked lovely with her dark soulful eyes flashing. A bit of Miss Willcox's hair came down and hung by her ear. Alison saw her feeling about for the pin that usually kept it up, and walked from her seat.

She picked up the pin that had dropped and put it on Miss Willcox's desk with one of her rather sweet smiles. Somehow the action and the smile soothed Miss Willcox.

'Thank you, Alison,' she said, using the deep voice that always thrilled Anne-Marie and Alison. 'You are always on hand to help!'

Anne-Marie felt jealous. She never liked it when Miss Willcox praised Alison in any way. She sat looking gloomy. The class was amused to see this little by-play.

After the reading of the play was finished, there were five minutes left. ' Has any one found anything interesting to read ? ' asked Miss Willcox, who always encouraged the class to bring any poem they liked or to quote any prose lines they came across, which pleased them.

Apparently no one had. ' We've been working too hard this week to read much,' said Hilary. ' We haven't time for anything till this awful exam. is over.'

' Miss Willcox,' said Anne-Marie, nervously smiling. ' Could I read the class a poem of mine, please ? I would so like to know if you like it.'

Miss Willcox was not really in the mood to hear poems by any one, since her own had been sent back. But the class, thinking that they could sit back and have a little rest for five minutes, applauded Anne-Marie's suggestion loudly. Anne-Marie flushed with pleasure. She thought they were welcoming her poem. It didn't enter her silly little head that the girls wanted a rest, and wouldn't listen to a word of it.

' Well,' said Miss Willcox, rather ungraciously, ' you can read it if you like, Anne-Marie.'

Anne-Marie got a piece of paper out of her desk, covered with her sprawling hand-writing, which was always far too big. She cleared her throat, and began, putting on a deep voice that was supposed to be a flattering imitation of Miss Willcox's own style.

' THE LONELY MILL
Lost in the wreathing mists of time,
Silent as years that are lost,
Brooding . . . '

Nobody but Angela listened. The whole class was bored to tears by Anne-Marie's pretentious, solemn and insincere poetry. Anne-Marie let herself go, and her voice rang quite sonorously through the classroom.

But she was not allowed to finish it. Miss Willcox had listened in a state of irritation, and stopped her half-way through. The poem was plainly an imitation of one of her own poems, in the book she had had published, and of which the adoring Anne-Marie had bought a copy.

Her poem was called ' The Deserted Farm ', and the whole plan of it was much the same as Anne-Marie's, even to the ideas in the different verses. As an imitation it was very clever—but Anne-Marie had not meant it to be an imitation. She had thought she was writing a most original poem, and had not even realized that she had drawn on her memories of Miss Willcox's own poem.

' Stop,' said the mistress, and Anne-Marie stopped, puzzled. She glanced at Miss Willcox, who was frowning.

' When you write something *really* original, something out of your own mind, something which isn't copied from *my* work or any one else's, I'll listen to it, Anne-Marie,' said Miss Willcox, putting on her deep, drawling voice again.

' But Miss Willcox—I didn't copy it from anywhere,' stammered Anne-Marie, horrified. ' I—I only tried to model it on your own style, which I admire very much. I—I——'

Even if Anne-Marie's poem had been as good as one by Shakespeare, Miss Willcox would not have admired it that morning, when she was still smarting from the sending back of her own precious collection of poems.

' Don't make excuses,' she said coldly. ' If I were you I should tear the poem up. Now—there's the bell. Put your books together and go out for Break. Alison, you can stay and help me for a few moments. I want these papers put in order.'

In tears poor Anne-Marie went out of the room—and with smiles Alison helped Miss Willcox. The other girls hurried out thankfully—what a nerve-racking English lesson it had been !

'YOU weren't sick after all, Claudine,' said Angela,
rather maliciously, as they went out.

'It passed,' said Claudine, airily. 'Happily Felicity
took Miss Willcox's attention, or I might have had to go
to Matron.'

'We'd better go and get Felicity out of her study,' said
Isabel to Pat. 'I wonder if she's written out the act of
that play. It's an awfully long one.'

They went to Felicity's study. Anne-Marie was there,
crying. She scowled at the others when they came in.

'Cheer up, silly,' said Pat. 'What does it matter what
dear Deirdre says about your poem ? I bet she's jealous,
that's all !'

'You don't know anything about poetry,' sniffled Anne-
Marie. 'I don't believe you heard a word of my poem,
anyway.'

'Quite right, I didn't,' said Pat. 'I'd listen if I understood what you were trying to say in your poems, Anne-
Marie, but it always seems to me as if you haven't got
anything to *say*.'

'You're all unkind to me,' sobbed Anne-Marie, thoroughly upset by two things—the fact that her precious
poem had been scoffed at, and that her adored Miss
Willcox had snubbed her.

'Oh, don't be such a baby,' said Pat, and turned to
look at Felicity, who was writing feverishly in a corner,
copying out the play in a nervous, very small hand-
writing.

'Bad luck, Felicity,' said Pat. 'Come on out now,
though. Do you good to get a blow in the air this morning. You look awful.'

'I don't know what happened to me in class today,'
said Felicity, raising her head for a minute. 'You

see, I've been working so hard on my music, and the tune I've been groping for suddenly came to me—and my mind just went after it, and I forgot everything else.'

' It's because you're a genius,' said Pat, kindly, for she liked Felicity, who put on no airs at all, and was not in the least conceited. ' Geniuses always do funny unusual things, you know. They can't help it. They like working in the middle of the night, they go without food for days sometimes, they walk in their sleep, they are absent-minded—oh, they're not like ordinary people at all. So cheer up—you can't help being a genius. Personally, I think you're working too hard.'

Anne-Marie listened to this sympathetic speech with sniffles and a discontented look. She thought herself just as much a genius as Felicity—but nobody ever talked to *her* like that! Nobody ever called her a genius, except Angela—and Angela really didn't know the difference between a nursery rhyme and a great poem! Life seemed very hard to poor Anne-Marie just then.

' Perhaps,' thought Anne-Marie, suddenly, ' perhaps if I do some queer things, like Felicity does, the girls will realize I'm a genius too. It's worth trying, anyway—so long as I don't get myself into a row. It's no good doing anything in Miss Willcox's class—after Felicity's performance it would be silly.'

She cheered up a little and went out for Break. Felicity would not go out. She was intent on finishing the writing out of the play, so that she could once more give her mind freely to the music that seemed always all around her. Felicity was finding things very hard that term. The work in the fifth form was more difficult than in the fourth, and there was the strain of the exam. to face. She was also working even harder at her music, and very often could not sleep at night.

Mirabel also was working very hard at the sports standard of the whole school. She wanted to raise the standard of the lacrosse so that even the fourth and third

teams would win all their matches. What a feather it
would be in her cap, if she did !

Gladys did not approve of all this intense drive for
high efficiency in games and gym. and running practice.
'You're trying to do too much too quickly,' she said to
Mirabel. 'You'll get much better results if you go more
slowly, Mirabel. Look at this practice list of yours for
the first form. You'll make them all fed up with games
if you insist on so much time being given to them.'

'Do them good,' said Mirabel, intent on the second
form list. 'These kids ought to be very grateful for the
interest I take in them. That Jane Teal for instance—
she is ten times better since she did what I told her and
put in more practice. She's the best catcher in the first
form.'

'Well, you can drive people like Jane Teal, who always
want to do the best they can for any one they like,' said
Gladys, 'but you can't drive every one. Some just get
obstinate. I think you're not at all sensible with some
of the fourth formers—and you really ought to know
better than to go after people like Carlotta and Angela
and Claudine.'

'I wish you wouldn't always find fault with me,
Gladys,' said Mirabel, impatiently. 'You're quite different from what you used to be. You used to like being
guided by me, you said I was the strong one, and you
quite looked up to me.'

'I know,' said Gladys, 'and I do now. I only wish
I had half your strength of will and purpose, Mirabel.
But as I accepted the post of vice-captain, which does
bring with it the responsibility of sharing with you most
of your decisions, I can't sit back and not say things I
ought to say. I don't *want* to say them—I know you
won't like some of them—but I'd be a very poor thing if
I *didn't* say them.'

Mirabel really was surprised at Gladys. Always she
had been the leader of the two and Gladys had followed
meekly and willingly. It was something new for Mirabel

to find Gladys sticking up for her own ideas, and actually going against her sometimes! Mirabel should have admired her quiet friend for this, but instead, glorying in her position of sports captain, she only felt resentful.

'I mean to make St. Clare's the best sports school in the country,' she said obstinately. 'I shan't listen to any excuses of over-work or tiredness from any one. They'll just have to put as much into their games as they do into their school-work.'

'Every one is not as big and strong as you are,' said Gladys, looking at the huge, strapping girl. 'I don't wonder you are going to train as a games-mistress. You're just cut out for it! You could take gym. and games the whole day long and then go for a ten-mile walk in the evening! But do, do remember, Mirabel, old thing, that youngsters like Jane Teal really haven't the strength to do all *you* do!'

Jane Teal had most conscientiously done all that Mirabel had asked her, for she was a loyal and hard-working girl. She felt proud when Mirabel told her that she was now the best at ball-catching in lacrosse in the whole of her big form.

But she had never stopped worrying about Angela, and she longed to make up the quarrel with her, and do things for her again. She sat in prep. and debated things in her mind. How could she become friends with Angela again? How could she do her jobs instead of Violet, who, after the upset with Antoinette, had been taken back into favour again. She could not for the life of her think how to get back into Angela's good books.

'You seem to be lost in dreams, Jane,' said Miss Roberts's voice. 'I can't think you are doing your maths., with that faraway expression on your face.'

'I—I was just thinking of something,' said Jane, embarrassed, and bent her head to her work.

The next day Violet went down with a very bad cold, and was taken off to the san. by Matron, sniffling and feeling very sorry for herself. She called to Jane as she went.

'Find that school-story for me, and my new jig-saw puzzle and bring them in sometime to me,' she said, and Jane promised she would. Accordingly she went to Violet's locker after morning school, and looked for the things she wanted.

She found them—and she also found two pairs of Angela's stockings, and two vests, all wanting quite a lot of mending. She stared at them.

Violet would be away from school for three or four days. Should she, Jane, do the mending, and take it back to Angela, and ask if she might take Violet's place till she came back ! It would be lovely to go to her study again, and tidy up the beautiful place, look at the pictures on the wall, fill the vases with water—do all the things she loved doing. Angela would smile at her again, and everything would be all right.

Jane mended everything beautifully, spending all her free time on the stockings and the vests. Some of her free time should have been spent in learning a part in a play the first form were doing. How could she learn it, when she had to go to bed early, like all the other first formers ?

'I'll take my torch to bed with me, and when the others are asleep, I'll switch it on under the bed-clothes and learn my part then,' thought Jane. She was pleased at having thought of such a good way out. No one would know. She did not think of how tired she would feel the next day !

She took the things to Angela that afternoon when Angela sent for Violet. She went in timidly, her heart beating fast, for she was afraid of Angela's sneers and snubs.

Alison was there alone. She was surprised to see Jane. 'Hallo, kid,' she said. 'Where's Violet ? '

'In the san. with a cold,' said Jane. 'I mended Angela's things instead. Where is she, Alison ? '

'Having a talk with Mirabel,' said Alison. Mirabel had been having serious talks with all the fifth form that day, asking them to help her in making the sports standard for St. Clare's much higher. She would certainly not have much success with Angela, who detested getting hot and untidy!

'Oh,' said Jane, disappointed, and put the mended stockings and vests down. Then her face brightened, for Angela came into the room and shut the door violently. She looked cross.

'That idiot of a Mirabel!' she said to Alison, not seeing Jane at first. 'She wants to turn us all into tomboys like herself, great strapping creatures, striding along instead of walking, shouting instead of speaking, playing . . .'

'Jane is here,' said Alison, warningly. Angela turned and saw her. She still looked cross, and Jane hastened to explain why she was there.

'Violet's ill, please Angela,' she said. 'So I have done your mending myself. I hope you don't mind. I—I— would like to do it for you again, if you'll let me.'

Angela stared at Jane unsmilingly. 'But what about dear Mirabel, and her anxiety to make you into a wonderful little sportswoman?' she said in a mocking voice.

'I can do both,' said Jane, anxiously. 'I can make time for my work, and my games and for anything you'd like me to do too.'

Angela knew it would annoy Mirabel if she heard that she was making Jane spend her time on all kinds of jobs for her. So she nodded her head and gave the girl a slight smile, which was heaven to Jane.

'All right,' she said. 'I'll have you again. I'm tired of that silly Violet anyway, with her big cow's-eyes. You can come instead.'

Filled with delight Jane sped off. Everything was all right again! The wonderful Angela had smiled at her! She didn't mind if she had to work in bed every night so long as Angela went on being nice to her.

MIRABEL was really making herself a nuisance just then, especially with the fifth form, who were working very hard indeed for the exam. She was trying to get them interested in the younger ones, to make them go and take practice games with them. They objected to this very much.

'It's a silly idea,' said Pat. 'Those babies much prefer to practise on their own. They don't like being chivvied about by us big ones.'

'Besides, we've got to *work*,' said Hilary, exasperated. 'I can't imagine when you do any extra work for the exam., Mirabel—I'm sure you spend all your evenings in your study, preparing your sports lists and list for matches, and goodness knows what.'

It was true that Mirabel was doing very little extra work. She was trusting to scrape through the exam., but she did not care whether she got good marks or not. Her whole soul was in the running of the school games, and she often annoyed the games-mistress intensely. But Mirabel's thick skin made her quite invulnerable to cutting remarks or snubs.

'She just drives on like a tank,' said Bobby. 'Nobody can stop her. She'll have us all trailing after her helping her in her sports ideas just because we're so tired of arguing with her.'

'You can't argue with Mirabel,' said Doris. 'She never listens to a word any one says. I doubt if she even listens to Gladys now. It's a pity Gladys isn't a stronger character. She might have some influence over our head-strong Mirabel!'

'Gladys *used* to have influence over her,' said Pat. 'Do you remember when Mirabel first came to St. Clare's

and was rude and defiant, and said she wouldn't stay longer than half-term, whatever happened ? '

' Yes,' said Isabel, remembering. ' She was simply unbearable—quite unreasonable. And it was the little Mouse Gladys, who got her round, and made her stay on, and become quite a decent member of St. Clare's.'

' But Mirabel has got swelled-head now she's sports captain,' said Bobby. ' Gladys can't do anything with her. I heard her arguing with Mirabel the other day, and all that happened was that Mirabel got angry and shut her up.'

' I have never liked this Mirabel of yours,' remarked Claudine, who had consistently got out of games and gym. whenever she could, all the time she had been at St. Clare's. ' She is always hunting me here, there and everywhere, calling upon me to do this and that.'

The girls smiled. Claudine usually found it quite easy to evade people who wanted her to do something she disliked, but few people were so persistent as Mirabel. No matter where Claudine hid herself Mirabel would run her to earth, produce a list of games and try to pin Claudine down to a practice.

' Yesterday, in my great despair, I went to speak to Miss Theobald,' said Claudine, raising her eyebrows and her shoulders in an amusing way. ' There was Mirabel close behind me, waving a great list, and there was I, taking to my toes.'

' Heels,' said Bobby, laughing.

' I run fast,' said Claudine, ' and I find myself outside Miss Theobald's door. What shall I do to get away from this dreadful Mirabel ? I knock at the door. I go in ! '

The girls were amused and wondered what Claudine could have found so suddenly to say to Miss Theobald.

' What excuse did you make ? ' asked Janet.

' I held a long conversation with Miss Theobald,' said Claudine, solemnly. ' Ah, we talked, and we talked, whilst the poor Mirabel, she waited patiently outside the door ! '

'What on earth did you talk about?' said Bobby,
curiously.

Claudine looked mischievous. 'There was no Miss
Theobald there!' she said. 'I talked to myself, and then
I talked again as if I was answering. The door was shut.
How could the good, patient Mirabel know that only I,
Claudine, was in the room?'

'Was Mirabel outside the door when you went out?'
said Bobby.

'Alas—Miss Theobald herself came to the door when
Mirabel was still standing there,' said Claudine. 'The
poor Mirabel! She must have been so surprised to see
Miss Theobald, as surprised as I was suddenly to hear her
voice outside the door. Me, I did not stay in the room
any longer. I jumped out of the window. The gardener
was there, and he too jumped—how do you say it—he
jumped out of his skin.'

The girls yelled at the thought of Claudine jumping out
of Miss Theobald's window, in order to avoid both Mirabel
and Miss Theobald. None of the others, except perhaps
Carlotta, would have thought of doing such a thing.

'You really are the limit,' said Bobby.

'What is this "limit" that you are always talking
of?' inquired Claudine.

'Never mind. What happened next?' said Hilary,
who always enjoyed Claudine's pranks.

'Ah, well—I went in at the side-door,' said Claudine,
'and I heard Miss Theobald and Mirabel being most
surprised at each other. Miss Theobald said "My dear
Mirabel, how can Claudine be talking to me in the drawing-room if I am here, outside the door? Do not be
foolish".'

The girls giggled. 'Didn't Miss Theobald open the
door?' asked Janet.

'Yes,' said Claudine, 'and there was no one in the
room. Ah, it was good to see poor Mirabel's face then!
So surprised it was, so puzzled. And Miss Theobald,
she was quite cross.'

'Did Mirabel ask you what had happened?' said Pat, grinning.

'Ah yes—she asks me so many times,' said Claudine. And I say, 'I do not understand, Mirabel. Speak to me in French. But the poor Mirabel, her French is so bad I do not understand that either!'

'Sh—here *is* Mirabel,' said Pauline, as the sports captain came into the room. You always knew when Mirabel was coming—she walked heavily, she flung doors open, and her voice was loud and confident. She came towards the girls.

'I say,' she said, 'I've just got Miss Theobald's permission to call a big sports meeting tomorrow night in the assembly hall. Seven o'clock. It's to discuss all the matches this term—and there are some jolly important ones. Seven o'clock, don't forget. And I shall expect every member of the fifth form to be there. The younger girls are all coming, of course, and it wouldn't do to let them see any of us slacking or not attending the meeting.

'Yes, but Mirabel—it's Saturday night, and you know we were going to have a dance,' protested Angela. 'You *know* that. It was all arranged. The third and fourth form were coming too. It was to be real fun.'

'Well, I put the meeting tomorrow night because the dance isn't a bit important and the meeting *is*,' said Mirabel. 'We can have a dance any other Saturday. But I've got quite a lot of new ideas to put before the school. I've been working them all out.'

'You might ask *us* if we would agree to exchanging a dance for your silly meeting,' said Alison. 'You're so jolly high-handed! I shan't come to the meeting. I've got better things to do.'

Mirabel looked shocked. How could there be better things to do than attend a sports meeting, and discuss the ins and outs of matches? She stared at Alison and frowned.

'You've got to come,' she said. 'Miss Theobald said

Claudine jumped out of the window

I could arrange the meeting, and tell every one to attend. It won't take long.'

'You always say that—but your meetings take hours,' said Carlotta. 'You stand up and talk and talk and talk. I shan't come.'

'I shall report any one who doesn't,' said Mirabel, beginning to look angry.

'Mirabel—put the meeting another time,' said Hilary. 'You're only getting every one's back up. You really are. We want a little fun tomorrow night. We've all worked hard this week.'

'I'm sorry,' said Mirabel, stiffly. 'The meeting will be held tomorrow night, and nothing will prevent it, not even *your* wish, my dear Hilary. You may be head of the form, but I am head of the whole school for sports.'

She went out and shut the door loudly. She knew the girls would say hard things about her, but she didn't care. She meant to have her way. The girls would thank her all right when every single match against other schools was won! She would put St. Clare's at the top.

'She has a wasp in her hat, that girl,' said Claudine, disgusted.

'A bee in her bonnet, you mean,' said Pat. 'How you do get things mixed up, Claudine! Yes, old Mirabel certainly has got a bee in her bonnet—its sports, sports, sports with her all the time, and every one else has got to be dragged into it too. I love games—but honestly, I find myself not wanting to turn out on the field now, simply because I know Mirabel will be there, ready to check all shirkers and late-comers!'

'Shall we *have* to go to this beastly boring meeting?' said Felicity. 'I wanted to work at my music.'

'And I wanted to finish my new poem,' said Anne-Marie at once.

'We'll have to go, if Miss Theobald has agreed to let Mirabel call the meeting,' said Hilary, reluctantly. 'I suppose she told Miss Theobald that we were all keen on the meeting. It's a nuisance—but we'll have to turn up.'

'Maybe the meeting will not be held after all,' said Claudine.

'Not a hope,' said Bobby. 'I know Mirabel. Once she makes up her mind about something, that something happens. She's a born dictator. She'll be appalling in the sixth form!'

'I think maybe the meeting will not happen after all,' said Claudine, looking dreamily into space.

'What do you mean?' said Bobby.

'I have a feeling here,' said Claudine, pressing a hand to her tummy. 'It tells me, this feeling, that something will stop the meeting tomorrow night. What can it be?'

Hilary looked suspiciously at Claudine, who was wearing one of her most innocent and angelic expressions. Claudine returned her look with candid wide-open eyes.

'Are you planning anything?' said Hilary. 'Because if so, don't. You can't meddle with things like school meetings, once you're a fifth former.'

'How true!' said Claudine, with a sigh, and went off to her study with Carlotta.

That night, when every one in Claudine's room was asleep the little French girl slipped out of bed and went along the corridor. She went down the stairs and soon returned with something that shone brightly each time she passed under a dimmed light. She deposited it in an unused chest outside the dormitory door, covered it with an old rug, and then slipped along another corridor to the dormitory in which her sister Antoinette slept.

She awoke Antoinette by a light touch, and knelt by her sister's bed to whisper.

'*Oui, oui,*' whispered back Antoinette, 'yes! Yes, Claudine, I will do as you say. Do not fear. It will be done!'

Claudine slipped back to bed like a little white ghost. She climbed between the sheets, grinning to herself.

Dear Mirabel, it will be difficult for you to hold your meeting tomorrow, poor Mirabel, you will be disappointed, foolish Mirabel, you cannot get the better of the little French Claudine! With these pleasant thoughts Claudine fell fast asleep.

12   THE MEETING IS SPOILT

THE third, fourth, and fifth forms were very much annoyed and upset by Mirabel's command to attend the sports meeting on Saturday night. They had looked forward to the dance so much—it was just like Mirabel to spoil everything!

' She walks about with those long strides of hers as if she owns the whole school,' said Belinda of the fourth form.

' I used to like games but now I'm getting fed up with them,' complained Rita of the third form. ' Mirabel ticks me off in public on the field as if I were one of the first form. I won't stand it!'

But she did stand it because Mirabel was a very strong personality determined to get her own way. She was using her power to the utmost and beyond.

The fifth formers all put away their various occupations that Saturday night as seven o'clock drew near. They grumbled as they shut their books, rolled up their knitting, put away their letters. But not one of them refused to go when the time came, for they knew that, as fifth formers, they must turn up even if only as a good example to the younger ones.

Mirabel was standing on the platform of the assembly hall, running through the list of things she meant to say. She glanced up as the girls came filing in, her quick eyes

watching to see that every one turned up. Woe betide
any unlucky first or second former who did not arrive!
Mirabel would be after them the next day!

Antoinette came up to Mirabel. The sports captain
glanced up impatiently. 'What is it, Antoinette?'

'Please, Mirabel, may the second form have a new ball
to practise with?' said Antoinette. 'It seems that we
have lost the one we had, and we are oh, so keen, to
practise hard for you.'

'Hm,' said Mirabel, rather disbelievingly, for Antoinette
could not by any means have been called keen on games.
'Why didn't Violet come to me about it?'

'Violet is in the san.,' said Antoinette.

'Well, come to me on Monday about the ball. I can't
possibly deal with matters like that now,' said Mirabel.
'You ought to know better than to come just before an
important meeting like this.'

'Yes, Mirabel,' said Antoinette, and sidled away.
Mirabel thought of her with exasperation. She was a
slacker, just like Claudine—but she would pin her down
and make her play games properly if it took her three
terms to do it!

The girls all filed in. Mirabel caught sight of Jane Teal
in the first-form benches, looking rather pale. Jane was
gazing at Angela, who was looking very beautiful that
evening. She had had her hair washed, and it glistened
like finest gold. Mirabel frowned. She wished that Jane
and the other first formers would stop raving about that
foolish Angela!

She ran her eyes over the fifth form. They all seemed
to be there—but wait a minute, where was Felicity?

Mirabel spoke to Anne-Marie, who was passing by the
platform at that moment. 'Where's Felicity?'

'She's coming, Mirabel,' said Anne-Marie, shortly, for
she, like every one else, resented giving up a jolly dance
for a dull meeting. 'She had some music to finish copying
out. She said she was just coming.'

'Well, I shall begin without her,' said Mirabel. 'She's

always unpunctual. Such a bad example for the younger ones! It's a minute past seven already.'

Every one was now in their seats. There was a great shuffling of feet, and an outbreak of coughing from the second form, who were a very lively lot this term.

Mirabel went to the front of the platform. She looked enormous there. She began very self-confidently, for she was seldom at a loss for words, when her beloved games were the subject.

'Good evening, girls,' she began, in her loud, determined voice. 'I have called this important meeting here to-night for a very special reason. I want to make St. Clare's the head of all the schools in the kingdom in their proficiency at games of all kinds. I want us to have hockey as well, I want us to . . .'

There came an interruption. A first-form girl stood up and stopped Mirabel.

'Jane isn't well. She says she won't leave the meeting, but she must, mustn't she?'

It was Sally, Jane Teal's friend. Every one turned to look at poor Jane, who, white in the face, felt quite faint with embarrassment.

'Take her out, Sally,' said Mirabel, rather impatiently. She did not like being interrupted in her opening speech. Sally helped Jane out. 'Are you going to be sick?' she asked in a loud whisper, which embarrassed poor Jane even more. She was terribly upset at holding up Mirabel's meeting, but she really did feel queer.

The two went out, and Mirabel resumed her speech, which went on for three or four minutes. 'I want us to win all our lacrosse matches, I want us to form a hockey team that is unbeatable, I want us to . . .'

But what else Mirabel wanted nobody ever knew. There came a sudden and unusual noise that made every one jump violently. It was the loud clanging of the school fire-bell!

Clang! Clang! Clang! Clang!

Mirabel stopped and listened, startled. Fire! This

was not just a practice alarm she was sure—Miss Theobald
would never choose a time like this for an unexpected fire-
practice ; she knew there was an important meeting being
held.

The first and second formers looked uneasily at one
another, and then looked for a lead from the older ones.
There were no mistresses present.

Hilary stood up, her face quite calm. ' Help me to get
the first and seconds out quietly,' she said to the twins
and to Janet and Bobby. ' We'll march them into the
grounds, out by the side door.'

Mirabel also took quick command. Her strong voice
rang out reassuringly.

' That's the school fire-bell. You all know what to do.
Stand, please.'

The girls stood, glad to have a leader. Mirabel saw that
Hilary, the twins, Bobby and Janet had moved across to
the younger girls, and she saw that she could expect the
utmost help from them. Some of the first formers looked
rather scared.

' Right turn ! ' roared Mirabel. ' Follow Hilary Wentworth. *March !* '

In perfect order, without any panic at all, the first and
second forms marched out, led by Hilary, who undid the
garden door and went into the grounds. It was a dark
night, but the girls knew the grounds well.

Pat and Isabel took out the second form. Bobby and
Janet, and the head-girl of the third form then marched
off with that form. The fourth formers followed with the
fifth, sniffing the air eagerly to see if they could smell
smoke.

' Where's the fire ? ' cried Belinda. ' I can't see a sign
anywhere ! '

Mirabel went out of the hall last, pleased to find that
she could handle an emergency so efficiently. Her loud
confident voice had at once instilled trust into every girl.
She wondered where the fire was.

The first of the mistresses to arrive on the scene was

Mam'zelle. Miss Theobald was out, and the French
Mistress had been left in charge for that evening. The
loud, distressed voice of Mam'zelle was heard long before
she appeared in the doorway.

'Ah! Where are the girls? Yes, yes—in the
assembly hall. To think that a fire should come when
Miss Theobald is out! Girls, where are you, Claudine,
Antoinette, show yourselves to me, I pray you! Are you
safe?'

'Quite safe!' came Claudine's amused voice, and then
Antoinette left the darkness of the grounds and went to
where Mam'zelle stood in the doorway. 'I too anf safe,'
she said in her demure voice.

Mam'zelle threw her arms round Antoinette as if she
had rescued her from flames. 'Ah, my little Antoinette!
Do not be afraid. I am here, your strong Aunt
Mathilde!'

'Where's the fire, Mam'zelle?' called a voice.

'Ah, the fire! Where is it?' repeated Mam'zelle, still
feeling rather dazed.

Then Matron appeared on the scene, and took command
at once. She had sped round the school immediately she
had heard the fire-bell, to see where the fire could be.
She had been to the place where the fire-bell was kept to
see who was ringing it—but the fire-bell was standing in
its place, and no one was near it!

She was puzzled, but as her nose, eyes and ears told her
that certainly there was no fire raging anywhere near she
felt sure that some one had been playing a joke. Matron
had been long enough at St. Clare's to smell a joke a mile
away by now.

'Girls, come in at once!' she said, in her crisp, cool
voice. 'There is no fire. But I must congratulate you
on responding to the bell so quickly and quietly, and
going out of doors in this sensible way.'

'Well, we were all at a meeting,' said Hilary, who was
near the door. 'It was easy. We just marched out.
But Matron—who rang the bell then?'

'We shall no doubt find that out later,' said Matron, dryly. 'In the meantime, please march indoors again.'

The girls all marched in. Some of them were shivering, for it was a cold night. Matron saw this and hoped the san. would not be inundated with people having colds the following week!

She looked at her watch and made up her mind quickly. 'You will all go to your common rooms and your studies at once,' she said. 'Head-girls, make up the fires in the common rooms, please, and see that the rooms are warm. In ten minutes' time come to the kitchen, two girls from each form, and there will be jugs of hot cocoa ready, which I want you all to drink as soon as possible.'

This was pleasant news. The girls hurried in, glad to think of warm fires and hot cocoa. But Mirabel was annoyed. She spoke to Matron.

'Matron, I'm sorry, but I'm afraid the girls must go back to the hall. We were just beginning a most important meeting. Shall I tell them or will you?'

Matron looked hard at the self-confident Mirabel. 'We shall neither of us tell them,' she said. 'You heard what I said to them. They've had a spell out there in the cold and I don't want them to get chills. There will be no meeting tonight.'

'Hurrah!' said one or two low voices, as the girls hurrying in heard this welcome news. 'Good old Matron.'

Mirabel ought to have known that one person she could never flout was Matron. She began to argue. 'But Matron—this is a most important meeting. I shall have to go to Miss Theobald, I'm afraid, and ask her for her authority to continue my meeting, if you won't give the girls permission.'

'Very well. Go and ask her,' said Matron, who knew quite well that Miss Theobald was out. So off went Mirabel, angry and determined, bitterly disappointed that her wonderful meeting was spoilt.

But Miss Theobald was not in her drawing-room. It

was most annoying. Mirabel hardly dared to go back and take up the matter with Matron again. She had not at all liked the tone of Matron's voice. Her spirits sank and she felt rather miserable.

Then her face grew grim. 'Well, I shall find out who rang that bell and spoilt my meeting, anyway! And won't I give them a dressing-down—in front of the whole school, too!'

13   WHO RANG THE FIRE-BELL?

MIRABEL went storming to her study. Gladys was there, warming herself in front of a cheerful little fire.

'Pity the meeting was spoilt,' she said, thinking that Mirabel would be in need of a little comfort about it. 'You were making a very good speech, Mirabel.'

'Gladys, who do you think rang that fire-bell?' said Mirabel, grimly. 'Is that cocoa in the jug? I'll have a cup. Not that I'm cold, but I do feel a bit upset at having the meeting completely spoilt by some silly idiot who thinks it clever to play a practical joke like that.'

Gladys said nothing. She had no idea at all who the culprit could be. Mirabel stirred her cocoa violently, and went on talking.

'Who wasn't there? Well, Felicity wasn't, of course! Gladys, could it have been Felicity?'

'Of course not,' said Gladys. 'I don't suppose Felicity even knows there is a fire-bell, let alone where it is!'

'Well—I shall certainly find out where she was all the time,' said Mirabel. 'This is really the sort of idiotic joke Claudine would play—but she was there all the time. I saw her myself—and Antoinette was there too, because she came up and spoke to me at the beginning of the meeting.'

'And she was out in the grounds with the others,' said Gladys, remembering. 'Didn't you see her go up to Mam'zelle and speak to her when Mam'zelle yelled out for Claudine and Antoinette?'

'Yes,' said Mirabel, frowning. 'Well, who else wasn't there? Violet is in the san. Every one else was there as far as I can remember. I ticked people off as they came in, because I wasn't going to let any one get out of the meeting if I could help it.'

Gladys offered no suggestion. Mirabel suddenly slapped the table hard and made Gladys jump. 'Don't, Mirabel,' she said. 'Don't be so violent.'

Mirabel took no notice. 'Of course—Jane Teal went out, didn't she—and Sally. Do you think either of them would have done it?'

'I shouldn't think so for a moment,' said Gladys. 'Why, Jane is very fond of you, and Sally is far too sensible to do a thing like that.'

'I shall find out,' said Mirabel, her face hard. Gladys looked rather distressed.

'Don't go about it too angrily,' she said. 'You'll only put people's backs up.'

'I don't care if I do,' said Mirabel, and she didn't. Gladys sighed. If only Mirabel did care a little more about other people's feelings, she would find them easier to tackle. She was always complaining that people would not co-operate with her or help her.

Mirabel gulped down her cocoa. 'I'm going off to Felicity's study first,' she said. 'See you later.'

She went out of the room. Gladys took up some knitting. She was making a jumper for her mother, and she had very little spare-time for it, with all her exam. work, sports work, and Mirabel's incessant demands to cope with. She couldn't help feeling rather glad that she had an unexpected hour to get on with her knitting!

Mirabel went into Felicity's study. Felicity was there, trying her violin softly, whilst Anne-Marie sat over the fire, a pencil and notebook on her knee, trying to compose a wonderful new poem. She kept frowning at Felicity's soft playing, but Felicity was quite unaware of Anne-Marie's frowns or even of Anne-Marie herself. She jumped violently when Mirabel came into the room.

Then, thinking she had come to see Anne-Marie, she went on with her soft playing. Mirabel spoke to her roughly.

'Felicity, why weren't you at the sports meeting this evening?'

Felicity looked startled. 'Oh, Mirabel—I'm so sorry. I really did mean to come, and I forgot all about it! I was playing my violin, and somehow forgot I had said I would go! How awful of me!'

'Where were you when the fire-bell went?' said Mirabel.

'Fire-bell?' said Felicity, looking astonished. 'What fire-bell?'

'She never hears anything but her music when she's really wrapped up in it,' said Anne-Marie. 'You know how she behaved in class the other day, Mirabel. I don't expect she heard the bell at all.'

'I didn't,' said Felicity, looking really bewildered now. 'Did it ring? Was there a fire? What happened?'

'Oh, you're hopeless,' said Mirabel, and went out of the study. Felicity stared at Anne-Marie, who made an impatient noise, stuffed her fingers in her ears, and tried to go on with her poem.

Mirabel went to find Jane Teal and Sally. They were in the first-form common room, Jane still looking rather pale, but better. She flushed when Mirabel came in, quite thinking that the sports captain had come to see how she was.

But Mirabel hadn't. She came straight to the point. 'Jane and Sally—did either of you ring the fire-bell when you left the meeting?'

The girls stared at her in surprise. It would not have occurred to either of them to spoil such an important meeting! Jane felt very hurt to think that Mirabel should imagine her to be capable of such a thing.

'Well—haven't either of you tongues?' said Mirabel. The whole of the first form had now gathered round the three, and were listening with the greatest interest.

'Of *course* we didn't,' said Sally, indignantly. 'As if we'd do a thing like that! Anyway, poor Jane was feeling awfully ill. She had a terrible headache. She's always having headaches.'

'Shut up, Sally,' said Jane, who knew that Mirabel did not look very kindly on such things as headaches.

'Did you leave Jane alone at all?' said Mirabel to Sally. 'Yes—you came back to the meeting without her, didn't you? Then she could easily have slipped out of your common room and rung the bell, couldn't she?'

'*Oh!*' said Sally, really indignant, 'as if Jane would do a mean thing like that! Yes, I did leave her here as she seemed a bit better and I went back to the meeting— and as soon as I sat down, the bell rang. But it wasn't Jane ringing it.'

Jane was terribly upset to think that Mirabel should even think she could spoil a meeting of hers. Her lips trembled, and she could not trust herself to speak.

'Now don't burst into tears like a baby,' said Mirabel to Jane. 'I'm not saying you *did* do it—I'm only saying that you had the *chance* to do it. It just puzzles me to know who could have done it, because everybody was at the meeting, except you and Felicity—and I'm pretty certain that Felicity didn't even know St. Clare's possessed such a thing as a fire-bell!'

'Well, it looks as if I must have done the deed then,' said Jane, bitterly, trying to keep the tears out of her eyes. 'Think it was me, if you like. I don't care!'

'Now that's not the way to talk to your sports captain,' said Mirabel. 'I'm surprised at you, Jane. Well, I suppose I shall find out one day who rang that bell.'

She went out of the room and shut the door unnecessarily loudly. The first formers looked at one another.

'Beast,' said Sally. 'I shan't do one single minute's more lacrosse practice than I can help!'

'Nor shall I,' said Hilda, and the others all agreed, Jane mopped her eyes, and the others comforted her.

'Never mind, Jane. Don't you worry about it. We all know you didn't do it!'

'I wish I knew who *had* done it,' said Sally, her eyes sparkling. 'I'd go and pat her on the back and say "Jolly good show!"'

The others laughed and agreed. It was queer how in a few short weeks Mirabel had changed from an object of great admiration into one of detestation.

Miss Theobald had to be told about the strange ringing of the fire-bell, apparently done by nobody at all. She was rather inclined to take a serious view of it and Mirabel was pleased.

'I am glad you too think it is a serious matter to have an important, pre-arranged meeting completely spoilt by somebody's stupid ragging,' said Mirabel.

'Oh, dear me, I was not thinking of your meeting,' was Miss Theobald's rather damping reply. 'I was thinking that I cannot have the fire-bell rung without proper cause. If it is, then the girls will not take warning when the bell is rung for a real fire. That is a very serious matter—not the interruption of your meeting.'

'Oh,' said Mirabel, rather crest-fallen. 'Well, could I have the meeting next Saturday night instead, Miss Theobald?'

'I'm afraid not,' said the Head Mistress. 'The heads of the third, fourth and fifth forms have already been to me to ask me if they may have the postponed dance then, Mirabel. I don't think we can possibly expect them to postpone it again. These forms are working very hard this term, and very well. I want them to relax when they can.'

Mirabel left Miss Theobald, angry and depressed. She went into her study and sat down at the table to do some work. 'What's the matter?' said Gladys.

'Hilary and the head-girls of the third and fourth have been to Miss Theobald behind my back and got her to say they could have their dance this coming Saturday,' said Mirabel, gloomily. 'It's absolutely the only chance I have of getting the whole school together on Saturday evenings, and they know it. Deceitful beasts!'

'Don't be silly,' said Gladys, feeling a wave of anger. 'They probably never even *imagined* you'd actually want them to give up *another* Saturday evening. Do be sensible, Mirabel. And look here—why have you left little Jane Teal out of next week's matches? She's very good and you know it. It will break her heart to be left out, when you've as good as told her she might play.'

'I'm not satisfied that she didn't have something to do with the ringing of that bell,' said Mirabel.

'*Well!*' said Gladys, exasperated, 'you might at least wait till you *are* sure, before you punish her like this. I think she's a very decent little kid, I must say, and I'm dead certain she wouldn't do a thing like that.'

'Look here, *I'm* captain, not you!' said Mirabel, losing her temper. 'I keep *on* having to remind you of that. I won't have you preaching at me and interfering.'

Gladys went rather white. She hated rows of any sort, and always found it difficult to stand up to Mirabel for any length of time. She took up a book and said no more. Mirabel took up a book too, and looked at it frowning. But she did not see a word that was printed there. She was turning over and over in her mind the same question—WHO rang that fire-bell?

She would have been interested in a little conversation between Claudine and Antoinette if she could have heard it.

'Very good, *ma petite*,' Claudine remarked to Antoinette. 'It was good to show yourself so well to Mirabel at the beginning of the meeting, and to appear out in the grounds when *Tante* Mathilde called us. There is no one who thinks of you, no one at all.'

'Clang, clang, clang!' said Antoinette, her dark eyes gleaming with mischief. 'I felt like the old town crier at home. Clang, clang, clang, the meeting will not be held, clang, clang, clang! Ah, it is a good bell to ring!'

'Sh. Here come the others,' said Claudine. 'Slip away, Antoinette. Be sure *I* will help *you* if you want me to, since you have done this thing for me.'

Some of the fifth formers came up. 'What mischief are you thinking of?' said Bobby to Claudine. 'You look pleased.'

'I was remembering how I said "I feel as if there will be no sports meeting",' said Claudine. 'And I was right, was I not, Bobbee?'

14   THE TERM GOES ON

THE girls soon forgot about the strange ringing of the fire-bell—all except Mirabel, who felt sure Jane must have done it. In fact, she went even further in her thoughts and suspected Angela of having put Jane up to doing it! She took no notice at all of poor Jane, left her out of the matches, and altogether made her life miserable.

Angela tried to make things up to Jane, delighted at the chance of making a fuss of somebody neglected by Mirabel. Poor Jane was in a great state of mind, upset because Mirabel was unkind to her, thrilled because Angela was sweet to her, and over-tired with all her learning in bed at night with the light of her torch.

She had headaches, felt terribly sleepy all the day, and could not see properly, for she was spoiling her eye-sight by reading in bed by the dim light of the torch.

She was not the only one with headaches just then. Felicity, always more or less afflicted with them, was having them almost continuously. Also, to Anne-Marie's alarm, Felicity had begun to walk in her sleep at night!

This was something that Felicity had done as a child, when her mind was over-taxed, and now she had begun to do it again. Anne-Marie slept in the bed next to Felicity's, and was awakened one night to see a dim white figure stealing out of the door. She sat up and switched on her torch. Felicity's bed was empty!

'Has she gone to the study to do some more work?' thought Anne-Marie. 'What an idiot she is! I'd better go and get her. She'll get into an awful row if Miss Cornwallis finds out.'

Anne-Marie flung her dressing-gown round her shoulders and went after Felicity. To her surprise Felicity did not go in the direction of their study. Instead she went down the stairs and into the assembly room. She climbed up the platform steps, and stood in the middle of the platform.

'Felicity!' whispered Anne-Marie, astonished. 'What are you doing? Felicity!'

Felicity took absolutely no notice at all. She bowed gracefully, took a step backwards and then raised her arms as if she was playing a violin. It was queer to see her in the light of the moon that shone through a nearby window.

Up and down went Felicity's right arm, as the girl played an imaginary tune on an imaginary violin. Her eyes were wide open, fixed and staring. Anne-Marie shivered to see them.

She went up the steps and touched Felicity on the arm. The girl made no response. She went on with her tuneless playing, and then bowed as if she had finished. Anne-Marie took her by the arm. To her surprise Felicity came quite readily with her.

'Are you awake or asleep, Felicity?' said Anne-Marie, fearfully, as they went up the stairs. There was no reply. Felicity was fast asleep, though her eyes were wide open.

Anne-Marie took her safely to her bed and got her in. Felicity cuddled down, shut her eyes and breathed deeply. Anne-Marie got into bed too, but lay awake a long time puzzling over Felicity's sleep-walking.

' It must be because she's a genius,' thought the jealous Anne-Marie. ' She does queer things, as all geniuses seem to do. Sleep-walking must be a sign of genius, I suppose. I wish I did unusual things too. Then maybe every one would think I was a genius—as I am ! Suppose I start a little sleep-walking of my own ? If only the girls would wake up and see it, it would be a good way of showing them I'm a genius too. But they all sleep so soundly ! '

Still, it was an idea, and Anne-Marie pondered over it a good deal, making up her mind that when a suitable chance came she too would sleep-walk !

Felicity did not remember anything about her sleep-walking the next day and was half-inclined to disbelieve Anne-Marie's account of it. She shrugged her shoulders, and went off to her music-lesson. She could not find interest in anything but her beloved music these days.

Anne-Marie was still trying her best to win back Miss Willcox's smiles—but as the only way she knew was by pestering her to read her poems, she was not very successful. She so badly wanted praise and admiration for her talents, that she did not see that Miss Willcox only had time for those who gave praise and admiration to *her* ! Miss Willcox was in many ways a grown-up Anne-Marie, posing and posturing, soaking up adulation and flattery from any one who would give it to her. She had no time for people like Anne-Marie, who also demanded it.

For this reason Alison was very much her favourite. Alison had a real gift for making herself a willing slave to people of Miss Willcox's type. Like Jane for Angela, Alison was pleased to do all kinds of jobs at all kinds of hours, if she could please her idol. Miss Willcox took advantage of this, and kept the devoted Alison quite busy.

Felicity raised her arms as if playing the violin

'It's a pity,' said her cousins. 'She's even beginning to dress like Miss Willcox—rather untidy and bitty!'

So she was. She would appear in class with a startling belt round her slim waist, or a scarf round her neck, and had even managed to get some pins rather like Miss Willcox wore in her hair—only Alison's were gilt-topped, not gold!

'Dear little Deirdre fan!' said Bobby, mockingly, when she saw the pins holding back Alison's pretty, curly hair. 'Golly, you and Anne-Marie really are a pair! Look at Anne-Marie, she's got on a brooch just like the big ones our Deirdre wears!'

It was really funny to see the way the two girls vied with each other to imitate Miss Willcox. But Miss Cornwallis was not pleased. She eyed the two girls each day, and said nothing at first, for the fifth formers were allowed more freedom with their clothes than the forms below.

But, when Alison appeared with two scarves of different colours twined round her neck, and Anne-Marie came with an out-size pewter brooch that had a brilliant orange stone in the middle, Miss Cornwallis could bear it no longer.

'Have you a sore throat, Alison?' she inquired politely. Alison looked surprised.

'No, Miss Cornwallis,' she said.

'Then why *two* scarves, Alison?' said Miss Cornwallis, still in a tone of great politeness, which rang a warning in the ears of the class. How well they knew that extra-polite tone! It always spelt Danger!

'I—I thought they looked nice,' stammered Alison, also hearing the warning in that cold, polite voice.

'Well, Alison, I had thought till this term that you had good taste,' said Miss Cornwallis. 'You always looked tidy and neat and dainty—well-turned out, in fact. But this term you look like a third-rate imitation of some little shop-girl who thinks the more colours and scarves and pins and brooches she wears, the better she looks.'

'Oh,' said poor Alison, scarlet in the face.

'And Anne-Marie seems to be going the same way,'

said Miss Cornwallis, looking at the would-be poet in a way that made her squirm and long to take off the enormous brooch. ' *What* is that dinner-plate you are wearing, Anne-Marie ? Do you really think it becomes you ? '

Anne-Marie removed the brooch with trembling fingers She could not bear to have any faults pointed out in public.

' That's better,' said Miss Cornwallis. ' I don't know if you are imitating any one, either of you—but let me tell you this—imitation is *not* always the sincerest form of flattery when you make yourselves look such silly little sights ! '

' Poor little Deirdre fans ! ' whispered Bobby to Janet. ' That was a crack at dear Miss Willcox ! I bet Corny knows all about what sillies they are over her ! '

That was the end of Alison and Anne-Marie trying to dress like Miss Willcox—but they still went on trying to imitate her deep, drawling voice, her graceful gestures, and her rather round-shouldered walk. The girls got very tired of it, and tried to tease them out of it.

But Alison, thrilled because her dear Deirdre was making such a friend of her, was not in a state to listen to anything the others said, and Anne-Marie was too obstinate. If Alison could imitate Miss Willcox and please her by doing so, then Anne-Marie meant to as well !

Tempers began to be rather short as the exam. drew near. Hard work and worrying about the exam. made most of the fifth form feel harassed and worn. Only Bobby kept cheerful, and Claudine, of course, did not turn a hair. Even Carlotta worried a little, for she wanted to please her father, who had said he would be proud if she passed this rather stiff exam. well.

Pauline worried a lot too. She was not brainless and could do quite well if she tried, but she did not like her study-companion, Alma.

' She's queer,' she told Alison. ' She doesn't seem to work at all, just sits and stares at her book and eats and eats, like a cow chewing cud. She's always grumbling too—says the food isn't enough here, and she wants more sweets and isn't allowed them. It's awful to swot over your work when a person like that sits opposite, glowering and grumbling and chewing ! '

' Poor old Pudding ! ' said Alison, thinking of the fat, dull Alma, who was always at the bottom of the form. The mistresses did not seem to be unduly upset at Alma's position. In fact, they rather seemed to take it for granted, which was queer. Miss Cornwallis always had a few sharp words to say to any of the others who stayed too long at the bottom of the form ! But she rarely spoke sarcastically to Alma about her work.

' It's awful to live with somebody like Alma all the time,' sighed poor Pauline. Carlotta heard her and made a suggestion.

' Come in and share our study with me and Claudine when you get too fed up,' she said, generously, for she did not really like Pauline very much. ' It's a bit bigger than most people's, so there'll be a corner for you if you like. But don't do it too often or you'll get Alma's back up.'

' Oh, thank you,' said Pauline, gratefully. ' It will make such a difference if I can sometimes pop in next door to your study, Carlotta. You will be cheerful company after Alma. She really *is* a pudding ! '

Carlotta and Claudine got on very well together. The younger girls who came to do jobs for them liked them very much. Antoinette often came, and strangely enough, never made the kind of extraordinary mistakes she had made in Angela's study !

One day Antoinette found her sister alone and spoke to her with dancing eyes.

' Claudine ! Our form is to have a midnight feast ! Do you remember telling me of the fine feast you had when you were in the fourth form—you had a midnight picnic by the swimming-pool.'

' Yes, I remember,' said Claudine, and she sighed. ' It is a pity to be in the fifth form. We are so good now. We do not have midnight feasts, we do not play tricks. You will enjoy your feast, my little Antoinette.'

'Claudine, could you tell us a good place to keep our cakes and tins and ginger-beer in?' asked Antoinette. 'We can't keep them in the common room, and we daren't hide them in our dormitory. Tell me where we can keep them in safety.'

Claudine thought hard. 'There is a big cupboard just outside my study,' she said at last. 'It has a key. You shall put your things there, Antoinette, and I will take the key! Then everything will be safe and I can give you the key when you wish for it. You have only to put your head into my study and wink at me—and I will come out with the key!'

'Oh, thank you, a million times!' said Antoinette. 'The second form will be so pleased. What a fine sister you are!'

She disappeared, and in due time the cupboard was piled full of eatables and drinks. Claudine removed the key. 'Now no one will find them,' she said, and hung the key on a nail in her study.

But somebody did find them, which was very unfortunate!

15   ALMA AND THE STORE CUPBOARD

ALMA did not at all like the way Pauline deserted the study they both shared in the evenings. Pauline would sit for a little while, trying to study, then, exasperated by Alma's continually chewing of chocolate, gum or toffee, she would gather up her books and disappear.

'Where are you going?' Alma would call after her. But Pauline did not bother to reply.

So Alma decided to see where Pauline went to. She popped her head out of her study door in time to see Pauline go into the next study, which was Claudine's and Carlotta's. She stood and frowned.

Pauline was not really friendly with either of them—so why, thought Alma, should she keep popping into their study? She sat and brooded over the matter. The next time that Pauline disappeared she made up her mind to follow her into the next study, after a while, and see exactly what she was doing there.

It so happened that Carlotta had had a big box of sugared candies sent to her by her grandmother, and, in her usual generous way, she opened it and laid it on the table in front of Claudine and Pauline.

' Help yourselves whilst you work,' she said. Claudine looked longingly at the delicious candied sweets. There were bits of lemon and orange and nut, all candied round beautifully. Claudine, however, thought a great deal of her complexion, which was very good, and she took only one sweet, meaning to make it last all the evening. But Pauline helped herself liberally. She had very little pocket-money to buy herself luxuries, and sweets of this kind did not often come her way.

Just as she was choosing her fourth sweet, the door opened and Alma came in. ' Could you lend me a maths. book ? ' she asked, rather self-consciously. ' Oh, *you*'re here, Pauline ! I say, what gorgeous sweets ! You never told me you had a lovely box like that, Pauline.'

She thought it was Pauline's box because the girl was helping herself to them. Carlotta gave Pauline no time to reply, nor did Claudine. They both disliked Alma, and were afraid that, seeing Pauline there, she might sit down and stay for the whole evening. Then there would be no sweets left !

' Here's the maths. book, Alma,' said Carlotta, and threw her one.

' Shut the door after you,' added Claudine.

Alma glared. She thought them very rude, as indeed

they were. But who could bear to have Alma sitting
there all the evening ? Pauline looked uncomfortable as
Alma went out and banged the door after her, almost
shaking the pictures from the wall.

'She'll be simply beastly to me now,' she said. 'I
suppose she spied after me and saw where I went. What's
the matter with her ? She's so terribly fat and pasty-
looking.'

'Just over-eating, I should think,' said Carlotta,
beginning to write an essay. 'Now shut up for a bit,
both of you. I want to think.'

Alma was very angry that the three girls in the study
had not asked her to have even one sweet. She did no
work at all that evening. She sat and brooded over that
enormous box of sweets. Alma had a craving for that
kind of thing.

'They're mean pigs,' she thought. 'Really mean. I
shall get even with them, though. I'll wait till Carlotta
and Claudine are out, and I'll slip in and help myself to
a few sweets. I suppose they're Pauline's, and she took
them in there to share with the others, instead of sharing
them with me.'

So Alma kept a watch to see when Carlotta and Claudine
went out. There was a little alcove some way up the
passage, over which a curtain hung. If she stood there
quite quietly she could see when the two girls left their
study.

Two evenings later her patience was rewarded. Pauline
had gone to a debate. Alma slipped into the alcove and
waited to see if Carlotta and Claudine would go to it at
half-time, as she had heard them say they would.

Sure enough, in a short while, the study door opened,
and Carlotta and Claudine came out. They went down
the corridor, talking. Alma waited till their footsteps
had died away. She was just going to slip out of the
alcove and into the study, when she heard footsteps
returning. She peeped out to see who it was.

It was Claudine hurrying back. She had just **met**

Antoinette, who had given her a tin of sugar biscuits to hide in the cupboard with the other things. Claudine ran into her study, took down the key of the cupboard, went outside and unlocked it, pushed in the tin, then locked the door again and hung the key on its nail. Alma watched in the greatest amazement.

Claudine hurried off to join the debate downstairs. Alma stepped out of the alcove, her little eyes gleaming. So that was where the fifth form kept their stores. They must be going to have a party of some kind, and they hadn't told her a word about it! Alma was trembling with rage.

How mean every one was! It had been bad enough in the starchy sixth form the last term, but really, the fifth form were even worse, the way they left her out of things. Alma walked into her own study and sat down heavily. She looked across at the cupboard there. There was absolutely nothing to eat, nothing—and it was ages till supper-time—and even then there wouldn't be much to eat.

She wondered where Claudine kept the key of that store cupboard. It would be fun just to have a peep inside and see what was there—not to *eat* any of it, of course—oh no, thought Alma, she wouldn't do that, mean though the others had been not to ask her to share. But she would dearly like to *look*.

There was no one about at all. She tiptoed to Claudine's study and pushed open the door. She looked round for the key. Could that be the one, hanging on the nail by the fire-place? She took it off and went to the cupboard in the passage outside.

With trembling fingers she slipped the key into the lock. It turned easily! It *was* the key. Alma opened the cupboard and looked inside.

The things that were there! It seemed as if every single thing she liked was there—sardines and tinned milk, strawberry jam and pineapple in tins, ginger-beer and a box of sweets, biscuits and chocolate.

It was quite impossible for Alma to resist the temptation to pilfer the cupboard. Just one of those chocolates —just a biscuit to go with it—just a sweet or two! Guiltily the girl helped herself, then, hearing footsteps, hurriedly shut the door, turned the key, and slipped back into her own study.

She waited till the footsteps had gone by, then ran into Claudine's study next door, and returned the key to its nail.

For quite a long time Alma sat and brooded over her discovery. She felt certain that the fifth form were going to have a party. She hadn't heard a word about it—but then, nobody ever told her anything!

Alma badly wanted the things in the cupboard. Her continual craving for food made her find excuses for the wrong thing she wanted to do. ' It's only right I should share! Even if they don't ask me, I'm a fifth former and I ought to share in their treats. Well, I *shall* share— but in secret, instead of with them at the party! That will punish them for their meanness. It will give them a shock to find a lot of the things gone.'

It was a curious secret to have, but Alma found great pleasure in thinking about that store cupboard in bed at night, and in class the next day. She hugged the secret to herself, and gave Claudine many triumphant glances, which the French girl was quite at a loss to understand.

Alma began to go to the store cupboard whenever Claudine's study was empty. She was very artful, for she was careful not to take things whose absence would be very noticeable. She did not take much of the barley sugar in the bottle there, for instance, because she knew it might catch Claudine's eye. But she carefully took all the bottom row of the box of chocolates, which would not be noticed till the first row was eaten. She took a few biscuits from each row in the big tin, not one whole row. She drank half of each ginger-beer bottle, but filled each one up with water so that it would seem as if the bottles had not been tampered with.

She enjoyed being cunning like this. Poor Alma—her whole interest seemed to lie in food, more food and yet more food. Fat, unwieldy and pasty-faced, with no friends, few brains, and a sly, suspicious nature, she was not a happy person.

She had a wonderful time pilfering the store cupboard. Claudine added a few more things to it, never suspecting that many had already gone. Alma was very clever at getting the key, and taking food when no one was about. If she had only used half as much brain in class as she did in stealing from the cupboard, she would not have been so far down at the bottom of the form.

Then one evening something happened. Pauline, Claudine, and Carlotta had gone down to the common room of the fourth form to discuss something with the girls there, and Alma, alone in her study, planned to take some biscuits and some chocolate—perhaps she might even take a tin of sardines, as there were now five or six of them. She could open them when she was alone in her own study.

She stole out and got the key from the study next door. She had just put it into the lock of the cupboard and turned it, when she heard some one coming. In a panic she fled to her own study next door, only just disappearing in time. But the key fell out of the lock with a clang and lay on the floor.

It was Alison coming. She heard the key fall, and was surprised. She picked it up when she came to it, and put it into the cupboard lock. The door swung open —and to Alison's surprise she saw the stores there! She was still staring in amazement when Claudine came along, gave an exclamation and slammed the door shut.

She glared at Alison. 'Did you get the key from my study? Well, really, Alison, I did not think it of you! What business is it of yours?'

Alison was puzzled. 'From your study?' she said. 'Of course not! Some one must have been at the cupboard and opened it when I came along, because I heard footsteps scurrying away, and then heard the key fall

out of the lock. I put it back, the door swung open—
and I saw the things. I don't want to know anything
at all about the food, Claudine, and I certainly shan't tell
any one—but it's obvious that somebody knows about
the cupboard, isn't it!'

Claudine believed Alison at once. Alison might be
weak and silly in many ways, but she was honest and
truthful. Claudine swung the door open and looked into
the cupboard very thoughtfully. So some one knew of
the stores—some one knew where the key was kept—
some one knew the secret!

It wasn't long before Claudine discovered that the
someone had also taken various things from the stores.
She shut the door and locked it, angry and puzzled.

'Some one's been at the things,' she said to Alison.
'but as far as I know only I and my little sister Antoinette
knew the hiding-place. The second form are to have a
midnight feast, and I have kept their food under lock and
key for them. Who could have found out the hiding-place
—and who could be dishonest enough to steal the things?'

'I can't imagine,' said Alison, amazed. 'It is such
a mean, low-down thing to do. Who ever did it is
absolutely despicable. It's unbelievable! Anyway,
Claudine, if I were you I'd keep the key somewhere about
your person. Then the thief, whoever it is, won't be able
to get it!'

16   ALMA—ALISON—AND ANNE-MARIE

ALMA heard all this conversation quite clearly. She
felt a wave of anger against Alison. Interfering little
busybody! Now she, Alma, would not be able to feast
herself on the hidden goodies any more. She sat per-

fectly still, hoping that neither of the girls would come into her study and see her there. She felt guilty, and was sure her guilt would show in her face.

But they did not come. It did not occur to either of them that the thief would be anywhere near. They felt sure she had run away. Maybe it was a second former —but how disgusting, whoever it was!

The next time Alma had a chance of tip-toeing into the study next to hers, the key was missing. She had feared it would be. She supposed that Claudine had it round her neck in safety. Now Alma would not be able to enjoy those delicious, deceitful little feasts any more!

The girl made a curiously big thing out of the whole happening, and for a few days thought of nothing else. She hated Alison for being the unwitting cause of depriving her of the food she craved for.

'I'll pay her out,' she thought. 'Spoiling things for me like this! I'll get even with her.'

Alma was strangely clever in underhand ways. Stupid people can often be cunning, and Alma was no exception. She set her wits to work, and Alison began to go through an unpleasant and most annoying time.

Things kept disappearing out of her study. Never Angela's things, but always Alison's.

'*Where's* my hair-slide?' wailed Alison; 'it's gone, and I only *saw* it on the window-sill this morning. Have you borrowed it, Angela?'

'Of course not,' said Angela. 'You've dropped it somewhere.'

Then it was Alison's hair-brush that disappeared from her dressing-table in the dormitory. She hunted all over for it, and then had to report the loss to Matron, who was not very pleased.

'How can you possibly mislay a *hair*-brush?' she said to Alison. 'I suppose you've been using it in a bedroom battle or something, and it's flown out of the window!'

'We fifth formers don't have bedroom battles,' said Alison, with much dignity.

Then her geometry outfit went. It completely and utterly vanished, and no amount of hunting brought it to light. Bobby had two and lent her one.

'But for goodness' sake don't lose it,' she said. 'You seem to be losing everything this term!'

The same day Alison's knitting needles disappeared out of the scarf she was knitting, and the stitches all pulled out loose when she took the work out of her bag.

'Now this is very queer,' said Alison, and she held it up to show Angela. 'Look—the needles are gone—and all the stiches are dropped. Angela—what do you think of that?'

'Well,' said Angela, 'I think some one's doing beastly things to you, Alison. I do really. And I bet I know who it is, too!'

'Who?' said Alison, feeling shocked and hurt.

'Some one who is awfully jealous of you,' said Angela.

'You don't mean—Anne-Marie?' said Alison, still more shocked. 'Oh *Angela*—surely she wouldn't do mean things like this! Do you think that she's been taking all those things of mine that disappeared too? Oh *no*—she couldn't be as low down as that.'

'People say that when any one is jealous they don't mind what they do,' said Angela. 'And you know Anne-Marie is awfully jealous because you are so well in with your dear Deirdre, and at the moment she isn't in Deirdre's good books. Why she can't see that her dear idol is bored stiff with her poems I really don't know!'

'She's a beast if she is really taking my things, and spoiling my knitting,' said Alison, almost in tears. The girl always loved to be liked by every one, and it hurt her very much to think that one of her own form could be so unkind. 'I shan't listen to a single one of her silly poems now.'

So, much to Anne-Marie's surprise, neither Angela nor Alison evinced the slightest interest in a long new poem, called 'The Weary Heart', which she went along to their study to read out loud that evening.

'We're busy,' said Alison, shortly.

'And you ought to be, too,' said Angela, virtuously. 'The exam. is coming jolly near.'

'It won't take long to read my poem to you,' said Anne-Marie, crest-fallen. 'This is how it begins . . .'

'Do get out,' said Angela. 'I'm doing maths. and they don't go with poetry, even if the poem *is* called "The Weary Heart", which is very descriptive of mine at the moment.'

'Why don't you write a poem called "The Missing Knitting-Needles?", said Alison, unexpectedly. Anne-Marie stared at her puzzled.

'Why knitting-needles?' she inquired at last.

'Well, you ought to know, oughtn't you?' said Alison. But Anne-Marie didn't. Thinking that Alison and Angela were rude and unkind, and a little mad, she went away, carrying her precious poem with her. She bumped into Miss Willcox on her way, and gave a gasp.

'Oh—Miss Willcox—please would you read this? I spent hours over it last night.'

Miss Willcox took the poem and glanced at it. It was the same kind as usual, pretentious, full of long words, solemn, sad and far too long. Miss Willcox felt impatient. She determined to be candid with Anne-Marie, now that she had her alone.

'Look here, Anne-Marie,' she said, in her deep voice. 'I want to give you a little advice—and I want you to listen to it carefully, and follow it.'

'Oh *yes*, Miss Willcox,' said Anne-Marie, fervently. 'I will, indeed I will.'

'Well,' said Miss Willcox, 'you can't write poetry, and you may as well know it. You can rhyme and get the metre right—but your ideas are rubbish. *Real* poetry has ideas in it, beautiful pictures, great feelings. Tear up all your poems, Anne-Marie, and set your mind on the coming exam. That is my advice to you. You think you're a genius. Well, you're not! You are just an ordinary little school-girl who has got swelled head, and thinks she can write. It is my opinion that unless your character changes considerably, you never *will* write a really good poem ! '

Miss Willcox swept off, glad to have relieved her mind of the irritation that Anne-Marie and her never-ending poems always aroused in her. Anne-Marie, struck absolutely dumb, gazed after her, too hurt even for tears.

Her knees felt rather weak. She went to her study and sat down. Felicity was there, conning over some music theory, humming softly to herself. She did not even see Anne-Marie come in.

It took a little time for all that Miss Willcox had said to sink in. Poor Anne-Marie had had the greatest shock of her life. All her great ideas about herself began to totter and waver. *Wasn't* she a genius ? *Couldn't* she write marvellously ? She began to feel as if she wasn't Anne-Marie any more—she was nobody, nobody at all. She gave a sudden loud sob that entered even Felicity's ears.

' What's up ? ' said Felicity, looking round.

' Oh, *you* wouldn't understand ! ' said Anne-Marie, bitterly. ' You're a genius, you don't seem to live in this world, you don't notice anything that goes on at all. You don't even know I'm here half the time. Well, what does it matter ? I'm nobody, not even Anne-Marie. I've had everything stripped away from me, everything I cared about.'

' Don't exaggerate so,' said Felicity, mildly surprised at this curious out-burst. ' Can't you find the right rhyme for one of your poems ? Is that what has upset you ? '

' Oh, you're im*pos*sible ! ' said Anne-Marie, and threw a book at Felicity, which surprised her even more. Anne-Marie went out of the room. Felicity was at once absorbed in her work again, little creases between her eyes, her headache bothering her as usual.

Anne-Marie was hurt, shocked and resentful. She wondered if Miss Willcox could possibly be right. After all, she knew about poetry, so she ought to know if Anne-

Marie's was good or bad. Anne-Marie thought a great deal about Miss Willcox that evening, and what she had said.

Her resentment made her begin to see the English mistress rather more clearly than usual. She remembered how the girls laughed at her posing and pretence, her vague ways and soulful looks. Almost in a flash her adoration turned to detestation. Poor Anné-Marie—all the things she cared for had indeed been reft from her suddenly. Her pride in herself and in her genius was gone, her hopes for the future, her confidence that Miss Willcox liked and admired her, even her poems now seemed worthless.

She half thought she would do as Miss Willcox had so coldly advised her, and tear them up. But a doubt still persisted in her mind about the teacher's ability to know, really *know* whether her, Anne-Marie's, poems were good. Suppose she tore them up, and wrote no more—and suppose after all Miss Willcox was wrong, and her poems *were* good—what a loss to the world they might be !

' If only I could find out whether or not Miss Willcox is as good a judge as she always sets out to be ! ' thought Anne-Marie, quite obsessed by the subject. ' But how could I ? I don't see *how* I could.'

Then a way came to her, and she thought so deeply about it that she didn't even hear Alison speaking to her as she passed. ' I'll do it ! ' thought Anne-Marie, exultantly. ' I'll do it ! I'll find some little-known poem of one of the very great poets—Matthew Arnold perhaps, or Browning—and I'll write it out in my own handwriting—and next time we have to write a poem for Miss Willcox, I'll send in, not a poem of my own, but a classic ! '

She got up to go to the school library to look through the books of poets there.

' If Miss Willcox praises the poem, I shall know she genuinely appreciates good poetry—if she sneers at it, thinking it is mine, I shall know she doesn't ! Ah, Miss Willcox, we shall see ! '

Anne-Marie was soon busy turning over the pages of Matthew Arnold, Tennyson, and Browning. She felt as if her whole happiness, her whole future depended on this. She must be careful not to choose a poem at all well-known, or certainly Miss Willcox would recognize it. She must choose one as like her own style as possible —something yearning and soulful and rather high-brow. Ah, Anne-Marie meant to test Miss Willcox, no matter whether she cheated or not in doing so !

Now that her liking for Miss Willcox had so suddenly vanished, Anne-Marie's jealously of Alison disappeared too. Silly little Alison, she thought, pityingly, as she shut one book of poems and opened another.

But Alison, not knowing anything about Miss Willcox's unkindness to Anne-Marie, and its result, still thought that the other girl was jealous of her, and put down the annoying disappearances of her things to spite on Anne-Marie's part.

Alma knew this and rejoiced. It made things much easier for her, if Alison so clearly suspected some one else ! She took a few more things, enjoying poor Alison's exasperation and annoyance. To Alma the loss of the hidden food in the cupboard was as great a blow as Miss Willcox's words had been to Anne-Marie !

17   MIRABEL IS VERY HIGH-HANDED

THE second formers decided to have their feast in their own dormitory, which was conveniently far from any mistress's quarters. They asked the first form to join them and there was great rejoicing among the younger ones at this.

' Jolly decent of them ' said Sally. ' I vote we get in a spot of food ourselves. Don't you think so, Jane ? '

Jane was not as thrilled as the others. She had been very quiet and subdued lately, hurt at Mirabel's neglect of her, and at her unjust suspicion regarding the ringing of the fire-bell, which mystery still had not been cleared up. She worked hard for Angela, finding comfort in the older girl's liking and praise, and still did a good deal of her work at night under the sheets.

' Cheer up, Jane ! ' Sally kept saying. ' You look like a hen caught in the rain. *Do* cheer up ! '

Jane tried to smile. She had been very afraid of suddenly bursting into tears lately, a most unusual thing for her to do. ' It will be fun having a midnight feast,' she said, trying to think it *would* be fun. But somehow nothing seemed fun lately. It was so awful to be left out of matches, when she knew she was better than the others. What was the use of practising hard every spare minute she had, when Mirabel kept treating her like this ? It wasn't fair, thought Jane, resentfully. It really wasn't.

Claudine had told Antoinette of the pilfering of the cupboard, and the second formers were annoyed and puzzled, for Antoinette had told no one of the hiding-place. Still there was plenty of food left, so never mind !

Antoinette went to Claudine. ' Claudine, we are to have our feast tomorrow night. Can I have the key of the cupboard please ? I and one of the others will come up here very quietly just before midnight, and get the things.'

' Here is the key,' said Claudine, taking it off a thin string she wore round her neck. ' Now don't make a noise tomorrow night, whatever you do. Have a good time ! I wish I was coming too ! '

Antoinette grinned. She was enjoying this first term at St. Clare's. Like Claudine, she had slipped out of things she did not like, had played many undetected pranks, and had enjoyed the fun and the jolly companionship. She took the key and went off. She hadn't gone far before she retraced her footsteps.

How many bottles of ginger-beer were there ? Would there be enough, now that the first form was coming ? She slipped the key in the lock and turned it.

Alma, in her study, heard the click of the lock. How well she knew it ! She peeped out of the door. Why, it was Antoinette at the cupboard, not Claudine. She went out of the door. Antoinette jumped violently and shut the door.

'What have you got in that cupboard ? ' said Alma, in a smooth voice. 'Let me see.'

Before Antoinette could object she grabbed the key from her and opened the cupboard. Then she pretended to be very surprised at the contents. 'Good gracious ! What is all this ? Does it belong to you, Antoinette ? '

Antoinette hesitated. She disliked Alma and did not trust her. But what could she do ? If she was rude, Alma might be most unpleasant.

'I see it is a secret,' said Alma, longing to take one of the tins of pine-apple. 'Give me one of those tins, Antoinette, and I will not tell any one of this at all. I suppose you are going to have a midnight feast ? '

'Yes, tomorrow,' said Antoinette, disliking Alma even more. 'I'm sorry I can't give you a tin, Alma. I should have to ask the others first. It is not a nice thing for you to ask, anyway—I do not like a bargain of this sort ! '

Antoinette shut the door firmly and locked it again, before Alma had made up her mind what to do. She took the key from the lock and stuffed it into her pocket, eyeing Alma defiantly. 'I will ask the others if you *may* have a tin of pine-apple, if you wish me to, Alma,' she said. 'But—surely you do not wish me to ? '

Alma scowled. Of course she could not have Antoinette telling the second form that she wanted a tin of pine-apple. She tried to laugh it off.

'Don't be silly ! I didn't really mean it. I don't like pine-apple. Well—I hope you enjoy your feast ! '

' You won't tell tales of us, will you ? ' said Antoinette, distrusting Alma more and more. ' You promise that, won't you ? The second form would think you were terrible to tell such a tale, Alma. You have the English sense of honour, have you not, this honour that always you English girls are talking of ? '

' Of course,' said Alma, walking off with what dignity she could muster. She went into her study. She thought of the food in that cupboard. She thought of Antoinette's half-veiled insolence. Probably she *would* tell the second formers about the tin of pine-apple she had asked for—and they would nudge each other when she passed, and giggle.

Alma wished she *could* tell tales, and get the feast stopped ! But who would listen to her ? She would not dare to carry tales to Miss Theobald or Miss Cornwallis, nor was she certain that Hilary, the head-girl of the form, would even listen to her !

Then a thought struck her. What about Mirabel ? Mirabel was so keen on sports—and there was a match the day after next ! She would not be at all pleased if she knew that the first and second form were going to have a midnight feast just before the match. Mirabel should be told about it, and maybe, in her blunt, overbearing way, she would stop it. That would punish Antoinette all right !

Alma did not dare to go to Mirabel direct. She printed a note, so that her handwriting would not be recognized, and did not sign her name at the end.

' DO NOT EXPECT THE THIRD TEAM TO WIN ITS MATCH ON FRIDAY,' said the note. ' THEY WILL ALL BE UP AT MIDNIGHT ! '

Mirabel found the note on her table in the study that evening. She picked it up in curiosity and read it.

' Gladys ! ' she said, tossing the note over to her, ' what in the world does this mean ? '

Gladys read it distastefully. ' It's a wretched anonymous letter,' she said, ' sent by some one who wants to tell tales and doesn't dare to do it openly. Beastly. Tear it up and put it in the waste-paper basket. Don't take any notice of it. That's the way to treat letters of that sort.'

'Yes, but Gladys—the third lacrosse team *won't* win their match if they are up at midnight,' argued Mirabel. 'And I do want them to. I've set my heart on it. I suppose they're going to have a midnight feast or something, silly kids. They'll be tired out next day.'

'Well, didn't *you* enjoy midnight feasts when you were in the lower forms?' said Gladys. 'Have you forgotten what fun they were?'

'We didn't have them just before an important match,' said Mirabel. 'We didn't, Gladys.'

'For goodness' sake don't think of stopping the feast, or whatever it is,' said Gladys, alarmed. 'You can't interfere like that, Mirabel, and be such a spoil-sport.'

Mirabel thought for a few moments. 'I know what to do. I'll send a note to Katie, who's head of the second form, and inform her that I have heard there is to be something going on at midnight tomorrow, and I would like her to see that it is put off till after the match. They will respect my wishes I am sure—then they can play the match properly without being tired, and have their feast afterwards.'

'Well, I shouldn't even do that,' said Gladys. 'I don't think the feast will really make much difference to the match—and anyway, only about a quarter of the girls are playing in it—hardly that!'

'You never back me up in anything now,' said Mirabel, frowning. She said no more, but busied herself in writing a short note to the head-girl of the second form.

Katie got it that day and read it in surprise. She showed it to Antoinette. 'However did Mirabel get wind of our plans?' she said. 'Have you told any one, Antoinette?'

'Well—only Alma,' said the French girl, and she told Katie what had happened at the store cupboard.

'How awful!' said Katie, shocked at the tale and at Alma's behaviour. 'I say—I wonder if she was the one who pilfered our stores!'

'Perhaps,' said Antoinette. 'She is not a nice girl, that one.'

Katie called a meeting of the second formers in the common room and read them Mirabel's note. It was, as might be expected, rather arrogant and peremptory. Evidently Mirabel expected to be obeyed, and that was that.

'I vote we have the feast tomorrow night as planned,' said Yolande. 'Mirabel has been throwing her weight about too much lately. I call that a most uncivil note. Anyway, what business is it of hers? She's always interfering now.'

Every one followed Yolande's lead. It was curious how unpopular Mirabel had become. She had tried to drive every one too fast, and now they were digging their toes in and refusing to budge!

'I'd better not answer this note of Mirabel's to-day, had I?' said Katie. 'I'll answer it *after* we've had the feast, then she can't stop it!'

Mirabel was surprised to have no answer from Katie, giving an undertaking to postpone the feast till after the match, but it did not occur to her at all that the first and second formers would dare to defy her. She felt puzzled and thought that Katie was not very mannerly —surely she knew that an answer should always be sent at once to any request from one of the top form girls?

The first and second form were getting excited. It was the first time they had had a feast at night, and to them it seemed a terribly exciting thing. Every single girl was going. Violet was back from the san. now after a bout of flu, and was looking forward to it too.

Jane tried to look forward to it, but she was feeling very unhappy. Then a dreadful quarrel blew up between her and Violet, and Jane felt as if she couldn't bear things any more!

Violet had come back from the san. expecting to do Angela's jobs as usual. She had been disappointed because Angela had not even sent a kindly message to her when she was ill. Never mind—Angela would be very glad to see her back, doing her cleaning and mending as before, thought Violet.

But Angela didn't want Violet mooning round again. She had got used to the quiet and efficient little Jane, who, so long as she got a smile and a word of praise now and again, seemed to be quite content. Violet was too talkative, and always liked to recount all her thoughts and doings, which was very boring to the self-centred Angela.

So, to Violet's enormous dismay, Angela did not greet her warmly, and merely informed her that perhaps she would like to go and see to Pauline's jobs, as Jane was doing everything necessary. Violet did not dare to argue with Angela, but rushed off to Jane at once.

'You underhand thing!' she said, her eyes sparkling with anger. 'You go behind my back when I'm ill— and worm yourself into Angela's good graces again—and do all the things she was letting me do. Jane Teal, I shall never speak to you again, and neither will half the first form!'

Jane tried to defend herself, but Violet had a ready tongue, and could say some bitter, cutting things. Jane was tired out and unhappy, and she burst into tears.

'Just like you!' said Violet, scornfully. 'You think you'll get sympathy just because you cry. Well—you just burst into tears with Angela, and see what *she* says! She can't stand anything of *that* sort!'

Jane could not help feeling that perhaps she *had* done a mean trick to Violet. She hardly slept at all that night, and in the morning she awoke with a sore throat and a headache, which made her feel more miserable than ever. 'It's a good thing I'm not playing in the match tomorrow!' she thought and wondered if Mirabel would ever put her name down for a match again.

Jane felt rather queer that day. She had a high temperature and didn't know it. She did badly on the lacrosse field and Mirabel ticked her off. She could not concentrate in class and Miss Roberts was not pleased. Violet avoided her and some of the other first formers, who were friends of Violet's, did not speak to her either.

' I wish I was at home,' thought Jane, longingly. ' If I could just tell Mother all about it I'd feel better. I can't write it in a letter. I wish I could go home.'

The idea grew and grew in her worried mind and at last Jane made a plan she would never have made if she had been quite well. Instead of going to the feast she would go home! Luckily for her, her home was actually in the next village, four miles away. Jane felt sure she could easily walk there in the middle of the night! Then she would see her mother, tell her everything, and things would be all right again.

She did not know she was beginning to have flu and had a temperature, she had no idea she was not normal just then. Sally could not get a word out of her and was worried. Poor Jane—she was not having an easy time just then. But never mind, she thought, I'll be home tonight!

18   A SURPRISING NIGHT

THAT Friday night was to be a most astonishing one for Mam'zelle, though she did not know it. She never forgot it, and, whenever she took a holiday in her beloved France, she would often recount the happenings of that night, to show her enraptured listeners how queer were the English girls!

It was the night of the Feast, and the first and second

formers were to have it at twelve o'clock sharp in one of
their dormitories. Antoinette had already secreted some
of the things on the top of a high cupboard in her dormitory, and meant to fetch the rest just before midnight.

Mirabel, unfortunately, had seen Antoinette hurrying
along the corridor outside her study, carrying various
suspicious parcels. She had called after Antoinette, but
Antoinette had thought it advisable not to hear, and had
scurried fast round the corner, almost knocking over Miss
Willcox.

Mirabel stared after the disappearing Antoinette in
exasperation. Really, these kids were getting too
uncivil for words. She went back into her own study
and frowned. *Could* those kids be going to have their
feast that night after all—when she had asked them not
to? Could they flout her request in that way—surely
not!

All the same a doubt persisted in Mirabel's mind, and
she could not get rid of it. She said nothing to Gladys,
but she made up her mind to keep awake that night, and
to go along to the first or second form dormitories about
midnight, to see if anything was happening.

'And if there is—won't I give them a talking to!'
thought Mirabel, grimly. 'I'll report them too. I'll
make them see they can't disregard *my* orders!'

Now Anne-Marie had planned to stage a sleep-walking
act that night. She had thought of quite a lot of things
to do which were extraordinary, and might make people
say 'Ah, she does those because she's a genius,' as so
often was said of the absent-minded Felicity. But she
rather doubted her ability to carry them off in front of
the sharp-eyed, quick-minded members of the fifth form.

It would never do to put on some sort of genius act,
and have the others roar with laughter, disbelieve in it,
and tell her it was all put on. It was getting to be quite
imperative to Anne-Marie to be thought really clever.
She had to do something to cancel out the damping effect
of Miss Willcox's words.

Who would be taken in most easily? She thought for a while, and then decided on Mam'zelle. She had heard of the many tricks the girls had played on the French Mistress through the years, and she felt sure she would take in Mam'zelle. Mam'zelle would exclaim, and waggle her hands, and tell every one. She would say ' Ah, *la petite* Anne-Marie, she walks in her sleep, she recites poetry as she walks, she is a genius! We must be careful of her, we must cherish this talented girl! One day she will be famous! '

Yes, certainly Mam'zelle would be the best one to impress. The middle of the night would be the best time. She would find some means of waking Mam'zelle, and bring her out in the passage, and then she would let her see her, apparently walking in her sleep, reciting lines and lines of poetry. Mam'zelle would be most impressed, and perhaps even Miss Theobald would think that Anne-Marie was a genius, and ask to see some of her poems.

Anne-Marie was really very pleased with her idea. She quite looked forward to putting it into practice that night. ' About half-past twelve or so,' she thought. ' That would be the best time. Every one will be asleep by then.'

She had, of course, chosen a most unfortunate night for her sleep-walking, for quite a number of people were going to be wide-awake! All the first and second formers would be revelling in their feast. Jane Teal would be stealing through the school, meaning to run off home. Mirabel would be on the prowl to find out if the younger girls were really having their feast. Alma would be snooping about to see if there was likely to be any food left in the cupboard. Antoinette and one or two others would be fetching the rest of the food.

And Felicity was to choose that night for sleep-walking too—but genuine sleep-walking, in her case. So there would be quite a number of people wandering about, though Anne-Marie hadn't the remotest idea of this.

All the girls went off to bed as usual at their ordinary

times. The first and second formers went first, giggling with excitement, vowing that they wouldn't sleep a wink till midnight. Antoinette and Sally were to be responsible for rousing any one who *did* go to sleep. It was thrilling to look forward to such an escapade.

The third and fourth formers went off to bed later.

The fifth and sixth could stay up till ten o'clock, and usually did. They all retired as usual, even Felicity, who often did not go till much later, lost as usual in her music. It was astonishing that no mistress had discovered her light burning so late in her study, but so far no one had.

Then the mistresses went to bed, yawning, having a last word together before they parted. Mam'zelle was the last to go. She had a pile of French essays from the sixth form to go through, and had left them rather late.

' I will correct these, and then go,' she thought, glancing at the clock. ' Half-past eleven already ! How slow I have been tonight ! '

At just about five minutes to twelve Mam'zelle went into her bedroom. At twelve o'clock she was getting into bed, and the bed was about to creak under her rather heavy weight, when some sound caught her ears.

It sounded as if something hard had been dropped on the floor immediately above her head. Mam'zelle sat on the side of the bed and pondered over the various possible causes of the noise.

It was not the cat. It was not the unexpected groan or creak that furniture sometimes gave at night. It was not any mistress on the prowl, because all had gone to bed. Then what could it be ? Mam'zelle thought hard. She knew that the fifth form studies were above her bedroom, stretching in a long couple of rows down and around two corridors. Surely no one could possibly be up still ? The fifth form must all be in bed !

Another small sound decided Mam'zelle. She had better go and investigate. It might be a burglar. Mam'zelle had a horror of burglars, but she felt it her duty

to find out whether there was one in the school or not.
Feeling extremely brave, and arming herself with a hair-
brush, she put on her dressing-gown and slippers, tied the
girdle tightly round her plump waist, and opened her bedroom door.

All the passages and corridors of St. Clare's were lighted
throughout the night, but with specially dimmed lights.
It was possible to see a figure, but not to make out who
it was. The corridors looked rather eerie to Mam'zelle
as she set out on her journey of investigation.

The first thing that Mam'zelle did was to fall over the
school cat, who was an enormous black fellow, much
given to wandering around at night. Seeing Mam'zelle
perfectly clearly, though she could not see him at all, he
advanced upon her, and tried to rub against her ankles,
delighted to see a fellow-wanderer in the night.

Mam'zelle gave a muffled shriek, and almost over-
balanced. One of her big feet caught the cat on its side,
and it gave one of its yowls. Mam'zelle recognized the
cat's voice, and was relieved to find that it was not a
burglar lying on the floor to catch her foot, but only the
cat.

'Sssst!' she said, in a piercing, sibilant whisper, and
the cat fled, grieved at Mam'zelle's lack of friendliness.

Mam'zelle went up the stairs to the next floor, where
she had heard the noise. Antoinette was up there, on
her third journey to collect the eatables with Sally. To
her horror she suddenly heard Mam'zelle's piercing
'Sssst!' noise from the floor below. She clutched
Sally.

'Somebody's about! Did you hear that? Oh, how
tiresome, Sally! What shall we do?'

'There's an alcove near here,' whispered Sally. 'Look
—where that curtain is. We'll get behind there with our
tins and bottles. Quick! Maybe whoever it is will
pass by. Don't sneeze or anything!'

The two girls pressed themselves behind the curtain,
their hearts beating fast. They heard Mam'zelle's foot-

steps coming along, making a soft swishing noise in her big bedroom slippers. They stood quite still.

Mam'zelle came to the alcove. She thought the curtain bulged suspiciously, and she put out a trembling hand. She distinctly felt some soft body behind it! She gave a gasp. Antoinette and Sally decided to make a bolt for it, and suddenly shot out from the alcove, dropping a ginger-beer bottle on poor Mam'zelle's toes. She gave an anguished groan, lifted her foot, and did a few heavy hops over to the opposite wall, putting out a hand to steady herself when she got there.

She caught sight of two figures racing down the dim passage, and round the corner. She had no idea whether they were burglars or girls. As she felt her corns tenderly, wrath swept over her. How dared people drop things on her feet in the middle of the night, and then run away without apologizing? Mam'zelle determined to chase the scamps, whoever they were, and run them to earth.

She did not see the ginger-beer bottle lying at her feet, and she fell over it as she went swiftly down the passage, stubbing her other foot this time. The bottle went rolling off and hit the wall. Mam'zelle stopped again and groaned.

She ran down the passage and came to the corner. There was no one to be seen there. The passage went completely round the third floor of the building, and came back again where it began, and Mam'zelle thought it would be a good idea to go the whole way and see if any one was about on that floor. So off she set, determined to run to earth whoever was up so late at night.

Pad-pad-pad, went her feet, and every now and again Mam'zelle set her pince-nez firmly on her nose, for they had an irritating way of jumping off when she ran. Pad-pad-pad—the chase was on!

ALMA was the next one to be dimly seen by Mam'zelle. She had been certain that Antoinette would go to the store cupboard that night, and would probably make two or three visits. Probably in between she would leave the door open. Then, thought greedy Alma, she might be able to pop in and take something for herself. A tin of pine-apple for instance. She seemed to crave for a tin of pine-apple!

So, making sure that the rest of her dormitory were asleep, Alma rose quietly from her bed, and went up the stairs to the third floor. She made her way to the cupboard just at the same moment as Mam'zelle, panting, came round the last of the four corners of the corridor, back again to where the alcove was. The store cupboard was quite near.

Mam'zelle saw a figure in the passage. Ah—there was *one* of the midnight wanderers, at least! Mam'zelle would teach them to drop things on her poor toes! She crept up behind the unsuspecting Alma, who was half in the cupboard, groping about for a tin of some kind.

Alma had the shock of her life when she felt a hand on her shoulder. She lunged out in fright and struck poor Mam'zelle square in the middle. Mam'zelle doubled up at once, and gave such a deep groan that Alma was horrified. She could not move an inch, but stood there, trembling.

Mam'zelle recovered rapidly. She felt certain that this must be a burglar rifling cupboards. He was dangerous! He had given her a terrible blow, the big coward! Mam'zelle was not going to come to grips with him. Giving Alma a sudden push, which landed her among the tins, bottles and old rugs, she shut the door firmly, locked it, and took the key.

'Ha!' said Mam'zelle, addressing the alarmed Alma in the cupboard. 'Now I have you under key and lock! I go for the police!'

With this terrifying threat she padded off to telephone to the police. She went downstairs, congratulating herself heartily on her smartness and bravery, and feeling her middle tenderly to see if she was bruised.

As soon as she got downstairs she saw Jane Teal, who had chosen that moment to creep away from the others, put on her hat and coat and go to find a side-door she could open quietly. But poor little Jane was now feeling very ill. The flu was sending her temperature high, and she felt as if she was in a dream. All she wanted was to get to her mother, and to do that she knew she must get out of St. Clare's and walk and walk.

So, hardly knowing what she was doing, she felt with a feverish hand along the wall to find the side-door. She muttered to herself as she went. 'I must find the door. That's the first thing. I must find the door.'

Mam'zelle heard the muttering and stopped in amazement and alarm. Could this be yet another burglar? Who was this person groping along the wall—with a hat on too! Mam'zelle could not see in the dim light what kind of a person it was, but having got the idea of burglars firmly in her mind, she felt certain this must be another— probably the second of the two she had first seen racing down the upstairs passage. She began to tiptoe cautiously after Jane.

Jane felt along the wall till she came to a door. 'Here is a door,' she muttered. 'I must open it and go out. I've found a door.'

But it was not the side-door, leading into the garden. It was the door of the second form games cupboard, full of lacrosse sticks, old goal-nets, a few discarded rain-coats and such things as this. Jane opened the door and went into the cupboard. Mam'zelle, triumphant, saw a chance of repeating her recent brilliance, and of locking this second burglar into a cupboard too.

She darted forward, shut the door and locked it, leaving poor Jane in the darkness among things that felt most extraordinary to her hot little fingers.

' I want to go home,' said Jane and suddenly sank down on to a pile of sticks and nets, for her legs felt as if they would no longer carry her. She lay there, feverish and half-dreaming, not knowing or caring in the least where she was.

Mam'zelle could not help feeling very proud of herself. What other mistress at St. Clare's could catch and imprison two burglars in one night like this? Mam'zelle began to think she was wasted as a French mistress. She should have been in the police force.

' Now I go to the telephone,' she said to herself, thinking with delight of the astonishment of the police when they heard her news. But she was not yet to broadcast her news, for, even as she went into the hall, she saw somebody else !

This time it was Felicity, walking in her sleep, trying to find the assembly room, so that she might once again mount the platform, and play her imaginary violin. She walked solemnly, her eyes wide open, humming a melody in a low, soft voice. She had on her white night-gown, and Mam'zelle was absolutely petrified to see this figure walking towards her, making a queer low humming.

' Tiens ! ' said Mam'zelle, and took a step backwards. For the first time she began to wonder whether the night's happenings were real or whether she might be dreaming. It seemed astonishing that so many people were about, in the middle of the night.

This could not be a burglar. It looked like something unearthly—a spirit wandering about, lost and lone ! Mam'zelle shivered. Burglars she had been able to deal with—but spirits were different. They faded away, they disappeared into thin air, if they were touched, and Mam'zelle did not like things of that sort.

She decided not to go to the telephone just then, as she would have to meet this wandering spirit face to face.

She would retire to her bedroom for a little while till the spirit had returned to wherever it had come from. So Mam'zelle turned tail and fled.

But for some reason Felicity, fast asleep as she was, seemed to perceive Mam'zelle as she disappeared towards the stairs. Into her dreaming mind came the idea that this person might take her to the platform, so that she might play her wonderful compositions, and she followed Mam'zelle up the stairs, her eyes glassy and wide open, her hands outstretched.

Mam'zelle glanced behind and was most alarmed to find the white spirit following her. She had not bargained for this at all. She almost ran to get to her bedroom on the second floor.

Felicity followed, seeming almost to float up the stairs, for she was tall and thin, and much too light for her age. Mam'zelle bolted into her bedroom and sat down on her bed, out of breath.

The door opened and Felicity came in, her eyes still wide open. As Mam'zelle had her light on, she saw at once that what she had thought was a frightening apparition was only Felicity.

'Tiens!' said Mam'zelle, putting her hand up to her forehead. 'Tiens! What kind of a night is this, when burglars and children walk around. Felicity, my child, are you awake?'

There was something rather terrifying about Felicity's white, unawakened face. Mam'zelle saw that she was sound asleep, and was afraid to wake her. She was more than relieved when Felicity, feeling the bed, drew back the covers, got into it and shut her eyes. In a minute or two she was apparently sleeping quite peacefully.

Mam'zelle stared down at the pale face on her pillow. To have two burglars shut into two separate cupboards and a sleep-walking girl in her bed was rather bewildering. She could not make up her mind whether to telephone to the police or to go and call Miss Theobald and show her Felicity. Mam'zelle had had enough experience of girls to know that sleep-walking was not a good thing—something had happened to make Felicity act in this way, and that something must be investigated.

There was a noise upstairs again. Antoinette and Sally had returned to the cupboard for eatables, and had found the door locked, the key gone, and a prisoner in the cupboard! In amazement and fear they fled back to their dormitory to tell the others. Mam'zelle, disturbed by the noise they made, went out of her bedroom, and, as an afterthought, turned the key in the lock, in case Felicity should try a little more sleep-walking.

She was just in time to see Antoinette and Sally, two vague figures in the distance, running back to their dormitory.

' *Tiens!* ' said Mam'zelle again, thunderstruck to find yet more people abroad that night. ' Do I sleep or wake ? Everywhere I go I see people fleeing in the night ! '

The next person Mam'zelle saw was Mirabel, who was creeping down the stairs to see if the second formers were holding their feast after all. Mam'zelle could not believe her eyes. Was the whole school wandering about that night—or was this yet another burglar ?

Mirabel was a tall, strapping girl, and she wore pyjamas. In the dim passage she looked as big as a man, and Mam'zelle felt certain this must be another of the gang of burglars that appeared to be infesting St. Clare's that night. She followed her, trying to make no noise at all. It was becoming quite a common-place for Mam'zelle to lock people up that night, and she fondly imagined she could somehow imprison this burglar also.

Mirabel went towards the second form dormitories. Mam'zelle, afraid that the burglar might scare the girls there, hurried her steps. The school cat reappeared at this moment, and tripped poor Mam'zelle up, so that she made a noise. Mirabel looked round, and slipped quickly into one of the bathrooms that ran opposite the dormitories. She did not want any of the second formers to know she was snooping round, in case by any chance they were *not* holding the feast after all.

Mam'zelle saw with great pleasure that once again she could lock somebody into somewhere. She began to think that burglar-catching was the easiest thing in the world—merely a matter of turning a key in a lock. She turned the key in the shut bathroom door—and there was yet another burglar accounted for !

Mam'zelle thought with delight of the surprise and admiration of the other mistresses when they heard of her exploits. She felt ready to imprison half a dozen more burglars into cupboards and bathrooms if necessary.

Mirabel was horrified at being locked in. She had no idea who had turned the key, but thought it was some silly trick of one of the younger girls. So she settled down to wait for the door to be undone. She felt sure no girl would keep her imprisoned all night long.

Mam'zelle decided that she would now go to Miss Theobald, as she felt that no policeman would be inclined to believe a telephone call from her about three locked-up burglars. So she padded along the passage to the stairs —but just as she was about to descend them, she caught sight of yet another night wanderer.

This time it was Anne-Marie, who was now putting on her sleep-walking act in imitation of Felicity, and was on her way to wake up Mam'zelle. Mam'zelle could not believe her eyes when she saw yet another sleep-walker. No, really she must be going mad ! There could not be so many people rushing about at night in the school passages !

Anne-Marie saw Mam'zelle standing under one of the dimmed lamps, and recognized her. At first she got a shock, for she had expected Mam'zelle to be in bed and not ambling about. But as soon as she was sure it really *was* Mam'zelle, she acted exactly as if she was walking in her sleep. She glided by Mam'zelle, her eyes set and staring just as Felicity's had been, muttering a poem.

Mam'zelle hesitated to grab her, for she had heard it

was bad to awaken sleep-walkers suddenly. So she did not touch Anne-Marie, but followed her, whispering under her breath.

'The poor child! Here is another who walks in her sleep! I will follow her.'

Anne-Marie led Mam'zelle a fine dance, and finally ended up outside the second form dormitories. The girl on guard there gave the alarm when she saw the two figures coming, and there was a terrific scramble as bottles and tins and plates were pushed under beds. The candles were blown out and girls got hurriedly into bed, those who didn't belong to that dormitory squeezing into wardrobes and under beds.

Anne-Marie, still acting, wandered into the second form dormitory, meaning to walk to the end and back—but she fell over an empty bottle, and gave an exclamation. Mam'zelle followed her into the room and switched on the light.

Anne-Marie, dazed by the sudden light, blinked in confusion, watched in amazement by girls in bed. Then, remembering her sleep-walking act, she once again became glassy-eyed and glided between the beds.

The girls sat up, giggling. 'She's pretending!' called Antoinette.

'Ah, no, she walks in her sleep, the poor, poor child,' said Mam'zelle. 'What can we do for her?'

'I will cure her, *ma tante*,' said the irrepressible Antoinette, and leapt out of bed. She took a jug of cold water and threw it all over poor Anne-Marie, who, angry and wet, turned and gave Antoinette such a ticking off that all the girls knew at once that she certainly had not been sleep-walking before, but only play-acting. Mam'zelle realized it too, and tried to haul Anne-Marie out of the room, scolding her vigorously, and telling her to go and change her wet things at once. So engrossed was she that she entirely failed to see any signs of the midnight feast, nor did she notice any of the girls squashed into the wardrobes or under the beds.

Antoinette threw the jug of cold water at Anne-Marie

'Golly!' said Sally, as soon as Mam'zelle had gone off with Anne-Marie, 'I don't believe she even *saw* the signs of our feast, not even that bottle that rolled out from under a bed!'

'Bit of luck for us,' said Violet. 'Come on, let's finish everything up quickly, and hide the things and get to bed before Mam'zelle thinks of coming back!'

The girls giggled. Mirabel, shut in the bathroom just opposite, heard them, and knew they were still enjoying their feast. She grew very angry indeed. She felt certain one of the second formers had locked her in, and she was determined to report the whole lot of them and have them well punished.

Mam'zelle took Anne-Marie to Matron's room, and woke Matron up, explaining volubly about Anne-Marie and why she was wet. Anne-Marie, her sleep-walking act quite ruined, wept copiously, fearing that she would be the laughing stock of the school next day.

'Now stop that silly crying,' said Matron, briskly giving Anne-Marie a vigorous rub-down with a very rough towel. She had long ago sized up Anne-Marie as a silly, swollen-headed girl, just the kind to act about like this.

'I must go,' said Mam'zelle, remembering the various people she had locked up that night. 'I have burglars to see to.'

Matron stared. 'What did you say?' she inquired.

'I said, I have burglars to see to,' said Mam'zelle, with dignity. 'I have spent the night chasing people round the corridors, and locking them up. I go to Miss Theobald now, and she will telephone to the police. Ah, the people I have chased tonight. You would not believe it, Matron!'

Matron didn't. She thought Mam'zelle must be dreaming. 'Well, you go and get Miss Theobald and the police and whatever else you like,' she said, rubbing Anne-Marie so hard that she groaned. 'But don't bring me any more wet girls to dry in the middle of the night. I don't approve of them.'

Mam'zelle went off. She came to Miss Theobald's
bedroom and knocked on the door. A surprised voice
came from inside.

'Yes? Who is it?'

'It is I, Mam'zelle,' said Mam'zelle, and opened the
door. 'Pardon me for coming at this time of the night,
Miss Theobald—but I have burglars locked up in cupboards and a sleep-walker in my bedroom.'

20   A LITTLE UNLOCKING

MISS THEOBALD listened to Mam'zelle's tale in the
utmost astonishment. It seemed to her as if all the
corridors of St. Clare's must have been peopled with
burglars, robbers, thieves, and others the whole of the
night—but what was even more astonishing was the
thought of Mam'zelle, who was terrified even of mice and
beetles, valiantly chasing the burglars and, more remarkable still, locking them up wholesale!

She could hardly believe it. She looked closely at
Mam'zelle, and wondered if the French mistress could
possibly have dreamt it all. She got out of bed and put
on her dressing-gown.

'I think, before I telephone the police, you had
better show me where you locked these men up,' she
said.

Mam'zelle trotted her off to the cupboard where she
had locked in little Jane Teal. There was no sound from
there at all. Miss Theobald was puzzled. She rapped
on the door. Still no sound. Jane had fallen into a
feverish doze. Miss Theobald suddenly heard the sound
of overloud breathing, quick and hoarse.

She felt sure it was no burglar there. She unlocked

the door, to Mam'zelle's dismay, and switched on the light inside the big cupboard—and there, before poor Mam'zelle's startled eyes, lay little Jane Teal, obviously ill, fully-dressed, even to her hat.

' This child's ill,' said the Head Mistress, feeling Jane's burning hot hand. ' 'Flu, I should think, and a very high temperature with it. What on earth is she doing dressed up like this, with hat and coat on ? Was she going out ? '

Mam'zelle was dumbfounded. She could not think of a word to say. Miss Theobald gently awoke Jane, and helped her to her feet. She could hardly stand. Between them the two mistresses took her to Matron's room, who, at one glance saw that Jane was seriously ill.

' I'll carry her to the san.,' she said. ' I'll sleep there with her myself tonight.'

Matron's capable, strong arms lifted the half-unconscious Jane easily, and bore her away to the quiet and comfortable san. where all the ill girls were nursed. There was no one there at the moment. Matron soon had Jane undressed and in bed with a hot water bottle.

' Well,' said Miss Theobald, thankful to have found poor Jane before worse befell her, ' what about your next burglar, Mam'zelle ? '

Mam'zelle fervently hoped that the next prisoner *would* prove to be a burglar, even if he leapt out at them and escaped ! She led the way to the bathroom opposite the second form dormitory.

The second formers were still awake and heard the footsteps and voices in wonder. As the footsteps passed their door, they sat up and whispered. ' Who is it ? What's up ? '

Antoinette leapt out of bed and padded to the door. She peeped out cautiously. To her enormous astonishment she saw the Head Mistress standing by the bathroom door, with Mam'zelle, her aunt ! Antoinette gaped as she saw Miss Theobald rap quietly on the door and say, ' Who's in here ? '

A voice answered something, an angry voice. Miss Theobald heard that it was a girl's voice and not a man's, and she unlocked the door. Out shot Mirabel, expecting to see a group of grinning second formers—and stopped short in amazement when she saw Mam'zelle and the Head Mistress.

Mam'zelle's eyes almost dropped out of her head. She had shut her biggest burglar—or so she thought—into the bathroom—and now it was only Mirabel, that big detestable, loud-voiced Mirabel, whose talk was all of games, games, and yet more games. Mam'zelle snorted in disgust.

'I want to complain,' said Mirabel, in a loud voice, surprised but unabashed by the sight of the Head. 'I came to see if the second formers were having a midnight feast, which I had forbidden—and one of them locked me in this beastly cold bathroom. I want to report them, Miss Theobald. I know they held a feast, and there's a most important match tomorrow. And I demand that the girl who locked me in shall be punished.'

'It was Mam'zelle who locked you in,' said Miss Theobald. 'You had no right to be wandering about at night like this. Mam'zelle thought you were a burglar and locked you in.'

Antoinette stifled a giggle and rushed back into the dormitory. She related in whispers what she had heard. The girls were half-amused and half-angry—amused to think that Mirabel had been locked up, and angry to think she had been sneaking round, and had reported them.

Then Mam'zelle's loud voice penetrated into the listening dormitory. 'What is this untruthful thing you say, Mirabel? The second formers had *no* feast tonight! Did not I go there to chase Anne-Marie, after I had locked you in, and the good girls were all in bed and asleep! Not a thing to be seen, not a tin, not a bottle! You are a bad untruthful girl, trying to get others into trouble to protect yourself from blame!'

Mirabel was speechless. She glared at Mam'zelle, and Miss Theobald hastened to intervene.

'Well, if Mam'zelle was in the second form dormitory, and the girls were in bed and asleep, it seems to me that you must be mistaken, Mirabel.'

'I'm not,' said Mirabel, rudely. 'Mam'zelle isn't speaking the truth. Go into the second form dormitory and ask the girls if I or Mam'zelle are right, Miss Theobald. Then you will see."

'I shall do nothing of the sort,' said the Head Mistress, coldly. 'Be more polite, Mirabel. You forget yourself.'

Mirabel, simmering with rage, dared say no more. 'Go back to bed,' said Miss Theobald. 'I will settle this tomorrow. I do not feel very pleased with you, Mirabel.'

Mirabel went back to bed with an angry heart. She knew she was right. Those second formers *had* had a feast, and Mam'zelle must be shielding them—because of Antoinette, she supposed. Well, she would get even with the little beasts. She would cancel the match next day! No one should play. She would show those youngsters she was sports captain, and make them toe the line!

'Well,' said Miss Theobald, looking at Mam'zelle, as Mirabel retreated, 'what about your next burglar, Mam'zelle?'

Mam'zelle took the Head up to the corridor that ran round the fifth form studies. She was feeling rather nervous now that her burglars were all turning into girls. It was really most extraordinary.

Miss Theobald rapped on the cupboard in which Alma was imprisoned. Alma's voice was heard.

'Let me out! It's awful in here!'

The Head unlocked the door, and Alma staggered out, stiff and cold. Miss Theobald looked at her in surprise. 'Why were you wandering about at night?' she said, sharply.

'I—er—I heard a noise,' said Alma, stammeringly' for she was afraid of the Head. 'And some one locked me in that cupboard.'

Miss Theobald switched her torch on and lighted up the inside of the cupboard. She saw at a glance that it had been used as a storing-place for food.

'You went to take food from here, I suppose, Alma?' she said. 'Was it your own food?'

'I wasn't taking any,' said Alma. 'I was—well, I was just *look*ing.'

'This girl is always eating,' said Mam'zelle in disgust. 'Always she chews something, always she sucks.'

'Go back to bed, Alma,' said Miss Theobald. 'I will see you in the morning.'

Alma scuttled off thankfully. Miss Theobald turned rather coldly to Mam'zelle. 'Any more burglars?' she asked.

'Oh, Miss Theobald, truly I am sorry to have made so many mistakes!' said Mam'zelle, passing her hand through her hair in bewilderment. 'I pray you to forgive me, to . . .'

'Don't worry about it,' said Miss Theobald. 'It is perhaps a good thing that all this has happened. It seems that a great deal is going on this term at St. Clare's that I must inquire into. Now—who is this girl you had in your bedroom—the one you found sleep-walking?'

'Felicity,' said Mam'zelle, fervently hoping that Felicity would still be there. She hurried down the stairs to her room, and unlocked the door.

Felicity was still there, lying asleep in bed. She looked very young and thin and, even in her sleep, her face wore a harassed, worried look. Miss Theobald looked at her for some time.

'This girl is obviously over-working,' she said, and sighed. 'Her music is too much for her, but her parents insisted on her taking her exams. I think, Mam'zelle, if you don't mind, we'll leave her in your bed. You had better sleep in the bed in Miss Harry's room—she is away for a few days. I suppose you have no more locked-up girls to show me tonight ? '

' No,' said Mam'zelle, looking so crestfallen that the Head smiled. She patted Mam'zelle's plump arm.

' You meant well,' she said. ' If they had all been burglars, as you thought, you would have done a good night's work. Anyway, it is a good thing that so many things have come to light. Good night.'

Miss Theobald went back to bed, worrying about little Jane Teal, Alma, Mirabel and Felicity. It looked as if Jane had been trying to run away. She must find out about that.

Mam'zelle got into a strange bed, cold and puzzled. Why had so many girls been wandering about that night ? Ah, that detestable Mirabel, how dare she say that she, Mam'zelle, was telling an untruth that night ? And that dreadful Alma ? Did she go snooping round every night to steal food from cupboards ? There was something wrong with her, that girl !

' Tomorrow I will talk with Claudine and Antoinette,' thought Mam'zelle, screwing up her eyes, trying to go to sleep. ' They have good sense, they will tell me everything. It is a pity that English girls have not the good sense of French girls. It will be a pleasure to talk to my good little Claudine and Antoinette—*they* do not wander round at night for me to lock up. Alas, to think that I made so many prisoners, and now not one remains ! '

21   A FEW UPSETS

THE next day the whole school knew the story of the night escapades, and how Mam'zelle had locked up so many girls. There was a great deal of giggling and chattering, and Anne-Marie had her leg pulled about her sleep-walking.

'How can I help sleep-walking?' she asked, trying to assume a dignity she did not feel. 'Felicity sleep-walks too, doesn't she? And you don't laugh at *her*.'

Miss Willcox heard about Anne-Marie's sleep-walking act and laughed too. She even teased her about it in class, which hurt Anne-Marie more than anything, and made her quite determined to get even with Miss Willcox if she could.

Felicity did not appear in class that day. It was reported that she had gone to the san. for a rest and would not be taking the exam. which was the next week. Jane Teal was very ill indeed. Sally had been allowed to see her and had come back rather scared.

'Matron's worried about her and so is the doctor,' said Sally. 'Her mother is there in the san., too. I'm not allowed in any more. Matron shooed me out. I heard Matron say that Jane's worried about something and she can't get out of her what it is. But *I* know! It's all this business with Mirabel and Angela, and I know Jane reads in bed late at night with a torch. She learns her English and Latin that way. She told me so.'

'Well—hadn't you better go and tell Matron what you know,' said Katie. 'She might put things right for Jane then.'

'She can't, silly,' said Sally. 'You know what worries Jane more than anything—she's upset because Mirabel believes she rang that fire-bell to stop her meeting, and that's why Mirabel is so beastly to her. If only we could find out who did ring that bell, and make them own up, it would take a great load off poor Jane's mind!'

Violet Hill was feeling uncomfortable that morning, when she heard how ill Jane was. She remembered her quarrel with Jane, and the unkind things she had said. She wished she hadn't now.

'It will be a good thing to play in the match this afternoon,' said Sally. 'Take our minds off everything! We'll feel better out on the field, playing or watching.'

But Mirabel threw a bomb-shell that morning. She put a notice on the board, and soon every one was round it, astonished and angry.

'The match today is cancelled, owing to the behaviour of the team members,' said the notice, and it was signed by Mirabel.

'Well!' said Sally. 'Would you believe it! How has she got the nerve to stick up a notice like that? And what right has she to cancel our match?'

'She's got the right because she's sports captain,' said Violet. 'Beast! I vote we send her to Coventry and don't speak a word to her, or smile at her, or turn up at any practices at all!'

Every one agreed. It was an unheard of thing for the lower forms to treat an upper form girl in this way, but they felt so indignant that not one member of the first or second form backed out of the agreement. Just because they had dared to have a feast in spite of Mirabel, she was treating them abominably, and putting up a notice in public to make them look small!

Gladys saw the notice and was shocked. She went straight to Mirabel.

'Mirabel! How *could* you put up that notice? Whatever were you thinking of? You *can't* cancel the match!'

'I can and I have,' said Mirabel grimly. 'I've sent a telegram to the school we were playing. They won't be coming. We shall have a practice match, instead. I have just written out another notice about that—the practice is to be at three o'clock, and every girl must attend from the two lowest forms.'

'Mirabel, you must be mad,' said Gladys, quite alarmed at her friend's grim face. 'You can't put all the girls against you like this, you really can't. You'll only get the worst out of them instead of the best.'

'I've told you before that I won't have you interfering with my decisions,' said Mirabel.

'Then what is the use of my being vice-captain?'
said Gladys. 'Not a bit of use! I can't help you,
because you won't let me!'

'Well, you're not much use, if you really want to
know,' said Mirabel, coldly, and went out of the room
to pin the lacrosse practice notice on the board.

The girls held an informal meeting about the practice,
and one and all determined not to turn up. It was
Saturday, and, if they wished, they could go for nature-
rambles. All the first and second forms decided to do
this, even Antoinette, who detested walking.

So, to the astonishment of Miss Roberts and Miss Jenks,
the whole of the two lowest forms went off in the sun-
shine together, taking with them nature notebooks and
collecting tins and jars, chattering loudly as they passed
by the windows of the mistresses' common room.

'*Well!*' said Miss Roberts, looking after the laughing
girls, 'what's come over them? Why this sudden,
violent and wholesale interest in nature? I thought
there was to be a match or lacrosse practice or something.'

Mirabel turned up on the playing fields at five to three,
grim-faced and determined. But nobody else arrived.
Mirabel waited till ten past three, and then, rather white,
went back to the school. One of the third formers, hardly
able to hide her smiles, told her politely that the first and
second formers had all gone out for a nature walk.

Then Mirabel knew that she had lost. It had been her
will against the wills of the first and second form, and
they had won. They had ignored her orders. They
had shown her what they thought of her and her authority.
She sat down in her study, feeling dismayed.

She saw a note on the table addressed to her and opened
it. It was a formal resignation from Gladys.

I wish to resign my post as vice-captain as I feel I cannot be
of any use to you.

GLADYS

Mirabel threw the note on to the floor. She felt unhappy and bitter. She had been so pleased to be sports captain. She had worked so hard for that position. She had had such high hopes of putting St. Clare's at the very top of the lacrosse and tennis schools. Now the girls had defied her, and even her best friend had deserted her. It was a bitter hour for Mirabel.

The girls came back from their walk, rosy-cheeked and merry. They heard from the third form how Mirabel had gone out alone to the playing field, and had waited there in vain. They also heard that Gladys had resigned as vice-captain and they were pleased.

'Good old Gladys,' they said. 'We always thought it was funny she should back Mirabel up in her unpleasant ways!'

When Mirabel appeared in public at all that week-end the girls carefully turned away from her. 'Almost as if I was in quarantine for something beastly!' thought Mirabel, bitterly. The girl was very worried and unhappy, but far too proud to appeal even to Gladys for comfort. Gladys was miserable too, and would have made things up with Mirabel at once if her friend had turned to her, or had admitted that she had been too high-handed with the younger ones. But Mirabel was cold and stand-offish, and gave Gladys no chance to be friendly.

The exam. was to be held the next week, and most of the girls were feeling the strain. Only a few, like clever Pam, or the placid Hilary, did not seem to worry. Felicity was not to take the exam.

A specialist had come from London to see her. He spoke to Miss Theobald very seriously.

'This girl is on the verge of a nervous breakdown,' he said. 'Her mind seems full of music and nothing but music. See how she plays an imaginary violin, and strains to hear the tune. She must do no more work in music for a year.'

Miss Theobald nodded. How she wished Felicity's proud parents had not insisted on their gifted girl working for that difficult music exam.! How much better it would have been for her to have dropped her music for a while, and to have entered into the ordinary, normal life of the other fifth formers, instead of losing herself night and day in her beloved music. Now her music might suffer because Felicity's brain had been worked too hard.

' Parents' fault, I suppose ? ' said the specialist, writing a few notes in his case-book. ' Why will parents of gifted children always push them so hard ? '

' Just selfishness,' said Miss Theobald. 'Well—you think we must keep Felicity in bed for a time—then let her get up and wander round a bit, without any lessons—and then gradually join in with the others, without doing any music at all ? '

' She can *play* at her music, but not work at it,' said the specialist. ' Let her enjoy it without worrying about it. She will probably do that anyhow when she knows she is not to work for the music exam. for at least another two years.'

Felicity's parents came to see her, worried and dismayed. They remembered how Miss Theobald had pleaded with them not to push Felicity on so quickly. They were frightened when they saw her white face and enormous, dark-rimmed eyes.

' Don't worry too much,' said Miss Theobald. ' We have stopped her in time. Her sleep-walking gave us warning. Mam'zelle discovered that, and so we have been able to deal with Felicity quickly. Soon she will be a normal, happy girl again, and when she knows she need not work night and day for her music exam., a great weight will be off her mind, and she will laugh and chatter and be as cheerful as the others.'

It was a rather subdued father and mother that went home that day. ' Miss Theobald might have said, " I told you so," to us,' said Felicity's mother. ' But she didn't. Poor Felicity—I feel we are very much to blame for all this.'

The other sleep-walker, Anne-Marie, was not having

a very good time. Whenever the first or second formers saw her coming, they immediately put on glassy stares, and with out-stretched hands, began to glide here and there. Anne-Marie hated this teasing, and when it spread to the fifth form too, and glassy eyes appeared there also, Anne-Marie was very near tears.

' It's beastly of you,' she said to Alison and Angela, who laughed at her. ' I know I shan't pass the exam. if you all jeer at me like this. It's mean of you.'

' Well, you're pretty mean yourself,' said Alison. ' You keep on doing beastly things to *me*, don't you ? Where have you put my geometry set you hid last week ? '

Anne-Marie stared in surprise. She hadn't the least idea what Alison was talking about.

' Oh, don't put on that wide-eyed innocent look,' said Alison, impatiently. ' We all know you can act, but don't try to take *us* in by it ! I know jolly well you're jealous of me because Miss Willcox likes me better than she likes you, and you're trying to get back at me by hiding my things and making silly bits of trouble for me ! '

' I'm not,' said Anne-Marie, her voice trembling with indignation. ' I wouldn't dream of doing such a thing. I haven't *touched* your things ! And as for being jealous of you, you needn't worry ! I've no time for Miss Willcox now ! I'm sure she's not as clever as you think. And what's more I'll show you she isn't.'

' Don't be silly,' said Alison. ' And don't talk about Miss Willcox like that. You're just plain jealous and you're taking my things and being beastly just to get even with me.'

' I tell you I'm not playing tricks on you, and I'm not jealous,' cried Anne-Marie. ' You can keep Miss Willcox all to yourself ! I don't ever want to see her again ! *Deirdre* Willcox indeed ! Her name is Doris, just plain Doris—I saw it written in one of her books. I bet she calls herself Deirdre just because she thinks Doris is too ordinary. She's a—a—silly pretender ! '

Anne-Marie flung herself out of the room, and Alison stared after her in rage. Angela laughed.

'You two amuse me,' she said. 'I'm glad I don't go off the deep end about any one like you do! Silly, I call it!'

'Oh, *do* you!' said Alison, in a cutting voice. 'Well, let me tell you, you're just as bad in another way—you smile sweetly at the lower form kids and get them all round you to wait on you—then when you're tired of them, you just tick them off—and they're as miserable as can be. I bet you're partly responsible for Jane Teal trying to run away!'

Angela opened her mouth to answer heatedly, but just then the door opened and Anne-Marie popped her head in again.

'I'll show Miss Doris Willcox up tomorrow, in front of the whole class!' she said. 'You see if I don't! Then you'll have to say I'm right, and you'll be jolly sick you didn't see through her. So there!'

The door banged and Anne-Marie disappeared. 'I'm tired of Anne-Marie and her silly ways,' said Alison, who still thought that it was she who was playing tricks on her, and had no idea it had been Alma. 'Let her do what she likes. I shall always like Miss Willcox!'

22   ANNE-MARIE TRAPS MISS WILLCOX

ANNE-MARIE had prepared her little trap for Miss Willcox, and she had prepared it very carefully. Every week Miss Willcox set the girls some kind of composition to do, and they sent in their entries, which were carefully gone through by her and marked.

This week the subject set was a poem. It had to be

only eight lines long, the first and third lines had to rhyme, and the second and fourth, the fifth and seventh and the sixth and eighth. The subject was to be ' Thoughts.'

The fifth form grumbled. They didn't like writing poetry, they *couldn't* write poetry, it was a silly waste of time for them in exam. week. It was just like Miss Willcox to set a poem for them to do ! So they grumbled and groaned, but all the same they managed to produce something that could be called a poem.

Anne-Marie had hunted through the poets for a lesser-known poem that would suit her purpose. If only she could find one that would just do ! And by great good fortune she suddenly found exactly what she wanted. It was a little eight-line poem by Matthew Arnold, called Despondency, which seemed to Anne-Marie to be just what she wanted.

She copied it out in her big, rather sprawly hand-writing. Really it seemed as if it was her own poem, it was just as sad as the ones she liked to write !

Anne-Marie sent the poem in with those of the others of her form. She signed her name at the bottom. Now, Miss Doris Willcox, we will see if you know good poetry when you see it !

The English lesson duly arrived, and Alison glanced curiously at Anne-Marie, who seemed excited. Was she really going to carry out her silly threat and do something to Miss Willcox ? Alison felt a little disturbed. Ought she to warn Deirdre ?

Miss Willcox arrived, carrying the sheaf of poems in her hand. She looked as soulful as ever, and wore a trailing crimson scarf round her swan-like neck.

The first part of the lesson was given to the reading of a play. Then came the time set apart for the commenting on the girls' own work. Miss Willcox pulled the sheaf of poems towards her.

' Not a very good set,' she remarked, slipping the elastic band off the papers. ' I suppose the exam. has had an effect on your creative powers. Pam's is the best—quite

a praiseworthy little effort, simple and honest. Claudine,
I can't pass yours. You may have meant it to be funny,
but it isn't.'

Claudine made a face, which fortunately for her Miss
Willcox did not see. Miss Willcox dealt with every one's
poems rapidly, quoting from one or two, praising here
and there, and condemning the efforts of Doris, Angela
and Carlotta.

Then she came to the last one, which was Anne-Marie's.
She looked round the class, a rather spiteful look in her
large eyes.

'And now at last we come to the poet of the class,
Anne-Marie. A sad, heart-rending poem as usual.
Listen to the wailings of our poet.

'THOUGHTS

The thoughts that rain their steady glow,
Like stars on life's cold sea,
Which others know, or say they know—
They never shone for me.

Thoughts light, like gleams, my spirit's sky,
But they will not remain.
They light me once, they hurry by,
And never come again.'

Miss Willcox read these lines out in a mock-heroic way,
exaggerating the feeling in them, making fun of the whole
poem. She put down the paper.

'Anne-Marie, why must you write like this ? It is all
so silly and insincere and quite meaningless. What for
instance can you possibly mean by " Stars on life's cold
sea ? " What *is* life's cold sea ? Just words that came
into your head and you put them down because they
sounded grand. Life's cold sea ! Ridiculous ! '

Anne-Marie stared at Miss Willcox steadily. She felt
very triumphant. That wasn't *her* poem ! It was written
by a great poet, not by Anne-Marie at all ! That just
showed that Miss Willcox didn't know a thing and wasn't
any judge of good poetry !

Miss Willcox didn't like the steady, queerly triumphant look on Anne-Marie's face. She felt a wave of anger against her.

'You have the scansion and the rhyming *quite* correct!' she said scornfully to Anne-Marie, 'but all the same I consider your poem the worst of the form.'

'Miss Willcox,' said Anne-Marie, suddenly, in a high, clear voice, 'I'm so sorry—I think I must have made a mistake in sending in that poem! I don't believe it is mine after all!'

The class turned to look at Anne-Marie. She sat tensely, still with that triumphant look on her face.

'What do you mean?' said Miss Willcox, impatiently. 'Not *your* poem? Then whose is it? I must say it *sounds* exactly like yours!'

'It's—it's very kind of you to say that,' said Anne-Marie, 'because you see—that poem is by Matthew Arnold, not by me at all. I'm glad you think his poetry is like mine. I feel honoured. Though I don't suppose, if he were alive, he would be at all pleased to hear the things you have just said about his little poem—it's queer to think you consider *his* poem the worst in the form!'

There was dead silence. Alison turned scarlet, seeing the trap Anne-Marie had set for Miss Willcox, and the prompt way in which she had fallen headlong into it. Anne-Marie pulled a volume of Matthew Arnold's poems from her desk and opened it at a certain page. 'Here's the poem,' she said, getting up from her desk. 'It's called "Despondency" not "Thoughts". I'll show it to you, Miss Willcox.'

Miss Willcox had gone white. She knew it had been a trap now—Anne-Marie's revenge for the cruel words she had spoken to her some days back. She had shown her up in front of the whole class. Oh why, why had she said that the poem was the worst in the form? Why had she said such spiteful things? Only to hurt Anne-Marie, and because she thought she wanted taking down two or three pegs.

Alison was terribly distressed. She hated to see Miss Willcox trapped like that—and she also hated to think that the teacher had allowed herself to be trapped because of her own petty spite. She looked with dislike at the triumphant Anne-Marie.

'You have cheated, Anne-Marie,' said Miss Willcox, trying to regain her dignity. 'I shall have to report you to Miss Theobald for a grave act of deceit.'

'Yes, Miss Willcox,' said Anne-Marie maliciously, and the English mistress knew that it would be no good reporting Anne-Marie—for Anne-Marie would also report her own side of the matter, and Miss Theobald would not think very much of a teacher who condemned lines by a great poet just because she thought they were written by a school-girl she disliked.

The bell rang, and never did Miss Willcox feel so relieved to hear it. She gathered up her books and sailed out. The girls rounded on Anne-Marie.

"That was a beastly thing to do!' said Hilary.

'I thought it was funny,' said Claudine.

'You would!' said Pat. 'It was certainly clever, but it wasn't a decent thing to do.'

'I know it wasn't,' said Anne-Marie, defiantly. 'But I wanted to get my own back. And I did.'

'Well, I hope you're happy about it,' said Alison, bitterly. 'Trying to humiliate a good teacher in front of the whole class.'

'Did she feel sorry for poor little Doris-Deirdre then?' began Anne-Marie, but Hilary was not going to allow any spite of that sort.

'Shut up, both of you,' she said. 'Maybe you won't be such an ass over Miss Willcox now, Alison—and perhaps, now you've taken your revenge, Anne-Marie, you'll cool off and try to behave decently for the rest of the term. Alison has complained to me about your behaviour to her, and it's got to stop.'

'I don't know what you mean by my " behaviour to Alison ",' said Anne-Marie, puzzled. 'She complains that

I take her things, and play tricks on her, but I don't. Why should I? I'm not jealous of her or anything. She can keep Miss Willcox all to herself if she wants to! I don't mind!'

Most of the class, although they thought it was not a nice thing to humiliate a mistress publicly, had secretly enjoyed the excitement. Alma certainly had, for she had often been held up to ridicule by Miss Willcox for her complete inability to appreciate any fine literature at all. She was glad to see her defeated by Anne-Marie—and she was glad too when she heard Alison openly accusing Anne-Marie of the tricks she, Alma, had been playing on the unsuspecting Alison!

'I'll play just one more and that shall be the last,' she thought. 'I know she had a box of sweets sent to her today. I'll slip in and take those when she isn't there, and she'll blame Anne-Marie again!'

But Alma tried her tricks once too often. When she slipped into Alison's study, it was empty, and she picked up the box of sweets quickly. She hurried to her own study and ran in.

To her dismay both Alison and Angela were there, waiting to ask Pauline something! Alison immediately saw the box of sweets in Alma's hand.

'Those are my sweets!' she said. 'You beast, you took them out of my study! Alma, you're a thief! I'm sure you were a thief before too—you pilfered the cupboard outside, when the second formers hid their stuff there. Angela, isn't she absolutely awful?

Alma stood there stubbornly, trying to think of some way out. 'I wasn't going to eat them,' she said at last. 'I was only playing a trick on you because I don't like you.'

'You were stealing,' said Alison, furiously. 'You know you meant to eat them! This will have to be told to Hilary. It's simply awful for a fifth former to be caught stealing.'

Alma sat down suddenly, feeling frightened. She had

had a solemn and very serious talking to by Miss Theobald about being found in the cupboard the other night, and it had been impossible to convince the Head Mistress that she had not been doing anything wrong. If this got to her ears, matters would be even more serious.

'I didn't steal them, Alison,' she said, desperately. 'I tell you, I was just paying you out because you stopped me going to the cupboard where the second formers put their food—though you didn't know it. I took your knitting-needles—and your geometry set—and other things. Only to spite you, though, not to steal them. They're all here, look !'

She unlocked her desk in the corner and before Alison's astonished eyes lay all the things she had missed during the last week or two !

'Bring them into my study,' said Alison, completely at a loss to know what to do or say. 'I'll have to think about this. What a beast you are, Alma—especially as you knew I was blaming Anne-Marie all the time.'

Alma took everything back, weeping. Alison took one look at the puffy, pasty face and turned away in dislike. How could a girl who had been in the top form do things like this? Perhaps that was why she had been dropped back into the fifth—maybe because of some disgrace or other !

23 A FEW THINGS ARE CLEARED UP

'WAIT till the exams. are over before you make any fuss about Alma,' said Angela to Alison. 'Oh dear—no wonder Anne-Marie didn't know what we were talking about when we kept accusing her of taking your things !'

'I shall have to apologize to her,' said Alison, gloomily.

'Blow Alma—what a first-class idiot she is, really! Isn't she queer? I don't understand her at all. Sometimes I think she's daft.'

The exams. were now pressing on the girls, and they were working feverishly. Only Pam appeared to find them easy. Hilary worked through her papers methodically, and so did Pat and Isabel, Bobby and Janet, but Carlotta, Claudine and Angela got very hot and bothered. So, queerly enough, did Mirabel, which was unusual for her, but she had given so much of her time to the organizing of the school games that she had not worked as well at her exam. tasks as the others had.

'These awful questions!' she said, as she read one after another. 'I can't seem to answer any of them!'

At last the exams. were over and the whole form heaved a sigh of relief. What a week it had been! The girls wanted to yell and laugh and stamp and rush about. They became very boisterous, even the quiet Pam. But the teachers turned a blind eye and a deaf ear on the yelling girls, and did not even appear to see Carlotta doing cart-wheels all round the gym.

'Thank goodness we haven't got to wait long for the results,' said Doris. 'I hate having to wait weeks. Miss Cornwallis says we shall know in a few days.'

'How's little Jane Teal?' said Pat, remembering the first former for the first time for a few days. 'Is she better?'

'She's over the flu,' said Isabel, 'but Matron says she's still worried in her mind. When she was so ill, she kept raving about the fire-bell, and Mirabel and Angela. I rather think there's going to be a few inquiries made about certain members of our form soon! Poor Jane— it's rotten to think no one ever owned up about that bell, but let Jane take the blame. It made Mirabel simply beastly to her. She is the only person that hasn't been to see Jane in the san. Did you know?'

'Just like her,' said Pat.

The exam. results came out and were posted up on the

board. Pam and Hilary were top with honours. The
others came in turn down the list. Carlotta was glad to
see she had passed. Doris just scraped through too, and
so did Claudine and Alison.

Three girls failed. They were Angela, Alma—and,
most surprisingly, Mirabel!

Alma had not expected to pass. Angela was amazed
that *she* hadn't! As for Mirabel, she was humiliated
beyond words. To think that she, sports captain of St.
Clare's, should have failed. She rushed off to her study,
filled with shame and horror. How every one would
sneer!

Gladys, who had hardly spoken with Mirabel since she
had resigned as vice-captain, stared in amazement at the
exam. results. Mirabel failed! She could hardly believe
her eyes. With her heart full of sympathy and warmth
she hurried off to find her one-time friend.

Mirabel was sitting by the window, her humiliation
almost more than she could bear. Gladys went to her,
and took her hand.

'Bad luck, old thing,' she said. 'I'm awfully sorry.
You worked too hard at the matches and things, that's
all. Don't worry too much about it. Two others have
failed as well.'

Mirabel was touched by Gladys's warm sympathy.
She had felt lonely and deserted. With tears in her eyes
she gazed at Gladys, and tried to speak.

'I can't bear it,' she said at last. 'They'll all laugh
at me. Me, the sports captain! They'll be glad to
laugh too. They hate me. Every one hates me. Where
have I gone wrong? I meant to do so well.'

'Let's be friends again, Mirabel,' said Gladys. 'You
need me, don't you? You wouldn't let me help you at
all this term—but let me help you now. The girls don't
really hate you—they admired you awfully at the beginning of the term, and there's no reason why they shouldn't
again.'

Poor Mirabel—and poor Angela! Both liked to shine,

and both had failed. What was the use of being sports captain, what was the use of being the most beautiful girl in the school, if your brains were so poor you couldn't even get as good marks as Doris or Alison!

Claudine had been rather quiet for a day or two. She had been to see Jane Teal and taken her a lovely little handkerchief she had embroidered for her. Then she sought out Antoinette and made a proposal to her that surprised that second former very much.

'What! Tell Miss Theobald that I rang the fire-bell!' said Antoinette, in surprise and disgust. 'Are you mad, Claudine?'

'Yes, perhaps,' said Claudine, thoughtfully. 'I am afraid I have caught a little of this English sense of honour, alas! I feel uncomfortable *here* when I think of Jane Teal worrying about the fire-bell, and of Mirabel thinking it is Jane. It is a great pity, but I fear I have caught this sense of honour, Antoinette.'

'Oh, is it catching?' said Antoinette, in alarm. 'I do not want to get it, it is an uncomfortable thing to have. See how it makes you behave, Claudine.'

'I will go to Miss Theobald and tell her it was all my fault,' said Claudine, at last. 'You do not need to come into it, Antoinette. After all, it was my idea, and you only carried it out. I will go and confess.'

She gave a huge sigh and went off. Miss Theobald was startled and amused to see Claudine arriving with a saintly and determined expression on her face.

'Miss Theobald, I have caught the sense of honour from somebody at St. Clare's,' announced Claudine. 'I have come to make a confession. I told my little sister to ring the fire-bell, when Mirabel was about to hold her stupid meeting. I did not mean to own up, but now I feel uncomfortable *here* about it.'

Claudine pressed her tummy, and Miss Theobald listened gravely. 'I am glad you have owned up, Claudine,' she said. 'It was a silly thing to do, but it became a serious thing when some one else was suspected of it.

Please tell Hilary. I shall not punish Antoinette, but
she too must own up to Jane Teal, and put her mind at
rest.'

Claudine went out, knowing that her real punishment
was to be owning up to the serious head-girl of the form.
Hilary did not favour misbehaviour of this kind now that
they were top-formers, and she had a way of talking that
at times made Claudine feel very small. She made her
feel small now.

'You don't realize that next term we shall all be in the
top form,' she said to Claudine. 'From there we go out
into the world. We can't behave like naughty children
in the first form now. We have to set an example to the
younger ones, we have to learn what responsibility
means!'

'You should be a preacher, Hilary,' said Claudine,
jokingly.

But Hilary was not in a mood to be joked with. She
took her position as head-girl very seriously, all the more
so because she knew she would not be head-girl of the
sixth. She was only staying one term more, and the
head-girl must be some one staying for three terms.
Every one was wondering who would be chosen.

Claudine went off, abashed, and found Antoinette, who
was highly indignant at being sent off to Jane Teal to
confess. But when she saw Jane's face, she was not
sorry she had gone.

'Oh,' said Jane, 'was it really you, Antoinette? Oh,
I'm glad you told me. You know, I really began to feel
it *might* have been me, I was so worried about it. Whatever will Mirabel say?'

Mirabel soon heard about it. Gladys told her. She
flushed uncomfortably, thinking of the hard time she had
given poor Jane because of her unjust suspicions. She
thought for a while and then went straight off to the
san., where Jane still was.

'Jane, I've heard who rang the fire-bell,' said Mirabel,
hardly liking to meet Jane's eyes. 'It wasn't you, and

I was sure it was. I was beastly to you—left you out of matches unfairly—and things like that. I'm—I'm sorry about it. I . . .'

'It's all right, Mirabel,' said Jane, eagerly. 'I don't mind now. Not a bit. All I want is to get up and practise hard for you again, and perhaps play in a match before the term ends.'

Jane's warm response and loyalty were very pleasant to Mirabel, who had been very miserable. She smiled at the first former, left her some barley sugar, and went back to her study, thinking how nice it was to have some one look at her with liking once again.

Mirabel's visit to Jane made a great impression on the lower forms. Jane soon spread it abroad, and spoke so glowingly of Mirabel's kind words to her, that the younger ones began to get over their dislike and defiance. They had deserted the practice field, and had shown little or no interest in games since Mirabel had cancelled their match—but now they gradually drifted back, and Mirabel found, to her delight, that they seemed as keen as ever.

Gladys took back her resignation, and Mirabel set to work humbly and happily to make out games lists again and to arrange matches—but she let Gladys do at least half of it, and was careful to listen to her and to take her advice when she gave it. The two were much happier than they had ever been before and Gladys was glad to see her friend learning from the bad mistakes she had made.

'Looks as if Mirabel will be a good captain after all,' said Bobby in surprise. 'Well, well—we're all turning over a new leaf ! There's Felicity back again, not caring two hoots about her music for a bit, and being quite one of us—and there's Anne-Marie gone all friendly and jolly since Alison apologized to her for suspecting her wrongly— and there's Alison behaving sensibly too, now that she sees through dear Deirdre—and Angela isn't being such an idiot with the younger ones since she failed in her exam.'

'No—that was a shock that pulled her together a bit,'

said Pat. ' She's working hard now. Did you know that Hilary gave her a most awful talking-to. She wept buckets of tears, and was furious with Hilary—but she certainly has been better since.'

' It's only Alma that's still a pain in the neck,' said Isabel. ' I hate speaking to her even. I know Hilary's gone to tell Miss Theobald about her taking those things of Alison's. I bet she'll be expelled or something if she isn't careful.'

But Alma was not expelled. Instead Hilary explained something to the girls that made them feel rather uncomfortable.

' I told Miss Theobald all about our trouble with Alma,' said Hilary, ' and she told me we must be patient with her and put up with her, because she can't help it just now. There's something wrong with her glands, that can't be put right for about six months. That's why she's so fat, and always hungry, and looks so pasty and funny. She was sent off from her last school in disgrace— but Miss Theobald wants to keep her here and help her, till she can have some sort of marvellous operation done that can put her right,'

' Poor old Pudding,' said Doris. ' She's her own enemy, I suppose—or her glands are, whatever they may be ! Well—I suppose we must put up with our Alma, and grin and bear it when she chews and sucks and gobbles.' Doris began to imitate Alma at a meal, and the girls screamed with laughter.

But there was no real unkindness in the laughter. One and all were ready to put up with Alma now and help her, even selfish little Angela, and wild Carlotta. They were growing up, they were fifth formers, they could behave decently. St. Clare's put its mark on you by the time you were in the fifth form !

24 WHO SHALL BE HEAD
OF THE SCHOOL?

AFTER the exam. the girls relaxed with pleasure and relief. The teachers gave them less prep. to do, and the fifth formers spent pleasant evenings in their own studies or each others', talking and laughing.

' Christmas will soon be upon us,' said Pat. ' The rest of this term will fly ! I always like the Christmas term— it begins in summer-time, when the September sun is still hot, and it often ends in snow, with Christmas beckoning round the corner.'

' You sound quite poetic,' said Doris. ' Anne-Marie used to say things like that ! '

Anne-Marie laughed. She had not written any poems for some time, for, after the success of her trick on Miss Willcox, she had felt rather ashamed of herself. After all, *she* had pretended too, just like Miss Willcox, *she* had tried to write poems that sounded very grand, but were quite worthless really. Now Anne-Marie was determined to wait till she had something to say, before she wrote poetry again.

She had had a talk with Miss Theobald, who had heard of Anne-Marie's ' cheating ' as Miss Willcox called it. The Head Mistress hadn't much time for the English teacher herself, sensing that she was insincere and rather conceited—but she could not allow any of the girls to flout authority, or be insolent, without reprimanding them severely.

So Anne-Marie had had a bad twenty minutes, and had come away a sadder and wiser fifth former, determined that she would write no more ' wonderful ' poetry until, as Miss Theobald said, she had something real and honest and sincere in her heart to put into her writing and make it worth while.

Mirabel had got over the shock of failing in the exam.,

and was trying to make the lower forms forget her stupid arrogance and harshness. Her voice was still loud and clear, but not haughty or dictatorial, and she no longer walked as if the whole earth belonged to her. She was a wiser person altogether, and the girls respected her for being able to change herself so completely.

Jane Teal was once again working hard for Mirabel, exulting in her returned health and strength, a great weight off her mind. Angela no longer gave the younger ones so many jobs to do, and she and Alison did their mending together. Hilary had made a great impression on Angela when she had ticked her off, and had really frightened her.

' You're a poor, poor thing, Angela,' she had told her. ' You use your pretty face and smile to save yourself trouble, and you are getting a lazy mind and a lazy body, letting other people do the things *you* ought to do. No wonder you failed in the exam.—and failed miserably too ! If you're not careful you'll go *on* being a failure in all kinds of ways, and people will laugh at you instead of admiring and respecting you. What do you suppose Jane and Sally and Violet and the rest of your lower form slaves think of their darling beautiful Angela now, when they see that she and Alma tied for bottom place in the exam. ! Pull yourself together a bit, for goodness' sake.'

Each term brought different things to learn, besides lessons. Those girls who faced their difficulties, saw and understood their faults, conquered their failings, and became strong characters and leaders would make the finest wives and mothers of the future. Miss Theobald watched the fifth formers carefully, and was proud of many of them.

She remembered them as silly little first formers, and a little less-silly second formers. She remembered Pat and Isabel O'Sullivan, the ' stuck-up twins ' as they had been called, when they first came. She remembered how Mirabel had vowed not to stay longer than half a term, and had misbehaved herself dreadfully in her first term. She remembered the wildness of Carlotta, who had come to St. Clare's from circus-life, untamed and head-strong.

She remembered Bobby, whose brilliant brains were once only used in mad and clever tricks—and Claudine, untruthful, deceitful and unscrupulous, who was at last finding responsibility and a sense of honour. Here were all these girls now, dependable, honest-minded, hard-working, and responsible. Truly St. Clare's was a school to be proud of.

Before the end of the term came the Head Mistress must choose the head-girl for the whole school. All the sixth were leaving, and the fifth were to go up, with one or two new girls. Hilary was the only one of the fifth who was not staying on for one more whole year. She was only to stay one term more, and then she was to go to India to be with her parents there.

Otherwise Hilary would have been head of the sixth, and a good responsible head she would have made. But now some one else must be chosen. The girls wondered who it would be. It was a tremendous honour, for the head-girl of the sixth would be the head-girl of the whole school, a person of great influence.

'It won't be me, anyway,' said Doris, comfortably. 'I'm too stupid.'

'And it won't be me,' said Carlotta. 'I'm still too wild.'

'Nor me,' said Bobby, grinning. 'I'm still too much given to playing tricks. Didn't Mam'zelle jump when she drank her glass of milk this morning and found a black beetle at the bottom?'

The girls giggled. It was a silly trick, but had caused a lot of fun. Bobby had popped a little tin black beetle into Mam'zelle's glass of mid-morning milk, and her horror when she had drunk all the milk and then had suddenly seen the beetle at the bottom had been most amusing to watch.

' *Tiens !* ' she had cried. ' What is this black animal I have almost drunk ? Oh la, la, that it should choose my glass and no one else's ! '

The girls recalled all the tricks Bobby and Janet had played on poor Mam'zelle—the way they had made the plates dance—the dreadful stink-balls—and many others. They had all been good fun, and Mam'zelle had always joined in the laughter afterwards.

' We break up in three days' time,' said Bobby. ' Then heyho for the holidays—and when we come back, we shall all be sixth formers, grave and serious and solemn ! No tricks then—no giggles—no messing about ! '

' Oh rubbish ! ' said Carlotta. ' We shan't suddenly alter just because we're sixth formers. We shall be just the same. I do wonder who will be head-girl. Perhaps one of the twins will.'

' I hope not,' said Pat, at once. ' I'd hate to be something Isabel wasn't, and she would hate it too. Otherwise we'd either of us love it. It's the thing I'd like best in the world at the moment. I love St. Clare's, and I'm proud of belonging to it. If I could do something for it I would—but I don't want to do something that I can't share with Isabel.'

' I feel the same about that,' said Isabel. ' But if we *did* have the honour of being asked, either of us, to be head-girl, we'd say no. Anyway, there are plenty of others who would make better head-girls than we should.'

At that very moment the matter was being decided by Miss Theobald, Miss Cornwallis and Mam'zelle. They were sitting together in the Head's drawing-room, dis- cussing the very weighty and important question of who should be the next head-girl. It was important because the head-girl had a powerful influence on the whole school, and was, in fact, typical of the spirit of St. Clare's.

They were going down the list of girls. ' Hilary can't be, of course,' said Miss Cornwallis. ' A pity, because she has had great experience of being head-girl in three or four forms. Still, perhaps it is time some one else had a chance of showing leadership.'

' Janet ? ' said Miss Theobald.

The others shook their heads. Janet could still be hot-tempered and wilful at times. She had not yet learnt to guard her sharp tongue completely. A head-girl had to have complete control of herself.

' Not Bobby, of course,' said Miss Cornwallis. ' Brilliant, trustable, but still a little unsteady. What about Gladys ? '

' Too gentle—not enough of a leader,' said Miss Theobald, who knew the characters of every girl in a most remarkable way. ' And Claudine I am afraid we must also cross out, Mam'zelle.'

Mam'zelle sighed. It had been a secret wish with her for two or three terms that Claudine, her little Claudine, might be head of St. Clare's, the school in which Mam'zelle had taught for so many many years. But even Mam'-zelle, biassed as she was, knew that Claudine was not fit to lead others.

' If she had been at St. Clare's when she was thirteen now,' said Mam'zelle, ' ah, then my little Claudine might have had time to learn enough to become head-girl ! '

Both Miss Theobald and Miss Cornwallis had their doubts about this. In fact, Miss Cornwallis thought that if Claudine had been at St. Clare's ever since she was a baby, she would still not have been suitable for a head-girl. But neither wanted to upset Mam'zelle, who adored her two nieces, so they said nothing.

' Alma, certainly not, poor girl,' said Miss Theobald. ' She is a most unfortunate child. Perhaps when she is in really good health, she will improve. Carlotta now—no, I think not. Still rather unaccountable and uncontrolled in her temper. I always feel she is still capable of slapping people if she doesn't approve of them.'

Mam'zelle remembered various slapping episodes in Carlotta's school-life and smiled. ' Ah, she would slap

the first formers hard if they did not behave ! ' she said.
' She would be an amusing head-girl, but perhaps not a
very good one.'

' Felicity, no,' said Miss Cornwallis. ' She will always
be apt to forget everything when her music fills her
mind. She will perhaps someday be one of the foremost
musicians or composers, but only in her art will she be
fit to lead others.'

' Angela and Alison—neither of them leaders in anyway,' said Miss Theobald. ' How good it would be for
both of them to be head-girls, and feel the weight of
leadership and responsibility on their shoulders—but how
bad for the school ! Alison is still such a feather-head,
and Angela has a lot to learn yet. Three more terms to
learn it in—well, maybe it will be enough.'

' Anne-Marie would be hopeless,' said Mam'zelle, ' so
would Pauline.'

' That leaves Doris, Pam and the twins,' said Miss
Theobald, looking at her list.

' Doris is too stupid,' said Mam'zelle. ' Still she cannot
roll her " R's " for me in the French way. Ah, she will
be a great success on the stage, that girl, she is so clever
a mimic. But she is stupid in all other ways, though a
nice, nice girl.'

The others agreed. ' Pam would make an ideal head-
girl,' said Miss Theobald, ' but she is too young. Almost
two years younger than the oldest in the fifth. She is
staying on two years, so perhaps she will be head-girl in
the future. A nice, hard-working, quiet and dependable
child.'

' That only leaves the O'Sullivan twins,' said Miss
Cornwallis, ' and I am sure that we cannot choose one
without the other. They are inseparable and always have
been. The other twin would feel very much left out if
we chose one of them.'

' Ah—I have it ! ' said Mam'zelle, suddenly, banging the
table and making the other mistresses jump. ' I have
it ! Yes, we will have *two* head-girls ! Why not ? Is

not St. Clare's bigger than ever it was? Has not the head-girl more than enough to do? Then we will have *two* head-girls, girls who will work together as one—so why not the O'Sullivan twins?'

Miss Theobald and Miss Cornwallis looked at each other. It was a good idea. Two head-girls who were twins would certainly work very well together, and could share the responsibility well. Pat and Isabel had consistently done good work, and had grown into splendid, trustworthy and sensible girls.

'Yes,' said Miss Theobald, at last. 'It's a very good idea indeed. The twins will make fine head-girls. It will do them a world of good, for they have never undertaken any kind of leadership here so far. They shall be joint head-girls. I will make the announcement to-morrow.'

So, when the whole school was called together for the head to announce the changes in the coming term, the names of the two new head-girls were given.

'We have carefully studied the question of who shall be head-girl of the school for the coming year,' said Miss Theobald. 'And I think there is no doubt that our choice is wise and will be very popular. St. Clare's is growing fast, and the head-girl has a great deal to do; sometimes too much. So we have decided to have *two* head-girls working together, and we have chosen a pair who have been with us from the first form, and have made their way up the school steadily and well, winning every one's respect and admiration. Next term the O'Sullivan twins will be our head-girls!'

There was a terrific out-burst of cheering, clapping and stamping at these words. Everyone knew the like-as-pea twins, everyone liked them and trusted them. Now they were to be head-girls together—splendid!

The twins were overwhelmed. They blushed scarlet, and when they heard the outburst of cheering, they felt sudden tears pricking their eye-lids. It was a wonderful moment for them. To be chosen to head the school, to lead it, to hold the biggest honour St. Clare's had to offer —that was something worth while.

'Thank you,' said Pat, standing up with Isabel, when the cheering had lessened. 'We'll—we'll do our very best!'

So they will—and their best will be very good indeed. And there we must leave them, about to have their dearest wish, head-girls of St. Clare's, the finest school they know.

Other Enid Blyton titles available in the series

THE TWINS AT ST CLARE'S

containing
The Twins at St Clare's
The O'Sullivan Twins
Summer Term at St Clare's

Twins Pat and Isabel O'Sullivan are dreading
going to St Clare's . Life is not nearly so easy as
at their old school and the 'stuck-up twins' have
several unpleasant shocks and arguments before
they realise their difficulties are of their own
making. Problems resolved, the girls soon find
friends and settle down. Each term brings more
fun and games, as well as plenty of new girls and
lots of surprises. Pat and Isabel don't regret for
a moment having gone to school at St Clare's!

MALORY TOWERS

When Darrell Rivers first arrives at Malory Towers, she has lots of exciting adventures in store! She makes many new friends, there are practical jokes and plenty of fun, but some problems too for Darrell in controlling her dreadful temper. We meeet Mam'zelle, a great favourite with the girls, trying to be strict but not succeeding, as well as lots of new girls who all have something special to add to life at Malory Towers.

BACK TO MALORY TOWERS

containing
Upper Fourth at Malory Towers
In the Fifth at Malory Towers
Last Term at Malory Towers

Darrell Rivers and her friends Sally, Alicia and all the others are back at Malory Towers, this time as senior girls taking their exams, but also having lots of fun organising the school pantomime, playing tennis and lacrosse, having midnight feasts and trying more tricks on Mam'zelle. Darrell's sister Felicity arrives with other new girls who bring their share of problems, but it helps to make the final three years more exciting than ever, before the girls finally have to say goodbye to Malory Towers.

MYSTERIES

containing
The Mystery of the Burnt Cottage
The Mystery of the Disappearing Cat
The Mystery of the Secret Room

In this collection of the first three adventures in
Enid Blyton's famous Mystery series, the Five
Find-Outers - Larry, Daisy, Pip, Bets and Fatty,
as well as Buster the dog - solve three exciting
Mysteries in spite of the efforts of PC Goon to
stop them...